"Magical."   —M. Isidora Forrest, author of *Isis Magic*

"In this account of the fate of Cleopatra's daughter in the household of Augustus Caesar, Dray reveals the same events we've seen in *Rome* and *I, Claudius* from a very different perspective, that of a teenage girl. Cleopatra Selene has unusual gifts and problems, but her struggle to understand herself and her destiny is universal. The glimpses of the cult of Isis leave one wanting to know more, and the story keeps you turning the pages until the end."

—Diana L. Paxson,
author of *Marion Zimmer Bradley's Sword of Avalon*

"*Lily of the Nile* is graceful history infused with subtle magic and veiled ancient mysteries, at a time of immense flux and transition. Cleopatra Selene—regal, stoic, and indomitable daughter of the legendary Pharaoh-Queen Cleopatra—carries on the spirit of her mother, the goddess Isis, and the soul of Egypt itself into the lair of the conquering imperial enemy. Selene, whose skin speaks the words of queen and goddess in blood, channels the dynastic pride that is her birthright, and seals the fate of the Roman Empire. Meticulously researched, thoroughly believable, this is a different kind of book, and a true achievement."

—Vera Nazarian,
two-time Nebula Award–nominated
author of *Lords of Rainbow* and *Mansfield Park and Mummies*

"With clear prose, careful research, vivid detail, and a dash of magic, Stephanie Dray brings true life to one of Egypt's most intriguing princesses."

—Susan Fraser King,
bestselling and award-winning
author of *Queen Hereafter* and *Lady Macbeth*

Berkley titles by Stephanie Dray

LILY OF THE NILE
SONG OF THE NILE

SONG

of the

NILE

A NOVEL OF CLEOPATRA'S DAUGHTER

STEPHANIE DRAY

BERKLEY BOOKS, NEW YORK

THE BERKLEY PUBLISHING GROUP
Published by the Penguin Group
Penguin Group (USA) Inc.
375 Hudson Street, New York, New York 10014, USA
Penguin Group (Canada), 90 Eglinton Avenue East, Suite 700, Toronto, Ontario M4P 2Y3, Canada
(a division of Pearson Penguin Canada Inc.)
Penguin Books Ltd., 80 Strand, London WC2R 0RL, England
Penguin Group Ireland, 25 St. Stephen's Green, Dublin 2, Ireland (a division of Penguin Books Ltd.)
Penguin Group (Australia), 250 Camberwell Road, Camberwell, Victoria 3124, Australia
(a division of Pearson Australia Group Pty. Ltd.)
Penguin Books India Pvt. Ltd., 11 Community Centre, Panchsheel Park, New Delhi—110 017, India
Penguin Group (NZ), 67 Apollo Drive, Rosedale, Auckland 0632, New Zealand
(a division of Pearson New Zealand Ltd.)
Penguin Books (South Africa) (Pty.) Ltd., 24 Sturdee Avenue, Rosebank, Johannesburg 2196,
South Africa

Penguin Books Ltd., Registered Offices: 80 Strand, London WC2R 0RL, England

This book is an original publication of The Berkley Publishing Group.

PRINTING HISTORY
Berkley trade paperback edition / October 2011

Library of Congress Cataloging-in-Publication Data

Dray, Stephanie.
    Song of the Nile / Stephanie Dray. — Berkley trade pbk. ed.
        p. cm.
    ISBN 978-0-425-24304-6 (trade pbk.)
    1. Cleopatra, Queen, consort of Juba II, King of Mauretania, b. 40 B.C.—Fiction.   2. Cleopatra, Queen of Egypt, d. 30 B.C.—Family—Fiction.   3. Rome—History—Augustus, 30 B.C.–A.D. 14.—Fiction.   4. Augustus, Emperor of Rome, 63 B.C.–A.D. 14—Fiction.   I. Title.
    PS3604.R39S65 2011
    813'.6—dc22

                                                                                    2011020553

To my mother and my grandmothers,
because like Cleopatra Selene,
I come from a long line of powerful and inspiring women.

Dear Reader,

It's often erroneously said that Cleopatra VII of Egypt was the last of the Ptolemaic queens. In truth, that title belongs to her daughter, Cleopatra Selene. Though Augustus would make Selene the most powerful client queen in his empire, she's typically overlooked by historians in favor of her notorious mother. It was suicide that helped to make Cleopatra so famous, but her daughter has always captivated me because Selene's story is one of survival.

Cleopatra Selene carved out a new destiny for herself in an uncertain land, but she seems always to have been looking behind her. She was a woman who forgot nothing.

I wrote this book so that we don't forget *her*.

As an author of historical fiction, one of my greatest joys is filling in the spaces the historical record leaves empty. While Selene is believed to have married King Juba II of Mauretania in 25 B.C., she doesn't appear on the coins of her realm for another five years. Her exact whereabouts during this time are unknown, but as a nominal member of the imperial family, she had a unique perspective from which to witness five of the most crucial years in Roman history and *religious* history.

Though Isis worship would eventually come to dominate the ancient world, the cult frequently came under attack even before it fell out of favor with Augustus. While the Romans generally tolerated foreign gods and goddesses, Augustus banned the worship of Isis within the sacred boundaries of Rome. Cassius Dio tells us that Agrippa also cracked down on the Alexandrine cult in 21 B.C. In spite of this, or perhaps because of it, Selene actively promoted her goddess. That she appears never to have been censured by Rome for this—or for any of the more politically provocative actions she took as queen—tells us that she enjoyed an extraordinary relationship with Augustus.

This novel imagines and dramatizes that relationship.

As in *Lily of the Nile*, I've adopted some conventions that bear explanation. To start with, I've embraced the most familiar spellings and naming conventions for historical figures and ideas. For example, I've used Mark Antony for Marcus Antonius and Cleopatra instead of Kleopatra. I've also used English words for Latin concepts whenever possible. One instance is my adoption of the word *lady* when the word *domina* may have been more accurate. Moreover, I've addressed Augustus as *the emperor* throughout the novel even though our modern understanding of the word differs greatly from the traditional Roman concept of an imperator. I stand by this choice because of Octavian's nontraditional use of imperator—a title he held lawfully in 43 B.C. and should have relinquished that same year but continued to use in front of his name until he acquired the new honorific of Augustus.

Whenever the historical record was in doubt, I've unabashedly adopted the slant most favorable to Egypt, Selene, her family, or the faith in which she was raised; the bias against Rome and Augustus reflects her views as I've imagined them, not my own. Also, Selene's relatively uncritical acceptance of the idea that native peoples must be "civilized" is not an endorsement, but simply the historical attitude of the time period.

Finally, though the weddings, divorces, battles, treaties, and imperial politics are all firmly rooted in historical fact, I've tried to respect this work as a novel more than as a biography. To that end, my choices and changes are explained in the author's note at the end of this book.

ACKNOWLEDGMENTS

There are many people I wish to thank. My wise-woman agent, Jennifer Schober, for her guidance and innate understanding of my work. My warrior-woman editor, Cindy Hwang, who taught me how to make this story more powerful. My amazing husband, for his infinite patience and encouragement. My wonderful friends and family—especially my in-laws—all of whom have been so supportive. My sister, for her friendship and tireless promotion. The Rovets for their hospitality. The generous bloggers and reviewers who have helped spread the word. Kay Dion for being the most unfailingly helpful librarian in the nation. Mallory Braus, Julia Drake, Shelly Dunlop, Tanja Pederson, and Anna Treece for assisting me with publicity so that I could focus on writing. Paul McEndree for help with sea snail mucus and purple dye. Jessica Cooley for last-minute edits. Victoria Janssen, Rachel Blackman, Craig Lammes, and Reggie Greenberg for their vivid recollections of Athens. Sheila Accongio, Christi Barth, Sharon Buchbinder, Mallory Cates, Sabrina Darby, Moriah Jovan, Michelle Sandmeier, Christine Rovet, Constance Chamberlain, Jen Lazarus, Kai Lawson, Joseph Kelly, and Stephanie Rice for critiquing early drafts of the manuscript. Becky Wilson and Jamie Michelle for reading the manuscript after I made changes—and the remarkable Gabrielle Carolina, who gave up sleep to help me with the book and with study guide questions.

I also couldn't have written this without Leah Barber holding down the fort and without my Divas cracking the whip over my head every day. Nor do I think I could have kept track of the enormous piles of research for this book without the help of Scrivener, upon which I'm hopelessly dependent.

I must again thank Duane W. Roller, Professor (Emeritus) of Greek and Latin at Ohio State University, who offered his expertise on Cleopatra Selene and Juba II. I'm also grateful to anthropologist and *Amazigh* activist Helene Hagen, whose work on Berber culture is fascinating. Both scholars patiently answered my questions, but any mistakes in this manuscript should be ascribed to me alone.

Mindful that footnotes distract and that my sources are too numerous to cite here, I would, nonetheless, like to credit several, including W. W. Tarn's scholarly paper titled "Alexander Helios and the Golden Age" as well as Duane W. Roller's *The World of Juba II and Kleopatra Selene*, Margaret George's *Memoirs of Cleopatra*, Wilbur Smith's *River God, Pharaoh* by Karen Essex, and the splashy Hollywood film *Cleopatra*, starring Elizabeth Taylor.

I'm again indebted to authors who have also tried to bring Selene's world to life, including Andrea Ashton, whose social awareness about the conflict of Berbers and Romans helped inspire several scenes in this book. Additionally, I want to thank Alice Curtis Desmond and Michelle Moran, whose influence can also be felt in this novel. However, it's Beatrice Chanler's 1934 novel, *Cleopatra's Daughter, the Queen of Mauretania* that inspired me most. My work is heavily influenced by her ideas, imagery, and lofty prose. In particular, Ms. Chanler's book captured my imagination because of its unusual theory that Cleopatra Selene and her twin brother were religious symbols—a theory that I've extended into the fantastic.

In adopting and modernizing this theory by reimagining Isis worship, I relied not just upon ancient sources and current scholarship but also upon the worship of Isis as it's currently practiced. M. Isidora Forrest's *Isis Magic* was invaluable on that count, as was Ms. Forrest herself, who kindly offered advice on rituals that Selene may have been familiar with. The calling prayer of Isis appears in this novel with her permission.

While it is a perilous endeavor to speculate about the sexuality of historical figures, I was emboldened by *Virgil in the Renaissance* by David Scott Wilson-Okamura and Saara Lilja's *Homosexuality in*

Republican and Augustan Rome. I've portrayed Selene's sexual morality through the lens of mythic Isiac fertility rites as explored in Merlin Stone's fascinating book *When God Was a Woman,* itself inspired by the work of Robert Graves. While no detailed record of Isiac mystery rites survives, I drew upon the legend that Isis herself had served as a prostitute in Tyre. I was also mindful of Herodotus's claim that female adherents of goddess cults gave themselves to a stranger at least once in their lives—an idea echoed by Strabo. And, of course, I must express appreciation for *The Metamorphoses* of Lucius Apuleius, an Isiac work and the only Latin novel to survive in its entirety. I blended all this information with extant accounts of the Eleusinian Mysteries.

Insofar as this novel is about Augustus, I relied upon ancient historians Cassius Dio, Suetonius, and Tacitus, freely adopting the latter's uncharitable views of Livia. When it came to reconstructing Berber culture as it may have existed in Selene's reign, I consulted Susan Raven's *Rome in Africa,* Paul MacKendrick's *The North African Stones Speak,* and *The Berbers* by Michael Brett and Elizabeth Fentress.

For additional sources, please see my website at stephaniedray.com.

The Court of Augustus Caesar

Augustus Caesar, or Octavian, Gaius Julius Caesar Octavianus, the imperator and victor of Actium

> **Julia,** his daughter by his former wife Scribonia, and his only child

> **Livia Drusilla,** his wife, scion of a powerful noble family, the *Claudii*
> *Tiberius,* her oldest son by her former husband
> *Drusus,* her youngest son by her former husband

Octavia, his long-suffering sister
> *Marcellus,* her son by her first husband
> *Marcella,* her daughter by her first husband
> *Antonia Major,* her eldest daughter by her second husband, Mark Antony
> *Antonia Minor,* called Minora, her youngest daughter by her second husband, Mark Antony
> *Iullus Antonius,* her ward, son of Mark Antony by his deceased wife, Fulvia
> *Ptolemy Philadelphus,* her ward, youngest son of Mark Antony and Cleopatra VII of Egypt
> *Alexander Helios,* her missing ward, son of Mark Antony and Cleopatra VII of Egypt, twin brother of Selene

Agrippa, his most powerful and trusted general

Maecenas, his political adviser and overseer of imperial artistic programs
> *Terentilla,* the beautiful wife of Maecenas and mistress of Augustus

VIRGIL, his revered poet and propagandist

ANTONIUS MUSA, his renowned physician, a freedman

The Court of Cleopatra Selene & Juba II

CLEOPATRA SELENE, Queen of Mauretania, only daughter of Cleopatra VII of Egypt and Mark Antony

JUBA, her husband, the Berber-blooded King of Mauretania and Numidia
Lucius Cornelius Balbus, his adviser, a Roman veteran
Circe, his mistress, a Greek *hetaera*

CHRYSSA, her Greek slave girl, a hairdresser and keeper of the wardrobe

TALA, her Berber attendant, sister of Maysar, a tribal leader

EUPHRONIUS/EUPHORBUS, her court physician, mage, and priest of Isis from Alexandria

CRINAGORAS OF MYTILENE, her court poet

MEMON, her captain of the Macedonian guard from Alexandria

LADY LASTHENIA, her adviser, a Pythagorean scholar from Alexandria

MAYSAR, her adviser, a Berber tribal leader

CAPTAIN KABYLE, her Berber-born ship's captain

MASTER GNAIOS, her father's famous gem cutter

LEONTEUS OF ARGOS, her court tragedian

LADY ANTONIA, also called Hybrida, her long-lost sister, a wealthy widow and daughter of Mark Antony
Pythodorida, her daughter

Song of the Nile

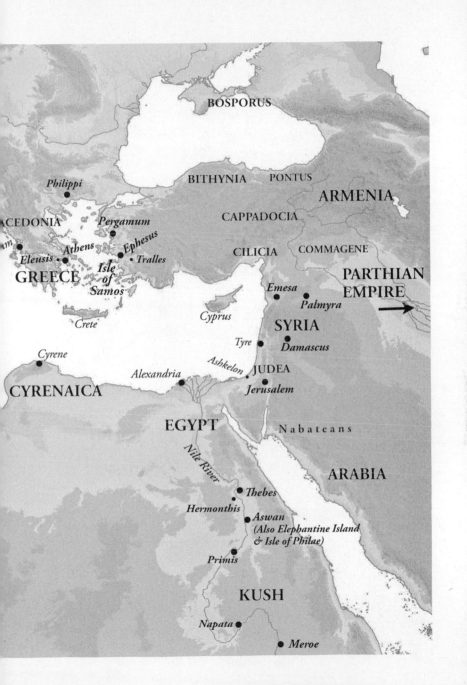

Prologue

❧

ISIS

I am nature. I am the mother of everything that has ever been or will ever be. I am all goddesses. And you know me, for I live inside you. I am in the part of you that feels magic when the wheat is harvested and cleansing wind separates golden grains from the chaff. I am in the part of you that sees a woman dance by firelight and understands the sacred power of her body. I am in the part of you that has suffered dark nights of the soul and survived to see the dawn.

You know me, because I am every strong hand that ever stretched out to help you. I am every soft kiss that soothed your tears. I am every warm meal that has filled your hungry belly. I have a thousand names, and yet, *you know me.*

I am the good goddess. Bona Dea. Call me Hecate or Cybele, Venus or Inanna, Neith or Tanit, Kore or Demeter. I will answer to them all. But I am properly known as Isis, for it is by this name that the world has best worshipped me.

They tell stories of how my husband was murdered and how I raised up my son to avenge his father. This story is true, but it is a son's story. A daughter's journey is different. That is why there are *other* stories they tell about me. Stories of how my daughter was taken, pulled down into the underworld, and how I refused to work my magic until she returned to me.

This is one of those stories.

One

SELENE

ROME

AUTUMN 25 B.C.

MY wedding day dawned rosy as the blush on a maiden's cheek. Like the sun peeking between pink clouds to warm the sprawling city of terra-cotta roofs below, I must also shine for Rome today. As morning broke, I surveyed the middling monuments that blanketed Rome's seven hills. I gazed to the Tiber River beyond, diamonds of dawn sparkling on its surface, and tried to see this day with my mother's eyes.

She was Cleopatra, Pharaoh of Egypt, a woman of limitless aspiration. And I was her only daughter. She'd wanted a royal marriage for me. She may have even hoped my wedding would be celebrated here in Rome. But could she have conceived that this wedding would come to me through her bitterest enemy? In her wildest dreams, could she have imagined that the man who drove her to suicide—the same man who captured her children and dragged us behind his Triumphator's chariot—would now make me a queen?

Yes, I thought. She could have imagined it. Perhaps she had even planned it.

Worn around my neck, a jade frog amulet dangled from a golden chain. It was a gift from my mother, inscribed with the words *I am the Resurrection*. On my finger, I wore her notorious amethyst ring, with which she was said to have ensorcelled my father, Mark Antony. It was now my betrothal ring, and I hoped it would steady me, for I was a tempest inside.

At just fourteen years old, I had neither my mother's audacity nor the brazen courage that allowed her to so famously smuggle herself past enemy soldiers to be rolled out at the feet of Julius Caesar. I had *heka*—magic—but had inherited none of my mother's deeper knowledge of how to use it. I didn't have her wardrobe, her gilded barges, nor the wealth of mighty Egypt. *Not yet.* But the Romans often said I had her charm and wits and the day she died, she gave me the spirit of her Egyptian soul.

Today I would need it.

It was early yet in the emperor's household; only the servants were awake, bustling about the columned courtyard, trimming shrubbery and hanging oil lamps in preparation for the wedding festivities. They were too busy—or too wary of my reputation as a sorceress—to acknowledge my presence beneath an overripe fig tree, where my slave girl and I made devotions to Isis. My Egyptian goddess was forbidden within the sacred walls of Rome, but no one stopped us from lighting candles and using a feather to trace the holy symbol, the *ankh*, into the soft earth. The Temples of Isis might be shuttered here in Rome, her altars destroyed and her voice silent, but my goddess dwelt in me and I vowed that she would speak again.

Once we'd offered our prayers, my slave girl and I strolled the gardens with a basket because it was the Roman custom for a bride to pick flowers for her own wedding wreath. The summer had been ablaze, so hot that flowers lingered out of season. I had my choice in a veritable meadow. Stooping down, I plucked two budding roses to remind me of my dead brothers, Caesarion and Antyllus, both killed in the flower of youth. I chose a flamboyant red poppy for my dead father, the Roman triumvir, who'd been known as much for his excesses as his military talent. Finally, for my mother, a purple iris because purple was the most royal color, and my mother had been the most royal woman in the world. The sight of a blazing golden flower, the most glorious in the garden, reminded me of my beloved twin. But Helios was only missing, not dead, and I refused to tempt fate by plucking that flower from its vine.

Helios promised me that we'd never live to see *this* day; he swore he'd never let me be married off to one of the emperor's cronies, but the day had come and Helios was gone.

A startled murmur of slaves made me turn and see a shadow pass between two pillars. It was the emperor. *Augustus.* The first time I ever saw him, he was a dark conquering god, a crimson-faced swirl of purple cloak and laurel leaf, ready to mount his golden chariot and bear me away as his chained prisoner. Today he wore only a broad-brimmed hat and a humble homespun tunic cut short enough to expose his knobby knees. But the smile he wore with it wasn't humble. This morning—the morning of the day he'd give me away in marriage—Augustus looked supremely smug.

He was without his usual retinue of barbers, secretaries, and guards. Even so, the slaves, including my Chryssa, all dropped to their knees and genuflected. He stepped over their prone bodies as if he were one of the Eastern rulers he derided for tyranny, for he was the master here. He owned everything in this garden: the Greek statuary, the marble benches, the colorful flowers, and the slaves. For four years now, I'd been his royal hostage and he believed he owned me too.

One day soon, I meant to prove him wrong.

"Good morning, Caesar," I said, sweeping dark hair from my eyes.

Understand that the emperor wasn't an imposing man. His power was all in the snare of his ruthless winter gray eyes, which now darkened with suspicion, as if he'd caught me trying to slip past his praetorians with their crested helmets and crimson capes. "What mischief are you up to, Cleopatra Selene?"

After all the opportunities I'd declined to run away from him, it was strange that he'd suspect me of it now. I wondered what accounted for his latest paranoia. "I'm only gathering flowers for my wedding wreath."

I showed him my basket, and seemingly satisfied, he glanced over his shoulder through the open doors to where he received clients and other morning visitors. The *tabulinum* was now empty except for the clutter of scrolls, brass oil lamps, and busts of his ancestors, the *Julii*, each painted to create the most lifelike rendition. "Walk with me," the emperor said, and I did, for no one refused him. "This morning I granted an audience to an ambassador from Judea, Selene. King Herod sends a last-minute wedding proposal. He wishes to take you as his junior wife."

The mere mention of Herod's name made my steps falter. The Judean king had been my mother's rival and had long urged the Romans to exterminate my whole family. The news that he wished to make me, the last daughter of the pharaohs, a part of his harem actually forced a gasp from my lungs. The proposal would have been more insulting if it were anything other than a pretext to kill me. Herod had already murdered his most beloved wife to make an end to her Hasmonean dynasty. He wouldn't lose a moment's sleep over my death. "Caesar, you cannot mean to give me to Herod. You swore to make me Queen of Mauretania!"

Augustus smiled. I think it pleased him to see me lose my footing, to see my confidence waver. "Trust in Caesar, Selene. You're already promised to another and in such an important matter as your marriage, I wouldn't cater to the whim of a Jew—even if he's already proved his loyalty, and you haven't. Yet."

I breathed, realizing that he'd told me this only to frighten me. To remind me of his largesse. To make me gasp with fear and then relief. Though Augustus was more than twenty years my senior, no wicked boy plucking wings off insects loved cruel games as much as he did. He stopped beside a small sphinx he'd pilfered from Egypt to adorn his garden. "Be grateful, Selene. By the end of this evening, you'll be the wife of a newly made king, and the wealthiest woman in the empire. Not even your mother could have asked for more."

Of course, she *did* ask for more. Offering her crown and scepter to him in surrender, she'd asked that her children be allowed to rule Egypt after her. Then she took her own life. My mother's suicide had been convenient for him in every way, and I'm certain that his advisers all breathed easier when she breathed her last, but

Augustus had been shocked by her death. Shaken by it. *Octavian always wants most what he cannot have*, she'd said, as if she'd known that it would ignite an obsession in him. He'd wanted her alive. He'd wanted her as a trophy. He'd settled upon me instead. "Half of Rome will be here for your wedding, Selene. Let my enemies bear witness to how kindly I treat Antony's daughter. Your father's partisans may whisper that I'm the descendant of slaves, but let them see how the grandson of a rope maker now gives away a royal princess in marriage."

There it was. The cavernous insecurity at the center of his character that drove his every action. It didn't matter that he'd vanquished all his rivals. Not his ever-expanding imperial compound with its marble and showy gardens, not the mountains of gold in his coffers, nor the might of his legions would ever conquer his fear that somewhere, someone was laughing at him. "Are you sure it shouldn't be a simpler wedding, Caesar? More in keeping with austere Roman values?" I asked, because I feared Roman crowds and knew from bitter experience that they could be dangerous.

He tilted his head, his eyes shadowed beneath the brim of his hat. "I mean for your wedding to be a *spectacle* and you're too ambitious to want it any other way. Today will make plain to Isis worshippers who foment dissent in Rome and rebellion in Egypt that they dare not oppose me, for I have a Cleopatra of my very own. Remember our bargain. Marry the man I choose for you and do as I command. Glorify me and I'll show mercy to your surviving brothers, your countrymen, and those who worship your loathsome foreign goddess. Be *my* Cleopatra and one day your mother's Egypt may be yours."

BY late afternoon, the slaves had stripped my room bare. The golden incense burners, the red and green tapestries, the painted oil lamps, and even the *kithara* harp I played to amuse the emperor— almost everything that had ever lent color or comfort to my room here—all packed into trunks and satchels. Turning my eyes to my dressing table, I thought of the loose brick beneath it, the one Helios used to pull out of the wall so that we could whisper to one another when the Romans slept. We'd never do that again, I realized. Even if the emperor's hounds hunted down my runaway twin brother and hauled him back to the Palatine, I wouldn't be here . . .

With a sharp knock at my door, the emperor's sister marched to my side. It was a mother's duty to dress her daughter for marriage and Lady Octavia was the closest thing to a mother that I had left in this world. She'd been my father's wife when he embarked upon his grand love affair with my mother. But after my parents were sealed in their tombs, Octavia had collected all my father's children. Though she was a rigid woman, I'd come to love her. Even so, it felt like betrayal to let her take my mother's place on this day. We were awkward together as we hadn't been in years. "Well," she said, both hands on her fleshy hips. "Let's get you ready, Selene."

She used a special comb to divide my hair into the six segments of the *tutulus*, the traditional hairstyle worn by Roman brides. "What a vicious little comb," I hissed, wincing as she tugged mercilessly. "Why is it shaped like a spear?"

"It's to drive out ill fortune," she said, cheerfully. "It's also to remind us of the Sabine women, the first Roman wives, forced to wed at the tip of a spear!"

"That hardly seems like something to be remembered with pride," I muttered.

Octavia only tilted my chin with a sentimental sigh. "Oh, Selene, you're going to be a lovely bride. Your father was always given to emotion, you know, and I think if he saw you, it would bring a tear to his eye." In spite of the many wrongs he'd done her, Octavia never spoke against my father, for which I was grateful. "I think you have Antony's best qualities."

This puzzled me because my father had been a big jolly man with a raucous laugh whereas I was slender and decidedly sober. "I can't imagine how I'm like my father."

"He inspired people and so do you," she said. "My daughters imitate you. Your royal poise, the way you hold your posture, and your piety. Because you work so hard at your lessons, the little ones study more. It's your gift, Selene. You lead everyone around you to aspire to something greater. Even me."

I stammered, because it was the nicest thing anyone had ever said to me. "E-even *you*?"

As the emperor's sister, Octavia had always held influence. Now that her son Marcellus had married the emperor's daughter, Lady Octavia was the most powerful woman in Rome. Wearing her distinctively severe hairstyle with its knot over her brow like a crown, she lifted her chin. "As the emperor's heir, my son is still young, untested. Marcellus will need guidance more than ever and I think *I* can help him. He and Julia need to win over the people so I'm going to find a way to fund a beautiful new theater as a gift to the city."

"They're fortunate to have an ally in you," I said, knowing how this would irritate the emperor's ambitious wife, Livia, whose role as First Woman in Rome Octavia had supplanted. Truly, it was a new day.

Octavia seemed to feel it too. "You've made a good match, Selene! And your story sounds so romantic. Two scions of African royalty. Two orphans saved by the emperor and adopted into his family, only to become stewards over a new land. Why, if I were your age, I might envy you this marriage. Your groom is such a handsome young man."

"I'm familiar with his virtues," I said, for Juba was no stranger to me. The deposed Numidian princeling was a scholar. Such a prodigy, in fact, that he'd been my tutor. Once I'd even counted him a friend. Now he was just the husband the emperor had chosen for me and the first step I must take on my path back to Egypt.

"You're a lucky girl," Octavia chattered on. "He's going to be a splendid, civilized king. *Rex Literatissimus*, they call him. And such a fine specimen of a man—no woman in Rome can avoid following him with her eyes. But remember that he *is* a man. No sweet boy like my Marcellus." Given the clumsy way her hands worked in my hair, and her unusually breezy banter, I realized that she was working up to something. "Selene, do you know what Juba will expect from you in the bridal bed?"

My cheeks burned. Everyone imagined my mother as a seductress with great knowledge of the sensual arts, but I'd been young when she died; she'd never shared any of that particular wisdom with me. "I—I think I can guess."

Octavia now looked sour, as if she were about to face a torment of the spirit. "This is what will happen. When you're alone in the bridal chamber, Juba will call you wife and draw you into his arms. But you mustn't go willingly or he'll think you're a *lupa*." A *she-wolf*, she said, but she meant *whore*. "You must shy away and struggle just enough to please him but not enough to make him angry. Then submit to him as your husband and your king."

Helios is my king. The thought came to me so suddenly and unbidden that I feared that I'd said it aloud. My twin was the rightful King of Egypt and dearer to me than I could dare admit. Some said that it was for his sake the city of Thebes had rebelled. But I'd bargained for my twin's life, so I'd have to submit to the emperor's wishes and to Juba too. I'd just have to remind myself every day how fortunate I was not to be married off to old King Herod of Judea.

When my little gray cat leapt onto the dressing table, upsetting a tray of hairpins and ribbons, Octavia cried, "Wretched creature! I won't be sorry to see that beast leave with you. I can't see why cats are sacred in Egypt. They're nothing but mischief." Bast took no notice of this insult, purring and burrowing into my arms while Octavia scowled. "Oh dear. I'm making a mess of your hair. My fingers aren't as nimble as they used to be. I'll let your *ornatrix* fix it."

My slave girl fixed my hairstyle, and then we dallied until dusk, trying to decide between two pairs of sandals, one of which was prettier but pinched my toes. At last, Chryssa helped me into my wedding garments. The white muslin *tunica* and accompanying girdle. The floral wreath and the orange flame-colored veil. This was the garb of a modest Roman bride, but in spite of all the years I'd lived amongst my father's people, it still looked foreign to me. When I glanced into the polished silver mirror, I groaned in dismay. Octavia had bound my hair in such a way that it smothered everything unique about me. The white muslin left me looking pale, hiding what beauty I possessed, and I was all but suffocated by the saffron veil. "It's horrible."

"No," Chryssa said, softly. "You're a beautiful bride."

But this was something people said to brides, whether or not it was true. I pulled the veil away. "I need . . . something else."

Chryssa's eyes widened. "It's almost time for the wedding. Half the city is at the gates."

This did nothing to calm me. Roman weddings were supposed to be small and modest affairs, simple contracts that required only a few witnesses. Mine would be different. The guests would be looking to see if I was just a Roman girl, the daughter of Mark Antony, or if I was Cleopatra's daughter, a sorceress whose blood made flowers grow, whose hands left crocodiles docile in her wake. As the foremost worshipper of Isis in Rome, stories about me had passed from temple to temple, tavern to tavern, amongst the slaves and the lower classes. I'd emboldened them. Perhaps I'd inspired them. So maybe I need not fear the crowds; I wasn't a prisoner anymore.

Be my *Cleopatra*, the emperor said, *and one day your mother's Egypt may be yours.*

Augustus was a grand actor in a pageant of his own creation and the only way to remain in his favor was to play my role. He wanted spectacle? Well, I would give him one. With deep resolution, I unwound the braids that Octavia had so painstakingly fastened, brushing out my dark hair so that it curled and cascaded, loose and free, over my shoulders. "I won't be a Roman bride," I said. "My mother was Pharaoh and I'll let no one forget it."

Chryssa's mouth formed a circle of surprise when I threw open my wardrobe chest, giving no care to the fact that the slaves had carefully packed it for the journey. I rifled through it until I found a beautiful diaphanous gown that Helios had given me. Octavia had tried to make it modest with stitches and brooches. Now I refashioned it. Removing the pins, I wrapped the gown under my arms and tied it between my breasts in the knot of Isis, the *tiet*, a loop with trailing sides that was a variant of the *ankh*. My wide-eyed slave girl watched me as if I'd gone mad. "You're going to give insult. You'll anger the emperor!"

"I know him better than you do." Since I was a little child, I'd learned to play all the emperor's games; this was just one more. *Be my Cleopatra*, the emperor had said, and I was young and foolish enough to believe I knew what that meant. "Don't stand there gaping, Chryssa. Help me!"

Reluctantly, she went to my dressing table, searching for the proper cosmetic pots, as I told her what to do. My mother had been a Hellenistic queen, and when she dressed for the civilized Greek-speaking world, she dressed accordingly. But she'd also been Pharaoh of Egypt. It was that reminder of Egypt I wanted now, so I urged Chryssa to draw the dark lines of the *wedjat*—the eye of Horus—on my eyelids with black kohl. Then she used the greens and blues and reds of Egypt to color my face. When she was done, I held up the mirror and peered at myself with the green eyes of a jungle cat, exotic and wild. "You need more jewelry," Chryssa suggested, finally warming to the idea. "Something sparkling to go with your little jade frog and betrothal ring."

I knew just the thing. Carefully wrapped in the bloodstained dress I'd worn as a prisoner was a golden snake armlet with gemstone eyes that my mother left for me when she'd foreseen her own death. I retrieved it from under my mattress, where I'd kept the bundle hidden for years, and slipped the armlet up until it hugged my bicep, its history merging with my skin. The effect was dazzling and scandalous. "You look like your mother's portraits," Chryssa breathed.

But I saw in myself someone entirely new.

Two

THEY were all waiting for me. At the edges of the vast peristyle garden, guests found their seats beneath the columned porticos. In the torchlight, the emperor's family gathered—the *Julii* and all their numerous friends and clients. Sitting apart was the emperor's wife and her family; as a Claudian, Livia descended from a nearly unbroken line of power-hungry maniacs and criminals, but in Rome their pedigree made them untouchable. The smell of their old aristocracy wafted on the air, just over the scent of burning torches.

I watched from beneath an archway as senators fiddled impatiently with their purple-bordered togas and ladies delighted in the confections served by passing slaves. The emperor's daughter arrived late, accompanied by her new husband. Julia's recent wedding had been a hurried affair, as if to prevent Livia's jealous interference. In fact, Julia's wedding had been nothing like this one. Her father hadn't even been present, but Augustus was here now, waiting for me.

My family was also waiting. The Ptolemies. Julius Caesar. My mother. My father. My butchered brothers and the only brother that still remained with me, my little Philadelphus, my mother's youngest son. The only one missing was the one I needed most. My twin wasn't here except insofar as he lingered in the prophecy of our shared birth. The Isis worshippers and others believed we'd bring about a Golden Age. All those hopes and dreams and expectations hovered in that courtyard. I had only to appear on the stage that the emperor had given me.

The moon that was my namesake hung in the sky like a pale ghost, its face only half revealed, like mine. I stepped out and everyone turned to see. I stretched my hands to the sides, like the paintings of my winged goddess on Egyptian tombs. They'd all expected that I'd go meekly to this wedding, shy as a slave on the block. They expected a bride in white muslin and orange veil. Some of the guests may have even supposed I'd marry in a Greek *chiton* with a royal purple cloak over my shoulders. None of them expected me to cast aside the respectable garments of a Roman bride in favor of a scandalous gown, a painted face, and hair flowing over my shoulders in dark ringlets.

The guests tittered. Some stood. Others sat down abruptly on couches. Two servants knelt in homage to me while a lute player missed his note. Then the musicians went quiet altogether. I knew the memories I conjured with my mother's coiled serpent upon my bare arm, my ruby red lips and the malachite on my eyelids glittering like a pharaoh's mask, firm breasts swaying beneath the gathered green folds of my thin gown. If my display weren't so deadly earnest, I might have laughed at the way women clutched at their modest garments, all scandalized by Cleopatra's daughter. My groom was scandalized too. The newly made King of Mauretania waited for me beneath the grape arbor, an angry expression upon his handsome face.

But my eyes were for Augustus, who was bedecked for this occasion in the *corona civica*, his oak-leaf crown. He'd been sipping at wine and chatting with his adviser, Maecenas, but stopped mid-conversation when the crowd opened a path between us. The emperor saw me and his eyes narrowed. Then he stilled.

In all the years since my mother's death, I'd been raised never to address a crowd of my own accord. Never to speak unless spoken to. Never to shout or lift my immodest eyes. To remember always that I was the daughter of the whore who'd plunged Rome into civil war and that it was only by the grace of Augustus that I lived.

But I knew the emperor loved a good show and I intended to give him one. With my arms still upraised, I proclaimed, "I am the eighth Cleopatra of the royal House of Ptolemy!"

The emperor handed his wine to Maecenas so abruptly that some of it sloshed out of the goblet. This brought an uncomfortable sputter from the wedding guests. Only Lady Octavia dared to speak. *"Selene!"* She thought I mocked her with this display. That I meant to spit upon all the modest virtues she'd taught me. She started toward me but the emperor lifted two fingers to stop her. This and the evening wind at my back emboldened me. "I am Cleopatra Selene, Queen of Cyrenaica," I continued. It was a title without power, for Cyrenaica was governed by Romans, but at the sufferance of the emperor, it was the only royal title I retained as my own. "I am Cleopatra Selene, daughter of Isis, and therefore *Thea Notera*, the Younger Goddess, the Maiden Goddess."

The emperor's jaw tightened. He didn't like that title, *Thea Notera*; and he especially didn't like my mention of Isis, his least favorite goddess. My *mother's* goddess. His praetorians tensed as if readying for battle and the *lictors* who accompanied him on formal occasions stiffened. Their axes were ceremonial, but I knew their blades could cut. Somehow I found the courage to press on. "I am Cleopatra Selene, *Thea Philadelphoi*, the Goddess Who Loves Her Brothers."

The emperor's nose lifted as if to scent treachery in the air. I could see the way his mind was turning, trying to divine whether or not I would declare myself the rightful Queen of Egypt and my twin Egypt's rightful king. Augustus could have me killed with a mere signal to his henchmen. With a simple flick of his wrist. Still, he let me come. I drew closer, my eyes never leaving his. "I am Cleopatra Selene, *Thea Philopatris*, the Goddess Who Loves Her People."

It had been one of my mother's appellations and a few of the guests jeered, which shook me. This same citizenry that had come to celebrate my wedding had bayed for my blood when I'd been dragged through the city as a child, so my fears raced alongside my heartbeat. Some faces in the crowd were awed. Others were hostile and whispered of my arrogance. I passed my brother Philadelphus, on my right. After my marriage, he would remain here in Rome to secure my good behavior. Already pale from a recent illness, he went paler at my bold display. The emperor's daughter glanced up at me and twitched, like a frightened fawn ready to bolt for the woods. My Roman half sisters, the Antonias, cloistered around her, both of them agape. And the emperor's wife looked as if she saw in me an apparition.

At last, I found myself standing before Augustus. He knew not what I meant to do but seemed mesmerized by the possibilities. I confess I enjoyed his discomfort. If I named myself the Queen of Egypt, everyone would know it for the truth, but it would also mean my end. I was so close to him, as close to him as I'd been on the day of his triumph, when he held my chin between his thumb and forefinger and decided to spare my life. I lifted that same chin and said, "As I come to this marriage to the King of Mauretania, I remain a friend and ally of the Roman people, loving and loyal ward of Augustus, Gaius Julius Caesar Octavianus, *Divi Filius*, Son of his Father, Julius Caesar, the God."

Then I lowered my head, bowing as a suppliant before him. The crowd roared its approval. They cheered, stomped their feet, and whistled. They sounded like the mobs in the stadium instead of an assemblage of wedding guests. I'd done all this to stroke the emperor's vanity, to honor my mother's legacy, and to speak the name of my goddess even where it was forbidden. But in so doing, I gave the emperor a gift he could have received from no one but me. I'd taken unto myself all the prestige of my lineage and laid it at his feet, giving him more power than he possessed before, letting him glimpse the glory that only I could bestow upon him.

He knew it, and avarice gleamed in his eyes. "I thank you for the tribute, Queen Selene." *Queen Selene.* He'd said it, and all the guests heard. Rising from my bow, I saw that he was also shaken. He hissed, voice low, "You risk much, you impudent thing."

"Fortune favors the bold," I whispered back, knowing it was Caesar's favorite motto.

The omens had already been taken from the entrails of a sacrificial ox and the day deemed provident for marriage, so the trumpeters heralded the beginning of the ceremony and officiates poured libations. If this had been a normal Roman wedding, we would have followed the priest into the emperor's mask room. We were foreign monarchs, though, so marrying under the wax death masks of the Julian family ancestors would have been very strange indeed. Thus, with his palm at the small of my back, the emperor escorted me to the fleece-covered couch where my groom waited. Augustus liked to think of himself as the kindly *paterfamilias* to all the orphans he'd taken into his care, but my real father should be standing here now. Would Antony have hugged me in his muscular arms? Would he have stroked my shoulders to calm me, his eyes dancing playfully as he gave me to my bridegroom? I would never know. My father was dead, and the man who claimed his place was the very one who had put him in his tomb.

At the feel of Juba's warm hand upon mine, I finally turned my eyes to the man I was to marry. A young Berber prince, his dark hair was curled in the style of a scholar. He was meticulously groomed, each clasp on his clothing perfectly positioned, freshly polished, and tightly fastened. He was trim, vigorous, and vibrant; more than a few women sighed with jealousy that I'd been given over to the newly made king. I was acutely aware of Juba, right down to the ridges of his fingertips on my hand, and remembered a time when I'd been fond of him. When—in my girlish infatuation—I'd welcomed his attention. He'd been my teacher and confidant. I might have been fond of him still, if I didn't know that Juba had helped the emperor defeat my parents. If only I didn't know that Juba, in his own small way, had been responsible for all the tragedy in my life.

The Romans had all manner of silly superstition against kings, so within the old walls of the *pomerium*, Juba couldn't wear a royal diadem upon his brow. Without it, it was difficult for me to imagine him as royalty, but the copper flecks in his irises made his eyes something more than ordinary brown. I saw hints of anger there, and through clenched teeth he said the simple Roman vow of lives intertwined. "When and where you are Gaia, I then and there am Gaius."

Where you are woman, I am man. When you are happy, I am happy.

It took a moment to find my voice. The officiant cleared his throat expectantly and I glanced up to see the emperor's intense stare. I swallowed, a wild hope that my missing twin was somewhere here in the crowd, torch in hand, determined to set the entire courtyard aflame and spirit me away. It was only a fantasy. I would know it if Helios was near. I would sense him. He wasn't here and I must marry Juba, so I forced myself to speak. "When and where you are Gaius, I then and there am Gaia."

Where you are man, I am woman. Where you are the father of a family, I am mother.

As the words fell from my lips, the emperor nodded as if Juba were merely the conduit between us—and an arc of dangerous electricity sparked the air we breathed. Augustus had once looked upon me as a mere child, a hostage, a political asset. Later, he came to see my mother in me and wondered how he might manipulate me for his own glory. But he'd never looked at me the way he did now. Something was happening between us, something that hadn't been a part of my plan, something that resonated with the darkest part of my soul. Something I was too young to understand and it made me deeply uneasy.

A piece of wedding cake was offered me and I took it, the spelt flour dry in my throat. The contracts were signed. Then it was done; as I've said before, Roman weddings weren't complicated affairs. Philadelphus was the first to embrace me. The rest of the family crowded round too. My Roman half sisters, the Antonias, my Roman half brother, Iullus, and my stepsister and stepbrother, Marcella and Marcellus. They'd all been my fellow orphans and childhood companions in Rome. When Octavia began to chastise me for my garb, it was the affable Marcellus who defended me against his mother's wrath. "Selene's gown is quite fashionable in the East, and she did wear a bridal wreath!"

Juba stood stiffly beside me, wincing at the thump of Admiral

Agrippa's hand on his shoulder. The emperor's most trusted lieutenant, and Rome's finest general, was a grizzled soldier who always looked ill at ease in a toga and today was no exception. Agrippa chuckled, his smile rueful but warm. "By Jupiter, I don't envy you the task of making this girl into a proper wife, Juba. But you'll never be bored."

Everyone laughed except for my new husband. Then Marcella kissed me warmly on each cheek. "I think you've bewitched my husband the admiral. I should be jealous." She said it without malice, for everyone knew that Agrippa couldn't be bewitched, not even by her. His heart belonged to his mother-in-law, the Lady Octavia, but we'd all learned long ago that Agrippa's love was always eclipsed by his devotion to duty, as he saw it.

The emperor's daughter threw her arms around me in heedless abandon, laughing. "Selene, you always find some way to steal all the attention for yourself, don't you? Now who is going to remember *my* wedding?"

Julia was my dearest friend and I was grateful for her affection in the face of the wicked gossip that now swirled around me. *Augustus has made this Princess of Egypt, this Queen of Mauretania, the richest woman in the world! How does he know she'll stay loyal to Rome?* Somewhere else I heard snippets of hushed conversation. *Is it true that she works magic? She's a witch. They say she charms crocodiles. How eager Lady Octavia must be to get rid of her!*

I'd expected some censure, but now that I was in the eye of the storm, heat flamed at my cheeks. I stumbled through the evening under the emperor's penetrating gaze. He was always staring at me, no matter to whom he was speaking. And while he was watching me, his wife was watching *him*. The serene smile Livia always wore in public didn't reach her eyes, and I had the strange sensation that I'd somehow made a terrible mistake.

HENCEFORTH, my wedding proceeded like an illusion. I didn't taste the food, though I ate it. The songs all ran together and the faces of guests blurred before my eyes. My world became a haze. In another River of Time, perhaps it would have been my twin that I took for a husband—to live and love and rule jointly over Egypt as was our people's custom. Perhaps in some other, happier, River of Time, I *had* taken Helios for my husband. But in *this* life, he'd abandoned me to the Romans, and so it was Juba's wife I'd become.

We dispensed with the traditional feigned struggle, where the bride was carried off and revelers cried out bawdy jests; such a performance would insult our dignity as royals. When we reached the bridal chamber that Octavia had made ready for us, I ritually adorned the door with wool and smeared it with oil. Slaves and freedmen should have carried me over the green garlanded threshold, but Juba lifted me and carried me to the large bed that dominated the center of the room. This wasn't the typical Roman sleeping couch, but an exotic Eastern-style bed, truly fit for a king and queen, its mattress piled high with tasseled purple pillows, its festooned frame inlaid with ivory and gold. Marble statues of stern-faced Roman gods and goddesses surrounded the bed in a semi-circle, as if to supervise what would happen here.

Outside, amidst the notes of the lyre and the shakes of rattles, the lingering laughter of our guests still echoed. Inside, our bridal suite was quiet enough that I could hear the erratic beat of my own heart. Alone for the first time since the ceremony began, we were as strangers. Juba folded his elegant hands in his lap and I straightened my gown over my legs. He unfastened his cloak, then rolled his shoulders as if to loosen them. I pushed myself up against the pillows, then adjusted my mother's famous amethyst ring upon my fourth finger, where the nerve was said to run straight to the heart. He started to utter my name, then cut himself off. He wouldn't even look at me.

Octavia told me that I must pretend to struggle, but I doubted I'd have to playact my reluctance if he should try to take me into his arms. Thankfully, Juba reached first for the laces of my sandals, unfastening the ties and dropping each shoe to the floor. I watched him do it, marveling at his grim concentration. When he was done, he shook his head, whispering harshly, "Who are you?"

"You know who I am, Juba. You're just angry with me for dressing this way."

"Do you know what you've done?" he snapped, rising to his feet. "You made them think of Cleopatra and Caesar!"

Rebellion swelled in my chest. "So what if I did? The world would be a better place if Augustus were more like Julius Caesar."

Juba whirled to face me. "Are you so naive, Selene? That was a public and political flirtation. You'll have Rome gossiping that you and Augustus are lovers."

Now I recoiled, holding back my indignation with one hand pressed to the base of my throat. "*Lovers?* What an obscene thing to say!"

"It *is* obscene." Juba was usually a man of the mildest temperament, but now he glowered. "All my life I've fought to prove that I'm no barbarian. I've become a scholar, trained as a soldier, and mastered Roman law so that no prejudice might be held against me for my Berber blood. Yet in one night, you've soiled my name. How will Rome believe I'm fit to rule a kingdom if I can't even rule my own wife?"

It was only because I'd also tried to prove myself to the Romans that I started to reassure him, but he held up a hand as if forbidding me to speak. "I can forgive you for humiliating *me*, Selene. I've suffered humiliations before. But how could you do this to *Augustus*? You and I both came to this city in chains, children of conquered kings and queens, yet he did us the kindness of making us part of his own family." *No*, I thought. *He kept us hostage.* The emperor never did any kindness that wasn't rooted in some other motive, but Juba left me no room to interrupt his lecture. "How do you repay him? By putting his life in danger!"

At this last accusation, I sputtered. "Just how could *I* put the emperor's life in danger?"

"Think, will you? Julius Caesar was assassinated by men who thought he'd been corrupted. He flaunted a foreign queen as his lover and they wondered if he'd destroy the Republic and name himself king. Now there's a new Caesar and the senators already whisper about how Augustus will destroy the Republic—"

"With good reason," I interrupted. "But that has nothing to do with me."

"Gossip doesn't deal in truth, Selene. Your performance today may have destroyed the reputation of a moral man!" If I'd ever wondered whether Juba's loyalty to Augustus was feigned, those doubts were now put to rest. Who else could earnestly describe the emperor as a *moral* man? It was true that Augustus worked hard, refrained from excesses of wine and food, and could live quite humbly without complaint. It was also true that darker passions swirled in the emperor's soul. He could be vicious and petty, murderous and cruel. There was an emptiness in him that no victory could fill. I knew all about the helpless girls who were brought to his bedchamber. Girls who left in tears. Having lived so long with Augustus, Juba should have known it too, but perhaps it was easier for him to shut his eyes to such truths. "Do you hate him, Selene? Do you hate him that much?"

Augustus was my mother's worst enemy, my father's false friend, and the murderer of my brothers. But at the hour of my death, even knowing that the gods would soon weigh my heart against a feather on the scales of justice, I might deny that I hated him, for he'd spared my life and still held in his hands the fate of everything and everyone I held dear. Yes, I would deny that I hated him, and not even I would know if I lied.

I shook my head. "Augustus showed no hint of fear for his reputation or his life, and if he isn't displeased with me, why should you be?" In lieu of a reply, Juba's gaze wandered up to the red and gold geometric patterns carved into the ceiling. He was silent. Brooding. "Juba, I'm sorry to have upset you."

Pushing a forelock of hair from his brow, Juba sat down beside me, the weight of his body settling on the bed. "Believe me, Selene, I don't want to quarrel on our wedding night. We were friends once, weren't we?"

We *had* been friends and I'd always been drawn to him. Now, in spite of myself, in spite of how I knew Helios would hate it, I wanted to forgive Juba. Maybe it was innocence or youthful pride, but I *had* married him and I wasn't like the Romans who so blithely wed and divorced at their leisure. "Juba, what differences lie between us, there are no remedies for . . . but I would like to be friends again."

"More than friends, I hope," he said, leaning close.

I closed my eyes and let Juba's lips touch mine. It was my first kiss. It felt forbidden—*alien*—to be this close to someone. His breath on my face was like the hot wind of the desert, and his shaved cheek was smooth against my own. There was a cloying sweetness in that kiss that left me wanting both to flee and to draw him closer. Not knowing what to do with my hands, I let them grip the bed linens, and when we broke apart, I made a nervous sound, like the quaver of a harp.

Juba chuckled, his bad temper fading. "You look like a startled hare, Selene. Haven't you kissed anyone before?"

"Of course not," I replied quickly, sounding very much like an indignant Lady Octavia.

His finger traced my lower lip, which still tingled from the kiss. "So you come to me untouched?" I let my potent glare be answer enough for him. My mother had been accused of promiscuity, even harlotry, so when I didn't come to him dressed in the saffron veil, all modest and weepy, Juba had seen me as the Romans had seen my mother: as an Egyptian whore. Taking hold of the edge of the bed linen, my new husband wiped at my face, removing the cosmetics, swiping at my *wedjat*-painted eyes, my red lips, and rouged cheeks. When at last he was satisfied, he leaned back and said, "Ah, now I can see the maiden in you . . ."

It disarmed me. My mask had been my armor. He kissed me again, and defenseless, I forgot to be angry. Longing welled inside me, a need I couldn't identify. It was some manner of wanting, one I felt certain I couldn't satisfy without Juba's help. We paused and afraid to speak, I bit my bottom lip, the taste of the kiss lingering there. "I've wanted to kiss you for a long time," Juba admitted, his chest rising and falling. "When you first came to Rome, you were such a spoiled little princess, a proud Ptolemy, eager to recite all the languages you knew. I couldn't blame you for it. You were a clever girl. I knew you'd make a fine royal wife. And you made me nervous. I wanted to woo you with poetry but could never write a worthy verse."

"I'm sure that isn't true," I replied, flattered that he'd wished to woo me with poetry. Astonished that I'd ever made him nervous. Unexpectedly pleased by the way his breath quickened when his eyes trailed down my body. "Everyone says you're a brilliant writer, Juba, never at a loss for words."

"Except when it comes to you," Juba said, drawing close enough to whisper in my ear. "I want us to be more than friends, Selene. Will you let yourself love me?" Over the rush of blood in my ears I wasn't sure I'd heard rightly. The Romans told me it was my duty to lie beneath this man and be a mother to his children, but it'd never been any part of the bargain that there should be words of *love*. I tried to hush him, boldly offering my lips for another kiss, but he didn't take them. "Selene, you count the emperor's daughter amongst your friends, and in spite of all your mother's animosity for Octavia, you found it in yourself to love *her*. Why resist the idea of loving me?"

Because I knew—I knew better than anyone—how dangerous love could be. Love had destroyed my parents. The emperor had also taught me that love could be exploited to make me obey . . . and what of Helios? I loved my twin more than anything in this world or the next, and being apart from him was an open wound. How could I love anyone else? It would be a betrayal, not to mention foolish, to allow myself to feel for Juba any more than was required. Yet he persisted, nuzzling a soft spot by my ear that made me shiver. "Say that you'll love me, Selene."

It was a strange request. Unnecessary. Un-*Roman*. I couldn't say it. My throat tightened. My tongue swelled in my mouth. Where I'd been pliant and curious only moments before, I now went rigid and his expression darkened. "I have a *right* to you." I forced myself to perfect stillness as his fingers worked at the knot of Isis between my breasts. He'd expected a different knot and left off after a few unsuccessful tries, a sound of frustration in his throat. It was all going wrong.

"Shall I unfasten it for you, Juba?"

"No," he said sharply.

I didn't think my cheeks could get any hotter, but they did. "I forgot to struggle. Is that what you want?"

Muttering a curse, he covered his eyes with one hand and rolled onto his back. "It's been a very long day, Selene. We're both over-tired. We should sleep."

I let out a breath I didn't know I'd been holding. Relief mingled with discontent. I should say something, make some apology, but I didn't know what to say. When I started to rise, Juba caught me by the arm. "Stay."

I was bewildered because not even the emperor and Livia shared the same bed at night. "Do you intend for us to *sleep* together?"

"Does that disappoint you?" Juba laughed, but it was a sound that lacked all merriment. "If you leave now, there'll be more gossip."

The wedding had left me weary, but my eyes remained open until the oil lamps burned out. If Juba slumbered, I didn't know. When sleep finally swallowed me up, I dreamed that I was swimming in the Nile. The god of the river came to me as a lover, singing, his body merging with mine. The god's limbs were all pale and youthful and I knew he was my true husband, but no matter where I turned my head beneath his reverent kisses, I could never see his face.

Three

I woke to an empty bridal bed.

Without retrieving my sandals, I went to the doorway, intent upon finding Juba. I thought better of that idea when Julia swept into the room with a tray of leftover spelt cakes. She'd been my first and best friend in Rome. Witty and vivacious, with a charming little smirk that she couldn't even suppress for the artists who painted her portraits, she was prone to spontaneous fits of laughter and mischief. No sense of decorum ever prevented her from flinging her arms around those she loved and some said that Julia and I were as different as two girls could be. The truth was we shared more in common than anyone knew. "So, now you're the Queen of Mauretania," Julia said, with a playful grin. "I hope you won't expect me to kneel for you in obeisance. We Romans don't do that sort of thing."

I sniffed in my most queenly manner. "I suppose accommodations can be made."

This made her laugh. "I wish your wedding breakfast would start already. I'm famished and can't wait to try the delicacies—it'll be nothing but the best for you. This morning I had to listen to Octavia make a dull accounting of how they're loading your baggage train with chests of gold, fabrics, and glassware. I'm told that you'll want for nothing because Juba has acquired artists and fawning courtiers and a veritable army of engineers and slaves." These last were bought and paid for by her father so that we could stamp the Roman seal into the untamed lands of Africa. Taking a bite of cake and licking crumbs from her fingers, Julia complained, "You know, if I'd done what you did yesterday, my father would've banished me."

She was probably right. For all that Julia could be impulsive and selfish, vain, and sometimes silly, I couldn't blame her for her resentment. I hated the way her father treated her and hated even more the idea that she might be displeased with me. "Please don't take me to task. Juba already scolded me."

"Did he?" Now Julia looked at me closely. "Oh, Selene, you poor thing. Your eyes! Did Juba hurt you?"

Whatever could be wrong with my eyes? I found a silver mirror upon the dressing table and examined my reflection, only to see that the kohl from the night before had smeared and made it look as if I'd wept. "He didn't *hurt* me," I murmured, reaching for a washcloth from the nearby basin. "He barely touched me."

Julia's eyes widened as she glanced at our bed. "Perhaps he's waiting to claim his rights until he's sure of a pleasant reception." I remembered the rush of warmth that had flowed through my body when Juba kissed me. I might have received Juba *quite* pleasantly if he hadn't asked me for something I couldn't give. "Or perhaps your groom hopes to reach some sort of arrangement with you, Selene."

I arched a brow. "An *arrangement*?"

At this, Julia snatched the mirror from me to admire her own delicate features. "Marcellus and I have an arrangement." The hairs at the nape of my neck rose in a way that reminded me of my cat's reaction to danger. "On the night of our wedding, I told Marcellus that I knew he played the catamite with older men like Virgil. That kind of bedroom play is well enough for a poet or a Greek, but for the emperor's nephew? Scandal!"

Of all the older boys in the household, Marcellus had always been the most agreeable. Moreover, Virgil, the emperor's poet, had always been a friend to my brothers and me. It pained me to think of either man brought into disgrace. "What did Marcellus say when you confronted him?"

Julia tossed her head, the green glass beads of her dangling earrings rattling together as she laughed. "Marcellus was actually *relieved* that I knew. He's never been with a woman. He can't bring himself to it. We've agreed to put out in public that we're happily wed and neither of us will interfere in one another's affairs."

I wanted to share in her laughter, but I couldn't even make myself smile. "Julia—"

"Oh, here comes a lecture, and it ought to be rich, coming from you, who just yesterday set every tongue wagging."

"Your father relies on you to give him an heir!"

"Then he should have married me to Iullus Antonius," Julia said, defiantly. When I put both my hands over my mouth to stifle my gasp, she said, "Don't pretend to be surprised. I love your stepbrother. I've always loved him. I always will. Besides, you're the one who prattles on about Egypt, where women are able to *choose*. You say women are as valuable to the world as men. And look! You've persuaded my father to make you a queen. Why shouldn't I shape the future to *my* liking?"

Just the day before, I'd proclaimed myself a goddess and Julia wondered why she couldn't simply be the mistress of her own destiny. Her thoughts were dangerous. Iullus was my father's son by the fearsome Fulvia, long since dead, but another woman the emperor loathed. Julia would have been hard-pressed to find a more insulting candidate for her heart. "Julia, do you know what your father would do to you if he caught you with Iullus? To both of you?"

She fluttered her eyelashes at me, the very image of innocence. "Why should my father ever find out? Someday the empire will belong to Marcellus. He'd gladly adopt my children as his own. He said so. After being forced to marry, we've found a way to be happy. Why can't you be happy for us?"

"Because I'm terrified for you." For Iullus too. My Roman half brother had made a misery of my childhood in Rome, but I never wished actual harm to befall him.

Julia poked at me with the hard edge of the mirror. "Don't give me your solemn expression. You'll have plenty of time to be solemn after a few years of chasing Juba's brats in Mauretania. You'll have to give him a whole litter, and you'll be so busy with motherhood, you'll forget all about your loved ones here in Rome."

At this, I bristled. "I never forget my loved ones." I didn't forget my living brothers or the ones that Augustus murdered. I didn't forget my father, who had fallen on his sword. Nor did I ever forget my mother and how she met her end. Those pains crowded my *khaibit*, the shadow part of my soul. I didn't want to make room for more.

MY husband arrived at the wedding breakfast without offering any explanation for his early-morning disappearance, and my attempt to engage him in conversation was drowned out by the din of the pipers announcing us. Juba stood tall, a hand at my elbow, turning me to the guests as if for display, but there wasn't anything improper about my ensemble this time. My hair twisted in a modest knot at the nape of my neck and a light blue *chiton* bloused low on my hips. It was a Greek garment, but it was still considered appropriate. Even so, it didn't prevent Livia's caustic appraisal. The emperor's wife leaned forward to whisper, "Do you expect everyone to forget that you dressed like a harlot for your wedding? Don't think you can embarrass me, as you did yesterday, without paying a price."

I detested the emperor's wife but knew better than to antagonize her. I was mindful that my little brother Philadelphus must stay behind in Rome. There were too many people I loved who would remain at Livia's mercy long after I left to rule my new kingdom, so I made no reply to the emperor's wife, giving all my attention to the swarm of guests. Surrounded by speculators and hangers-on seeking our patronage, Juba and I were overwhelmed with gifts. Vivid paintings framed with precious wood, engraved gemstones, expensive Greek sculptures carved from the finest marble. More practical gifts too, including couches with golden feet arched in the shape of eagle claws, tall braziers studded with carnelian, and oil lamps that served as a canvas for fanciful creatures painted in black and ochre.

Amidst all this treasure, Lucius Cornelius Balbus approached us boldly. The *Cornelii* were a famous patrician Roman family, but this man came from one of its plebeian branches and was an inveterate survivor of the civil wars. He hailed from Spain and had been one of my father's soldiers—one of the many who deserted. Nonetheless, I resolved to treat Balbus with gracious regard because many of those who would come with us to Mauretania were veterans of Actium. Some of them might remember my father kindly and be well disposed to me. So I said, "Good greetings, Lucius Cornelius."

In reply, the stout man unfurled a glorious purple cloak over my knees. "Queen Selene, I bought this for you with the riches of my plantations in North Africa," he boasted. The cloth flowed over me like liquid and I couldn't help but test the smoothness of it between my fingers. "I hope your husband will make me richer still by keeping the barbarians off my land!"

Some laughed at Balbus's comments, but most of our guests stared with slack-jawed amazement at the costly gift. The cloak had been dipped several times in the *ruinously* expensive Tyrian purple dye and the covetous glances of the crowd gave me the impression that the garment was worth a small city. Even the emperor seemed impressed, motioning for me to join him on his couch. "Come show me!"

Normally an abstemious eater, Augustus today ate with gusto. He feasted upon dormice seasoned with honey and poppy seeds. He poured a generous amount of the peppery fish sauce called *garum* on his eggs. As he ate, I balanced unnaturally on the farthest edge of his couch with the garment clutched in my lap, my fingers tracing the golden embroidered edge. Augustus didn't glance up at me until he'd finished chewing. "This purple cloak is ostentatious, isn't it? It suits your tastes, Selene. Like your mother, you have a fondness for Eastern decadence."

I didn't hear a note of displeasure in his voice, but I was always wary when he mentioned my mother. The pipers and laughter guarded our conversation from eavesdroppers. Still, I lowered my voice. "Augustus, I'm sorry if I offended you with my bridal costume yesterday."

He examined the cloak more closely, or pretended to. "As long as you remain loyal to me, I can forgive you such extravagances." His gray eyes met mine, thin lips twitching in the semblance of a smile, and I could see that my performance at the wedding had flattered his vanity and lifted his spirits. Was it only my imagination that his eyes roamed over me in a way that was anything but fatherly? I wished the wicked notion away, trying to convince myself it was born only of the vicious suggestion Juba had made the night before. "Don't you care for your breakfast, Selene? I haven't seen you eat."

I pulled my shawl over my shoulders in sudden awareness of Juba's frosty scowl from across the room. What would he have me do? Refuse to sit by Augustus when summoned? "I'm not hungry, Caesar."

"Why not? What could trouble you? Haven't I given you everything a girl could ever ask for?"

No. He hadn't given me Egypt, but I wasn't so foolish as to remind him of it now. Glancing around the room at the guests, I saw some of them whisper to one another behind jeweled hands, their eyes sliding in my direction. Did those low murmurs carry rumors about the emperor's fondness for me? How I wished Juba hadn't filled me with doubt!

"Let's play a game, Selene." Augustus had always tested the children in his household. Especially me. I was, after all, his most unlikely apprentice. "Excluding the two of us, who is the most important person here?"

It was a difficult question to answer. With all her powerful Claudian connections, the emperor's wife gave him the status that his mostly base blood denied him. He'd thought Livia important enough to marry while she was pregnant with another man's child, important enough to keep as his wife, though she couldn't bear him a child of his own. Still, I knew the emperor would never concede that a woman was more important than a man, so Livia couldn't be the answer to his riddle . . .

Propped up on elbows upon various couches were Roman senators, each of whom would publicly claim only to be the equal of his colleagues. They all harbored secret ambitions and it was tempting to choose one of the rich ones who'd returned recently with loot from the provinces. However, if the most important man in the room was the wealthiest, I must name Maecenas, the emperor's shrewd political adviser. He was a balding man with a hawkish face and served as the vizier over all the emperor's artists and propagandists. It was also rumored that Maecenas had a house in every city on the Mediterranean coastline and I didn't doubt it. Just as I was about to name him, the emperor broke in with, "Come, Selene, not even a guess?"

Something about his tone made me hesitate. This was my wedding breakfast. Perhaps Augustus meant to make some point about its significance. "Is it my husband, your newest client king?"

Augustus grunted. "No. Juba is loyal. Useful. A valuable friend. But he cannot be more important than a Roman."

That did narrow the choices. "Marcellus, then. Your nephew, your son-in-law, the last male of the *Julii*."

"Not yet. He'll still have to prove himself." Plucking a spear of green asparagus from a silver platter, Augustus pierced the air between us. "You disappoint me, Selene. If you wish to wield power, true power, you must learn from me. Always know the most important person in the room."

I took an agate cup of watered wine from a passing slave to reconsider my answer, and peered over its striated rim. By the entryway, Agrippa shifted from foot to foot, eager to leave. He was the emperor's trusted soldier and strategist, the true enforcer of all his power. Aside from the emperor, he was likely the most important person in the room, but I was suddenly hesitant to say so. Indeed, the banquet was filled with more luminaries than I could name, and I hesitated to set one above the other without knowing the emperor's purpose for fear of condemning a man as a rival. At my hesitation, the emperor growled. "Too slow, Selene! The answer is *Lucius Cornelius Balbus*, the man who gave you this fine purple garment. He'll be accompanying you to Mauretania and he's the most important person here because of what he represents."

"So, it was a trick question." Then again, with the emperor, they always were.

"You're clever enough to grasp it. Balbus is a veteran. The loyalty of the legions has been at the core of my victories. Now all these ambitious soldiers need to be settled and appeased. My veterans will be there for you to call upon if the natives rise up, but you'll need to win their confidence. Otherwise, I'm better off making Mauretania a Roman province."

"I dispute none of that," I said, finally settling upon my own answer. "But I think the most important person here is Julia."

"Julia?" He laughed as if I'd told some grand jest.

I braved explaining myself. "You need her because of what *she* represents. Haven't you called Rome yet another wayward daughter for you to govern? When citizens measure how you treat Julia, they gauge what kind of father you'll be to the empire." I said this both because I believed it and because I noticed the way Julia and Iullus flirted, feeding one another grapes at the far end of the hall, laughing at some private joke between them. Julia's arrangement with her husband had filled me with foreboding. There might come a time when the emperor wished to punish Julia, and even if he forgot all paternal love for her, perhaps he'd remember her political significance if I pointed it out to him now.

Augustus shifted to face me, letting the asparagus fall back to his plate. "You're right about one thing. Everyone is always measuring me, judging me. Thanks to your twin, this city is filled with malcontents, agitating to steal from me all that I've won. Look at these people eating my food and availing themselves of my hospitality as if they weren't waiting for me to stumble . . ."

I shouldn't let him dwell on those who resented his power. It made him paranoid and vengeful. "They'll praise your name when the grain flows again and that's something I can make happen as Queen of Mauretania."

"You're too sure of yourself. Mauretania isn't like Egypt. It's uncivilized. You and Juba could fail to turn it into the breadbasket and port of trade I need . . ."

Because no one was listening, I dared to say, "But if we succeed, you must agree that I could rule Egypt even better."

He caught me with a shrewd sideways glance, and for a moment

I worried that I'd pushed too far. Then he laughed. "You'd think I'd tire of your single-minded greed, Selene, but if you ever ceased angling for things out of your grasp, I'd worry you were up to some treachery . . ." He leaned back, eyes searching the crowd. "Sadly, I seem to have overestimated your twin's affection for you. I hoped Helios might interrupt your wedding or try to smuggle himself into the breakfast, where my guards could catch him."

With the emperor, there were always layers upon layers of intrigue. I found it strangely comforting to know that I'd been used as bait for my brother. Not long ago, incensed that Helios had escaped the imperial compound and outraged at rebellion in Egypt, the emperor had insisted Helios be denounced before the Senate as a traitor and enemy of Rome. Since then, his temper had cooled and he'd changed his mind. There were those who said Helios hadn't run away at all; that Augustus had simply had him disappeared. I desperately needed to believe otherwise, so I took comfort in the idea that the emperor was still laying snares. "You want to capture Helios *here*?"

"You should want it too. I've put out that the rebellion in Thebes is only a tax revolt. I've kept your twin's name out of it, so that I may be merciful to him and to Egypt, but I've done this only for your sake." I didn't believe that it was for my sake. Legions were still bogged down in Spain, Egypt was rising up, and the Republican faction in Rome grew increasingly restless. There might be another civil war if my father's old partisans knew that the son of Antony and Cleopatra was in rebellion. Those who knew the prophecies that a savior would come to purge Rome by fire might see in Helios the bringer of a Golden Age. Consequently, the emperor gained nothing by acknowledging Helios as his enemy; it was far more advantageous for my twin to simply *vanish*. "Make no mistake, Selene. If the Prefect of Egypt can't put down this rebellion in Thebes, I'll ask you and Juba to raise legions in Mauretania. You'll help me end this."

He thought he could make me fight against my own brother and my own people. I could never let it come to that. Fortunately, I was spared the need to reply when the emperor's poet rose to recite some verses from the *Aeneid*—a special piece of propaganda the emperor was keen to have him finish. Virgil had been working on the epic longer than I'd been in Rome, like Penelope at the loom, weaving words by day, and striking them out at night. The *Aeneid* told the story of Aeneas, the defeated Trojan who abandoned the powerful Carthaginian queen Dido. Ah, yes, dutiful Aeneas, unmoved by the plea of a pleasure-seeking, goddess-worshipping foreign queen. It was a scarcely veiled condemnation of my mother and father, and I loathed this poem. But when Virgil finished his recitation and the applause died down, the emperor's eyes were filled with tears. He liked to affect emotion in a crowd like this, to persuade them that in his chest beat a compassionate heart. He was a showman; if this poem touched something inside him, it was his ambition.

It was then that Virgil introduced his friend Crinagoras of Mytilene, whom I knew by reputation to be a master epigrammatist. Crinagoras was sleight of build, with soft, almost feminine features, and when he smiled, his warm eyes crinkled at the corners. "I'm pleased to meet you," I said when he bowed before me. "Your name precedes you, Crinagoras."

"As well it should, *Your Majesty*," the little man said with a boastful smile. "Think of the esteem my reputation will bring to your royal court. You should hire me at once before some wiser monarch steals me away."

I'd never met such a bombastic self-promoter. "Are you asking for a position?"

Crinagoras smirked. "There's no need to ask. You're already charmed, *desperate* to have me glorify your reign."

I stifled my laugh because I knew better than to let a courtier think he had the upper hand. "And why should we hire a court poet when there's more serious work to be done in Mauretania?"

"Majesty, you must have a court poet, or no one will ever know about your serious work," he replied, and I followed his eyes to Virgil, catching his meaning at once. The emperor was already seeing to it that his rule would be immortalized in a way that suited him. He was shaping history and making certain that he had a voice in it.

I wanted a voice too but said, "We'll have to hear your work before we can make a decision of such consequence."

"How very fortunate that I've already composed a toast in honor of your marriage!" Crinagoras waved his hand theatrically and the wedding guests gathered round. It was just the opportunity I'd been waiting for. The chance to slip away from the emperor's couch and return to Juba's side. The musicians quieted, and everyone leaned in as the poet recited, *"Great bordering regions of the world which the full stream Nile separates from the black Ethiopians. Ye have by marriage made a destiny common to both, turning Egypt and North Africa into one country. May the children of these princes ever again rule with unshaken dominion over both lands."*

At these words, my body tightened like a bowstring. I was the rightful Queen of Egypt and through this poem, Crinagoras reminded everyone of that fact. Even the emperor seemed stunned by the man's nerve. With his gray eyes narrowed, Augustus said, "Crinagoras, how good of you to remember the majesty of Selene's past."

"And her future," the poet said boldly. I might have choked on my wine if I hadn't already swallowed it. Did the little poet care nothing for his own safety? I had the emperor's goodwill, but I couldn't protect him. Still, Crinagoras went on. "Isn't the House of *Julii* powerful enough to encompass all the greatness of the Ptolemies?"

It was exactly what I wished the emperor to believe—that he should restore me to Egypt where my power could only swell his own. I couldn't have fashioned better propaganda if I'd tried. But I *hadn't* tried and I worried when the emperor turned to me as if this were a plot. "Ah," Augustus said. "You see, Juba and Selene? Your match has captured the imaginations of the people; they find it fitting. Your marriage is the kind of news that should spread all over the empire. Even to Thebes."

Even to my twin, I thought. The emperor wanted Helios to know that I married Juba. He wanted Helios to believe that I'd betrayed him. And perhaps I had.

Four

AT length, the banqueters filled their napkins with treats to bring home. Meanwhile, Juba and I stood side by side, making our farewells to the guests. "I'd like to offer Crinagoras a place as our court poet," I said.

Without looking at me, Juba replied, "Crinagoras is no Virgil; he lacks a grand artistic vision."

"Yet his wedding verse today indicates that he has *political* vision. Did you disapprove?"

"Of the poem? No." Juba's jaw tightened. My new husband obviously disapproved of *something*. Most probably me. "Selene, if it pleases you, I'll extend an invitation to Crinagoras. Just be ready to travel at dawn. I'm going into the city tonight and can't say when I'll return." Then he turned with a swirl of his toga and walked away.

So it was to be like this between us, then.

Eager to work the knots of tension from my shoulders after the festivities, I hastened to the private baths, where steam made my skin damp even before I undressed. Chryssa followed me into the water with her reed basket of sponges, oils, and scrapers, just as she did the first day I'd come to Octavia's house. "Will Juba be joining you, my lady?"

"No," I said, trying not to sound embarrassed by the question. Egyptian weddings involved a ceremonial bath, but I found it difficult to imagine being naked with Juba after this morning's cool words. It was only natural that he'd want to say good-bye to his favorite teachers, fellow scholars, and dearest friends. Besides, Juba had—in some sense—given me a reprieve on our wedding night and I ought to be grateful. Soon, though, he'd expect to claim me as his wife. Nervously, I fanned my fingers over my belly beneath the water. I had to know what to prepare for because I didn't want to let out an undignified cry at the crucial moment. "Chryssa, when the emperor took you to his bed, was it painful?"

For a moment, the trickling of fresh water out of the fountain mouth of a gilded lion was the only noise in the room. "He—he wasn't," she stammered. "He wasn't physically cruel."

No. That wouldn't be the emperor's way. The deepest wounds were those he inflicted on the inside. And I was no better, for I'd been thoughtless and selfish to ask her this question. She'd gone unwilling to the bed of Augustus and been horribly ill used. Why had I made her remember it? I turned to apologize when I saw Chryssa clutching the *strigil*. It was only a scraper, meant to slough off sweat and oil. It wasn't very sharp, but Chryssa's white-knuckled grip made it cut into her skin. "You're bleeding," I said softly. She hissed as if only now realizing it and let her hand drop into the water between us, where the red droplets of her anguish mixed with the bathwater. "He won't touch you again, Chryssa. I'll take you away with me to Africa, and you'll never have to see him again." Her expression went carefully neutral in the way of a slave and together we watched the reed basket of sponges float across the murky water, like a sailing ship gone adrift. "You don't want to go with me," I said, realizing it for the first time. "You want to stay here, in Rome?"

"It's just that I have a sister," Chryssa said. "I wish I wasn't leaving Phoebe behind."

I was being forced to leave my little brother Philadelphus; I didn't have to imagine Chryssa's inner torment. "Maybe I can find a way for Phoebe to come with us . . ."

"No. There's nothing to be done. My sister belongs to Lady Julia now and considers herself quite fortunate. She's had cruel mistresses before who beat her with the lash. She wouldn't want to risk her new station."

Such were the terrors of slaves. Chryssa's back was also striped with scars from the lash, for she hadn't always belonged to me. "I'll find a way to let you stay here with your sister, then. Perhaps Augustus will allow me to grant you your freedom. I mean to do it anyway, the moment we get to Mauretania."

I was surprised to hear her gasp with dismay. "What would become of me? Do you think it's easy for a woman on her own in Rome? How would I feed myself?"

I felt foolish and confused. "You're a skilled *ornatrix*. Besides, I have money now. I'd help you."

Chryssa seemed angry, or at least as angry as a slave ever allowed herself to seem. "Do you know how many barbarian slaves have been brought into the city? It would be cheaper to buy ten of them than to pay me a wage. I was once Chryssa, slave of the emperor's wife. Then, Chryssa, slave of the Egyptian prince Helios. Now I'm Chryssa, slave of the Queen of Mauretania. If you set me free, I'm nobody at all."

"That isn't true. You'll always be Chryssa, a child of Isis."

My goddess opened her arms to slaves, and thus had many followers even where the conscript fathers had deemed hers a dangerous foreign cult. But Chryssa only said, "Without you here, Rome is no place for those who honor the goddess."

I bit my lip, worried about what might happen to the worshippers of Isis in my absence. Until I could return Isis to the throne of Egypt, perhaps I could make a safe haven for her worshippers in Mauretania. I tried to offer Chryssa some comfort. "My new kingdom isn't so far. With the right winds, Mauretania is just days away. I promise you can visit Rome—"

"No." She glanced over her shoulder as if she could see Livia and Augustus and all the others who had tortured her. "I'll never want to come back."

FOR weeks now, I'd been consumed with the wedding and all that attended it. It was only now, in the quiet aftermath of the celebration, that my imminent departure became a painful reality. Knowing this to be my very last day in Rome, I ushered Philadelphus to the schoolroom. Because my littlest brother was far more prone to pranks and frivolity than a Ptolemy ought to be, I rummaged through the scroll-cases that lined the wall, searching for parchment and vellum works on history and mathematics that I thought it especially important he study. With a roll of his eyes, Philadelphus said, "You aren't my tutor. Let's not spoil our last hours together with serious things."

I winced, knowing that he was no longer the baby brother who hid in my skirts. No longer the boy who cried with fear when the Romans took us prisoner, nor the boy who shook with sweat and fever. He was eleven years old now, as old as I'd been when I came to Rome. Even so, leaving him here as a hostage for my good behavior felt like the worst kind of betrayal and I hated myself for it even if I had no other choice. "Promise me that you'll study hard to make yourself useful to the emperor, Philadelphus."

"Oh, stop fretting," Philadelphus said with a brave smile. "Come be a sister to me. We'll play knucklebones until Juba returns." Like my father, Philadelphus possessed an easygoing charm. With his thick auburn curls and aquiline nose, he looked every bit the Roman boy, and I hoped this would protect him when I was gone. I let his brave smile melt my resistance and followed him back to the bedchambers that he'd once shared with Helios. We sat together on his sleeping couch and the cat jumped up between us, watching my brother rattle the *tali* dice inside a wooden cup. "Are you going to take Bast with you, Selene?"

Reaching down to pet her soft fur, I remembered that our cat belonged more to Helios than to either of us. Maybe that's why I so badly wanted to bring her to Africa with me. Now I pushed away that selfish urge. "She should stay with you and watch over you . . . You know that I don't want to go without you, don't you? I don't want to leave you, Philadelphus!"

"But you must," my brother said, fingering the Collar of Gold amulet at his throat. Like the jade frog I wore, it was the last thing my mother had ever given him. The moment she put it around his neck, he seemed to possess the gift of sight. "I've seen it in the Rivers of Time, Selene. You always leave and I always stay in Rome."

Philadelphus's hidden power was strong, but I refused to believe he saw truly. "You're wrong. Someday, we're *both* going back to Egypt."

He smiled weakly, swirling the dice. "I think I've almost seen it that way once . . . Nothing in the future is certain but the more often I see something, the more likely it's true. I've seen you become a great queen. You help to bring about a Golden Age. You feed the people and save Isis."

I saw his eyes slide away. "Is that the only thing you've seen? Will I be forced to fight Helios?"

He shrugged, letting the dice fall to the mattress between us. All ones. The Vulture. The lowest throw. "I don't know, but sometimes I've seen that you're a cause of war in Egypt . . . and that your life ends too soon."

We both shuddered and I scooped up the dice, putting them back in the cup and laying my hand over the top. "Don't look into the Rivers of Time anymore, Philadelphus. You know how the Romans feel about magic. I won't be here to protect you."

"It's not something I can control." I knew what he meant, for my own powers—when I had them—were wild and beyond my grasp. Hieroglyphic messages from Isis carved themselves into my hands when I touched the blood of the faithful, but I hadn't been able to control the winds that sometimes swirled when I was upset. I'd used them once, when Livia slapped me, to throw her to the ground, but since my bargain with the emperor, the winds had been still.

"Just be careful, then, Philadelphus. Write me letters. Lots of letters. If I don't hear from you, I'll assume the worst." He must understand how fragile his safety was. As he grew older, he'd be seen as a danger—a son of Antony and Cleopatra for all the emperor's enemies to exploit. "We're the last of the Ptolemies. Do whatever you must to survive. If you ever need to betray me, I'll never blame you for it. If I fall from the emperor's favor and he asks you to condemn me, don't hesitate!"

He jerked back as if I'd slapped him. "Selene, I would never betray you or condemn you. Just as I know that you'd never betray Helios." Now Philadelphus was crying and I was consumed by guilt. How would I ever leave him behind? They'd have to tear him from my arms in front of everyone.

"If you see me off in the morning, I'll fall apart. I'll simply fall apart."

"Then we'll say our good-byes tonight," he agreed. "We'll stay up all night together. I won't sleep."

But he was still a boy. Hours later, with Bast curled up under his chin, sleep finally closed his eyes and I let that be our parting.

I was surprised to find Iullus in the hall. "You weren't looking for me, were you?"

"No," Iullus said. "I'm going to see Augustus."

Oil lamps burned low, casting shadows over the painted walls. One sputtered out. "At this hour?"

My Roman half brother gave me a sharp look from under dark brows. "I'm going to ask him to annul Julia's marriage and give her to me."

I nearly stumbled in shock. Iullus had been my childhood nemesis, but we shared blood, so I gripped his arm to keep him from turning away. "What can you be thinking? If the emperor doesn't laugh in your face he'll have you shipped off to fight the Cantabri in Spain. That is, if you live so long. If he doesn't kill you himself, Livia will see you dead by dinner!"

Like all my father's sons, Iullus was well formed and handsome. At eighteen years old, he'd already served in war at the side of Augustus. He could have swatted me away with one strong arm, but instead he glared. "If Augustus can give a crown to Cleopatra's daughter, why not give a great marriage to Antony's son?"

Octavia had said it was my gift to inspire people to reach higher, but it seemed more like a curse. "Because I'm a *girl*. Augustus thinks I'm an ornament. An interesting amusement that suits his purposes. You're Antony's *Roman* son. If you tell the emperor that you want his daughter, he'll think you're trying to plot against him, trying to declare yourself his heir."

"You just don't want Julia and me to be together," he said, but I saw he was wavering.

"You're wrong." I loved Julia and would begrudge her nothing. As far as I was concerned, Iullus's secret affection for Julia was his only redeeming quality. "I only worry about you. In spite of everything, we're family. That means something to me."

"It's because you worry about *everything*, Selene. You think you're some savior. That you can go round and make everything right. Well, you can't." His criticism was too close to the truth for comfort, so I didn't stop him when he stalked away. But I noticed that he returned to his room, and I prayed he had the good sense to stay there.

JUBA never came home that night, and I don't remember that I slept. By morning there was nothing left to do but dress and take one last turn around the grounds. I passed the spinning room where Octavia had taught me to turn baskets of white fleece into spools of thread. Where Julia and I had worked the looms and woven cloth for tunics and togas. I walked through the courtyard where they'd first told me about Caesarion's death, then through the gardens where I'd married Juba. So many slaves had been ordered to help prepare for our departure that there had been few left to clean up after the wedding. Remnants of the marriage feast were still scattered about, goblets tipped upon the stones. With a disapproving expression, Lady Octavia surveyed the mess, and I realized she was waiting for me, my wedding gift from Balbus draped over her arm. "I brought your cloak," she said, reaching up to cover my shoulders. "You'll want to wear it in the highlands of Africa. Give a care for your modesty and remember that even queens can catch a chill."

"I'll remember," I said, grateful for the warmth against the cold morning air.

"Best that you do, because everything is going to change for you, Selene," she continued, tugging at the fabric of my cloak so she could fasten it with a fibula pin. "You'll be queen of a wild and untamed place. Keep your mind on your duty and don't distract yourself worrying about Philadelphus. I'll watch over him as if he were my own."

I looked up, meeting her eyes, and saw that they were red-rimmed with tears. *I love you too*, I thought. She was the emperor's sister and I was Cleopatra's daughter. It was something neither of us could say, but I saw it in her eyes, and I hope she saw it in mine. "I'll honor you always, Octavia."

"Just do your duty to Rome and to Juba," she sniffed, straightening the drape of my gown. "Make me proud."

Under the archway, beneath a canopy of vines, Julia appeared. "Selene, they're waiting for you."

I went down the stairs with her and peeked through the bars of the gate at the impressive caravan. Wearing his finery, Juba mounted his dun stallion with the ease of an expert rider. He and Augustus would lead the procession, side by side, and if either man gave a thought to my presence, I had no reason to know it. Meanwhile, Crinagoras and some of the other courtiers climbed into wheeled carriages, readying for travel. Agrippa was there too, sweating and surly. He shouted at hapless soldiers who piled furniture, supplies, and armaments onto carts. "Load it up, laggards!"

"I'm dying of envy," Julia said, grasping hold of my fingers and squeezing. "You're going on an exciting adventure, whereas I'll never see more of the world than what you can glimpse from the Palatine Hill." Her bravado came crashing down then. Her lower lip trembled and she threw her arms around me. "Oh, Selene. I don't want you to go."

"I'll come back to visit," I promised.

"You're too clever for that," Julia whispered, holding me so tight I thought I might bruise. "You've finally found a way to escape. You'd be wise to stay away." With that, Julia turned and fled back into the house.

"Julia!" I cried.

"Let her go," Octavia said. "Her destiny is right here in Rome, but yours is across the sea."

WHEN I first came to Rome, dragged as a chained prisoner behind the emperor's chariot, the people spit at me and threw rocks. Now the Romans threw flower petals in the path of the snow-white horses that pulled my gilded carriage. A sort of fervor for all things Egyptian had taken hold of the city in my honor. Women scented themselves with lotus perfume and adorned themselves with jewelry featuring sphinxes and crocodiles. Men wore scarab rings and thick gold bracelets, if they could afford them. Perhaps it was merely the fashion, for the emperor's own fascination with obelisks and other Egyptian treasures had set the trend. But these might be Isiacs too, come to wish me well.

Today I was the daughter of the *good* Queen Cleopatra who had been beloved of Julius Caesar, not the *bad* Queen Cleopatra the seductress. Today I was the daughter of their Antony, the *good* Roman general who had avenged Caesar and was merciful to his enemies, not the *bad* Antony who was enslaved to an Egyptian whore. I was the loyal Roman girl, ward of Augustus, rewarded with a kingdom. So they all cheered.

When the carriages, the wagons, the standard bearers, and the litters passed through the city gates onto the Via Ostiensis, the breath went out of me. I was leaving! I threw back my head and took in a great gulp of air wondering if Helios passed beneath this same canopy of umbrella pines and if he'd felt the same swirl of emotions I felt now. Anxiety and joy, sadness and triumph, regret and hope. I couldn't be certain if the invisible shackles that bound me would break or tighten. I only knew that against all odds, I'd emerged from that stifling brick city with my life, queen of a new world.

Five

A few hours into our journey on the open road, some commotion stalled our rumbling procession. Shouts rang out, and even from the confines of my carriage Chryssa and I thought we heard weapons clashing. Wood against wood, fists against bone. It happened quickly, followed by the clatter of galloping horse hooves on the stone road. Curiosity made me pull back the curtain to see Augustus dismounting his horse. He joined me in my carriage, dismissing Chryssa to follow on foot, and then we were moving again. My heart jumped to my throat. "What's happening? What's wrong?"

The emperor's expression was distant as he took the seat across from me. "Nothing for you to concern yourself about. It was a protest. Yet another crowd come to demand things of me."

"What did they want?" I asked, hugging myself against an unexpected chill.

"It doesn't matter. Restoration of the Republic. Restoration of the Temples of Isis. More grain. Reform. It can be anything or nothing that stirs the hearts of these malcontents." His lips curled. "I'm only glad they won't trouble me again."

The menace in his tone filled me with foreboding. The wheels of my carriage rolled on and the scent of carnage told me there'd been bloodshed. I saw men dead in the grass, eyes wide and empty, gaping wounds shining with blood, glistening entrails in the dirt. A noxious stew of horror churned in my belly and boiled up to my throat. To keep myself from retching, I pressed the back of my hand against my mouth. I could scarcely make my lips move to utter the words, "You executed them."

"They were nobodies." Augustus yanked at his decorative cuirass as if the weight of the breastplate pained him at the shoulders. "Not even citizens. Just fools and madmen to get in my way on a day like this. My praetorians made short work of them. And if you mean to rule, Selene, if you mean to be a true queen, you'll need a stronger stomach."

No matter how many people he killed, I'd never be able to shrug indifferently as he did now. Murder never gave him pause, but he wasn't an indiscriminate killer. The dead men must have threatened his power in some way, and like the monster he was, he simply cut their lives short. It was a sharp reminder of how dangerous a game it was I played with him. It gained me nothing to let him see how his ruthlessness sickened me. It wouldn't help these poor dead strangers and it would only mark my weaknesses for Augustus to exploit. He was right. If I were to ever be his equal or ever triumph over him, I'd have to choke back my bile. So I turned my eyes away from the dead men on the road. "Did this have something to do with Helios?"

"No. I'm no longer worried about your twin. The Prefect of Egypt assures me that he'll crush the rebellion in Thebes shortly." My mouth went dry as I stared out at the funereal monuments that lined our path. We lurched and bumped our way down the road in silence until the emperor said, "My temper is in need of soothing and it occurs to me that I'll miss you when we're apart. Who will play the *kithara* for me?"

"You can hire a skilled harpist."

He smirked indulgently. "She'll cost me far less than you. Not every musician demands a throne as her price."

I lifted my chin with Ptolemaic pride. "Not every musician is Cleopatra's daughter."

His lips twisted in amusement. "Let's play another game. You're Greek. You'll enjoy this one."

My blood was Macedonian, which wasn't precisely the same thing as Greek, but I said, "I'm Egyptian."

"A fact you never let me forget," he said, showing only mild annoyance. "Now tell me, of these three historic figures, which one do I most resemble? Odysseus, Theseus, or Alexander the Great?"

The emperor had been the boy everyone had discounted. He'd risen to the consulship of Rome at the age of nineteen and now held most of the world in his palm. To find victory where all other Romans had failed, he was planning a campaign against the Parthians, so I knew he wanted to be compared to Alexander. He was never content to be himself. Within him still was the sickly boy my father had ridiculed. He was, and would always be, the insecure youth who relied on Agrippa to do his fighting and who felt compelled to kill my brother Caesarion for fear of a rival with the same name. He wanted to be Caesar. He wanted to be Alexander. But I wanted an answer that would please him even better. One that might turn his mind from war and killing. "I say that you are more like Aeneas than any of those three. Like Aeneas, who carried his ailing father out of a burning city, you've honored Julius Caesar. Whereas Aeneas built Lavinium, you wish to build a new Rome out of the ashes of the civil wars. *Aeneas.*"

"Selene," he uttered my name in warning, as if I'd spoken something too close to his heart. Then, in a flash of motion, Augustus pulled the curtain shut, plunging the carriage into darkness. It felt strange to be alone with him in such close quarters, closed off from the outside world. I blinked, able to make out only his silhouette, a shadow of himself. "Aeneas had *sons*, Selene. He had sons to rule after him. I don't. And you once predicted that my heirs will never inherit my empire."

"It wasn't my prediction. Those were the words of Isis," I said, for my goddess had sent that warning scrolling in blood and hieroglyphs down my arms. *As you refuse Isis her throne, be assured your descendants will never inherit yours. Deny me, and your ignoble name will fade to dust.* It had been a threat in retaliation for his mistreatment of Isis worshippers, but he'd believed it was my mother reaching for him, sparring with him from the afterlife. Now, he seemed at last to have accepted that my mother was gone. When he looked for her, he looked to me. "Isis never promised it would be your destiny, Caesar. Honor my goddess and change your fate."

His gray eyes were lupine in the dark. "Why isn't it enough that I honor you, her sorceress?"

Years ago, such a question would only have been put to me in threat, for the Romans had a fear and loathing of magic. But the emperor valued any power I had—whether it sprang from magic, religion, or my heritage—and he wanted to possess it for his own ends. "I'm not a sorceress." That much wasn't a lie. What powers I had, I didn't know how to control. Not yet.

"There's a woman who says otherwise, Selene. She tells everyone who'll listen that you put your hands upon her and made her fertile again. She was barren, and now she's with child."

I squinted, adjusting to the darkened interior, seeing his face knit in concentration, in expectation that I must disappoint. "Such things happen. It's the will of the gods."

"I need a son, Selene. I need you to make Livia's womb fertile again."

How like him to bring up such a thing with men lying dead behind us in the road. "I can't help you."

He made a dangerous sound, the snort of an animal. "Your mother worked fertility magic for Caesar. It was easy to say her child was of some other man's get, but I looked at the boy's face after he died. He was Caesar writ small."

It shocked me to hear him admit my eldest brother's true parentage. "Whatever magic comes to me, comes from Isis. I'm spent of it. I can't help you. Neither you nor Livia share my faith."

"*Faith,*" he said, as if the word always puzzled him. The Romans built great temples to their gods and made bloody sacrifices, but they didn't forge personal relationships with the divine. They didn't pray, at least not without great ritual and fanfare, and rarely in the way that I called upon Isis in moments of solitude and reflection. "Livia could make an offering," he said. "It wouldn't do for her to publicly honor a goddess whose worship I've banned, but she could do it in secret."

"Livia is past the age of childbearing. It isn't within my power."

Even if it were, I wouldn't wish Livia as a mother upon any child. If she'd ever given a kind word to either of her sons that wasn't calculated to advance her own ambitions, I'd never seen it. The carriage rumbled to a stop. Soldiers shouted to water the horses and if I had any sense at all, I would have let the conversation end there. But I said, "If you want a son, Caesar, take a new wife."

At that very moment the curtain drew back and Juba stood outside the carriage, offering to help me down. My new husband cleared his throat as my words died away, and in the awkward silence I noticed Livia nearby, standing beneath the shade of an umbrella pine, her eyes narrowed in a murderous stare.

WHEREAS Rome was a chaotic warren of narrow streets, the port city of Ostia was an orderly assemblage of brick shops, some of them covered in white stucco. Colorful mosaics graced the walkways in front of each building, the tiles depicting the trade of the place. Grapes in front of the wine warehouses, leaping fish before the seafood markets, and so on. The bustle was such that even the sailors, stacking sacks of wheat at the docks, were too busy to greet the emperor.

The screech of the gulls called my attention to the harbor, where I saw the masts of great ships, one of which would carry me back to Africa. The scent of grain captivated me. Oats, barley, and wheat all mingled in the ancient, earthy notes of civilization. I closed my eyes and imagined the threshing floors in Egypt, where all this grain found its source. Alas, there was too little of it, the merchants all said. The crops had failed this year and much of the rest was spoiled by vermin. In Africa, I must find a way to feed Rome, the way my mother did before me. The way Isis had fed the world since the dawn of time . . .

It was good that the emperor's most trusted political adviser was extremely wealthy, because hosting the imperial entourage would cost Maecenas a fortune. We descended upon his seaside villa en masse. To my astonishment, an entire set of apartments overlooking the ocean had been made ready for me. My sleeping chamber adjoined Juba's bedroom on one side and a room for Chryssa on the other. Without my having to command it, Chryssa capably directed the other slaves who carried my trunks. Her tastes could put lesser royalty in Asia to shame, and as we settled in I caught her appraising the decorative *amphorae* and each stick of gilded furniture with approval. "By the gods! This statue of Venus is an *original* Praxiteles," my slave girl breathed.

I stopped to admire the work of the famous sculptor, wondering if Maecenas had adorned my bedchamber with a statue of the goddess of love to honor my marriage. Two nights had passed since the wedding, and I had no right to expect Juba to be patient much longer. He might even come to my room tonight. Was the sudden gallop of my heartbeat fear or excited anticipation? It seemed when it came to Juba, I never knew my own mind.

IT rained that night and the gentle splashes against the roof lulled me to sleep. It rained in my dream too, like the tears of Isis falling on the desert. Beneath my bare feet, sand slipped between my toes like silk. My hands stretched to catch the raindrops. My lips were wet with kisses. It was a god who wrapped his arms around me, singing a magical little song. When I looked up to see his face, I saw only the rays of the sun, which broke through the rain to form a rainbow. It was rapture. I was overcome with a feeling of wholeness. *"Who are you?"* I asked, but my divine suitor didn't answer.

A sinuous shadow rose over us, a viper in the mist. It swelled, hood expanding, until my rapture turned to dread. It was an asp, the Egyptian cobra—the snake that had killed my mother and now came for me. I bolted upright, out of sleep. Wet with sweat, my hands clammy, and my heart racing. That's when I heard the knocking. I thought it must be Juba come to make a wife of me. "Selene?" someone called softly from outside, but it wasn't Juba.

Chryssa emerged from her chamber, wiping sleep from her eyes. "I think it's Lady Livia."

That made me sit up straighter. Chryssa unbolted the door, and Livia stepped inside, a mist sweeping in behind her. She held an oil lamp in one hand, and her hair was damp beneath her cloak. "The emperor wants to see you. There is news."

I lost my wits. For Livia to come for me, the news must be urgent and terrible. Philadelphus had taken ill again. The war in Thebes had taken a terrible turn. Helios had been captured. A thousand stories of tragedy played out in my mind. It took me three tries to properly fasten a robe over my sleeping gown and then I trailed behind Livia like a wraith in the fog of night. As we walked in the shadows of fabulous gilded lions and marbled athletes, Livia donned her otherworldly posture of serenity; it gave her a kind of frightening beauty, thin and ethereal.

The house was unfamiliar to me, and I can't say how many passages we navigated before we reached the emperor's chambers. We were met by one of the praetorian guards, a man named Strabo, and though he shared the same name as Juba's friend, the highly regarded Greek historian and geographer, this Strabo was all brawn. He admitted Livia without question and I followed in her wake. To my great surprise, we found the emperor settled into bed. The room was dark. A single brazier burned. "What is it?" I gasped, the words bursting from my lungs.

Livia went to the emperor and whispered something in his ear. He caressed her arms and she stroked his forehead. I'd never seen so much as a kiss pass between the two before; they considered public affection to be vulgar. Now, in the darkened room, I saw their silhouettes close and intimate. I watched, paralyzed. "You said there was news . . ."

Livia drew away from the bed, her hand lingering in the emperor's until their fingers broke apart, like a rope unraveling. She gave me a look that would have made me shiver even if my nightclothes weren't damp. "Remember," she whispered, venom in every word. "I warned you there'd be a price for embarrassing me."

"Come here, Selene," the emperor called to me. His voice was strange, throaty and unnatural.

Livia put her hands on my shoulders, nails digging into my skin like talons. "Obey him."

If I'd been fully awake, if I had any *heka* left in me at all, I'd have forced her to release me, but I drowned in confusion. "Come here, Selene," the emperor said again, and I took a few steps to him. Livia closed the door, leaving us alone, and Augustus rose to his feet. Then he circled me, like one of the beast hunters in the arena. "Look at you shivering like an innocent maiden . . . but we both know better, don't we?"

His eyes were half-lidded and he stumbled as if drunk, crowding me, edging me nearer and nearer to the brazier. My mouth went dry as he brought his face to mine, close enough to kiss me. It was madness. In spite of everything I knew about the emperor, I could make no sense of this moment, a strange dream. Truly, neither of us seemed fully awake. "Don't look at me that way," I said.

"Why not? You dressed like a whore for your wedding. I couldn't look away, and why should I have? You wanted me to look at you, Selene. You wanted me to stare."

"I wanted you to see the queen in me," I protested, suddenly apprehending the awfulness of my situation. With the emperor in front of me and the brazier behind, I was trapped between fire and ice.

He left me no retreat. "I saw your shoulders bare, Selene, with that golden snake wrapped around your upper arm. Your hair loose. You issued an open invitation for me to take you . . ."

I'd never seen him this way. He'd been my enemy, my savior, and my mentor. Never a seducer. Never! "You're mistaken."

"Did you use your magic to enchant Juba as he worked between your legs that night?"

"No!" I cried as much in shock as offense.

"Did you try to convince him that he was the first?"

"He will be!"

"Are you saying you're innocent?" the emperor asked, his gray eyes as foreboding as the stormy sky outside. "Prove it to me. If you cannot prove your innocence, then I'll let Juba divorce you as an adulterous slattern."

I could think of no proof to offer. I turned, intent upon fleeing, but he seized me by the shoulders. Those hands that had spared my life now grabbed my robe as if it were an army between us that must be conquered. He gripped the cloth until it bunched in his fists. His face was twisted, as if he were caught in the jaws of a monster, as if passion escaped like a chained creature from the depths whose existence he couldn't admit even to himself. I thought he might kill me in his next breath. "I'll see if you're lying to me," he growled, stealing his fingers beneath my gown. I flailed, trying to escape the sudden invasion. He wasn't the strongest of men, but he had a soldier's training and I didn't. The surprise, the shock, the horror of his hand probing my most secret places made me cry out. Dry fingers pushed into my sex and when he found some barrier, the murderous frost in his eyes melted away. He released me. Dazed. Astonished. "You're a virgin."

My legs gave out and I sat down hard on the edge of the bed, waves of nausea rolling over me. I put my hands over my face, squeezing the tears against my palms. "Are you satisfied now?"

He reached with a trembling hand to stroke my hair. "Oh, Selene, you were true to me. You never played me false. You really *are* my own Cleopatra."

"Stop it!" I cried, my voice near hysteria. Was he drunk? His eyes were bloodshot and unfocused, though I smelled no wine on his breath. Had he finally gone *completely* mad?

"You're as fecund as your mother, aren't you? You can give me the son that I need." He pushed me back against the bed, the wiry hairs of his legs scratching mine. "Beg," he said, tugging my gown up around my waist. I tried to clamp my legs shut, but his knees were between mine, bruisingly hard. "Beg me like the first time I saw you. I love when you beg, Selene. And cry. I want you to cry."

I didn't want to give him one more tear, but as he pushed my legs apart I couldn't hold back my sobs. "Isis, help me," I whispered, and the faintest flicker of *heka* blew from my fingertips, but the winds I summoned were only enough to make the fire in the brazier blow out. In the darkness, in desperation, I struck him full across the face.

We both froze. I'd actually hit him and we both knew that he'd killed men for less. He said, "Yes, just like a good Roman bride. You may struggle, Selene. You have my permission. And you must cry when I take your maidenhead. *Cry* like all innocent little virgins do." Trapped beneath him, my entire body quaked with disgust. He hitched up his tunic and I battered his shoulders, writhing to find an avenue of escape.

There was none.

He thrust up into me and I confess that I didn't struggle after that. He was already moving inside me, a violation so profound it didn't occur to me he could do worse. I lay there, dazed, thinking that this couldn't be happening. This was only a nightmare. Did nightmares burn with pain? He speared me over and over again, as if stabbing at my womb. I smelled my own blood and whimpered with each jerk of his hips, wondering how much longer it could possibly last.

"It's supposed to hurt, Selene." The words gave him renewed pleasure. Or maybe it was my tears that aroused him, for they flowed freely over my cheeks. "You're going to give me a son," he whispered, pumping faster, making the straps on the bed creak. His skin slapped against mine as his fingers dug hard into my breasts, clawing at them until they too were on fire. "You're going to carry my child, you little Egyptian whore!"

His body lurched and strained, his face tightening into a rictus as warm fluid flowed from his body into mine. Mercifully, he made only a few more rude thrusts. Then he collapsed on top of me, his finger over my lips. "Shhh. It's all a dream . . ."

The blood and sweat and seed trickling down my inner thigh wasn't the stuff of dreams, but I saw the emperor withdrawing into this fiction, the rabid animal he'd let loose slowly being pulled back on its tether. It was still raining outside and the pitter-patter of the water against the stone made a melancholy music. "Go to bed now, Selene. It was all a dream."

I can't say what hour it was that I stumbled back to my chambers, but the sun wasn't up yet. Even so, Chryssa was awake and fully dressed. The haunted shadows in her eyes told me that she knew what had happened to me; it had happened to her too. "Forgive me!" she cried. "When I realized it was Livia who came to fetch you I should have gone with you—"

"Be silent!" I hissed through clenched teeth. I didn't want her to look at me. I was a wounded animal, bruised and battered, though I doubted anyone could see where it hurt. What had happened to me happened to slaves everywhere. It had happened to Chryssa, and if she acknowledged it, I couldn't bear it. Instead, I pushed past her, climbed into the bed, and huddled there facing the wall, my throat filled with bile, my heart filled with hate.

EGYPTIANS say you can sense the presence of a serpent in the room before it strikes. So it was that I sensed Livia's presence even before I awakened to find her at the foot of my bed, her hair pulled back smooth, her slender shoulders adorned with a tasteful blue shawl. "Aren't you feeling well, Selene? Perhaps there's an illness in the house. The emperor is suffering from a grievous headache this morning." I didn't answer. "Well, no matter," she said, reaching to adjust the blanket under my chin. "I trust that you've learned to cover up from now on."

I slapped her hands away. "Don't touch me."

"That's a common reaction. Though I expected more tears. You do like to create a scene . . ."

Through bloodless lips, I asked, "How could you do it?"

She tilted her head, as if amused. "Easily. I've seen how he looks at you. How you toy with him. I couldn't allow it to continue. I couldn't let you leave for Africa with the fantasy of you lingering in his mind, or he'd become your slave as surely as Antony was Cleopatra's."

So she gave me to him. She let him have me.

Livia smiled when she saw that I understood. She'd been planning this for a very long time. She'd chosen her moment. She'd waited patiently until I was no longer under Lady Octavia's protection. She'd waited until we were out of Rome. And I'd gone with her like an unwitting fool. "You're a vile woman, Livia."

She laughed, the sound of it wicked. "And you're just a plaything for a petty princeling of an isolated and unimportant Western province. The emperor will never do anything you ask. He won't make you Queen of Egypt. He won't be fool enough to spare Helios when we catch him. In fact, once you're in Mauretania, my husband won't even think of you again except to remember some fleeting pleasure from this night, and if he drank deeply of my tonic, he won't even remember it well."

"You drugged him," I said, remembering the glazed look in his eyes. "I'll tell him. I'll tell everyone."

Livia smiled, giving a delicate shake of her head. "You won't tell *anyone*, because if your new husband asks me about last night, I'll reassure him that it wasn't your fault. The brutish Thracian slave I saw staring at you when our caravan arrived must have done it. It was so dark and rainy out. A girl could get lost in the passageways and be attacked by such a man."

"It was the emperor who did this to me."

"Oh, Juba!" Livia said in clever mimicry, putting her hand over her heart as if she were speaking to him. "The poor girl is in such shock. Of course she thinks it was the emperor. What princess could accept the shame of having been taken by a filthy slave? If she were any true royal wife, she'd kill herself rather than live with the dishonor of having been raped by an animal, but I must take Selene's part in this and insist the culprit be crucified!"

Raped. The word was nearly as ugly as the deed. I couldn't bear to hear it said, and turned away. "You're heartless."

"Not entirely," Livia said, nodding toward a cup by my bedside. "I've provided you with an honorable exit. It won't be as dramatic as your mother's end, but unless you have the power to conjure up Egyptian cobras, a goblet of poisoned wine will suffice."

I stared at the poisoned wine, surprised at my sudden thirst. Then Livia leaned close, her voice a mere whisper. "Your influence over the emperor is done. Your glamour, your mystique, your hold on him— it's over. You're nothing more than a little trollop in rumpled bed-clothes. You're *ruined*. I'm told your family motto is *Win or Die*. Well, Selene, you didn't win, so that leaves only one choice, doesn't it?"

Six

YOU'RE *ruined*.

That's what Livia had said to me with that satisfied grin, believing she'd destroyed me. As if my whole worth had been a maidenhead that Augustus breached like a besieged wall. She thought that in the emperor's one depraved act, he'd looted everything valuable inside me and left me in smoldering ruins. Maybe she was right, because here I was, huddled and tear-streaked beneath a blanket like some refugee of a plundered village, a cup of poison in my shaking hand.

You're ruined.

She was right when she'd said there was no one I could tell. If I went to Juba, Livia would spin her lie about the Thracian slave, and my new husband would believe it, because he'd *want* to believe it. Juba had always idolized the emperor and suspected me; I didn't need to test my sad little fraud of a marriage to know whose side Juba would take. Worse, what if Livia was right? What if lust was all that bound the emperor in his promises to me? What if I'd lost my chance to win back Egypt? What if I'd suffered all this and still not saved the lives of my brothers?

You're ruined.

She'd said that, knowing that the emperor had done to me the worst thing that could be done to a woman. Was it the *very* worst thing? I'd faced death the day I first came to Rome as a chained prisoner, a sacrificial knife poised above me. Roman matrons killed themselves when disgraced, but I wasn't Roman. My mother had killed herself when she was conquered, but I wasn't my mother either. In fact, I'd endured the humiliation meant for her. I'd been called vile names and spat upon and pelted with stones. I'd been forced to watch the Prince of Emesa die for me, his blood spattered all over my feet. Remembering the heat of his blood as it poured out of his body, I put the poisoned cup down. Shoved it away. I'd survived every trial Augustus and his wife had ever fashioned for me; I'd find a way to survive this too. And, oh, how I'd make them both regret it.

I soaked until my toes puckered and paled beneath the water. Then I scrubbed and scraped until my skin was livid, all in a fruitless attempt to get clean. Sometimes Romans opened their veins in hot baths like this. They claimed that the heat of the water disguised the pain as they bled their lives away. Maybe that's why I didn't feel the sting of the tiny lacerations that opened on my hands. It wasn't until the water clouded crimson that I drew my palms up to the light where I could see my wounds pulse with the slow and steady beat of my heart. *Blood.* I let the steam settle into my lungs as symbols swam before my eyes. The sharpest blade couldn't have cut so precisely into my fingers and palms, bright red outlines of vultures, double-reed leaves, owls and vipers. These were hieroglyphics and I could read them. These were the words of my goddess, come back to me.

Child of Isis, you are more than flesh.

These were *her* words, reaching for me in my dark hour, and a small sob of gratitude escaped me. There were nine parts of the Egyptian soul, of which my body was only one. The emperor had violated my flesh but he hadn't touched the rest. There were parts of me that he couldn't reach, could never touch, and had no power to defile . . .

The symbols on my hands changed. The needle-fine cuts healed themselves and opened again, with a new message entirely. I rose from the bath, pulling on a dressing gown, then padded barefoot out into the broad hallway. My hair was wet and wild and I held my arms out, blood trailing behind me, vivid red droplets on the white marble. "By the gods!" Strabo cried when he saw my frightening visage, bright blood running down my pale arms.

"By the *goddess*," I replied.

This put the emperor's praetorian in white-faced terror. Like most of the Romans, he'd heard the rumors about me, and he must have seen something in my face that made him step aside. I pushed into the emperor's chambers and found him sitting before an array of maps and battle plans for the invasion of Parthia. His lids were at half-mast and he was unshaven. He actually startled to see me and not because I was bleeding. I'd tucked each hand into the folds of my gown. I was overly aware of him. I could still smell his acrid sweat in the room. I was conscious of his every accursed breath. "Go away, Selene," he said in a voice like gravel. "I'm unwell."

"Is that your way of expressing regret?"

He crumpled a scrap of papyrus on his desk. "It's my way of telling you that you should know better than to come to a man's bedchambers. There are limits of propriety that must not be crossed. Even by you."

My laugh was bitter and I felt cold, all the way to my bare toes where they curled against the tiles. "You want to speak to me of propriety, after what you did last night?"

"I did nothing to you last night." Avoiding my gaze, he cradled his head in his hands as if a storm were pounding behind his eyes. "You must've had a vivid dream."

"Did I dream the bruises your knees left on my thighs?"

He couldn't look at me. "I've never laid a hand on you."

"You did last night." It hurt to speak over the rising lump in my throat. "You've spent your whole life lying to yourself, but you can't lie to Isis." With that, I revealed my hands, holding them in the light where he could see the shapes carved into my palms. He'd seen this before—the way the goddess came through me—but he still paled.

I began to read from the scroll of my own flesh. *"I am Isis. I am nature. I am the mother of all things. No man has a son but through*

*me, and I will not give you one, for you are an instrument of Set the
destroyer, the infertile god of the desert whose envy burns away everything he loves. You are a rapist, an enemy of women, and a destroyer
of faith. You have closed my temples, persecuted my worshippers, and
violated my daughters. Until you repent and make amends, you are
cursed. The Julii will come to nothing. You'll live long enough to watch
your heirs fall, one after the other, until your empire rests in the hands
of those who despise you."*

If I hadn't felt the goddess in me, I would have had the presence
of mind to be afraid. The emperor stood, knocking the stool out
from under him, and was upon me in two strides. Too late, I shrank
back, bracing myself in case he might throw me down and force me
again. Roughly grabbing my shoulders, he cried, "Why do you
condemn me for one moment of weakness! You're a wicked temptress, just like your mother. What man can resist such a young
nymph forever? Even Apollo was seduced by the virgin huntress
Cyrene. Am I to be stronger than a god?"

I was struck with horror at his words. Apollo was the emperor's
patron god, and like me, Cyrene had once been Queen of Cyrenaica. The kingdom was given to her by Apollo after he raped and
impregnated her. That Augustus should mention this story told me
that maybe he wouldn't have done it if Livia hadn't slipped something into his drink, but he'd been toying with the idea of forcing
himself upon me for quite some time. Livia had only made it easier
for him to have what he wanted. She'd only given him an excuse to
do to me what he'd done to so many other girls. Only this time, it
was no slave he'd taken. "You needn't worry about *my* condemnation," I said as the small wounds closed, flesh knitting over flesh.
"*Isis* condemns you."

The whites of his eyes widened with defiance. "Well, I've chal-
lenged Egyptian gods before and won. I'll put my faith in Roman
gods, who are stronger."

"And which Roman god countenances the violation of another
man's wife?"

He shook me by the arms. "Don't you know that you're mine to do with as I please? When I captured you in Egypt, I could've made a slave of you. I could've forced you into a brothel. Instead, I gave you a throne. I'm sending you to Africa with income from mines and deeds to plantations, with chests of gold and silver bars, with treasure enough to humble the proudest royalty in Asia, so don't cry to me about your spoiled virtue. I've taken from you no more than I've fairly purchased."

His words demeaned me, made me feel filthy, just as he'd intended them to, and I pressed my hands on his chest to push him away. He released me, staring down at the bloody handprints I'd left on the stark white folds of his toga. What guilt and remorse he was capable of feeling now welled up in his eyes. "I won't see you again," he whispered hoarsely. "Tomorrow, you and Juba will go to Africa without me. You'll find a way to forget this. I vow by Apollo that I'll *never* set foot in Mauretania."

Good, I thought, because I never wanted to see him again. I never wanted to smell him, or hear his voice, or have him breathe the air of any land I ruled. An ocean between us wouldn't be far enough, but he was Augustus. He was Caesar. He *still* held in his hands everything I ever wanted and the lives of everyone I loved. "But what of our bargain?"

"This changes nothing, Selene. I'll spare your brothers if you remain a loyal queen. But this will be the end of it."

"No," I said, a bitter taste in my mouth. "Now there will never be an end of it between us."

STUMBLING out of his rooms, my arms covered in blood, half delirious with both the joy of my goddess championing me and the unbearable pain of her leaving again, I was certain that I'd spoken truly. He wouldn't be rid of me with a royal dowry and a promise to stay away. I was a Ptolemy, the kin of Alexander. He thought that like a length of cloth dipped in royal purple dye, he could stain himself with the glory of my maiden's blood. But I hoped my blood would be a toxin to him. A slow poison that would eat at him for all our days.

"Gods be good!" one of Maecenas's slaves cried. "Where are you hurt, my lady? Have you been stabbed?"

"Hush!" Chryssa said, rushing to my side, breathless as if she'd been searching the villa for me. "Isis has been here. Now the *heka* sickness remains. We need to get her to her chambers before she falls."

I let them put me to bed, drifting asleep to a familiar song. The melody was so far away that I couldn't make out the words, but it was a man who sang to me, his voice like the rushing of water, strangely alluring over the notes of a plucked harp. He sang like a lover whose hands wouldn't hurt me but would coax warmth from my skin. Of other, sweeter sensations that would make my heart pound not from fear but from the pleasure of skin against skin, breath upon breath, the tangle of my fingers in his hair. It was a promise from my goddess to me, that a lover would come to purify me, like the Nile washes over Egypt and makes it new again. A promise I'd find someone who would take the pain away.

I awakened to see Juba hovering over me. Was he the lover my goddess promised? I'd married him. It would be only right if he were the one to make me feel safe and whole. So why did I flinch when his hand touched my shoulder? "Selene . . ." Juba had once seen my blood blossom to flowers on the temple floor. He'd tried to stop me from running into a pit of crocodiles. It had frightened him. I could see he was frightened again now. "How is it that you're working magic again?"

His gently spoken remonstration wasn't meant to be a question, but I wondered myself. How *had* Isis come to me? Always before, she was moved to speak when I'd touched the blood of her worshippers. Only now did I remember how Chryssa had cut herself with the *strigil*, her blood in my bathwater. "My goddess is moved by suffering."

"What torments you?" Juba asked, rubbing at the stubble of his beard. "Why does your goddess come to you like this?"

How could I tell him without confessing what the emperor had done? I wanted to trust him with the truth, but I remembered what Livia had said. Juba wouldn't believe me. How much worse for him it might be if he did! What if my new husband took my part, raging like a lion, thundering down the hall to the emperor's rooms, pounding upon his doors and demanding satisfaction? It would cost Juba his throne, if not his life.

As Juba searched my eyes for an explanation, I said nothing. He couldn't know. I didn't want him to know. I didn't want *anyone* to know. That the emperor had forced himself upon me was a wound so deep it might be fatal to expose. For now, I must give this pain to my dark shadow self, with all my unworthy thoughts, all the wrath that Isis warned against. I let my *khaibit* hold my atrocities— the ones done to me, and the ones I wished to do—knowing they'd be there for me another day.

AS the skipper led our small armada out of port, I stood at the rail, refusing to look away. From the shore, Augustus watched me go. I've always said that his power was in the cold treachery of his gray eyes, with which he could hold me perfectly still. Now, after four long years, his eyes were fading into the distance, his figure getting smaller on the horizon. His grip was loosening and I wanted him to remember me like this. Let him look at my cloak billowing behind me like the aura of a goddess. Let him wonder about the curse Isis had laid upon him in my name.

The sailors busied themselves with ship's tasks and my attendants saw to my berth. I thought I was quite alone at the rail, watching the milky green waves pass beneath us until Juba murmured, "Is it done between you?"

My breath caught in my throat. "I'm sure I don't know what you mean."

The sea breeze whipped his dark hair against the grim set of his jaw, and there was a shadow in his eyes that I'd never seen before. "The night it rained, Selene, I came to your room. You weren't there. Where were you?"

I turned away. I'd already resolved not to speak about that night. Not to Juba. Not to anyone.

He put his hand on my arm, a harmless gesture, but I was still too raw to be touched. When I yanked away, Juba winced as if I'd slipped a dagger past his defenses to wound him. "Am I really such anathema to you, Selene?"

"Juba, you misunderstand—"

"Where were you that night?" he demanded, eyes narrowed.

I shook my head. I wouldn't tell him. Perhaps I *couldn't* tell him. My throat closed with emotion and Juba's expression turned to stone. Snapping his gaze away from me, he stared out to the sea as if it might swallow us both up. The harbor of Ostia was receding now, all its warehouses getting tinier with every stroke of the rower's oars.

"I'll find a way to forgive you," Juba said at length, his voice cold. "Just tell me that it's done."

He shocked me into saying, "You think I went willingly?" I turned to stare at him.

"Don't!" His grip on the rail tightened until his knuckles went white. "Don't pretend you didn't seduce him, Selene. You used the occasion of our wedding to make a whore of yourself, and I endured it, so don't lie. If not your loyalty, you at least owe me the truth."

Each word drove into me like a dagger. I'd known he wouldn't believe me, so why did it hurt so much? And I remembered that Juba had asked for my love, but he'd never promised his. "What of *your* loyalty?"

"First and always to the emperor," he said, without any hesitation at all.

Looking deep into Juba's troubled amber eyes, for one horrifying moment, I wondered if he'd somehow been complicit. "You left me a virgin. Were you saving my virtue for your master?"

He snorted. "It was *you* who went rigid on our wedding night."

"What about the night after?" I asked only to lash out at him, to cause him as much pain as he was causing me, but a flicker of guilt passed over his features and what he said next stole my breath away.

"One doesn't take from Augustus what he wants for himself."

Though wind filled the billowing sails overhead, I couldn't seem to get enough air. Until this moment, I hadn't known what kind of man Juba was. Not truly. Both hands went to my cheeks, fingers over my ears, as if I could *unhear* his words. "You knew . . ."

"I'm not blind," Juba said. "Of course I knew what he wanted from you."

Then Juba had betrayed me. *Again.* "Why didn't you defend me? Why didn't you protect me?"

"Protect you?" Juba asked, eyes ablaze. "It's what you wanted, Selene. Now you've had your way."

"It's not what I wanted. Shall I show you the bruises?" I reached for my skirts to yank them up.

Juba caught my wrist, stopping me. He wouldn't look. He wouldn't *see*. And whatever might have been salvaged between us was now shattered. Blinking back stunned tears, I wrenched my arm from Juba's grasp, hating the white indentations his fingers left in my skin. I didn't want him to touch me. I didn't want any man to touch me ever again. There wasn't a man in the world I could rely upon. No one but Helios had ever protected me, and now no one else ever would. I must always and only rely upon myself. The realization left me frightened, furious, and torn asunder. When I found my breath, I spat, "You're a coward, Juba."

He blanched, his throat bobbing. "I ask you again, is it done between the two of you?"

For him to ask such a question, he mustn't have known me either. "No. It isn't done. I'll never let it be done."

Another man might have struck me or demanded a different answer from his wife, but as I turned to go Juba merely followed me to the tiny cabin on the deck that had been specially prepared for us. Inside, Chryssa vomited into a brass pot. Juba hovered in the entryway. "If she's going to be seasick the whole journey, I might as well find another berth."

I didn't even glance at him. "You might as well."

Seven

THEREAFTER I shut myself up with my slave girl in a cabin that smelled of vomit. I'd taken to scratching at my arms with my fingernails, as if I could scrape off the emperor's filth. That Juba had known, and let it happen, defiled me twice over, and I feared that all the water in the sea couldn't wash the shame away. So while Chryssa retched, I wished I could heave up the poison of humiliation in my own belly. All that comforted me was the memory of my goddess and her words.

Child of Isis, you are more than flesh.

"I'm going to die," Chryssa whispered late on the third night of our voyage, her eyes bloodshot, hair clinging in tendrils to the back of her sweating neck. She groaned as the waves tossed our ship like a gambler tosses knucklebones. "Promise that when I die, you'll commend my spirit to Isis."

"I promise no such thing as seasickness isn't fatal," I said, though her waxy complexion did nothing to convince me. Still, my tone was sharp and I hated the way my own despair made me mean-spirited and selfish. At the thought of her death, all I could think was that everyone else had left me. My parents. My brothers. Even my new husband had abandoned me to the clutches of a depraved fiend. I couldn't lose Chryssa too. "You're not allowed to die, Chryssa. I can't be burdened with the guilt of having dragged you across the sea to meet your end."

The next day, convinced that Juba was engaged elsewhere on the ship with his new advisers, I finally coaxed Chryssa out of her sick-bed to take lunch on the stern deck. We enjoyed a pleasant meal of dried dates and savory cheese wrapped in bay leaves, and Crinagoras sidled over to amuse us. Wary of male company, I remarked, "King Juba fears that you don't share Virgil's vision, court poet."

Crinagoras smirked, making a gift to me of an ingenious little feather fan. "It's true that my vision is clouded with the perfume and glitter of royalty. Remember, madam, Virgil is Augustus's poet, whereas I am yours. Augustus uses his poets to shape his reputation; I intend to help shape yours."

My twin had loved all things nautical, the transport ships and their banks of oars, the ports and the sea itself. He'd spent the better part of his youth sketching war galleys and river barges; but when the skipper offered to give me a tour of the ship I declined in favor of a nap. Arranging myself beneath the billowing square sail of our big-bellied craft as it rode the waves to Mauretania, I dozed. Hence, it was with my eyes half closed that I first spotted land, and when my eyes fluttered back open I gaped in astonishment, letting the fan fall from my hand.

What I saw was no strange Berber land at the west end of the sea. This was *Alexandria*. Her towering lighthouse rose up from Pharos Island, winking fire to greet me, and I saw the Heptastadion too—that jetty connecting the island to the mainland and shelter-ing the harbor, where dock workers unloaded cargo. Beyond that, broad avenues lined with swaying palm trees and the Great Library where scholars strolled, debating the questions of the day. *Alexandria*. My birthplace, home of Isis, whose temple shone brightly in the sun. I jolted up, the words exploding from my chest. "How have we come to Egypt?"

"This is Mauretania, Majesty." The skipper must have thought I'd lost my wits.

I blinked once and Alexandria was gone. A small untamed island off the coast led into the neglected harbor of a colorful village. Mountains broke through the clouds to loom over the blue sea and I was so disoriented that I forgot everything. "What is this town?"

"It was the capital city before old King Bocchus died," Crinago-ras replied.

"It looks barbarous," Chryssa said, surveying the rocky coast-line with a wary eye. "Is it just the first stop on our journey or are we meant to make it our home?"

"Not our home," I said to reassure us both. "It's only a *mansio*. A place to stay until I return to Egypt."

I hadn't meant for Crinagoras to hear my ambitions spoken aloud, but he seemed not the slightest bit surprised. "The natives call it *Iol*. It means 'Return of the Sun.'"

The sun was my twin's namesake, and the thought that this place might reunite me with Helios lightened my heart. A pod of porpoises leapt in our wake as if to celebrate my return to Africa and I realized that not even the emperor could steal all the joy of this moment from me. If Helios had returned to Egypt by sea, he too would have swallowed with emotion, his heart pounding as mine did now. We'd left Egypt together as prisoners of war, two children clinging to one another at the rail. Now, without think-ing, I reached for my twin's hand, grasping only empty air.

While the skipper barked out commands, it became apparent that Iol's harbor couldn't accommodate a ship such as ours and that we'd have to be rowed out, ferried to shore with the rest of our belongings. The smaller ships in our flotilla went in before us and as our officials made landfall, the people of Iol leaned out under tattered awnings, streaming out of flat-roofed buildings and thatched huts, hastening to the docks to greet us.

"We'd better dress in our finery," Chryssa said, urging me back to our berth.

The sight of land seemed to have worked remarkable curative powers on my slave girl, who insisted that I wear a curve-hugging gown and the expensive purple cloak. When she tried to fasten pearl earrings on me, I stopped her. "I don't want to be a peacock."

Chryssa dared to argue with me. "They're expecting to see their new queen! Why shouldn't you want to look beautiful?"

Because the emperor and Juba both claimed it was the way I'd dressed on my wedding day that had driven Augustus to violate me. Chryssa, of all people, had probably guessed it, so why did she harry me? "It doesn't matter how I look; they'll all say that I'm beautiful to curry favor."

"What will they say when you aren't listening? They want to see Cleopatra's daughter. Do you want your new subjects to think that you're some dowdy Roman matron?"

"Better that than an ornament on Juba's arm." It'd only been days since I'd been held down against my will, less since I'd learned my husband's part in it. "I refuse to be the pretty plaything of a petty king!"

"Majesty," Chryssa began cautiously, her world-weary eyes meeting mine in a direct stare that most slaves avoided. "When slaves are flogged, the first thing we do is reach for clothes. We want to hide the injury, hide the shame, but we can't suffer the cloth against our wounds. It makes it worse. The cruel masters know this. They count on that extra humiliation to break us. But you're no slave; you can't hide in shame and you can't let anything break you."

I tossed my head in denial; she had no right to speak to me this way and tears stung my eyes. It was as if she could see through me, like clear water, and I worried she might actually speak aloud what the emperor had done. I'd do anything to keep her from naming what had happened to me, so I blinked my tears away and surrendered silently, allowing her to make me presentable. I couldn't wear the sleeveless dress because I'd scratched my arms red and raw, so Chryssa draped me in a white *chiton*, sleeves fastened with golden pins. I wore the pearl earrings and let Chryssa fasten my hair in a circlet of gold. Thus attired, I made ready to meet my new subjects.

Lucius Cornelius Balbus offered me a hand, helping me down into the rowboat, and I found myself face-to-face with my husband. Juba gave me a curt nod of acknowledgment. I gave him a cool stare. Once on shore, I knew we must stand together, but we wouldn't have to clasp hands as Romans considered open affection between a husband and wife to be unseemly. These thoughts so consumed me as we made landfall that I was taken entirely by surprise by that first unexpected pleasure of planting my sandaled foot upon the soil of Mauretania.

It all rushed to me. Sea and salt, sun and sand. The lowing camels made strange music beneath the voices of the people in the crowd. The spice market must not have been far, for my senses were assailed with the scents of mint, lavender, turmeric, marjoram, mustard, oregano, and rosemary. Delighted, I stifled my sputter of amazement.

Had we been in Alexandria, crowds would have mobbed the deck at the sight of royal banners, throwing flower petals and holding their hands out for coins, but here in Mauretania, the crowd was merely curious. Dark and sandy-skinned merchants gathered, many of them wearing Greek or Roman garb. Some of our subjects were startlingly fair. These weren't Arabs or black Ethiopians. These were camel-mounted Berbers, native Africans who claimed descent from Hercules. They were ferocious-looking men in striped tunics, colorful head coverings, animal skins, and flowing burnoose cloaks. Some were desert nomads. Others were hardy mountaineers. Their interested stares slid from us to the vast treasure being unloaded from the belly of our ship with the seemingly endless stream of slaves.

The Berber men wore swords on their belts. I wasn't frightened, though, and the sight of Roman soldiers holding the crowd back only served to anger me. These soldiers were members of the Legio III Augusta, the Roman legion from the nearby province of Africa Nova. I wasn't grateful for them. Nor was I grateful for Juba's stance in front of me, as if to protect me in case the crowd would surge forward and attack. If they did, I'd sooner jump into the sea than seek shelter in Juba's arms.

Officiously, we alighted a small podium that had been hastily erected for us, and then Juba cleared his throat to speak in Latin. "*Salvete*, Mauretanians! I come to you the son of King Juba, restored to my patrimony." Of course, his father had been a Numidian king, not Mauretanian, which forced him to use my name to bolster his claim over the kingdom. "My queen is Cleopatra Selene of House Ptolemy, Princess of Egypt, so be confident in a prosperous reign. We're both children of the line of Hercules and will rule justly. May the gods bless our glorious undertaking here!"

When he repeated his speech in Greek, only some of the crowd applauded. "*Sweet Isis,*" Chryssa murmured. "Are they hostile or don't they know *Greek*? Have we been sent amongst savages?"

"Don't call them that," I whispered harshly. This wasn't Egypt. These weren't my people. But I'd asked to rule over them and I would honor them as I hoped they would honor me. When Juba finished speaking, I stepped forward to say a few words of my own, but he caught me by the arm. That he should touch me again was more than I could bear and I gave my husband a baleful look that stopped his tongue, midutterance.

In the king's silence, Balbus was bold enough to say, "It isn't proper for you to speak, Queen Selene."

Was I to take lessons on propriety from Romans? It seemed so. Balbus was a big man who blocked my path just long enough for most of the courtiers and government officials to turn their attention to our processional. It would have taken a trumpeter to get their notice again. Angry that I'd missed this first opportunity to speak to my subjects, I wanted to throttle Balbus but steadied myself with a deep breath of the intoxicating air. This land was hallowed and, somehow, as familiar to me as the palm trees that swayed in the breeze. I felt as if I'd come here to find the missing part of myself. As if Helios were standing right beside me.

A little girl dressed in brightly colored scarves came forward carrying a garland of flowers, and I stooped so she could put it around my neck. I gave her a small token of favor, a little bag of coins, then sent her back to her mother, whose hands were decorated with brown tattoos that whirled into flowers and crescent moons. "Beautiful," I said, first in Greek, then in Punic, which the woman seemed to understand, because she smiled.

At length, a Roman commander introduced us to the local garrison officers, and then Juba and I were ushered into litters with our entourage. Carried through the humble streets, we passed a charred and gutted apartment building, metal grates bent away from burned and crumbling bricks. Balbus was our self-appointed tour guide, and he explained that since the death of old King Bocchus, the city had fallen into decay. From what I could see of the streets where barefoot children played, Iol hadn't been much to speak of at its peak. Yet I felt charmed by every resilient patch of swaying grass and each brave wildflower that blossomed between the neglected paving stones. We passed an open-air market where colorful awnings shielded a multitude of traders wearing fringed leather and striped cloaks. An escaped goat zigzagged through the shoppers, a bell ringing loudly on its neck as several merchants gave chase. I smiled at the rusticity because it reminded me of the little townships in Egypt, but Juba put his face in his hands. "We'll need a new market," he said.

"Hopefully the locals will welcome it," Balbus said. "It's good that we brought slaves because if the tribesmen don't like a project, they won't work. These Berbers, the Mauri and the Gaetuli and others, they're the most backward and bullheaded barbarians you'll ever encounter."

I bit my lip, for Juba was himself a Berber, but if the new king took offense, he didn't show it. Perhaps Juba had become accustomed to such disparagement, or perhaps he'd never considered himself anything but Roman. A subtle tug of sensation made me turn my head and open the curtain of our jostling litter. On the street, I spied a little group of musicians, pounding drums and shaking rattles. Beyond the music, there was something else that drew my attention. It was faint but exotic. In Egypt, I'd learned the scent of magic while trailing behind my mother and her court mage, Euphronius. I knew this wasn't the floral scent of light magic nor the metallic scent of dark magic. *This* magic was some combination of the two, tinged with something more bracing, like mint. Sagging against its stone pillars, a crumbling temple leaned into view, and I had no doubt it was the source of the magic I'd scented. The temple's broad wooden doors were carved with a symbol that looked very much like the looped cross of an *ankh*, but with a wider base. A bronzed crescent moon sat atop the building, forcing me to exclaim, "Oh! A temple to Isis . . ."

"It's Tanit's temple," Juba corrected me, adopting the same tone he'd used when I was a child in his classroom. "She's the Carthaginian mistress of the moon."

It didn't matter by what name they called her. I knew my goddess anywhere and by any name. "I wager she's mistress of more than the moon, isn't she? She's a mother goddess, and a maiden, and a *magician*."

Juba arched a brow. "So they say, but the tales of this goddess are dark ones, Selene. The Carthaginians gave children in sacrifice, though the Berbers claim Tanit brings forth souls into new babes when women ask for her blessing. Her temple certainly isn't much to look at, here amongst the squalor of the street vendors."

"Where else should it be?" After all, my goddess was no indifferent Olympian, to be viewed from afar on some high hilltop. She was a goddess for all the people and heard their prayers. Though lacking in grandeur, this temple held so much magic that it seemed to seep out of the bronze-studded doors and the hairs on my nape rose in response. I wanted to go inside. To feel powerful again. To wield magic again. To worship Isis and thank her for delivering me from Augustus.

But it would have to wait.

Our procession moved on and Juba gritted his teeth every time a new side street came into view. "It will take a *lifetime* to turn this place into a modern city," he said, and when our litter arrived at the squat homestead of Mauretania's last king Juba's mood only worsened. The dilapidated mansion may have once housed royalty, but cracks in the plaster now gave way and the red-tiled roof sagged like an old man's jowls. Vines had overgrown the gate, their wild leaves scrambling over the ironwork like an army in assault. Juba sighed to Balbus. "This is hardly a place suited to my wife's Ptolemaic pride."

I didn't want the Romans to dismiss me as a spoiled Easterner. "My royal husband is overly solicitous of my comfort, Lucius Cornelius. I assure you, I'm content with this homestead."

Juba seemed dubious. "We don't have to stay, Selene. Augustus wants us to build our new harbor here, but we can rule from Volubilis, inland to the west. Or from the imposing cliffside city of Cirta, in Numidia."

Curiosity overcame me. "Do our lands extend that far?"

The king was forced to shrug. Though everyone said we were to rule the largest client kingdom in the Roman world, the borders of our territory seemed amorphous and subject to change no matter which map we consulted or official we spoke to. Perhaps Augustus wanted Juba to be able to claim that he now ruled his father's lands, when the truth was that Numidia had been almost entirely absorbed into the Roman province of Africa Nova.

As we climbed out of our litters, Roman soldiers hastened about. Our swift arrival seemed to have caught them unawares. Had no one told them we were coming? If we were to be a sovereign kingdom, these Romans would have to leave.

A menagerie of dead animals crowded the entryway. A giant rug of leopard skins stretched over a cracked tile floor and the skin of an elephant, ears and all, hung from the wall like a drab gray tapestry. I swallowed to disguise my aversion.

The staff stumbled over themselves to make obeisance, prostrating fearfully before Juba, for it had been his father's name too, and a name they feared in a king. Several of the girls peeked up at me with an expression of awe. The name Ptolemy still held power, and the name Cleopatra bespoke glamour, so I was very glad that I'd agreed to let Chryssa dress me in my fineries.

At length, my new lady's maids came forward, but exhaustion defeated my best intentions to remember their names. Seeing me sway on my feet, a pregnant servant, a Berber if I wasn't mistaken, asked in thickly accented Latin, "You want bath? Can fill tub."

"A *tub*?" Chryssa yelped, unable or unwilling to disguise her dismay.

Like me, she was accustomed to the Roman luxury of running water and heated baths but I desperately wanted to feel clean again, so we would simply have to make do. "A tub will do nicely."

The servants showed me through the rotting latticework doors to my chambers. Chryssa seemed eager to take charge, and I found myself grateful for her newfound sense of authority. With the noise from the courtyard, the scampering of lizards on the windowsill, and the strange aromas coming from the direction of the kitchen, this place was foreign to me. Yet I felt as if I'd found a refuge where everything that was broken in me might be healed again.

This wasn't only because of the temple and the magic I'd scented, but because, in the way of a twin, I sensed Helios near.

Eight

IF I'd hoped for a lavish palace and majestic coronation, I was to be disappointed. We'd invaded Mauretania like a small army and our reward was the old royal mansion, with its soot-stained walls. Our artists and other retainers all needed accommodation. The surveyors, engineers, and slaves needed lodgings too. There wasn't enough room for them, so some bedded down with the soldiers and others were forced to pitch tents on the grounds. To feed the multitude, our new cooks roasted meat on spits outside and boiled vats of porridge in the kitchen from morning till night. One afternoon, pushing away his bowl, Crinagoras leaned to me and said, "This gruel doesn't inspire me, Majesty. I do hope you intend something grand here in Mauretania, because this is no suitable place for a poet of my stature!"

Juba overheard, and though it was plain to me that Crinagoras was teasing, my husband gave him a sharp look. In truth, I wondered how either of them could have greeted the prospect of this new adventure so glumly. Unwilling to let them spoil my mood and eager to explore the grounds, I summoned the Berber woman to give me a tour. She was enormously pregnant, her bulk emphasized by bright clothing, flowery henna tattoos, and a mysterious blue sheen to her skin. The blue was a fascination to me, but I hesitated to ask about it lest I offend. Moreover, the Berber servant and I had difficulty understanding one another. She seemed to have some authority over the others and spoke better Latin—but that wasn't saying much.

"I am Tala," she said, showing Chryssa and me to an overgrown garden courtyard where a cistern-fed fountain snorted up muddy water. "You are king's *only* woman?"

Chryssa huffed with indignation. "She's your queen. Not the king's woman. She's his *wife*."

I was neither in truth, but Tala didn't seem impressed. "Numidian kings keep . . . much . . . wives."

"*Many* wives," Chryssa snapped. "King Juba will have only one. He's a Roman citizen. Learn to speak more respectfully, you insolent barbarian!"

I hadn't ever seen Chryssa in such a temper and Tala was a big woman—bigger because of her pregnant belly. She towered over my slave girl and I worried that the two might come to blows, but Tala turned her attention to me and said, "Carthaginians come, then go. Romans come, but they will go. This queen, she is Greek. Or Egyptian. She will go too. Always, only *Amazigh* remain."

Not even as a captive in Rome had I allowed servants to speak to me in this manner. "Tala, I'll be Queen of Mauretania for as long as the goddess wills it. Now, either tell us why every corridor has animal tusks protruding from the walls or leave my presence at once."

Tala gave a sullen shrug. "Old king liked hunt. Gave many animals for Roman arena."

It was a reminder of our obligations to Rome. There must be lions and elephants aplenty for the gladiators to fight. We'd be expected to provide them, and though it sickened me, it would enhance the prestige of our kingdom.

Later, when we were alone, Chryssa's temper hadn't cooled. "Why didn't you dismiss that impudent savage immediately?"

I earnestly pondered her question. It had been my deeper instincts that told me not to send Tala away. "Chryssa, I must win her over. If I can't win the love of my household staff, how can I win the rest of Mauretania?"

* * *

THAT night, the servants brought me a plate of flat bread and a board of goat cheese with a knife to cut it. I read from a scroll in my lap while I ate, leaving the oil lamps burning, never dreaming that Juba might take the glow under my door for an invitation. He knocked briefly, letting himself in and waving all my servants away. "What is it?" I asked, not rising to greet him. "News?"

"Nothing from Thebes, if that's your concern." Juba's eyes fell upon the scroll on my lap. "What are you reading?"

I fingered the vellum, for I liked its texture. "A copy of Mago's treatise on agriculture."

Juba looked suitably impressed. "In Punic? I knew that you'd learned a few words but not that you'd mastered it."

"I haven't yet," I admitted, wondering why he'd come. I didn't want him here. I hadn't forgiven him. I was certain I never would. "I'd do better with a translation, but I'm trying to learn the language of our people."

"Punic isn't the original language of the Berbers," Juba said, sitting beside me at the low table near the remains of my meal. "They speak it here in the cities, but in the highlands, they speak a thousand dialects. Better that we make our subjects learn Latin or Greek. Still, if you're determined, I'll send you a teacher and perhaps I can help you practice myself."

"That's very considerate," I allowed. "But you're a king now. You've more important things to do than tutor me."

An awkward silence fell between us until he cleared his throat. "Selene, I've given some rational thought to our situation. I understand how unhappy you are in this marriage, but you must also remember that Mauretania fell into the hands of the Romans because the king died without heirs. We're here to forge a new dynasty. We represent a second chance—perhaps Mauretania's *last* chance—for independence."

"I am aware," I said, anticipating a lecture.

"Then you must know that we have a duty to our new kingdom.

Given your age, I hoped to wait some years, to give you some time to grow into womanhood. Unfortunately, we cannot wait. We must have children and we must have them soon."

How could he speak of it now? Memories of the emperor's bony knees bruising my thighs raised a cool sweat on the back of my neck and nausea rose in my throat.

Juba must have noticed because his posture stiffened. "I can plainly see that you find me too lowly a prince for your affections, but I'll endeavor to make the act of conception as pleasant for you as I can."

Embarrassment singed my ears. "And what if I'm already carrying the emperor's child?"

Again, I said it only to hurt him, to wound him as he'd wounded me. But Juba must have considered the possibility already, because he didn't flinch. "I'll claim your child, Selene. It's no fault of the babe that it should have to endure the taint of illegitimacy."

I stared up at him in surprise and the scroll fell from my hands. "You'd do such a thing?" I'd been called the bastard brat of Antony more times than I could count. That Juba would spare a child that pain softened me toward him.

Juba nodded once, his fingers lacing together in quiet reserve. "Our reign can only benefit by raising the offspring of Augustus. If you're already with child, I'll simply wait a respectful interval before getting my own sons upon you. Motherhood will be good for you, Selene. It'll give you something useful to do."

He was trying to be reasonable. He was trying to be generous and conciliatory. It only drove me to rebellion. "And if I should refuse to let you 'get your sons upon me'?"

Just like that, the pretense of magnanimity vanished and Juba's lips thinned. "Don't play the Vestal Virgin, Selene."

He made a gesture that I mistook for an intention to grab me. "Don't touch me," I cried, my voice not nearly as steady as I wished it to be. I scrambled to the other end of the table, upsetting cups and plates along the way.

Seeing me flee from him in white-knuckled fright, Juba put his face in his hands as if he needed to master himself. When he finally looked up, his eyes hardened. "All your life, you've known me as a solicitous tutor, Selene. You should know that I'm a soldier too. I descend from King Massinisa of Numidia and my father was Juba the warrior king. You don't want to test me. I *can* be ruthless for the greater good."

At his displeasure, I should have lowered my head meekly the way Lady Octavia had taught me to do, but he was threatening me, and that was beyond endurance. "Just because you can ride a horse doesn't make you a soldier," I seethed. "And we both know you're a coward besides."

This time, he *did* reach for me. Though I gave it no conscious thought, my fingers wrapped around the hilt of the table knife. I was almost as astonished as Juba when the tip of my blade pressed against his belly. The knife stopped Juba short and we both stared at one another over the sharp edge. My chest rose and fell, rage making my hand shake, but I didn't lower the blade.

Eyes wide, hands slightly raised, Juba said, "You're as vicious as a she-wolf!"

He could have disarmed me, but he didn't try. Instead, he retreated and I called after him. "Think twice before you lord your barbaric ancestry over me, Juba! I'm a Ptolemy and you may trust that you'll be found dead in your bed before I ever let another man force himself on me."

THE next afternoon, swarthy desert men rode up to the gate. Their leaders dismounted effortlessly, swinging bright burnooses over their shoulders. There were other riders too, dangerous-looking men with braided hair, clad in animal skins, and carrying daggers and shields of rawhide. Some were dark-skinned, others were fair, and yet they were all allied tribesmen who eyed the Roman guards with hostility. Though we were unprepared for guests of any kind, it would have been insulting not to receive them, so Juba and I stood together in the audience chamber, not sparing each other a glance while the Berbers bowed before us. We had little to offer them for supper, so we served spare quantities of capers, yogurt, brown bread, and grilled lamb in juniper sauce. We shared this modest meal at low tables and one of the Berber chieftains rose to his feet.

Like Tala, his skin shimmered blue in the creases of his elbows, his hands, and some of the lines of his face. Lifting a goblet in salute, he introduced himself as Maysar of the Gaetulian tribes, then went on in passable Latin. "Juba son of Juba, the Gaetulians, the Musalamii, and the Mauri tribes bring to you an offering of horse stock, some of the finest steeds in this land."

Juba's expression lightened for the first time in days. "I'm honored by this gift! Horses are a passion of mine."

The chieftain glinted a pearly smile. "May these horses sire a royal cavalry that will be the fear of all nations!"

"To the greater glory of Rome," Juba said, for he couldn't show military ambition in front of so many Romans. Even I understood this, but some of the tribesmen scowled, conferring with their heads close together.

To distract from the angry murmurs, I asked, "Do you have a wife, Maysar? After so fine a gift as horses, it seems only right that I should gift your wife with a token of my esteem."

"I have a wife, just not . . . at the moment. She's in sanctuary. We're divorced tonight, but will remarry upon the morrow."

Sure that I'd misunderstood his words, I turned to Juba, who said, "It's a Berber custom."

"When our women wish for fortune or healing," Maysar explained, eager to teach me, "they spend the night in a tomb of our ancestors. Failing that, a cave or other sacred space. Whatever she dreams there will come true. Only unmarried women can go into sanctuary. Since we're a practical people, a married woman ritually divorces before she goes, then remarries when she returns."

This fascinated me. "Perhaps I should go into sanctuary, to bring good fortune and blessings upon this land."

The Berber chieftain tilted his head in surprise, a glimmer of pleasure in his eyes at my suggestion. At the same time, the Romans scoffed, and it was no secret that their opinion mattered more to Juba than mine. The king smiled tightly, swirling some of his watered wine in his cup. "I'm not sure it's fitting . . . My queen isn't Berber."

"But it's *most* fitting," Maysar argued. "Since our tribes and the Numidian tribes of your father are all Berbers, we greet you as a *brother* as well as a king. Your wife should share our customs."

Juba was clearly uncomfortable to be reminded of his heritage in this manner, and in the awkwardness, Crinagoras rose to recite an amusing epigram in which he maintained that he was himself a more revered poet than Homer. The guests all laughed, and the tension dissipated, for which I was grateful.

Later, when the men broke into groups, some to discuss commerce, others to plan construction, and still others to gossip, I sought out Maysar and his group of warriors. He bowed. "Queen Cleopatra."

It was my name but my mother's too. "You may call me Queen Selene. Your men don't much like the Roman soldiers, do they?"

At this, the Berber's smile faltered. "We're eager for them to be gone. We rejoiced to hear that a Berber king was being sent to us. Then we saw all the Roman settlers and all the slaves . . . We call ourselves the *Amazigh*. It means 'free people.' We won't bend easily under a yoke and we don't like to see others bent."

"What of your women?" I asked, drinking from a tisane of mint leaves steeped in hot water. The infusion was refreshing and I called for another cup.

"You've met Tala, haven't you? She's one of my many sisters and always free to speak her mind."

Sweet Isis! The proud servant who'd been unafraid to show her disdain for me was the chieftain's sister? She hadn't mentioned it and now I was glad I hadn't sent her away. "She's with child. Does she have a husband?"

Maysar's brilliant smile faded. "My sister Tala is a widow. Her husband was killed in a raid by the Garamantes."

"I'm sorry to hear it," I said, and I was. No wonder Tala was so unpleasant; she'd suffered a terrible loss.

"Berber women of her status seldom serve," Maysar explained.

"It is only because she's so heavily pregnant that I'd rather have her here in the city than helping to shepherd our tribe. With us, the women are the spiritual leaders. Some tribes keep their women cloistered. In others, women fight with the men or become crafts-women and magicians."

It was the word *magician* that caught my attention. I was about to ask him about it, when a young messenger burst into the room. Juba leaned close to the newcomer. After a few whispers my new husband rose from his table. He uttered some vague words of apology before retiring. Then his advisers all followed him out of the hall.

OUR first official dinner in Mauretania had come to an abrupt end and now, behind closed doors, something important was happening. Something I should be privy to. Shut out, I paced, hearing voices but unable to make out words. Balbus was loud and aggressive. Juba maintained a measured tenor. If only I knew what they were saying!

Coming upon me in the dingy corridor, Crinagoras made a sweeping bow that involved much dramatic waving of fingers. "Majesty, it's fortunate I was there to entertain the desert chieftains, but even a man of my talents can't make them stay when their monarchs flee the room."

"Of course," I murmured, only at half attention, straining to hear the men in the room beyond.

"Will you go in?" Crinagoras asked, glancing at the unguarded doors.

A bitter taste filled my mouth. "They shut the doors in my face. I wasn't invited."

Crinagoras shot me a sideways glance. "Why should you be? You're only the wife of the king. A veritable child-bride at that. A girl with no experience of the world and no concerns beyond cosmetics and hairpins and expensive jewels."

"You taunt me," I said crossly.

A grin split his face. "I knew you'd be clever enough to deduce as much. You must have also gathered that I'm only repeating words spoken by the men behind those doors. Majesty, have I ever mentioned that the first line of a poem is the most important? The first words, nay, the first *word*, the first *sound* as it rolls off the tongue, is crucial. It sets the tone for the whole piece."

He wasn't talking about poetry, and though I didn't care for his irreverent manner, he was right; if I didn't establish my place now, I might always be excluded. Without another word, I pushed the doors open to find Juba drumming his fingers upon a polished citrus-wood table. Balbus sat near him, alongside a number of Roman military officers and a few Greek diplomats. They were all big men, many of them warriors, and I forced myself to brave their irritated stares. "What news, gentlemen?"

Juba glanced up, clutching some missive in his right hand. "Go to bed, Selene. We'll talk in the morning."

My spine stiffened. "If the business of Mauretania must be conducted at this hour, I'll stay awake to hear it."

"Heed your king," Balbus snapped at me. "This is no place for a girl."

"But I'm not a girl." I took a steadying breath. "I'm the queen and you must accustom yourself to my presence."

Someone murmured something about how I was truly my mother's daughter. Then the room went silent. I made no move to leave. Seeing he wouldn't dissuade me, Juba finally waved a hand in surrender. One of Agrippa's engineers stood to make a place for me, and when I was seated, Juba said, "Selene, the revolt in Thebes has been put down. The Prefect of Egypt has crushed the rebellion."

It was with great difficulty that I didn't lurch forward. "When?" My voice was a rushed, shaky whisper.

The young courier cleared his throat. "Weeks ago, Majesty. A missive was sent to Rome, but it must have passed you on the sea. I came over land but was delayed for some time by the Garamantes in Numidia and was unable to carry this message until ransomed by superior officers."

The poor courier had been taken captive trying to get this message to us. A gracious queen would have asked after his well-being, but I was too stunned. What had I been doing the day the rebellion in Thebes was put down? While Egyptians were fighting Romans, had I been playing the *kithara* for the emperor? Had I been choosing gowns for my wedding chest? It seemed impossible that I might not have felt the clash of armies in my body the way I felt the words of Isis in my blood and pain. "And what of Alexander Helios, Prince of Egypt? Is there news? Has he been captured?"

The uncomfortable silence that blanketed the room told me that this question had already been asked. The courier shook his head and all eyes turned to Juba, including mine. The king's gaze fell to the scroll in his hand, and he swallowed. "Selene, there are reports that Helios was seen wielding a sword in battle. Gallus writes that they're still sorting the dead but that your brother will be found amongst the corpses."

Nine

I went limp. Then every part of me trembled. I should have cried out. I should have screamed. I should have felt the blackness of grief close its bony hand around my throat. But if Helios were dead, wouldn't I know it? He was blood of my blood, bone of my bone, my companion in this life and all the others. If he were dead, the sun itself would go dark in the sky. My heart couldn't possibly pulse with life without the answering echo of Helios's heart somewhere in the world. I knew this. I *knew* this as surely as I knew the sound of my own voice. "How can they still be sorting the dead?"

Juba sat back, his shoulders slumped, regret in his voice. "Because Thebes has been destroyed."

I couldn't make sense of this. Thebes—the city that had once been the capital of both Upper and Lower Egypt—destroyed? Thebes had been great before Alexander set foot on Egyptian sands. And the Romans had destroyed it? I tasted sand, envisioned toppled towers, and smelled the smoke as Thebes burned. I quaked at this madness. "What have you Romans done?"

Most of the men stared blankly, keeping the stiff professional disinterest of the Roman soldier, but some cringed. Perhaps they'd heard the whispers that I was a sorceress who held crocodiles in my thrall. Maybe they were afraid of me. Maybe they *should* have been afraid because I felt a terrible rage and a gust of dry wind howled through the old building, rattling the doors.

"Gods be good, let's hope it's not the sirocco," someone said. I didn't see who.

Juba seemed to sense danger. "We'll retire for the night. My queen needs time to grieve her brother's death."

His words sent me into a wilder fury. Helios wasn't dead and Juba couldn't simply say it and make it so. My twin couldn't be dead. Not after everything I'd endured to save him. If anything, I felt him nearer to me now than in all the months since he ran away. I should have been with Helios. Together, perhaps we could have saved Thebes. What was I doing here while officials sorted the dead in Egypt? My mother's Egypt. I rose from my seat and another blast of wind rattled the house.

"You're dismissed," Juba said to the men. "Go!" They scattered into the hall, leaving Juba and me alone. "Selene, I'll send word to the Prefect of Egypt and tell him not to burn the body. You can build Helios a tomb in the custom of your people . . ."

He meant well by it—I know he did—but I lashed out anyway. "Don't pretend you care. Helios isn't dead. If he was, certainly the prefect would have recovered his body. One day, Helios will rule Egypt. It's his destiny."

"No, Selene." Juba made me look at him and compassion colored his features. "Trust me, Helios is dead. If not in Thebes, then somewhere else. Augustus had a thousand agents seeking him out, and I can well imagine their orders. Do you think the Prefect of Egypt would have razed Thebes on his own initiative?"

I shook my head violently. "No, that wasn't the emperor's plan. He sent me with you to—"

"To get you out of the way. You were a dangerous girl to have in Rome where Isis worshippers invoked you as their champion. A dangerous girl to have in the East where your parents still have allies and friends. A daughter of Antony was too dangerous to keep in Rome, a daughter of Cleopatra too dangerous in the East. So he sent you here, to Mauretania, to the other side of the world."

Distraught, I brought my hands up to my face and Juba's hard expression crumbled, as if he regretted saying these things to me.

Tears spilled over my lashes. "I don't understand. The emperor promised mercy for Egypt. Mercy for Helios. The emperor promised me. He gave me his vow."

Juba reached for my chin, cupping it tenderly. "Oh, my poor Selene, you actually thought you could save him."

The pity in his voice was horrible. Unendurable. I broke away, fleeing the room. Somehow the news had already reached Chryssa. On her knees in my chamber, she was sobbing. Her cries echoed in my ears from somewhere very far away. "Stop it. Helios lives! I know it. I know he lives still."

Chryssa rocked herself and made a keening sound. "How can it be? I know the stories of Carthage. When Romans destroy a city, they kill every warrior, they put every building to the torch, and they salt the fields."

She'd been my brother's slave before she was mine. She'd loved him. Worshipped him. I found myself sinking down beside her, to offer her comfort. "It's true that the Romans are destroyers, but they're also *liars*. If Helios is dead, then why do I sense him here in Mauretania? Why is it that every time I turn a corner, I feel as if he'll be there?"

"Because you're one soul!" Chryssa wept, clasping my hands. "Now that his body breathes no more, the rest of his spirit must have come here to rejoin with yours."

THE winds blew that night and into the next morning, snapping sail lines, jostling fishing boats in the harbor, and sending sprays of water into the air. It was a stiff wind that roared hour after hour, carrying with it a dry and oppressive heat. The Romans saw it as a bad omen, more portentous than lightning or the entrails of the sacrificial beasts. *It bodes ill for our mission here*, some said, and wondered which ancient god we'd offended. Meanwhile, Berbers wondered if this storm had been sent to drive us away.

Outside, servants braved the scouring winds to haul fresh water from the well, dragging huge clay jugs into the house as if preparing for a long siege. The ladies in my chamber busied themselves closing shutters, pulling dusty tapestries from the walls and fitting them around the windows. I sat in the center of this whirlwind, hands tight on the arms of my chair. I was thinking. Turning this puzzle over and over. Had I been sent to Mauretania only because I was too dangerous to keep in Rome? I remembered the men Augustus killed on our way to Ostia. Had they come to see me? I'd thought to help Egypt with my newfound power as a queen confirmed by Rome, but perhaps I'd merely been sent into exile.

Though the howling winds buffeted us with hot air, my fingers were cold. My toes, my ears, my nose all ice. I hadn't eaten. I hadn't slept. I was scarcely aware of Juba's presence until he grabbed the arms of my chair, demanding, "Is this storm your doing?"

The blue-tinted Berber woman tried to explain, "It's the sirocco. First come winds, then sands from the Sahara—"

"Leave!" Juba cut her off as he'd seen my magic before and she hadn't. But I didn't care if he shouted and I didn't care if the winds blew. I didn't believe that Helios was dead. Still, at war with my heart was my reason. A dark, terrible, stormy reason that swept everything from my mind. What if Chryssa was right, and Helios's spirit was here, right here in this room with me, waiting for me to breathe for the both of us when I couldn't seem to breathe at all . . .

"Selene," Juba said, stooping in front of me. "Are you making these winds blow?"

I felt for the little frog amulet at my throat. It wasn't warm. I didn't feel *heka* flow through me. I felt drained. I felt *nothing*. A strange sound, almost like a laugh, escaped me. "I don't know."

Juba rocked back on his heels. "How can you not know?"

"In a world without Helios, how can I know anything?"

He cursed in Latin, pushed to his feet, then ran both hands through his hair. "I know we've been angry with each other. I know that this hasn't started well, none of it. Still, I wouldn't see you in such pain. Tell me what I can do to help."

Outside, the wind continued to howl, gusts of sand scrubbing buildings as it passed. I wanted to go out into it; maybe I'd finally get clean. "Let me go into sanctuary."

Juba was aghast. "I'm not sending you into a storm to stay by yourself in some primitive cave."

I tried to adopt a reasonable tone. "What do you think our new subjects will read into a storm arriving just as we take our places as king and queen? At least, if we follow their customs and the winds stop, they may think we bring them fortune instead of doom."

Juba couldn't argue or perhaps he simply didn't know what else to do with me. "Where would you go?"

"Tanit's temple could serve as a sanctuary, can't it? It has big doors to shut out the sand. I'll go with some covered skeins of water . . . maybe I can find some comfort for my grief there."

Juba sighed elaborately. "I suppose you want me to go through with the mummery of some ritual divorce?"

"There's no need, Juba. Both of us know this is no true marriage."

TO my surprise, it was Tala who objected most strenuously to my leaving. As the winds blew harder, the blue-hued woman said, "Foolish! When sand comes, you'll be stranded. No servants to cater to you. Sirocco cares nothing for royalty. Will swallow up even spoiled little queen."

Even Lady Octavia would have put Tala out into the street for speaking with such disrespect, but I'd let no one distract me from what I felt compelled to do. When Tala saw I was determined, she sighed and put her hand over her belly. "I take you as far as temple, then I turn back."

"I have guards to take me," I said, motioning to the assembling group of soldiers wearing plumed helmets and scarlet capes.

"*Roman* guards," she snorted, pulling a veil over her face. "I am *Amazigh*. I know this storm."

We rode camels to the temple because camels were the animals best suited to survive a full-bore sandstorm and would provide shelter if we were caught in one. I clung to the animal's hump as it swayed in its graceless gait, not liking the scratch of its fur, not daring to complain. My cloak flapped wildly behind me as I leaned into the wind, which howled down every alleyway like some ancient demon, and by the time I rushed up the steps of the temple into the relative shelter of the outer chamber, I was breathless. In the lamplight, Tala said, "I leave bedding. Sealed jars of olives and dates. Fresh water too." Then she handed me a stoppered bottle of olive oil. "Put it in nose and in mouth, to keep moist."

"Thank you, Tala. You may go now before the storm gets worse."

Her jewelry jingled as she turned to leave, but then she stopped at the doors. "Maybe Romans gave us brave queen. Good for *Amazigh*. We'll see."

THE inner chamber of the temple was dark, but I wasn't afraid, because Tanit—this Punic version of my goddess—was a mistress of the night. My footsteps fell softly upon the stone floor to a simple pallet with some blankets, but I didn't lie down. *Heka* drew me to the altar. Magic hummed in the stonework of the stelae and danced in a fountain that flowed over a ledge and dropped in a sheet to a murky pool below. The water tumbled, frothing over itself, misting the air beneath the candlelit statue of the goddess. She was a maiden beauty with a garland at her neck and a bed of flowers at her feet. She was foreign but familiar, and I let out a sigh of exultation.

The goddess had been waiting here for me and I waded into the pool so she might embrace me as her daughter. If there were crocodiles or sacred animals, I didn't fear them. Mere weeks had passed since the emperor put his filthy hands upon me, and as the water floated my gown up around my waist, I lolled there in the water, half awake, half asleep. I closed my eyes, feeling weightless, safe as I was in the womb. I rested my head on the ledge of the pool, breathing sweet air through my veil.

My goddess had suffered. Her brother-husband had been murdered by the dark god Set, his body mutilated. She'd wandered the world, gathering the pieces, using her magic to put him back together and bring him to life again. Somehow, I must do the same for Helios. The spell Isis cast, a simple prayer, was one I murmured now.

> *"I call you to me.*
> *I call you by the breath of your body.*
> *I call you by the truth of your soul.*
> *I call you by the spark of your mind.*
> *I call you by the light of your spirit."*

In the corners of the temple, little clouds of sand seeped through the stonework, snuffing a few candles out. It became darker, and I was so sleepy. So very tired. So completely exhausted with grief. I closed my eyes and must have slept. Berber women believed that whatever they dreamed in such sanctuaries would come true.

I dreamed that I wasn't alone.

I couldn't hear my own breath over the rush of the waterfall, but somehow I heard *his*. I opened my eyes and let them drift to each alcove, searching the shadows. Behind a pillar, I made out the shape of a young man. He emerged through the cascade of water, like a curtain pushed aside. Even with the spray of water in my eyes, I would have known him in any temple, in any part of the world, in any lifetime. "Helios," I whispered and rushed to him, throwing my arms about his neck. He crushed me against him and I recognized his scent—the sea-swept notes that were his and mine alike. He felt solid, but when he didn't speak I knew he was only a spirit body, my Osiris, from the realm of the dead. His hands pushed back the wet hair from my face. Our eyes met, and everything I wanted to say flowed out of me in a rush of tears. "How could you leave me?"

Then this spirit I'd conjured did speak. "I'm sorry," Helios rasped. "Sorrier than you'll ever know."

"You swore to me that you'd take me to Egypt, that you'd never let me be married off, that you'd always defend me. That you'd always, always, defend me. But I had to defend everyone. You, Philadelphus, Egypt . . . and I didn't know what to do."

I regretted saying these things because they seemed to pain him more than they did me. He shuddered, every part of him sagging with defeat and sorrow. "I'm so sorry, Selene. So sorry."

"The emperor hurt me," I whispered.

His shoulders rose again and he gripped my arms. "What did he do to you?"

At last the truth escaped me. "He raped me."

There it was. I'd spoken it aloud, and in the speaking, made it real. I'd given voice to the filth and shame and now I was fragile. I'd been called a whore and a seductress and a schemer, and borne it. If Helios doubted me, even this spirit version of him, it would break me. I'd shatter into a thousand pieces and no one and nothing would ever be able to make me whole. But Helios offered no recriminations. Instead, he cried out in rage. Then his voice dropped low and deadly. "I'll kill him. I'll make him pay for this as he's never paid for anything else in his life. If I could reach Octavian tonight, he wouldn't live to see the sunrise. I've made other promises to you, Selene, but this one I'll keep. By Isis, I vow to you, that I'll kill—"

"Don't," I whispered quickly. "Don't promise violence in a temple. Not even if you aren't real."

"I'm real enough . . ."

"You can't be. They told me that you were dead!"

He lowered his head. "Better that I were."

"If you're better off dead, then I am too," I told him, hot tears scalding my cheeks. "We've always been together and I can't be alive without you. I can't do anything without you. I can't even get clean . . ."

"You *are* clean," Helios said, pale eyes squinting.

"No." I shook with each sob, my shoulders heaving. "Since that night, I've scrubbed my skin raw, but I can't wash him away."

Helios looked stricken, his throat working as he fought back tears of his own. He pressed his forehead to mine and we stood like that, breathing each other's breath, until he said, "I'll wash him away for you." Making a cup of his hands he scooped up water from the pool, then let it trickle down my neck. He did it again. Then he poured water over each shoulder, as if in sacred ritual. It must have been, for I felt the magic wash over us. Here in this temple, I heard the chants of the priests and the sounds of rattles from eras gone by. Here a thousand women had brought their sacrifices and a thousand candles had been lit. I didn't recognize the chants or understand their words, but like me, they'd all come here in human frailty and need.

Pain was a universal language.

Together we knelt and my gown floated on the water ghostly white. Helios washed my shoulders, my arms, and my trembling belly. He *bathed* me. He went on and on, slowly and methodically. He ran his hands through my hair, combing his fingers through it, thumbs massaging my scalp. And stroke by stroke, drop by drop, the salt water of my tears mingled with the sacred water until I was wrung out, rinsed away of pain. I hadn't been able to do it alone, but with Helios all things were possible. In the water, the flow of *heka* rushed up from the floor, spreading like warm honey in my veins. With my fingers still tangled with his, I pressed them against a supporting pillar. The paint in this temple had faded but the magic inside it hadn't. *Heka* flowed through our fingers so strongly, I could taste the green malachite on my tongue. "Can't you feel that?" I asked. "Years of sorrows and worship, magic stored here for us to use. It was here waiting to bring us together."

This sharing of *heka* was intimate and Helios seemed surprised by the intensity of it, dipping his head. "Selene . . ." His voice was tortured. "You're too close to me."

"How can I be too close?" I asked, tasting the tears of generations. "Like the sun and the moon, we were always meant to be in the same sky."

"Selene," he said again, as if it hurt him to speak my name. That's when I realized that he *wanted* me. Perhaps he'd always wanted me. Not abstractly, as a king who wants a queen, but with burgeoning, potent sexual desire. He shied away, as if ashamed. He shouldn't have been. For hundreds of years my family had practiced brother-sister marriage like the Egyptian pharaohs before us. The Romans judged it a wicked thing for a man to take his sister as a wife, but Helios wasn't a man and I didn't come to him as a woman or as a sister.

I'd said the calling prayer. I'd drawn him back from the underworld just as Isis had called back her brother-husband. In this sacred space, he was a youthful god and I was a maiden goddess. He was the husband that had been promised me in my dreams. The one who would take the hurts and soothe them, the one who would take what was broken in me and make me whole. It wasn't Juba. Helios was the lover who sang to me. It was his face I dared not name, even to myself. My skin glowed like the pale moon and reflected silvery off the face of the goddess above us. I was the goddess and he was the golden god that overflows the Nile's banks, cleansing the earth, filling the cracks in the soil with the seed of life.

I kissed him and he startled when our lips sealed together in soft reverence. I wrapped my arms around his neck and tasted the salt on his skin. I ran my fingers through his leonine hair and realized he was vulnerable to me. His body fell easy prey to my touch. I could take him as my lover or cast him away. It was my choice. *Mine.* And I chose him.

Ten

I was clean.

He'd made love to me upon a flower-strewn altar. He'd stroked me softly, worshipfully, as if only my skin could offer him salvation. He didn't curse me or demand that I love him. He didn't have to. Every tremulous touch had brought me closer to wholeness. Trembling hands washed away cruel ones. Sweet, tentative kisses drowned unrelenting dark memories.

After, I awakened to a crash in the outer chamber—maybe an urn or potted plant that couldn't withstand the storm. The winds were still blowing. I squinted into the dimness, coughing in the dusty air. Someone had wrapped me in a blanket and I clutched it. Helios was here. More worldly, less perfect. Still here. With a tunic wrapped around his waist and a cloth over his mouth, he crouched over an oil lamp, using his fingers to give rise to a flame. My eyes widened in amazement when I felt a strange pull in the *heka* and realized that he was *using* it to make fire. "How are you doing that?" I asked.

He glanced up, then held his arm out to show me his birthmark, the one shaped like a cobra, the *ureas*, the spitter of fire. "I can take flames into me or let them out. You can do the same with wind."

My own birthmark was shaped like a sail, and I stroked it now, fascinated by each freckle. "Does that mean . . . Is this storm my doing?"

"I don't know. Fire seeks me out. It may be the same for you with wind." He came to my side with a skein of water and brought it to my dry lips. I drank eagerly, realizing only now that my throat was parched. I should have used the oil the way Tala told me to, but from the moment I'd entered this temple, nothing had seemed real. That was all changing now.

During our lovemaking, I hadn't noticed the bandage wrapped round his ribs. But then spirits and gods couldn't be wounded. So he was no shadow or double. "You didn't die at Thebes . . ."

"I should have," he said, bracing his back against the stone wall. "There weren't many survivors, but what few there were, my men and I evacuated to Hermonthis." It was strange to hear him talk of *his men*, as if he were a military commander like Agrippa. As much as I'd changed in the time since we'd been apart, Helios had changed even more. He looked like a young fighter, one of the boys they enrolled in the legions. "Magic and faith can't win wars, you said, Selene. Only soldiers can. You were right and I was wrong about everything . . ."

After the Battle of Actium, in defeat, my father had brooded in a cabin by the water and when he finally emerged there was a hollowness to him. Some kind of death before death. I'd never thought to see such a thing again, but when I looked at my twin now, I glimpsed that same abyss and knew I wasn't the only one who'd come to this temple all broken inside. "What happened to you, Helios?"

I reached to inspect his wound and he pulled away. "It's nothing. A glancing blow." He unstopped an amphora of olives and the two of us ate in silence. When he finally spoke again, he said, "I learned of your marriage . . ."

I flinched, staring down at my betrothal ring. "I didn't want to marry Juba. It's no true marriage."

"You don't have to justify yourself to me, Selene. I didn't come here to accuse you."

"Then why did you come?" I asked, still half certain that I'd conjured him.

"I had to see you one last time."

I hated the sound of that. "How would you know to find me in this temple? How could you know that I'd come?"

"When I heard of your marriage to Juba, I knew you'd make landfall in Mauretania. Once I arrived, I passed this crumbling little temple and knew you'd find it too . . ."

It still seemed too dreamlike. I had to lean against his shoulder to reassure myself of the warmth and substance of him. "Who knows that you're here?"

"No one," he said with a shake of that golden head. The heat of the storm had dried his curls and mine. "There's a back entrance to the basement where they store old offerings. I broke the chain . . . Selene, I meant to come back for you at the head of an army, to liberate you and Philadelphus the way we used to dream Caesarion would. I knew you were clever enough to stay alive until I returned." Well, I'd done that. I'd survived. I was good at that. Helios bowed his head. "I failed. In this River of Time, I failed. I know you can't forgive me, but I *am* sorry."

Sheltered beneath the statue of the goddess and all the magic her worshippers had left here, I tangled my fingers in his hair. "Of course I forgive you."

"If you saw Thebes, you wouldn't—you *couldn't*. This Prefect of Egypt, this Cornelius Gallus, wasn't content to win his victory and loot. He dismantled the temples. He burned the houses. He took women and children and . . ." He broke off, seeing it all again.

"Hush, it's all done now." I stroked his hair as if he were a child. "Surrender to Juba and it can all be over. The emperor said you might be allowed to live *here*, in Mauretania, with me."

At that, his chin jerked up and he met my eyes. "You know better, Selene. Augustus won't spare me. He'll kill me. You know that." How could I argue when the emperor had broken almost every promise he'd ever made to me, not least of which was the unspoken promise of any civilized man that he wouldn't force himself upon a woman? "He thinks he *must* kill me, Selene. The Sibylline Books say a woman shall rule and subdue Rome. A woman like our mother. Then Rome would be purged by fire with a coming savior, a sun god like Helios-Horus, a child of Isis. So I burned Rome."

"Did you really set fire to Virgil's house too?"

He swallowed. "Virgil made an accidental arsonist of me. I only meant to burn his poem. But fire leapt from the hearth into my hands and my command over it faltered. I learned my magic in those mistakes, and those fires in Rome, at least the first ones, they were my doing. I thought I was fulfilling the prophecy."

Rome scourged by fire . . . and then a savior comes.

Of the Sibylline Books, those oracular writings that the Romans feared and revered, I knew only that which had been taught to me by Virgil, who busily refashioned those prophecies to cast Augustus as Rome's savior. It was no accident the emperor had chosen Apollo the Sun God as his patron deity. He'd tolerate no rivals and Juba's words came back to me. *Oh, my poor Selene, you actually thought you could save him . . .* Juba knew what I hadn't: Augustus would never allow Cleopatra's son, a boy named Helios, to come of age. "Then you have no choice but to raise an army to fight and make you King of Egypt."

"I'm already King of Egypt," Helios said, and it was true. He didn't wear a diadem, but he didn't need to. His face, so beloved to me, carried echoes of our parents, of my brothers, and of all our ancestors. *Traces, even of Alexander,* I thought. Royalty and responsibility were written in his every gesture. "But I don't *deserve* to be king."

I reeled back. "Of course you deserve to be king! No one in this world loves Egypt more than we do. Egypt needs a pharaoh. Egypt needs you."

"No," he said, taking a long drink of water. "Enough people have died for me. I'll never ask anyone to fight in my name again. The Romans think I'm dead. Some part of me is. Let them believe it."

Then what would he do? Live in obscurity? I was a Ptolemy. I couldn't conceive of it. "There has to be another way. A place for you here, until we can go home. Maybe you can hide yourself among the Isiac brotherhood and become an even more powerful magician."

Helios scowled. "I'm done learning magic. Whatever star I was born under, whatever destiny our parents saw, whatever Golden Age the Isiacs hope to have of me, it's not in *this* River of Time."

It was like blasphemy. "How can you say that?"

Holding both his hands up in the candlelight, he said, "Our mage taught me to throw fire, to send pillars of flame rolling down a hill at the enemy, but still the Romans came in formation, with their shields held high. I knew then that the prophecies about me must be a lie."

The mention of our mage, my mother's court wizard, captured my attention. "Where is he?"

"Safe, I think," Helios replied. "When defeat was certain, I sent Euphronius to find you. Perhaps he can teach you what you need to know. He served me to the best of his ability, Selene. Now you must care for him as you care for me . . . and I need you to carve my name in stone so that the gods know me, here in the West, where Egyptian kings go when they die."

My mouth worked but it took a moment before I found my voice. "I don't understand. What's to become of you?"

"Do you remember our mother's funeral?" Helios asked, turning to me. "When I performed the Opening of the Mouth, the crowd chanted. 'He is Horus—he is Horus the Avenger,' they said. That's what Egypt needs from me. I'm a son who couldn't save his parents and a brother who couldn't protect his siblings. I can't also be a king who fails his country."

"But you just said that you wouldn't ask anyone to fight—"

"I said that I'll never ask anyone to fight in *my* name," he interrupted. "Egypt needs someone to fight for *her*, not for a throne. The Romans steal grain and tax the people besides. Raping the countryside—" I winced at the word and he noticed, his rage fueling the torchlight in the hot, cavernous temple. "By Isis, I'll make them pay for all our family's spilled blood, for every offense against our faith, and for everything they've done to you!"

It wasn't just idle talk of a traumatized boy king. He meant it. He'd come here only to say good-bye, and it sent a jolt of anger through me. "You can't leave me again. I won't let you go. I'll scream for the Romans, and they'll capture you."

He leaned forward. "You'd never betray me, Selene."

"But I did," I said, tears welling in my eyes. "I kept secrets from you. I made you run away."

"I only ran because I thought they'd use you against me. And they would have."

I was blind with need. "Then we'll go, together, both of us. Let the Romans think I was swallowed in a storm. Take me with you!"

Helios cupped my chin. "Trust me, I *want* to, Selene. But that isn't what's best for Egypt."

I knew then, that he was a better king than I was a queen. "I don't care."

"Yes, you do. We can't forsake Philadelphus. We must think of him too. Make it easier for me, Selene. The Romans think I'm dead. Make them believe it. Build a tomb. Mourn for me. I've lost my name, but the House of Ptolemy lives on in you."

He wanted me to agree, to give him up for dead. How could I? I put my face in my hands, trying to think of some other way. Some escape from this labyrinth. "Where will you go? Am I never to see you again?"

Helios laced his fingers with mine. "We're one *akh*, Selene. We'll always find one another."

He meant that we'd be reunited in the afterworld. That in every realm of the soul, we'd been together before and would be again. "But I need you in *this* lifetime, Helios."

He smiled softly. "No, you don't. Look what you've done all by yourself. You were a prisoner and now you're a queen. You made that happen, not me. It all rests on you now, Selene. I know that if there will ever again be a pharaoh of Egypt, it'll be you."

The admiration I saw in his eyes broke my heart. "You don't know the lies I've told. All the unforgivable things I've done—"

"Don't you know that there's nothing I wouldn't forgive you for? None of it matters. You kept Philadelphus safe, didn't you? And Chryssa?"

"She's here with me," I admitted.

At that, he smiled again. "I knew you'd take care of her."

"Well, you gambled there," I said, guilt-ridden and bitter. "I resented her because you trusted her . . . loved her . . ."

His cheeks flamed. "There's no one I love the way I love you."

I didn't want to be like Juba, pressing him to feel something he didn't, but oh, greedy heart, I wanted more. For Helios, maybe what we'd done here in this temple had been a thing apart. Maybe he wouldn't have done it except as a farewell, dreamlike, the god in him and the goddess in me, and now we were merely mortals again. I had to know. "How do you love me?"

He took my hand and pressed it to his chest, on his breastbone, so I could feel his pulse. "You're my queen." He started to say something else, but his words were cut off by the crackle of thunder. "The storm is getting worse. I don't know if the temple can withstand it."

"It can," I whispered. "This place does more than shelter us. *Heka* is in the floor, in the stones, in everything. Teach me to use it."

Gathering my clothes, which had baked dry in the hot air, I fastened the clasps, laced my sandals, and pulled my veil in place. We pushed aside a curtain that must have once been vibrant red but was now filth-splotched, insect eaten, and reddish brown. I followed Helios down a narrow staircase, descending into a darker part of the temple where I felt the crackle of some energy force. Helios felt it too. "The *heka* is deep in this temple," he said. "I think we've been drunk on it . . ."

Is that how he'd explain the kisses we'd shared and the way our bodies had merged?

At the end of the passageway, the wind howled. Sand leaked around the old bronze-studded door. Helios kicked aside the broken chain then pushed the door open and we were struck, both at once, by a swell of sand that whipped into our faces. We stepped outside and my gown billowed around me. I shielded my eyes with one hand. A smashed fruit wagon had overturned on the street, dates and pomegranates spilled, rolling all over the ground. Shards of pottery clacked against the buildings and shattered things in the distance. Palm fronds lashed overhead like a cruel slaver's whip.

This land was hurting. Mauretania suffered my pains. "Can I make it stop?"

Helios came up behind me, his chest tight against my back. His hands, always larger than mine, lifted my wrists. "You have to find the *heka*. Sift through the scents and sounds and tastes until you find it and draw it in. You have to swallow the wind, without being swallowed."

"How is there room for it inside me?" I wondered.

"Under your skin, between your bones, there's space for other, more fluid things. Like blood. Like *heka*. Like fire and wind . . ."

I closed my eyes and breathed in the desert, along with the loam of Africa, groping for its magical core. My lungs swelled. I tasted Helios's breath in that wind and heard the creaking ships as they rolled in the harbor. Layer upon layer. Sounds, scents, and smells battered at me as I ventured into the storm. I reached for the *heka*, but it was just outside my grasp. I waded further into the sea of noise. Soon, I was inside myself, drawing the wind in.

Very distantly, I heard Helios call my name, but I couldn't see him. The wind was inside me and I was inside it, the thread of it slipping through my hand. I grabbed hold tighter. I caught the core of the storm, and it lashed angrily. I heard the snap of branches as it leveled trees but the sounds were dim and faint, a world away. As I swallowed the storm, I delighted in the rush of voices. Laughter of a tribal marketplace. The clink of coins. Clacking carts, horses neighing, a thousand different languages. The taste of plums soaked in wine, like the ones Julia used to steal from the pot during Saturnalia.

But as the sounds and scents and tastes came faster, my delight turned to fear. I heard the women of Thebes screaming. The taste of their blood was in this storm too. Slaves crying and men dying on battlefields. Elephants stampeding. All this horror was being pulled into me with this storm and I was whisked away. Swirling, down, down, down into myself. I tried to exhale but no longer knew how. Frantic, I flailed for some familiar sound or scent. I lost my hold. If I had a body anymore, I did not know. I drifted. I drowned.

I call you to me.

These words I knew and reached for the sound.

I call you by the breath of your body.

Was the voice my own, echoed back to me? No, it was Helios. I swam to him, toward his prayer.

I call you by the truth of your soul.
I call you by the spark of your mind.

Yes, there it was. His voice. I grabbed on to it like a drowning swimmer, in desperation. He'd found me, somehow, in this ocean of *heka*, and now he drew me back to myself.

I call you by the light of your spirit.

Helios was kissing me, drawing me back from the void. Giving me back my breath. I came back to myself, finding my arms, one outstretched toward the sky and the other rigid at my side. I gulped at windless air. My heartbeat pounded in my ears, and slowly, I realized it was the only sound. The *only* sound. *Thump thump. Thump thump.*

My eyes fluttered open, and I saw that I'd somehow made my way to the heart of Iol. Sand settled in a thin blanket across the land, and the sun warmed the cloudless sky. The air was still. At length, a dog barked somewhere in the distance. The next sound was a murmur as people opened their windows and doors. My veil had blown away and my cheeks were red and stinging, the tendrils of my hair still lifted on the storm I'd taken into myself. I blinked over and over again, afraid to move, for fear I'd collapse.

"It's the queen," someone said, astonished.

The storm was gone—and so was Helios.

Eleven

IT'S strange to remember how little Juba said to me when I returned. I'd come in straight through the front doors, *heka* still coursing through my veins, my cheeks raw and my hair a fright. We stood together in the main hall, where carved lions stared down at us with dead eyes. I'd come in not just from the storm but from the arms of a lover, so I wondered how I should answer Juba if he questioned me, but he asked me nothing.

Juba only called for servants to attend me, then retreated to the cramped room he'd claimed as his private study. I was grateful, because I needed time to make sense of my changed world. Chryssa broke open a waxy green leaf, smearing sticky aloe onto my cheeks to soothe my wind-burned skin. I didn't want to share the truth of what happened, but I knew that Chryssa still grieved for Helios and believed him dead so I whispered, "I've seen him."

She shuddered, her hands trembling. "Isis gave you a vision?"

"No vision, Chryssa. I saw *him*. Helios is alive, but no one must know it."

She gave me a pitying look, as if she thought I'd gone mad. "Oh, my poor queen." She didn't believe me. Should she have? It was all too unreal. And when I woke the next morning, the skies were bright and blue as if the storm had never been.

* * *

SORCERESS.

This was the word spoken most often of me in the days that followed. The Romans whispered the word with fear and loathing. The Greeks, like Crinagoras, mused upon it with skepticism. The Berbers uttered it with a hushed reverence. That I'd gone into sanctuary in their custom pleased them; the rumor that I'd come out of sanctuary to command a storm filled them with awe.

To my surprise, I wasn't touched by the slightest trace of *heka* sickness. Only heartsickness. I grieved for Helios as if he were really dead. I mourned the boy with the golden future who must now lose his name and his legacy. I grieved to be separated from him again, and more important, I grieved that his spirit had been broken. The Prefect of Egypt, Cornelius Gallus, had done that, and now I traced his name on papyrus. Cornelius Gallus. *Cornelius Gallus.*

Names held power and I wanted power over this man, but I couldn't decide how to retaliate. If only I knew how to destroy the destroyer of Thebes! What could I do? Egypt was half a world away and even if I still had partisans there, how could I reach out to them without putting them in danger? Frustrated, restless, and in need of diversion, I fixated upon Mauretania. Until I could think of a way to have my revenge, I wanted to know more of this land that had reunited me with my twin.

Late autumn and early winter was the planting season in Mauretania, when farmers drove teams of oxen to pull their plows, digging furrows in the earth. I watched them at their work and learned that the best fields were reserved for delicate wheat, but barley could be grown aplenty on less choice land. While Juba remained cloistered with his advisers, refusing to allow me into the makeshift council chambers, I took a small retinue of servants and courtiers into the sun-drenched hills and inhaled the unique scent of Mauretanian soil in all its infinite complexity. The old king's orchards now belonged to us and from beneath an olive tree, I had an excellent view of the Roman engineers in the harbor, working a remarkable bit of sorcery of their own. In large vats they mixed volcanic ash from the Bay of Naples with lime to form a concrete that actually hardened under water.

While we watched them build piers with this miraculous substance, Chryssa examined the olive trees of my orchard, which were dry and rotting in the sun, the victim of some pestilence. "It's a shame," Chryssa said, running her hands over the gray bark as if it confirmed her belief that Helios was dead and all the world was dying with him. "We might have amassed a little fortune."

My slave had an acute awareness of every commodity's value—maybe even her own—but she didn't know everything. "The olive trees aren't dead yet," I said, firmly. "They'll fight their way back. Meanwhile, the grapes should have been harvested. They might have made a fine vintage. Next year they will."

Crinagoras plucked a withered overripe grape from its vine. "Our queen speaks as a veritable fertility goddess already. Luckily, I'm on hand to memorialize the epic story of her battle with the sirocco." I could tell from the way he wagged his eyebrows that he didn't believe I'd swallowed a storm. That wouldn't stop him from writing about it.

TALA'S child came the next night, in blood and sweat and pain. The Berber woman's screams echoed down the dark passageways, beneath the hunting trophies. It was a hard labor, a battle fought upon the birthing chair, one that nearly defeated the midwife with all her elixirs and rubbing oils. After many hours, Tala made a small triumphant sound, sagging as her babe squeezed between her thighs in a rush of fluid.

Tala's son was a squalling infant whose lusty cries convinced us he would live. His mother, however, lingered between life and death. Before dawn, all the women knelt down before a small stone altar in the garden to make an offering to their goddess for Tala's health. They left barley cakes and drizzled them with honey, poured milk libations onto the dry earth, and clutched at amulets bearing a circle with a wide triangular base. To their astonishment, I knelt down with them as they chanted their ritual. "Your goddess is my goddess too," I said, explaining that the symbol of Tanit, narrowed only a little, was an *ankh*, a sign of Isis, a mark of eternal life.

"Queen," they whispered. "Sorceress. Will you use your magic to heal her?"

I knew no healing magic, but the women pleaded with me to go to Tala's side, so I did. I found her contorted in bloody linens, her body robbed of all its color but the distinctive blue stain. Her hair hung in sweat-soaked ringlets, clinging to her bare shoulders like black coiling snakes. I feared that Anubis, the jackal-headed god of the dead, was near, so I prayed with her, telling her that childbirth was sacred to Isis and that the goddess would help her through her trials.

She listened, then struggled to make each Latin word she spoke very clear. "Don't let Romans put my son in the hills when I die. Take the baby to my brother."

It wasn't only the Romans who exposed unwanted babies, leaving them to starve, freeze to death, or be eaten by predators. Few in the palace would see the point in sparing an orphaned child of a Berber serving woman, even if she was the sister of a tribal chieftain, but I vowed, "I won't let anything happen to your baby. If Maysar won't keep your son . . . I will."

It was an impetuous promise, but I meant every word. The way Tala's eyes widened, this was more than she expected. She reached out for me in gratitude and began to cry. I hated this, for I'd never been able to bear watching strong people crumble. "Stop it, Tala. Don't embrace death because you think your son doesn't need you. Know that if you die, I'll give your baby over to Chryssa to learn Greek. He'll never learn to ride a horse or wield a Berber sword because she'll make sure that he spends all his time in the library, and he'll be as spoiled as you say I am. Do you want that?"

Her weak laugh mingled with her tears. "You're so spiteful, little queen?"

"Oh, Tala, you have no idea."

* * *

TALA survived the birth but never regained her strength. She was weeks abed, and even when she was urged to activity, she moved slowly, her vitality stripped away. The Roman wives at court urged me to dismiss the big Berber woman from my service, for she'd never been respectful and was no longer strong enough for hard tasks. What with a babe on her hip, she was no fit companion for a queen anyway, they said. Worse, she was the sister of a Berber chieftain, no doubt sent amongst us to spy. I didn't care what they said. I refused to send Tala away. Though the Berber woman didn't like me, for some reason I liked her, and as a vessel of Isis, I wouldn't dismiss a widow and her orphaned child.

ONE morning in early winter, Juba rode out from the palace on one of his fine new horses to inspect the aqueduct work of the Legio III Augusta. Thus, it fell to me to greet newcomers to the palace, and when a delegation arrived at the gate, I was stunned to learn that they'd come all the way from Alexandria. Excitement and apprehension warred inside me. "These are Egyptians from the finest city in the world! What will they think of this dank old building?"

"All Egyptians are spoiled like you?" Tala asked. Her customary rudeness had lost its hard edges but reassured me that her health was improving. "Just bespell them to admire this place."

"It doesn't work that way, Tala."

"Why not?" she asked, opening her gown so that her babe could latch on to a swollen brown nipple. "You are sorceress. I name my son Ziri, after moonlight. Like Selene. Means moon, yes?"

I nodded, touched, feeling a kinship with her, even through the barrier of her insolent glare.

At that moment, Chryssa rushed in, her cheeks pink. "The Alexandrians are waiting. We found a throne chair and dragged it into the receiving room for you. Come!" I followed, my nerves a jumble. Not since my father made me a queen in the Donations of

Alexandria—the very act that had predicated the war with the emperor—had I taken my place upon a throne.

This one was decidedly feminine, inlaid with ivory and pearls. I ran my fingers over the smooth iridescent arms, marveling. "Whose throne was this?"

It was Tala who answered. "Belonged to Queen Eunoe. King Bogud's wife, mistress of—"

She broke off and I knew why. "It's all right, Tala. You can say it. Queen Eunoe was Julius Caesar's mistress." Queen Eunoe hadn't been my mother's rival. Not truly. After all, it hadn't been Eunoe's statue that Caesar placed in his family temple. Eunoe hadn't given him a son. Nor had he taken Eunoe to wed in the ancient tradition. It was my mother that Caesar had loved. Still, I was intrigued by the queen who had come before me. I settled into the cushion, beneath the watchful gaze of a statue of hulking Hercules—that one ancestor that Juba and I both had in common if one credited the claims of his father and mine. "Was her affair with Caesar considered shameful in Mauretania?"

"Only by King Bocchus. Queen Eunoe was his brother's wife . . ."

The two Mauretanian kings, Bocchus and Bogud, had ruled jointly. But when Roman civil war broke out, Bocchus supported Pompey and Bogud supported Caesar, going so far as to lend his wife to the cause. After Caesar's assassination, the two brothers were forced to divide their loyalties yet again. Bocchus supported Octavian and Bogud supported my father. It was a common enough story. Wise families put a son in each camp during Roman civil wars so that at least one of them would end up on the side of the winner. It pit brother against brother, the kind of tragedy that Juba always pointed to when he insisted that the world would be better off when Augustus was the only man who held real power. I admit, it would have been easier to hate Juba if he didn't make such arguments sound so reasonable.

Our guests entered with the distinct bearing of Alexandrians, some draped in Greek *himations*, others wearing Egyptian cosmetics and wigs. The easy mix of cultures was a hallmark of the city in which I'd been born. These were my mother's old courtiers, several of whom wore mourning clothes for her. Or maybe it was Helios they mourned, though they could never say so openly, not even here. Standing before me was Master Gnaios, a talented gem cutter who'd worked for my father. Also the Lady Lasthenia, an esteemed Pythagorean philosopher who traveled with a number of her students, eager to find a place at my royal court. Memnon, the commander of my mother's formidable household guards, led a troop of Macedonian soldiers, scarred veterans, fair-haired and brawny, not to be confused with more typical Greeks. My heart swelled as they presented themselves, their eyes shining a reflection of my mother's gloried days.

Memnon appraised me with an open stare, as if he didn't recognize in me the child I'd been when the Romans took me prisoner, but I remembered him and how he'd scolded my brothers and me to make us behave. We'd been afraid of him; now his face was dear to me. "We offer our services as your personal bodyguard," Memnon said, and my throat tightened with emotion. To have armed men accountable only to me was a blessing.

"I'll try not to make it too difficult to protect me," I said, and they all grinned.

Lady Lasthenia laughed richly. "Majesty, if you'll have us, we'll be a veritable Ptolemaic court in exile."

I knew I shouldn't invite them without consulting Juba, but these Alexandrians remembered my mother as the strongest monarch in the world; I couldn't bear for them see me as only *the king's woman*. "We'll gladly have you," I replied, and should have given some flowery speech of welcome to these men and women who'd traveled so far to join me, but I detected the fragrant scent of light magic swirling together with the metallic tang of darker sorcery and faltered for words. Chryssa shot me an alarmed look and I followed her eyes to a figure cloaked in bright white.

Euphronius! I knew him on sight. Because the wizard had appeared amidst a delegation from Egypt, the Romans didn't seem suspicious. To them, he was one more foreigner, a priest of Egypt of no account. Even so, I didn't risk saying his name. I didn't wish to call attention to him in any way.

Once the Alexandrians had taken their leave, I flew down the hall to my chambers and sent Chryssa to fetch Euphronius at once. At length, the old mage shuffled into my presence. I'd grown taller or he'd grown smaller, I couldn't say which, but whereas I'd always looked to him for guidance, now he surrendered his divination staff—an iron rod carved at the top to resemble a hooded cobra. Such staves were common enough in Egypt, but they recalled to me the most devastating moment of my childhood.

Laying the staff at my feet and kneeling before me, Euphronius said, "Forgive me, child."

I was gratified that he didn't pretend all was well between us. "I'm not a child anymore."

"I see that," Euphronius said. "You're nearly grown. You have your mother's look but with the edges softened, like polished stone. I've missed you, Princess."

The title recalled to me happy days, learning at his knee. But those days were done. "Where is Helios?"

"Gone," he said.

"Where? Thebes would still stand were it not for you. I don't know that I can forgive you if you tell me that you don't know where to find my twin."

"I don't deserve your forgiveness," Euphronius said, his voice breaking. "I can only tell you that I haven't seen him since the battle in Thebes. Now he's gone from this world."

"You're wrong. I give you glad news that I've seen Helios in the flesh, in this world, alive."

The old wizard exchanged a glance with Chryssa. They didn't believe me and the mage filled his voice with compassion. "If you saw your twin, Princess, it was only his *akh* come to find you."

I tried, and failed, to quell my temper. "You're wrong. Wrong as you were when you said Augustus would die in Spain and that we should escape. Wrong as you were to encourage Helios to rebellion." I'd touched Helios and let him touch me when I couldn't bear the thought of any man's hands. He was *real*. "Helios is no spirit. No ghost. I saw him as I see you now. Work your magic. Look into the Rivers of Time and you'll see for yourself."

"I dare not," Euphronius replied, sadly. "As you've said, I've been wrong before about what I've seen. I failed your mother and your brother both, and when Alexander Helios saw the battle in Thebes was lost, he sent me away."

"You mean that you *left* him."

The mage's eyes glistened with tears. "Majesty, he was my king and he commanded me to go find you. I couldn't disobey his last request."

I wanted to shake the old man's trembling shoulders. "It wasn't his last request. Helios lives. Now he means to become Horus the Avenger."

Again, Euphronius exchanged a look of concern with Chryssa. "Princess, we must let him go . . ."

My fists clenched at my sides. "Then there goes the King of Egypt, though none but the three of us may ever know it!"

They waited for my temper to pass, perhaps fearing what I might do next. I only stood there in impotent rage until Euphronius bowed his head. "What I know—what all the world knows—is that you're Egypt's rightful queen. I offer myself into your service, if you'll have me."

My nostrils flared as I bit back unkind words. I wanted to banish him from my presence, but couldn't. "It's too dangerous to have you at court as yourself. Refashion yourself as a wise man or scholar. Take a new name. Claim that you were one of my father's freedmen. But don't hold yourself out as an intimate of mine, because I cannot bear to even look at you."

COMPARED to my mother's grand palace by the sea in Alexandria, the mansion in which I held court was a crumbling hovel. Our wine was only passable, and when it came to luxuries we had none but what we carried with us from Rome. In such circumstances, the Alexandrians must have thought their princess had fallen low. In truth, I knew that I was fortunate to rule any kingdom at all. Mauretania was my opportunity to rise back up like a phoenix and reclaim what was mine. In time, they'd see this, and I'd make them glad to serve me.

In honor of our Alexandrian guests, we held a dinner at which Crinagoras recited his poem about the sirocco. He couldn't have had a more appreciative audience. After dinner was served, my mother's wizard presented himself to Juba as Euphorbus, a learned physician, botanist, and scholar of the magical arts. I worried the Alexandrians would point out his deception. No one did. In truth, it was only a slight reshaping of his identity. After my mother's fall from power, it may have surprised no one that her magician should want to embrace a different name and calling.

Juba welcomed the old man to our retinue, even going so far as to recommend he tend me for ailments of the spirit. "My queen's grief for her twin has quite consumed her. Perhaps you can offer some elixir to comfort her."

"It would be my honor," Euphronius replied, but when the old mage bowed in my direction, I turned away.

It was actually Lady Lasthenia who caused the greatest stir. When she presented the king with the writings of Pythagoras and introduced herself as a philosopher, several Romans laughed and Juba arched a brow. "My wife maintains that some women work as scholars in Alexandria. Do you expect it to be the same here in Mauretania?"

Lady Lasthenia straightened her very plain gown, unperturbed. "Majesty, I expect nothing, but hope for much. I come to you from the Museum of Alexandria, the institute of the Muses. I've lectured at the Great Library. It's my understanding that you intend to create a center of learning here in Mauretania, which is why I've come."

Juba's eyes fell to the scrolls that Lady Lasthenia offered. Copies of Herodotus and Sallust, whose historical and geographical writings he prized. To turn her away would be to turn away precious gifts, so I knew her position was secure. Indeed, the king seemed grateful for the influx of culture from Alexandria. He missed those scholarly days of leisure when he could teach and research and write. And by the end of the evening, he was plainly enchanted by the tragedian, one Leonteus of Argos, who engaged the king in a lively debate over whether or not lowly cooks were actually the civilizers of society. While the two men bantered, I slipped away with Lady Lasthenia to receive news of home.

"Are things so difficult in Egypt that it's made exiles of those who served my mother?" I asked when we were alone.

The scholar, whose pretty dark hair was always a little unkempt, was frank. "The Romans put several of your mother's adherents to death, but most escaped punishment. Her court physician, Olympos, has retired to write a history of your mother's life."

Now that was something I should like to read. "And Fat Mardion?"

Lady Lasthenia smiled. "Your mother's eunuch sends his warmest regards."

"I worried . . ." I covered my mouth with both hands for I hadn't believed that my mother's closest minister would have been spared.

"Oh no," Lady Lasthenia fiddled absently with the frayed end of her braid. "The Romans would've been fools to put him to death. Mardion knows far too much about how the Greek and Egyptian systems work in tandem. The Prefect of Egypt needs him to keep the country from falling into disorder."

"The prefect. Cornelius Gallus." I forced myself to say the hated name. Offering Lady Lasthenia hot mint water, I said, "Tell me about him."

Pouring herself a cup, she said, "He's a vain man who fancies himself a poet, but he's enamored with wealth and power. He's looted the temples, of course, but to impress the emperor he's persecuted the Isiacs and terrorized the priests. To defend themselves against his ruthlessness, some have carved his name and likeness into the stelae as if he were Pharaoh."

Such shame! It mortified me that Egypt should honor such an

unworthy man—one who wasn't even the conqueror. Say what I would about Augustus, he hadn't demanded that we acknowledge him as Pharaoh. Gallus dared what the emperor had not, and now I hated him even more than before.

"When Thebes rose up," Lasthenia continued, sniffing at the mint tisane in her cup, "there was a glimmer of hope, but then Gallus destroyed the city, which prompted a riot in Alexandria. Worshippers of Isis, the zealous ones, and even the quietly faithful like Memnon believe that Isis must have a throne in this world. When rumors spread that your twin was killed . . . well, you're now the last hope for those who believe in a Golden Age."

As a Pythagorean, Lady Lasthenia studied mathematics and pondered theories about the transmigration of the soul. I somehow doubted she'd come to Mauretania seeking religious refuge. "And what about you, my lady?"

"I'm part of a vast network of worldly individuals who wish to have influence. My students and I can be your eyes here, in Rome, and in Alexandria."

"Why would you risk it?" I asked.

She smiled, taking a deep swallow from her cup. "Because, Majesty, we all believe you'll be the next Queen of Egypt."

Twelve

MAURETANIA
WINTER 25 B.C.

CORNELIUS *Gallus.* Everything Lady Lasthenia had told me about him further enraged me. He was a man of that knighted class that wasn't even noble by Rome's dubious standards. He'd destroyed one of the world's oldest cities, killed Egyptians, and broke my twin's spirit. But Helios wasn't the only one who could wield a weapon in vengeance, was he? I'd learned from the emperor that you could wound a man's reputation without ever taking to the battlefield, and sometimes that wound was fatal. A pen could be as sharp as a sword, ink as deadly as venom. Choosing carefully from a sheaf of blank papyrus rolls, I prepared to write to Augustus.

As the ink swept across the papyrus, I observed all the proper courtesies and salutations, then wrote: *You promised mercy for Egypt and for my brother. Now Helios is dead*—I stopped, shuddering at having committed those words to paper. It was a lie, I reminded myself, and there was no lie I wouldn't tell to have my way. I started again. *You promised mercy for Egypt and for my brother. Now Helios is dead and Thebes is no more. You refuse to make me Queen of Egypt, but you let Cornelius Gallus carve his name into the Great Pyramids. He demands the worship of the people as if he were their conquering god. I told you that Egypt needed a Pharaoh, but how bitter to know that you've given the title to a mere equite!*

The emperor would never lose a moment's sleep over the death of my twin or the destruction of Thebes, but he tolerated no rivals. He believed his own propaganda that my father's ambitions had been fueled by Egypt's mystic sands. In making him suspect that Gallus had fallen prey to the same Egyptian grandeur, I aimed a poisoned dart precisely where it would do the most damage.

The courier I found to carry my letter informed me that I should have a scribe make copies. Military dispatches would be sent even during winter, he said, but the seas were treacherous. Messages sent overland from Mauretania might never reach Rome because of the hostilities on the border. "The Garamantes have conducted devastating raids in the countryside, Majesty. They don't want to be ruled by either the Romans or a Numidian king."

I'd heard nothing of recent raids but knew Tala's husband had been killed by Garamantes. I guessed that *these* were the meaty matters Juba discussed with his advisers when I wasn't present. Appalled, I went straight to the king's study, nearly tripping over the stone threshold, which had come loose. He'd been writing—for Juba was always writing—and he cleared his throat in surprise. "Selene . . ."

From the doorway, I asked, "Who are the Garamantes?"

Juba twirled his reed pen between two fingers. "Have you returned to me as a pupil?"

One should never be too proud to admit ignorance, but his tone galled me. "When dispatches arrive, when you receive advice from Balbus and the others, I should like to be there."

The king gave a bark of mocking laughter. "Should you?"

Though my cheeks burned, I bit back my pride. I'd marched here to make demands, but in some ways I had less influence in Mauretania than I'd had in Rome. Juba had soldiers at his command. He had men who honored his authority, whereas I had only a handful of bodyguards, maidservants, poets, and a mournful old magician. "I want to learn; I'll listen quietly in council."

He snorted. "No, you won't. You'll never hear me disparage your quick wit or even your good intentions, but the fact remains that you'll meddle in *everything* and you're a girl with no experience in governing *anything*."

As my attempt to be reasonable failed, my temper flared. "And what experience do you have beyond governing a schoolroom?"

He dipped his pen back in the inkpot with a wry smile. "I'm sure most of the empire is asking the same question. I must pretend that I wouldn't rather be in Rome, debating scholars. I must pretend that I wouldn't rather be writing my books than practicing statecraft. Why not enjoy the freedom you have, Selene, unburdened by these concerns?"

"Juba, I'm a Ptolemy. I wouldn't need to pretend that I'd rather be doing anything else in the world. I was born to rule. I *want* to be involved with these matters."

Wiping a stray spot of ink from his finger, he shook his head. "The Garamantes are a warlike tribe and their rebellious spirit needs to be crushed. Their leaders need to be captured and crucified. Do you want to be a part of that? War is no proper concern for queens and I should think your mother's example would've taught you that."

His words stung me. I'd quietly endured the disparagement of my family in Rome, but must I endure it here too? "What my mother's example taught me is that but for some bad weather and a lack of concern for her reputation, Cleopatra might have ruled the entire world. How am I to fare in her shadow?"

He let out a long, frustrated breath. "Selene, I don't begrudge your desire to make a mark. Perhaps we can find a building project to interest you . . ." Pondering, he ran a hand through his dark hair, something he did often, and this habit annoyed me almost as much as his attempt to distract me. To send me off to do something somewhere I couldn't be a bother.

But perhaps I could turn this situation to my advantage. "I'd like to build a temple to Isis."

"Selene!" His teeth snapped together. "You know that isn't possible. Your goddess is out of favor with Augustus. He'll take offense. Put that thought out of your head."

I would never put that thought out of my head, but I could see that I wouldn't be able to change his mind. At least not now. He and the emperor had used me as a game piece since I was a child; well, I had a game of my own and there were several moves to make. "Then I want to build a mausoleum." It was the task that

Helios set for me. *The Romans think I'm dead. Make them believe it.
Build a tomb. Mourn for me.* "You said that I could bury Helios in
our tradition. Let me carve the name of Alexander Helios in stone,
so that the gods might remember him."

Juba's eyes softened such that I knew he wouldn't refuse, and in
the morning he sent architects to meet with me. Their sketches
lacked artistry, so I described the kind of tomb I wanted to memorialize my twin. Circular in foundation, with an Ionic facade and a
stepped cone like a pyramid on top. Very much like my mother's
tomb and not dissimilar to the one that Augustus built for himself.
The architects seemed stunned by the scope of it. "I studied under
Vitruvius himself," one of them said, puffing out his chest. "So I
know it can be done. But this would be something on a much
grander scale than we'd envisioned for . . . for . . ."

They wouldn't even say my twin's name. No one would. Helios
was neither a traitor nor a hero. His rebellion never mentioned. His
fate, not even whispered. Helios had simply vanished from the
house of Augustus. He was being *erased*, which was, in itself, a
death of part of his Egyptian soul.

When Juba saw the plans, I thought he'd complain of the
expense, but he gave his full-throated support. "We'll make it a
royal mausoleum. It'll make a fine statement about our dynastic
plans; it'll give the people a sense of our permanence here."

So he believed that I meant to stay here with him. That I'd live
and die here in Mauretania. That my mummy would be sealed in
this mausoleum. But the remains of my twin wouldn't rest in this
tomb, and neither would mine. Isis willing, I meant to return to
Egypt, no matter the cost.

IT was a strange thing to see Memnon and his men snap to attention outside my rooms. Holding round Macedonian shields, each
painted red and adorned with my initials, these guards were a
fearsome-looking lot, all awaiting my command. "I want to be
alone at night," I said to Memnon, remembering the way Livia had

come to fetch me in the dark and how I'd awakened the next morning to find her offering me poisoned wine. "Can you prevent anyone from coming into my rooms at night? Even the king . . ."

It was a peculiarity; it wasn't done. Wealthy persons of any station were attended in the night by slaves and servants who slept in niches and on bedding on the floor. What's more, I was a married woman. The king would be expected to visit my bedchambers. My desire for privacy at night, one that I would cling to all my life, was a suspicious thing, so I was grateful when Memnon nodded his understanding without judgment or dispute. "As you wish, Majesty."

Winter in Mauretania was pleasant. The evenings were cool enough to warrant a fire, but the days were warm unless it was raining. For my part, I didn't much mind the rain, for it reminded me of the season of inundation in Egypt. Just as Helios had bathed me in the Temple of Tanit, these rains washed the world clean. For my subjects, they also meant the difference between a full belly and starvation. Without the rain, the grain wouldn't come.

Since winter storms rendered the sea too dangerous for travel, we received few guests and there was time for personal indulgence. I chose planting urns to grace the grounds of my twin's empty tomb and Tala spent her days weaving a beautiful rug. The Berbers were skilled in such things, so it surprised me to see her struggle at the loom. I'd spent the better part of four years toiling in the sewing room with Livia, Octavia, Julia, and the rest of the Roman girls, so I lent my hand to the task. "Try it like this," I said, and all the women startled at the sight of their queen taking up weaving work.

Tala seemed more than startled and actually pushed my hands away. "*I* must do it."

"It's their way of grieving," Chryssa explained. "Berber widows must make something to remember their beloved husbands and shun the company of men until it's finished."

I too was making a memorial to my beloved so my hands fell away. "I'm sorry. I didn't know."

Tala nodded, grunting. "You're still strangers here. Ignorant."

Chryssa sniffed. "At least we're not *blue*."

I shot Chryssa a glare, but Tala barely glanced up from her work. "*Indigo*. Like my gown. We spread dye paste on fabric, then pound with stones until it shines like metal. Powder comes off on skin and stains. Is sign of status."

Chryssa laughed. "A high price to pay for status. You're *blue!*"

"I wouldn't laugh," I said. "If Tyrian purple stained, royalty would still pay a fortune for it."

ONE sunny winter afternoon, I accompanied the surveyors to the site of the mausoleum. It would have been more comfortable to make the trip in a litter, carried by the matched slaves we'd brought with us for just such a purpose. But whereas oiled slaves dressed in leopard skins inspired envy and respect in Rome, such a sight seemed to engender hostility amongst the native Mauretanians. For that reason, I chose a carriage, which jostled Chryssa and me together as we traversed the mostly unpaved roads. Euphronius trailed behind us on foot, though I hadn't invited him. "Why does he follow me like some beaten dog?"

"What else has he to do?" Chryssa asked. "He's a priest of Isis in a land that doesn't worship her, going by a name that isn't his own, serving a queen who won't even speak to him."

"I might've known you'd take the wizard's part," I said, lips pressed tight in irritation.

She glanced up at me from beneath fair eyelashes. "You make no secret of the fact that he's out of favor. It rouses suspicion."

I pretended as if her words were of no import, but it's always a slave who knows best how to pierce her mistress with self-doubt. Our carriage stopped below a hilltop upon which there were foundations of some older structure—perhaps some long-abandoned project of past kings. While the surveyors stretched ropes over the hard earth and tied them to pegs, I noticed Euphronius walking strange patterns through the grass. I'd seen him do this when I was young but didn't realize he was working a spell until I felt a slight tug of *heka* pull me toward him.

I didn't want to speak to him, but my curiosity overcame my resentment. I stepped over fragrant rosemary bushes to come to his side and asked, "What are you doing?"

He bowed deeply, his eyes alight. "Majesty, I'm searching for evil spells that might have been laid in this place . . ."

"Do *I* have the power to do this?" I wondered aloud.

He nodded, leaning against his divination stick, the serpentine eyes of which seemed to taunt me. "In Egypt you'd be able to do this and much more. Yet another reason we must see you safely home, Princess. Here, I don't know the limits of your powers or mine."

I bit my lower lip, admitting, "I don't know how to control my powers *anywhere*. Whenever I use them, the *heka* sickness comes, except for the last time, when I took a storm into me."

"There's no price to be paid for taking *heka* into you, but to let it out in a rush? It'll ravage you. *Heka* flows into your body and wants to remain there. When you release it to work magic, it carves its way out."

"It carves itself . . . in my flesh?" I wondered. "In blood and symbols?"

"When the goddess wills it," Euphronius said, seeming to measure the shadow of his staff. "Even if you can't see the wounds, the magic does cut you. You must give it a channel to flow away."

I resented taking instruction from him, but the old mage was my only link to the lost magic of Egypt. Given what little I knew, his words made some sense. "And my amulet. It isn't the source of magic . . ."

"Your frog amulet gives shape to your *heka* and serves to help you control it, but you could wield magic without it."

"Will you show me? I want to draw a light breeze."

He surprised me by asking, "To what end? Majesty, the *heka* you draw from the temples is left there by people who seek salvation. The magic is born of their hopes, their fears, their tears. Every bit too precious for experiment."

I didn't want to be lectured. Not by him. "Then how can I learn?"

"Why not commune with this spot? Make sure this is a good

place to build a tomb. Let the hill speak to you. If there are curses upon this place, you'll know it. Kneel down." The Romans builders were too busy exploring the foundations to pay much attention to me, so I gathered my skirts and lowered to the ground. "Now," the old man said. "Press your hands to the earth and push a bit of the *heka* inside you into the soil, then draw it back in again. Let it flow through you, but hold yourself aloof, and when it grows too intense, push the rest into your amulet."

Several ducks flew overhead and the blinding sun turned them to dark dots against the blue sky. I blinked my eyes shut, feeling the tingle of *heka* at my fingertips. The scent of grass was in my nostrils. The salt of the sea upon my tongue. I heard the gulls call to one another, and the rustle of stub-tailed monkeys playing on the far side of the hill. The soil beneath my fingers wasn't like the silken desert sand. Not like the black earth of Egypt either. It was something else entirely. I thought about all my wishes for Mauretania, my hopes for its people, and made a narrow channel through which my *heka* could flow.

"Yes," Euphronius said, and when my *heka* touched the hill it met no resistance. No hostility. No evil spirits or curses or enchantments. If anything, the soil welcomed me and drew me closer. "No, not so much, Majesty. Not so much!"

I pulled up, breaking the connection to the earth, clutching at my amulet to take the excess of magic. Then my eyes flew wide. All around me the grass had grown taller, greener, with red flowers woven into its verdant fabric. Caper blossoms opened in all their showy glory. From the tree above, olives burst forth, having ripened from purple to black. The surveyors dropped their tools and Chryssa ran to us, sighing with wonder at the grass that grew taller with her every step. It was the cusp of winter, but the hill had responded to me as if I were the incarnation of springtime. "Was that supposed to happen?" I murmured.

Stunned, Euphronius drew his white cowl over his head. "Not unless . . . Majesty, I believe that you must be with child."

Thirteen

RETURNING to my rooms, I called for the midwife. She put her hands on my belly and sniffed at my breath and asked me about my last moon's blood. I could tell her nothing with certainty. My last menses came before my wedding. Before the emperor violated me. Before I'd found my lover in the sirocco. Months ago, I told her. Maybe two. No more than three. I couldn't remember!

She departed, saying it was too early to tell. But I knew. I *knew!* And it was a calamity. I wanted to believe that what quickened inside me was a gift from Helios . . . that, like Isis revived Osiris, I'd brought Helios back from death in the guise of a babe. But it might well have been the emperor who fathered a child upon me and I shuddered at the very idea that something grew inside, unwanted, a threat to my life. How I regretted taunting Juba about the possibility of carrying the emperor's child. Had I tempted cruel fate by speaking the words aloud? Remembering Tala's ordeal, I wished it away a thousand times! Even if I survived the birth of this child, it would be a living reminder of all that the emperor had done to me and mine. I told myself that I'd never hold against a child the sins of its father, but what if I looked upon an innocent little face and felt nothing but loathing?

With reluctance, I sent for Euphronius and said, "I don't want a child. As a priest of Isis you know the herbs I must take."

"Princess, tread carefully," the old man warned. "What would happen to you if it were discovered you tried to rid yourself of . . . a royal heir?"

His slight hesitation made me gasp. He was still a mage. Did he know that the child wasn't Juba's? Did he guess at what the emperor had done to me? What if, in the Rivers of Time, he'd seen Helios and me upon a flower-bedecked altar? No, if he'd seen that, surely he wouldn't persist in telling me that my twin was only a ghost. "Royal heir or no, I don't want it!"

"Princess," Euphronius cooed. "There's risk in the herbs that would rid you of the child. Are there so many Ptolemies left in the world that we can do without one more? With the death of our beloved Helios—"

"Get out!" I couldn't bear that he should speak his name and tell me he was dead. Again. "Get out, get out, get out!"

WINTER rains flooded the streets with mud and sometimes forced construction to a standstill. No messages or dispatches arrived from Rome. We were effectively trapped here in this new land—as trapped as I was inside a body that was changing every day. Tenderness swelled in my breasts and the nipples darkened. My skin burned hot even when others complained of a light chill. My frog amulet, which had so often lain at the base of my throat, lifeless and inert, now gleamed green with expectation. "When will you tell the king that you're with child?" Chryssa asked.

Since the night I'd threatened him with a table knife, matters between Juba and me had been frosty, so I waited until February, when the Romans would be celebrating the Lupercalia, to tell him. I went to the stables, where the king had just returned from a ride on one of his favorite Barbary steeds, and let the words tumble out in a rush. I thought he'd quip something dark and bitter. That he might comment on how pleased Augustus would be. Juba only nodded and, for a moment, I wondered if he'd even heard me. "Are you angry?" I asked, wary of the king's equanimity.

Brushing his horse, a task he should have entrusted to a groom, Juba shrugged his shoulders. "What purpose would my anger serve? I'd prepared myself for it." It was the reaction that I'd hoped for, but now I wished he'd throw a fit of rage and fling ugly words and accusations. His quiet acceptance of my condition made me feel strangely objectified, as if I were merely a horse who had been ill bred this season but might foal offspring of a more desirable pedigree next time. "Allow that Alexandrian physician, what is his name? Euphorbus? Let him tend to you."

"I don't care for him," I said, not wanting to argue about the old mage. "A midwife will suffice."

Juba went on, my opinion of no consequence. "Euphorbus is a learned fellow of excellent temperament. He's been helping to identify plants for me. He'll deliver you of a healthy child."

"The child will need a proper nursery," I said. "We'll have to displace some of the servants."

"I have a better idea." Juba rubbed the horse's muzzle. "This place is falling apart. We need a new palace. We might as well start building one now. I don't suppose you have any suggestions for it . . ."

I was surprised at how this eased my despair. "Can we build it on the shoreline overlooking the harbor? It should have a view of an enormous lighthouse on that island, like the Pharos in Egypt!"

"I don't see why not, but remember that this city is to be like Ostia—a trade port for shippers and grain merchants."

"That doesn't mean it can't be a cultural center too. How much grain comes through Alexandria? Yet she's the finest royal city in the world. Besides, Iol is beautiful. At least, we can *make* it beautiful." I wanted to make a fine royal city but not simply because of my Ptolemaic ambition. Iol. *Return of the Sun*. I wanted this city to be a monument to that.

SERVANTS placed brass pots underneath holes in our leaky roof to catch the rainwater, while Juba and I sat cloistered with our architects, planning a new palace. I'd sketched what I remembered of my mother's royal enclosure and what I didn't remember, my Alexandrian courtiers described in detail. Juba did nothing to curtail my desire to replicate the palace in Alexandria. In fact, the time we spent together with our architects was unexpectedly pleasant. Juba could be good company and had an eye for expensive things. Hours passed in excited discussion of our plans without my remembering to be angry with him.

Augustus had made us rich, so we spared no expense. We wanted green diorite columns polished to a high sheen and agreed that some columns should be carved like women, caryatids like in Delphi and Athens. It was Juba's idea to order pale Luna marble from Italy, white and silvery, but my innovation to accent it with a yellow marble from quarries in Numidia. *Moonlight and Sunshine*, I mused, my twin brother never far from my thoughts.

Between rainstorms, I shopped in the market, where Berbers haggled over baskets overflowing with nuts and olives and the fleece of shorn sheep. I purchased new tapestries to hang on the walls, lamps and couches too. My ladies pointed to my enthusiasm for a more comfortable home as evidence of my readiness for motherhood. Only Chryssa seemed to know how much I dreaded the coming of this child. If I knew Helios to be the father, perhaps I'd have taken some comfort in it, but fortunate happenstances were rare in my life. Swelling so fat and miserable could only be the result of the emperor's doings.

Everyone whispered about the good fortune of the young king to have already sired a child. Juba took in due course the ribald jests about his virility, and when we were seen in public, I always behaved as if we were happy. In truth, I was only fifteen years old and the prospect of a child clinging to me for its every need struck me near dumb with terror. Tala assured me that motherhood would come naturally, but what if I was one of those *unnatural* women who couldn't care for her own child?

The Berbers gossiped that I'd give birth in summer, in the month named after Julius Caesar, a prospect I found detestable, and my resentment seemed to swallow me whole. A time came when only Crinagoras could cheer me. The Greeks loved his cutting wit. The Romans enjoyed his verse. The Berbers admired his spirit and applauded wildly when he told the story of how their young queen defeated the sirocco. The incorrigible jester flattered, fawned, and amused even me on my darkest days.

One afternoon, Crinagoras announced, "Majesty, I've decided to compose a poem comparing you to Kore, the maiden daughter of Demeter. The Romans call her Proserpina."

Unwilling to let him think me ignorant, I said, "I've also heard her called Persephone." I reached for a fig. Since my mother's death, I had a loathing for figs, but now, big with child, I couldn't eat enough of them. Something satisfied me about the texture of the sweet fruit, the seeds against my teeth. I craved them night and day. "If you're going to make a goddess of me, why not Isis?"

He sliced open a pomegranate with relish. "Because I write whatever inspires me and no person of civilized tastes questions my genius."

Though he had a boyish nature, Crinagoras had lived a very full life. He'd served as an ambassador in Rome when Julius Caesar wooed my mother. He was acquainted with every king from Mauretania to Parthia, not to mention most of the Roman generals since Pompey. He wasn't as afraid of powerful people as he should have been, and I was still too young to appreciate how valuable that made him. "I'm quite civilized," I said, reclining against an embroidered pillow. "I'm a Ptolemy."

Crinagoras grinned. "But have you been initiated into the Mysteries at Eleusis?"

He knew how to prick at my pride. Every two years, pilgrims from all over the world set sail for Athens to honor Demeter and Kore. Even Isiacs honored the festival, for it was said to have originated from an Egyptian rite. "Some day, perhaps I shall become an initiate, but none of this explains why you're inspired to compare me to Kore."

"Doesn't it?" Crinagoras asked, popping a handful of pomegranate seeds into his mouth and sucking at their red juice. "Kore was the maiden goddess who was kidnapped by Hades and dragged down into the underworld, bringing such grief to her mother that the earth plunged into winter. She's the youthful incarnation of your Isis. Like Kore, isn't Isis wed to the lord of the dead? Doesn't Isis possess the magic to bring forth our souls into salvation and to rise from the underworld to make all the crops grow?"

He was a cynic, so I couldn't tell if he was mocking my faith, but this syncretism, the merging of goddesses, was nothing new. Isis had a thousand names and I'd just found her in the guise of Carthaginian Tanit. Still, I found myself arguing, "Isn't Isis more like Demeter, the mother goddess who searches the world for her lost loved one?"

"They're aspects of the same," Crinagoras said, as if he were a great authority. "You're not yet known for being more than Cleopatra's daughter, a child stolen from Egypt. So I'll compare you to Kore, kidnapped and held prisoner in the underworld of Rome while famine looms—"

"You don't dare!" I cried, knowing full well how it might offend the Romans to hear Augustus compared to Hades. It was also far too close to the truth. Kore had been raped by Hades, who offered her seeds of pomegranate, the fruit of fertility, so he'd always have a hold on her ever after. Though Kore returned in springtime to her mother's realm, she was never free of the lord of the underworld. Just as I would never be free of Augustus. As this child grew inside me, our lives entwined, and nothing would change that now. Like Kore, I had eaten the pomegranate seeds.

THE baby wasn't the only thing moving inside me. In my blood, the sirocco still swirled restlessly. I knew that I should learn how to use my magic, but I was too mistrustful of Euphronius. Though workers erected a tomb to Helios, I wouldn't accept that he was dead, and I refused to have the old wizard near enough to tell me otherwise. To take my mind off my woes, I busied myself overseeing the work of the stonemasons and tile layers in the new palace. The architects liked my aesthetic sensibilities, though I'd become aware that people would flatter me because I was queen. I approved plans for a columned entrance and an enormous fountain in the main hall. A large garden too, with grape arbors and a sea of lavender.

When springtime came it was safe for travel again and every manner of fortune seeker flocked to Mauretania. With them came an infusion of gold and gossip. We learned that King Herod vowed to build a new city in the East simply to keep us from attracting the finest engineers to Mauretania. We also learned that under the most mysterious circumstances, Cornelius Gallus, the Prefect of Egypt, had been recalled to Rome and forced to commit suicide.

I didn't smile at this news, though it had been exactly what I'd hoped for. Had the emperor ordered his death because of my letter? If so, it had been appallingly easy to convince Augustus to kill on my behalf. Gallus deserved to pay with his life for what he'd done to Thebes, but I was shaken by my own capacity for vengeance, and my realization that Augustus was still my own deadliest weapon.

I only regretted that it changed nothing; the emperor simply sent another Gallus to rule over Egypt—this time, Gaius Aelius Gallus. I learned this from Julia, who wrote, *I weep for your loss, Selene. We hear rumor that Helios was killed in Thebes, but my father denies it, saying only that your twin must have perished in a sea crossing. I think he's content to let your brother's name pass unmarred so that no taint of treason touches you.*

I doubted that. Augustus didn't want Helios to be a rallying cry and so wouldn't acknowledge him as a foe.

Julia also wrote that her husband had been elected *aedile* for the coming year—a public administrator responsible for games and public works. It was a position Marcellus was too young to occupy, so I assumed that Augustus had rigged the election in favor of his heir or that Lady Octavia had convinced him to do so. Julia also told me that while the youngest of the Antonias wished to remain unwed until she was older, my eldest Roman half sister Antonia had been married off to Lucius Domitius Ahenobarbus. I saw Lady Octavia's hand in that marriage arrangement too. As First Woman in Rome, she could arrange the finest marriages for the children in her household. It must have vexed the emperor's wife and I worried that Livia would find some new way of taking revenge.

Julia ended her letter by saying, *My father hasn't been himself since you left; everyone has noticed it. He complains of every manner of ailment.* It was too much to hope that the emperor suffered from an attack of conscience, and heavy with child, I couldn't find it within myself to feel sorry for him.

At last, a letter came from Philadelphus, the papyrus stained as if by tears. When I read how he grieved for Helios, I was deeply troubled. Philadelphus saw clearly into the Rivers of Time, didn't he? He must know that Helios was alive. Was this tearful letter for the benefit of the Romans? Yes, that must be it. No letter from Philadelphus would reach my hands without being seen by a dozen of the emperor's toadies. I could almost imagine the wily Maecenas reading it forward and back, looking for a cipher . . . but what if Philadelphus truly grieved? I called for Euphronius. "Do you know some spell to send a secret message to Philadelphus?"

"If I did, I'd have used it by now," the old mage said.

I sighed, flinging the letter down. "I keep making the same mistake of thinking you'll be of some use to me."

"WHY can't you forgive him?" Chryssa asked once Euphronius had gone.

I turned to her, my palms outstretched. "How can you wonder? I once thought him wise, but now I know he's a charlatan. Look at what his false visions have wrought. You know what he's done to Helios. What happened in Thebes is his fault. I won't let him fill my head with false hope and foolish plans."

"I'm the one who made it possible for Helios to escape the emperor," Chryssa reminded me. "I showed him the tunnels underneath the Palatine. If you blame Euphronius, you ought to blame me too. You *did* blame me. So why forgive me and not a holy man?"

"Because you're a slave. You weren't free to do anything other than what Helios told you to."

"Is that what you think?" Chryssa was good at disguising her emotions, but a flick of her eyes showed me that I'd deeply offended her. I'd trivialized her love, loyalty, and the risks she'd taken for my brothers and me.

"I'm sorry," I said.

She turned away to fold my linens. "You're a queen and sacred to Isis. You've no need to apologize to a mere slave."

"You're no mere slave." We'd suffered much together. Our bond was deeper than I'd been willing to admit to myself before now. "I know that Helios would probably have run away from Rome without anyone else's help . . ."

"Then why can't you forgive the mage?"

"I don't know," I said, feeling an old familiar emotion coil inside my belly. It was the wound at my core, spilling forth a toxin that ate me from the inside. "Maybe it isn't just because of Helios or Thebes or all the disappointments. Maybe it's also because when I was a little girl, he made me carry a basket of figs into my mother's tomb." This was known only to my brothers, our wizard, and me. I'd never confessed this secret to anyone else, and my hands trembled to tell the tale. "There was a serpent inside that basket. A deadly asp, I think. Maybe a magical one. It killed her. Euphronius made an unwitting killer of me. And I couldn't save her . . ."

Chryssa put down the linens and covered my trembling hands with hers. "No one could save her."

I can, I thought. My mother gave up her life so that my brothers and I might rule Egypt in her stead. If I could make her dream reality, then my mother would never die. Not truly. Perhaps I could never put the lid back on that basket, but I could make true the last words she ever spoke. *In the Nile of Eternity, I shall live forever.*

"I shouldn't have told you that story," I said.

"Your stories are my stories," Chryssa said, and it touched me. "I'm your slave."

"You needn't be. I can manumit you and there's no law in Mauretania to stop me. You'd still have your position here with wages if you wanted it."

She shook her head. "I haven't saved up enough for my *peculium*."

I hadn't known she was saving the formal sum by which she could buy back her freedom, but I should have guessed. "You misunderstand. I'll happily *give* you your freedom."

Her gaze shifted to the curtains as they swayed in the breeze, and she shook her head again. "You're a vessel of Isis, so I'm indebted to you for the salvation of my soul, but I want to owe my freedom to no one."

Somehow I understood. All the vast wealth that the emperor had bestowed upon me was but a fraction of my stolen birthright. Even so, I wanted resources that were mine alone, which I might use to help me win back my mother's throne. "Then we'll both have to find a way to make ourselves rich."

Chryssa made a disgruntled noise. "You're already the richest woman in the world!"

"Though she hides it, I think Livia may be wealthier." Having spent summers at Livia's country estate, I knew there wasn't an inch of land that she left idle. She grew edible plants for decoration and sold the eggs of her famous white hens. I hated few people more than I hated the emperor's wife, but I made a point to learn from my enemies. "We'll need to create some industry." Chryssa eyed me with more interest now. "If there's money to be made, it's in some luxury the Romans want badly but not badly enough to steal it."

"Timber, pearls, citrus wood?" she suggested. "Or maybe fish sauce, wine, or horses for the circus."

We had all these things in plenty, but whatever I'd been about to say in reply was immediately forgotten with the sensation of movement inside me. I put both hands on my belly, marveling at the pain. "The child is kicking me."

"Does it hurt?" Chryssa whispered, the lines of her face creased with worry.

"Oof, yes, it hurts. I'm under attack!" My dramatics were apparently convincing. Hearing my cry, Tala came running with such haste that her jewelry was still tinkling when she burst into the doorway. With her baby boy in one arm and a drawn knife in the other, she looked like a gladiatrix ready to defend me. I panted, half doubled over with laughter and pain. "Oh, Tala, I think you're starting to like me."

Surmising there were no intruders, Tala huffed, "I'll never understand Easterners!"

Chryssa laughed. "Why not, Tala? Babe on one hip, dagger in the other, you're like some tattooed Amazon."

"Don't look down your long Greek nose at me, slave girl!" Tala turned to storm out, but when she grabbed for the old latticework door, it collapsed from its hinges, cracking into three pieces. I don't know why this should have seemed so very funny to us, but when we tried to smother giggles, it only made the three of us explode with laughter.

THERE'S one thing about the Romans I'll never criticize; they're the finest, most efficient builders in the world. Set them to a construction task, and they'll have workers in organized groups swarming beneath the sun by day and under torches at night. We'd only commissioned a new palace in February, but by high summer a small wing was already habitable. Eager to abandon the old mansion with its animal skins and disintegrating woodwork, we moved in with all our belongings. The sounds of hammers against wood and chisels against stone echoed through the halls from dawn to dusk, but with the ocean waves crashing just outside my bedroom terrace, I still slept soundly.

The summer harvest season was upon us, and wagonloads of grain rolled to the harbor where Roman ships waited to carry it all away. There wouldn't be enough, Balbus warned. Even if Mauretania produced a bigger crop next year, our granaries were disorganized, and until the harbor was finished the largest ships must seek port elsewhere. Meanwhile, dispatches arrived from Rome daily.

None from Augustus. Though he'd forced Cornelius Gallus to suicide, he'd never answered my letter. His cold-blooded elimination of the Prefect of Egypt was the only sign that the emperor had received my message or still thought about me at all. I'd said that it would never be over between us, but I began to wonder if Livia had been right. In delivering me to his bed before sending me into exile, perhaps she *had* broken his fascination with me. Perhaps Augustus gave no thought to the fact that my forthcoming child might be the bitter fruit of that accursed night in Ostia.

Perhaps he believed the child was Juba's. Certainly, everyone else did. Philadelphus wrote with much joy at the news of my pregnancy, and I reread his letter several times, searching for secret messages, finding none; though he was a Ptolemy, Philadelphus was no schemer. A missive from Lady Octavia assured me that I should rest throughout my pregnancy and that Philadelphus was applying himself to his studies. I received congratulations from Virgil, written in pastoral prose. I wrote replies to all of them, and when I went looking for a courier I came across Juba on the terrace.

"Don't trouble the queen with this news," he was saying. "We don't want to upset her when she's so near to childbirth."

I didn't bother to conceal myself—how could I, when my huge belly announced me before I entered a room? "What news is this? Tell me."

The hapless messenger looked between me and Juba, not sure who to obey, and the king let out a long-suffering sigh. "Selene, there's a new Prefect of Egypt."

"*Another* one so soon?" I asked, frustrated that such news always reached us weeks, if not months, after the fact. "What happened to *this* Gallus?"

Juba shook his head. "He made a disastrous expedition into the Arabian Peninsula and barely escaped with his life."

"How unfortunate," I said, wishing the new prefect hadn't escaped at all. "What was he doing in Arabia?"

Juba leaned back against the marble balustrade, his arms folded over his chest. "He was lured by tales of treasure. Frankincense and myrrh. He took a fleet of ships across the gulf. There may've also been some mercenaries involved. Then the heat of the desert crossing debilitated the army to the point of utter defeat. He had to turn back. Now he's trying to cover up his incompetence by claiming he was betrayed by his guides and some outlaw called Horus the Avenger."

Helios. I held my breath. They'd all tried to convince me that my twin was dead, but here was proof he was alive! Who but Helios could be responsible for the Roman defeat? If my suspicions were true, I'd helped rid Egypt of one terrible Roman overlord, and Helios had destroyed the next. How difficult it was to hide my deep-felt satisfaction. "So the Prefect of Egypt is being replaced *again?*"

Juba watched me carefully. "Augustus has no choice but to get rid of him. Such a defeat might encourage the Egyptians to rebel."

"Augustus *does* have a choice," I argued, heat prickling along my skin. "He can name me Queen of Egypt. After all, *I'd* never have made war on the Arabians without cause."

"Selene, you're upset. This is exactly why I didn't want you to know—"

I cut him off with a shriek. Pain clutched at my belly, clamping down with the ferocity of a crocodile's jaw. I staggered as the pain moved to my back and Juba hastened to steady me. I cried out again, and he shouted, "Send for the midwife!"

Fourteen

MAURETANIA
SUMMER 24 B.C.

WHEN they strapped me onto the midwife's chair, I felt like a condemned criminal sent to crucifixion. The child was coming and I was helpless to do anything but endure it. With every contraction, sweat ran like a river down my spine. I gripped the arms of the birthing chair until my fingers ached. I cried out in agony and between puffing breaths, I rolled my head from side to side, wondering how any woman consented to do this thing. I didn't want to be attended. Like a wounded animal, I wanted to crawl off into some corner by myself until the ordeal was over. But in this my wishes were completely ignored. Chryssa stayed at my side, sponging my face and wetting my lips while the midwife made preparations. Tala remained too, singing Berber songs and adorning me with henna. "What kind of barbarian symbols are you painting on her belly?" Chryssa demanded.

"Markings of the *Amazigh*," Tala said with a proud toss of her head. "The free people. You would know nothing of this since you're just a slave." I noticed that her Latin had much improved but I was too weak to command them to stop quarreling.

Still, I was young and healthy; I didn't flirt with death. The blood didn't pour out of my body in torrents, soaking my thighs as it had when Tala gave birth. Yet the writhing and panting and pushing tempered me as metal is tempered in a forge.

*   *   *

HOW foolish I was to ever think I wouldn't love her. With my infant daughter squirming in my arms, I tested each of her tiny pink fingers against my own, and some new magic happened I'll never be able to explain. I felt like a whole person for the first time. If Helios and I were each one half of a soul, then this baby was the mystical tendril that held us still connected. A tuft of shocking blond hair curled on her little head, and her eyes sparkled blue. I'd been fair as a child but my hair darkened, whereas Helios remained golden. I knew, as I hadn't known while I carried her, that she was part of me and part of him. Part of all we had ever been or would ever be.

Even if Helios wasn't her father, I didn't care. She was a Ptolemy. That made her *ours*, and I loved her as I'd never loved anything or anyone. It terrified me. I was sure that my enemies would know in one glance that harming her was the surest way to wound me. Is it any wonder that Isis hid her baby in the reeds? Where could I hide my daughter to keep her safe? Perhaps my mother had known this fear, embracing the bite of an asp to free her from it. I would always make a different choice. Cuddling my baby close, I promised, "I'll never leave you. I'll never, ever leave you."

When the king came to call upon me, I received him wearing a simple dressing gown. Subdued, Juba remained standing, hands folded at the small of his back as if afraid to touch my daughter, who mewled like a kitten in my arms. "What will you name her?"

"Isidora," I said at once. *Gift of Isis*. "Cleopatra Isidora."

We both knew that to give her a name of my heritage instead of Juba's would be taken either as an admission that my bloodline was far more prestigious than his or that he wasn't the girl's father. Even so, Juba didn't argue. He actually looked *relieved*. Had he thought I'd name her Cleopatra Augusta as my mother had named her child Ptolemy Caesar? He looked down at Isidora and I imagined that he was enraptured by her tiny pink lips and soft little ears. "Selene, I told you that I'd find a way to forgive you, and I have. Your twin is dead and Augustus is across the sea. We never have to speak of it again." I wet my lips, nodding only to forestall the inevitable argument and put an end to this conversation. "I blame myself, Selene. A man should know how to control his wife and make her find pleasure in submitting to him. I'm an able horseman. I should have known better how to approach a skittish creature."

"Juba, I'm not a *horse*," I said, though I was too tired to take much offense.

Juba reached out a hand and placed it over mine. "I shouldn't have threatened you when we first arrived in Mauretania. It'll be better between us now. This can be a new beginning for all three of us."

One might think that I scoffed at this offer or threw it back in his face. After the unforgivable things that Juba had done, perhaps I should have closed my heart to him forever. However, with a babe in my arms, everything looked different to me. I wanted to make a world for Isidora in which she could be safe and happy. If that meant accepting Juba's forgiveness for a crime I hadn't committed, was that too large a price to pay?

MY daughter's first six months were a time of unexpected tranquillity. I fed her from my own breasts, though it wasn't considered queenly to do so. And I tried to be of a more forgiving, generous nature, for I never wanted her to taste my hatred of the emperor in my mother's milk. I learned to soothe my daughter when she cried and though my servants were eager to give me a respite, I loved caring for Isidora, pressing my lips to her brow and inhaling the scent at her temple where her baby smell was strongest.

"You should give her over to me," Tala said one morning. "Let the little princess be a milk-sister to my son."

Princess. It was the first time I'd heard the title applied to anyone but me. My mother's advisers might always see me as the Princess of Egypt, but by rights that title now belonged to Isidora, and I shivered, because I knew that now I'd only see myself as the queen. Though my father had crowned me as a girl and Augustus had given me this kingdom as a dowry, it was my daughter who at last made me a queen in truth.

"For once, I agree with this savage," Chryssa said. "Your seclusion makes it easy for the king and his advisers to forget you."

That's when she showed me the newly minted coin. Clutching it in my hand, I hurried down the marbled hall, stepping over toolboxes and dodging workmen, until I found Juba in his new study—a room draped with crimson curtains and lit by giant braziers shaped like wheat sheaves. Juba rose with courtly grace to greet me, but I held up the evidence of his true intentions in my hand. "What's this?"

The king's smile swelled with pride as the metal caught the light. "It's the new coinage of the realm. It isn't the best portraiture of me, but your father's old gem cutter has promised to make a better likeness next time."

"Where is my portrait on this coin?" I asked. "Anyone who saw this would think you were sole ruler of Mauretania."

Juba knitted his brows and a sound of exasperation caught in his throat. "Women don't belong on coins." My father had been the first man to ever put a woman on a Roman coin—and he'd done it more than once. He'd made coins for Fulvia, for my mother, and even Octavia. He'd taken the women in his life as partners, not subjects, and it disturbed me that Juba wasn't that same kind of man. At my obvious distress, Juba adopted a conciliatory tone. "Selene, haven't we been friendly since Isidora's birth?"

Yes, we had been friendly. He'd indulged me with lavish gifts of jewelry and perfumes. He'd sat with me in my chambers, helping me to learn Punic and never pressing me for intimacy. I'd begun to think of him as a generous and gentle man again. But all the while, he'd been planning this accursed coin. "Juba, I'm not some kitchen girl to be wooed with sparkling trinkets. I'm a sovereign queen. When we first arrived here, you invoked my name to assure the people that they'd be well governed, but you and your counselors don't listen to a word I say!"

"I *do* listen to you," he protested. "This palace and the lighthouse are all being built to your specifications. My counselors agree that you have a good instinct for forming a proper royal court. Confine your interests to such things. Isn't your mother's example enough to teach you how disastrous it is when women involve themselves in politics?"

How often must I hear this argument? It seemed that I'd been fighting all my life for my own place. Even when I rushed here clutching this coin in my hand, I was filled with offense for the insult it did *me*. Now my anger went beyond what men were trying to steal from me; I thought of my daughter too. Her future should be shaped not simply by the fact that her grandmother had been an extraordinary woman. If we were ever to return home to Egypt, Isidora needed me to be strong too. "Juba, from this day forward, I'm going to act either in agreement with you or upon my own authority."

His cheeks reddened. "Such arrogance! Do you think it's easy to govern a kingdom, Selene? You're a child; the council won't work with you."

"Then I'll form my own counsel. So don't be surprised to find a giant Iseum being erected in the middle of the city." It was a threat without teeth, for the soldiers respected the king's commands, not mine. But Juba must have feared that I'd persuade others to my cause, because he came out from behind his writing table to confront me.

"If you build such a temple, you'll start a public quarrel with the man who has given us all this," he said. "We have to please Augustus. We have to show our *gratitude*."

And Juba had condemned *me* as the emperor's whore? Not wanting to have the same argument over and over again, I smiled sweetly. "If he needs a show of gratitude, let's rename the city. We'll call it Iol-Caesaria in honor of the emperor." Or so it would seem. The name also belonged to my murdered brother. I hadn't been able to give Caesarion a funeral, or to lay his body to rest in the Soma with the other Ptolemies, nor even to place him in my mother's tomb. I couldn't perform the Opening of the Mouth ceremony to help him breathe again in the afterlife, but I could name this city after him and not even the emperor would object.

"It's a good idea," Juba admitted. "*Iol-Caesaria*. Augustus will like that and it will confirm to every other client monarch that we're a rising power. No Iseums, though, or Augustus will turn Mauretania into another Roman province. Besides, who knows if the natives will accept Isis. She's a foreign goddess."

"*We* are foreign and they've accepted us," I said, but that wasn't wholly true. We'd come to this place with an army of slaves. The members of our court hailed from Rome, Egypt, Greece, and even farther than that. But where were the Berber advisers in our council? Though Tala was reluctant to tell me the complaints of her people, I knew they were growing angry with our high-handedness and it was time that something be done about it.

THE winter solstice had come again and the whole world was celebrating. In Greece it would be the Haloa, to honor the return of Demeter's lost daughter. In Egypt, they feasted for Isis and the Nativity of Horus. Though I'd been born on the solstice and proclaimed one of the holy twins, harbingers of a Golden Age, I knew better than to celebrate my sixteenth birthday with an Isiac pageant. Juba wasn't wrong when he told me that building an Iseum would insult Augustus, but Isis was a patient goddess. She'd hidden from Set until her child was strong enough. Isis would wait for me too.

In Rome, they celebrated the Saturnalia, so we'd celebrate that here in Mauretania too. I hoped it might provide a note of commonality. The Berber goddess Tanit had taken a sun god as her consort and because this sun god carried with him a sheaf of wheat and looked grandfatherly, the Romans reinterpreted Ba'al Hammon as their Saturn. With this in mind, I invited not just every prominent Roman family in the city to our banquet but also the Berber chieftains and their wives.

Our Saturnalia would be my first great entertainment as queen, the first thing I arranged on my own, without Juba's approval. I fretted, afraid to misstep. If I entertained too lavishly, the Romans would condemn me as a hedonist. On the other hand, if I erred on the side of frugality, my guests might take insult. I decided upon a middle course; I let Chryssa manage the funds for the banquet, and we decorated the new hall with pine wreaths and golden curtains. From the tribes of the Atlas Mountains, Tala purchased thick woven Berber rugs, dyed in beautiful shades of indigo. Silver plates and goblets graced every setting, and much to Chryssa's dismay, I decided that we'd send this silver home as a gift with each guest. She was only slightly mollified by my decision to serve Mauretanian wine from native grapes. Though the Romans complained it wasn't as fine as other vintages, it certainly wasn't as expensive.

That night, Chryssa helped me into a blue gown of transparent Coan cloth, wrapping it around my body many times so as to make some attempt at modesty. I liked the way it made my green eyes even greener, how lightly the gossamer fabric rested upon my skin, soft as Helios's caresses had once been. And I reminded myself that a woman should be able to dress as she liked without a man hurting her . . .

"You almost make me pine for a child," Chryssa said, cinching the gown. "Look what it's done for your figure."

I made a face. My hips had widened and my breasts were larger, but I didn't like the tiny lines pregnancy had left on my belly. What's more, while my mother had been a petite woman, I was growing tall like my father. I worried I'd become an unfeminine giantess. "*Sweet Isis*, listen to it rain," I said, stealing a glance at the terrace, where fat drops of water splattered the marble and made the bushes shake. "Do you think anyone will even come?"

Chryssa sniffed. "They'll all come. Every Roman plantation owner looking for favor will attend. Every artist seeking your patronage, and every hungry mouth that salivates for the wagonloads of oysters and mussels near the kitchens. Did we really need twelve different fish dishes to celebrate the new harbor?"

Of course we did. I looked to Tala. "Will the tribal chiefs come?"

Smoothing down my daughter's unruly curls, the Berber said, "Yes, but I hope you have enough couches and cushions, for they'll bring all their wives, and some of them have more than one. They'll bring their daughters too, who may offer themselves as concubines to the king."

I felt no twinge of jealousy upon hearing this. No matter how gently Juba wooed me, I hadn't invited him into my bed. The truth is that I couldn't imagine ever willingly joining with another man, skin to skin. Helios had made me into a goddess. In Juba's arms, I didn't ever want to be anything less. So if some other girl could divert the king's attention from me, I told myself I'd be grateful.

When we swept into the banquet hall, servants were already passing great platters of fishes and amphorae of warmed wine to our damp but spirited guests. The majordomo announced us and the crowd rose to its feet, giving a collective sigh of satisfaction at the sight of my golden-haired baby girl. They raised cups to the king, cups to the gods, and some of them even raised cups to me. Then the musicians took up their tunes and someone shouted, "Io Saturnalia!"

The night seemed sure to be a great success, with revelry and feasting. The women danced, weaving patterns with their henna-tattooed hands, jerking to drumbeats with zest. In Rome, men and women mingled freely during the Saturnalia. The custom seemed perfectly amenable to some of the tribesmen, but others kept their women at the back of the room. I thought to join these veiled and cloistered women, to encourage them, when I spotted the Mauri and the Gaetulians standing opposite a group of Roman settlers amongst whom Lucius Cornelius Balbus stood out in a magnificent burnoose and blue paint upon his face. With a wide, silly grin, he said to the Berber chieftains, "See, I look like you now. So we too are *brothers* and you shouldn't trespass on my lands."

The Saturnalia was a festival of pranks and tomfoolery, so Balbus's mockery wasn't out of place, but as I floated toward the knot of men I could see that the tribesmen weren't amused. One of them addressed Balbus hotly and I recognized him as Tala's brother, Maysar. "When did they become *your* lands?" he demanded.

"When your old king bequeathed his kingdom to Rome," Balbus replied.

"Then learn our ways like a good steward," Maysar argued. "We graze our animals on the lowlands—"

"You graze them in *my* fields where *my* slaves are trying to grow crops!"

"After the harvest, what fool objects?" Maysar asked, an enormous sword swaying at his belt. "When we take our animals to the highlands, the farmers are free to grow whatever they want. Farmers sell us grain, we sell them meat, and everyone is happy. We've been doing this long before any Roman stepped foot here."

Seeing that Juba was locked in conversation with the aqueduct engineers and didn't sense the trouble, I hurried between the men just in time to stop a red-faced Balbus from making some blustery retort. At my approach, he checked himself and made a correct bow, which every Roman considered a trial. The Berbers also bowed, the tinkling of their jewelry a pleasant sound as they rose back up again. "I'm so honored that you all came to celebrate the Saturnalia," I said, and knowing that Tala's brother had lost his wife to illness, I reached for his hands. "Maysar, I hope we can share in your joy for the new year as we shared your sorrows in the one past." In Egypt, where it was forbidden for strangers to touch the royal family, no queen would do this. But the Berbers might not come to love me if I held myself apart and I wanted them to love me. I needed them to love me. I'd learned from Cleopatra, Antony, and Augustus; I knew how important it was.

Maysar clasped my hands briefly, his eyes dropping in grief, and then he pressed the palm of his hand over his heart. "Come celebrate with us, Majesty."

I sat with the Berbers, listening to their stories. They were very polite and fiercely independent and generous with their praise when they learned that they were to keep their silver plate as a gift. Still, I sensed in them a tension that not even the rain or the freely flowing wine could dilute. It all came to a head when talk turned to the Garamantes. Balbus's nose was redder than usual and I suspected he was deep into his wine. "Mauretania must raise troops to fight," he said to Juba. "We can squeeze the Garamantes raiders between our soldiers and the ones in Africa Nova."

"We?" Maysar interrupted. "Will your sons fight or do you mean that the sons of Berbers should fight?"

The Romans prided themselves on enrolling their own sons in the legions, so I didn't think it was a fair critique. Moreover, we'd need to raise native Mauretanian troops, Garamantes or no; we couldn't rely upon Roman legions forever.

"Afraid of fighting, are you?" Balbus asked hotly. "The Garamantes refuse to acknowledge Juba as king. Your own brother-in-law was killed during a raid. If you don't want war with them, you're a coward."

"Coward?" Maysar was on his feet, and several other men rose with him. Then everyone started to speak at once and I had trouble following the argument.

"We avenged my tribesmen, then made peace—"

"You have no authority to make agreements—"

"The Garamantes aren't trustworthy—"

"Enough!" Juba shouted. My husband so seldom raised his voice that it silenced the room. Then the king waited for all eyes to settle upon him as he took a sip of wine to fortify himself. "We're building a kingdom. If there is to be Mauretanian independence, we must negotiate peace together, and if that fails, we must fight together too. Berbers and Romans, together."

This didn't go down easy. The chieftains grumbled their dissent, but Maysar suggested, "King Juba, son of Juba, perhaps we can send an envoy to the Garamantes to negotiate peace. I will go."

"It's too late," Juba said flatly. "The Garamantes have killed Roman citizens. They must pay for it in blood."

These weren't Juba's words, I knew. He was repeating something he must have heard from Balbus or one of the veterans, or perhaps even from one of the dispatches he received from Rome. Worse, I didn't know that he was wrong. I doubted that my mother would have dealt peacefully with raiders. War was an evil but perhaps, sometimes, a necessary one.

"If we raise a Mauretanian army for war with the Garamantes," Maysar ventured, "who will lead these troops?"

"Lucius Cornelius will lead our army," Juba said, and Balbus's expression was smug. Oh, how I wished the king hadn't made this announcement. Not here. Not now. The tribesmen were furious. Several slammed down their cups and others stood to leave. Some muttered curses and I knew enough of their language now to recognize it. Juba did too and tried to explain himself. "Balbus will be able to take a tribal cavalry and create an effective auxiliary force for the Roman legions."

"So much for the independence of Mauretania," Maysar said, spinning on his heel so that his burnoose swirled around him. Then he stormed out of the banquet.

I chased the widowed Berber chieftain down the long pillared corridor. My running steps were most undignified but entirely necessary, and the disquieting looks of the servants would have to be endured. *"Maysar, wait!"*

When I caught up, Maysar growled, "We thought this king would be different. But Juba is *worse* than a Roman. He's a changeling. He's a creature of Rome sent to defile our sacred lands. And though my sister praises you, you're just another Roman wife."

"I'm no Roman wife!" I cried, deeply offended. "I'm an Egyptian. A Ptolemy. I'm Cleopatra's daughter. There's no one who knows better than I do how the Romans destroy and defile sacred lands."

Now he stopped, his eyes snapping to mine. "There it is, madam. You're an *Egyptian*. Mauretania is but a sojourn for you. I've heard the talk of your haughty Alexandrian contingent. It's only a matter of time before you're restored to Egypt, they say. Then what's to become of us?"

"I'll still be your queen," I said, though I couldn't be sure of it.

He turned in the torchlight so that the hint of blue dye on his skin seemed like a menacing shadow. "Now you're going to give me honeyed words about how the Romans are only here to help us . . ."

"The Romans are here to steal from you," I said, and since he looked taken aback by my bluntness, I pressed on. "They have a voracious appetite that can never be filled. Even now, they're gorging themselves on Egypt. I hope they choke on it."

Maysar's hazel eyes narrowed, the weathered lines of his warrior's face tightening, wary of a trap. "You're here to stop them?"

"I can't stop them," I admitted. Deciding then and there, I said, "But I mean to ensure that for every single thing the Romans take from you, they give something back. Right now, all you see is this palace and a harbor for Rome, but it's only the start. With Roman money, we'll build roads to connect the cities and villages. We'll build aqueducts to carry water into the desert. We'll build markets in which every Berber can profit. We'll build an army, using what the Romans have taught us about fighting so that—"

"So that we become just like them," Maysar interrupted.

I clasped my hands, searching for the words to explain. "Rome is triumphant now, she's ascendant, but things change. Fate turns. In the hills and the desert, the Berbers have always bided their time. As your sister is fond of pointing out to me, the Phoenicians who built their Carthaginian Empire on these lands are gone, but the Berbers are still here. Aren't you strong enough to outlast the Romans?"

I saw the hint of a smile. "The king feels this way too?"

"The king is ill advised," I said carefully, not wanting to do more damage to Juba's reputation. "That's why I can't let you stalk off into the night. That's why you must stay. Serve as an adviser to me and to the king as well."

"And serve with that swine-faced Balbus? Never. My honor would never endure it."

He stared at me, waiting for a gesture of dismissal. I almost gave him leave to go. Then I changed my mind. "For four years I lived with the man who destroyed my family. I ate with him, shared his wine, and played a *kithara* harp to entertain him. For the good of all that I cherished, I endured it. You're a chieftain. For the sake of Mauretania, can't you tolerate Balbus?"

"No," he said, slowly, then showed me his teeth. "But I'll join your council and enjoy forcing Balbus to tolerate me."

Fifteen

WINTER was always quiet in Mauretania. To the southwest, winter snows crowned the Atlas Mountains, but here on the coast cypress, juniper, and aloe still covered the world in a green mantle. The almond trees were bare, but sun-drenched flowers bloomed in pots and the warm breeze that stiffened the banners over our palace carried a light perfume. We received few guests and even fewer letters. No more orders from Rome about the maps we must make, the aqueducts we must build, the grain we must send. Until the sea opened again, we were free to spend our efforts building the palace.

I hoped it would be the envy of every monarch in the empire. Bright and luxurious, it would be a reproduction of the home I'd left in Egypt. Carved marble niches waited with high arrogant brows, as if they knew Juba would acquire only the best artwork for them. Terraced gardens and brilliant mosaic floors—all inlaid with translucent glass tiles of green and blue—gave way to airy passageways. Draperies in the terrace doorways swished with every sea breeze, and though rain-fed fountains sprayed with fanfare in the entryway, there were more placid blue pools too.

I couldn't build a temple to Isis, but even Juba allowed that I must not be faulted for a private shrine to my goddess. If the Romans could house their *lares* and *penates* in the storeroom, I could build a private enclosure in my rooms for Isis as the patroness of my reign. Therefore, I oversaw workmen as they installed an alabaster altar with niches for burning candles or sacred herbs. Painters gave life to my goddess in bright green, red, and yellow—depicting her in the Egyptian style, with wings, an *ankh* in one hand, and wearing a headdress shaped like a throne. I swelled with pride to see it. If Isis lived in me, I was bringing her back home to Africa, step by step.

Meanwhile, Juba's Roman advisers now treated me with a modicum of respect. This may have been because I now looked more like a woman and less like a girl. It may have been because I was a mother. Or perhaps it was because Juba made no objection when I stated my intention to attend the council meetings.

Like all the greatest leaders, my family embraced the Hellenistic ideal of *harmonia*, a concept of community and cooperation. Tolerance for cultural differences. A goal of partnership between different peoples from all walks of life. This is why Juba had invoked my name to assure the Mauretanians that they'd be well ruled. Now I hoped to make good on that unspoken promise. I arrived early at the council chambers, ascending the stairs of the marble dais to my pearl-studded chair. It was smaller than Juba's, dwarfed by his golden throne, but mine had history, and I liked it. I thought Isis would have liked it too. I never forgot that Isis was the throne upon which I sat. It was by her providence and with her love that I must learn to rule.

The counselors arrived in groups, bowing to me as they found their seats. Some wore elaborate Roman togas draped over their arms. Some wore traditional Greek *himations*. One wore an unfashionable brown gown, for I'd invited Lady Lasthenia, and her presence here irritated the men almost as much as mine did. When Euphronius took his seat wearing stark white robes, more than a few of Juba's advisers raised their eyebrows. Still, none of them complained openly until Maysar strode into the chambers, his bright Berber garments sweeping the floor behind him.

Balbus drew his brows together, muttering something to his companions that I couldn't hear, and a general murmur of disapproval was cut off by the announcement of the king. Before Juba could settle onto the cushion of his throne or call our meeting to order, Balbus was on his feet, one finger pointed directly at the Berber chieftain. "What is he doing here?"

I gave Balbus my most charming smile. "Lucius Cornelius, thank you for giving me the opportunity to introduce our newest councilor, Maysar of the Gaetuli. He's here at my invitation."

My charm was clearly lost on Balbus, who turned to Juba. "Gaius Julius Juba, isn't it enough that we have to endure the queen in our council but also foreigners, most of whom aren't even citizens?" His fellow Romans thumped their feet in agreement and Maysar tensed, hand on the hilt of his sword. I didn't turn to look at Juba but sensed his alarm at this sudden mutiny. Balbus squared his shoulders, encouraged by the other Romans. "Why should we welcome a barbarian?"

My lips parted to answer, but I wasn't the first one to speak.

"Why should you?" Juba asked, voice steady and clear. "Because we say so."

If Juba's words surprised me, they positively stunned Balbus. Juba had used the royal *we*, and it seemed to remind Balbus that he stood before a sovereign king. "Majesty, I urge you to reconsider."

Juba's long arms stretched at his sides, tendons tight. "Lucius Cornelius, my wife and I were both raised within the household of Augustus himself, who set us here in the highest authority with his full confidence. You may trust in our decisions and you will remember yourself."

Juba and I were unlike any other client monarchs in the Roman world. We didn't have to send ambassadors to treat with Augustus, nor await intermediaries to express his will. Outside of Agrippa and Maecenas, there was no man within the emperor's circle trusted more than Juba. Balbus knew it, and though he blustered on a few more moments, he eventually took his place, brooding silently.

What we discussed that day I cannot now recall, though I'm sure it had something to do with raising troops to secure the frontier against the Garamantes. I only remember that Juba and I left the chamber together, and everyone stood until we were gone.

On the terrace at this end of the palace, the mist of ocean spray sometimes wet the tiles and made them slick, so Juba offered me his arm and I took it. "Thank you," I said as we walked. "It means a great deal to me that you supported Maysar . . . and me."

Juba drew me closer, but said, "I didn't do it to please either of you. I can't have men like Balbus test me and find me wanting."

I agreed. "He's ambitious and hard to manage."

"Somehow he's easier to manage than my wife." Juba's tone was lighthearted, an amused tilt to his lips. I didn't expect that. I wanted to read his thoughts, feel his emotions, but he wasn't my other half. He was, and would always be, in some part, a stranger. "Selene, I'm told that other men's wives concern themselves chiefly with their households and the gentler arts."

"I'm not one of those wives," I replied, encouraged when Juba didn't scowl. "And though you might deny it, I suspect you wouldn't be happy if I were. Perhaps we ought to encourage Balbus to find his glory elsewhere. There are opportunities for advancement in Africa Nova."

Juba shrugged off my suggestion. "I'm going to ride, Selene. Why don't you come with me?"

As I could think of no good reason to refuse, I accompanied him to the stables. He chose a white horse for me—one of an ancient, all-but-extinct breed with gray stripes on its legs. Taking our mounts down the road, I urged my horse to step clear of rain puddles. Memnon and a few of our guards rode behind us. When it came to horses, Juba was a native son. While I struggled to stay astride, Juba coaxed his horse into an easy gallop past some Berber washerwomen who were too slow to give way to our royal entourage. A spatter of mud doused the oldest woman amongst them, and when she turned to see that it was the king who had splashed her, she cried, "You Romans make a mess of everything!"

At that, Juba wheeled his horse around. "What is the trouble?"

She splayed her dirtied gown so we could all see it. "You're the trouble, Majesty. Look what you've done! You and your muddy hooves."

"Madam," Juba sputtered, hand on his heart. "Do you take me for a *centaur*?"

We all broke into uproarious laughter. Me, Juba, the guards, and even the mud-spattered woman. We gave her some coins for her trouble then rode to the shore where the rocks at last gave way to the sandy beach. "A centaur!" I cried, bursting into a fresh round of laughter. "You knew what she meant."

Juba stopped his horse, leaning forward. "Yes, but I wanted to make you merry."

As always when Juba wanted to please me, I was guarded. "What makes *you* merry, Juba?"

"Not much these days." He looked away, his gaze on the mountains to the south. "I've sent expeditions into the wilds, but I think I'd like to see more myself. Once things are more established here, I'd like to take a journey."

He often boasted that he'd been given back his patrimony, but his father's cities remained in Roman hands; I wondered if he longed for home as I longed for Egypt. "Will you journey to Numidia?"

"No. I want to explore the interior of Mauretania. To see the lions and the elephants and find—Selene, you oughtn't let him do that."

I'd been too lax with my horse, who stretched his neck to bother a shell in the surf. It was some manner of sea snail, and the horse was pawing at it, and nipping with his teeth. "Is the snail poisonous?"

"No, but look at the pink froth on your mount's lips. If left in the sun, it might stain him purple."

"Purple?" I asked, suddenly alert. "Is that snail a murex?" And when Juba nodded, I realized that my horse was worrying the tiny creature that created the most expensive dye in the world. "Here?"

"Don't get too excited . . . There's a dye works in Numidia, in Chullu, but its purple is considered inferior to the Tyrian, the recipe for which is a closely guarded secret."

Other spiny shells littered the beach, albeit without live inhabitants, and I dismounted to gather some. Juba climbed down from his horse and collected a few shells himself. They were golden in color and whorled at the end with a low spire. Smaller than the kind children put to their ears to hear the ocean inside. In the russet sunset, Juba and I walked together on the pebbles that had washed ashore, their once-angry edges washed smooth by the waters of Mauretania.

* * *

WHEN I returned to the palace with a handful of shells, Chryssa hoarded them like gold. "You said we must make ourselves rich! This is how we can do it."

"Juba says that the Tyrian purple can't be reproduced. We'll never be able to make the same shade."

"Only a Greek would know the difference," Chryssa argued. "To the barbarians, purple is purple!"

I might have debated the point, but I was distracted by my daughter's cries. Tala tried giving her a damp cloth and a wooden ring to teethe on, but it hadn't helped her pain, and near my wits' end, I called for Euphronius. When he entered the nursery, I asked, "Can you stop my daughter's tears?"

Euphronius lifted Isidora from her cradle, handling my child like the precious jewel she was. "Her gums hurt. It's natural for her to cry. These things are always more difficult for the mother than the babe."

"But she's suffering," I said, feeling guilty for having been away from her for most of the day.

"I could give her a pinch of white willow bark powder, but there may be a spell . . ." He took his finger and rubbed it slowly on her lips, letting her gnaw him as she was wont to do.

Tala tutted. "Old man, how can we teach her not to bite when you encourage her?"

"Hush, Tala," I said. Like a cat senses an intruder, I felt the *heka* as the old mage whispered some words in the ancient language. The scent of magic was in the air. Then Isidora hiccuped through her tears, and calmed.

"That's our little princess," Euphronius cooed, lowering her back down in her cradle, utterly spent. He sweated and panted as if he'd made the run to Marathon. Then all at once, my mage keeled forward, collapsing to one knee.

"What ails you?" I asked, rushing to help him up.

Euphronius got to his feet only with difficulty, abashed. "I'm old. It's an ailment of its own."

I could never remember a time when the priest of Isis had *not* been old. He'd been old when he was our tutor, old when we were taken by the Romans, and older still when he urged us to run away from Augustus. Isiac priests and priestesses lived long lives and I never thought that he'd be an exception. He never ate the flesh of animals. He subsisted on fruits and vegetables, breads, cheeses, and nuts. He took bracing baths and long meditative walks. He'd always seemed hearty and hale until recently. "Is it *heka* sickness? Did you forget to do as you instructed me and make a channel for it to flow away?"

Euphronius shook his head. "It's like squeezing blood from a stone, Majesty. I have very little *heka* left inside me."

"Then visit the Temple of Tanit and be replenished," I said, wondering if he'd lost his wits.

"Majesty, I am not like you. I'm a priest of Egypt and Isis doesn't come to me in every incarnation. Besides, there is little *heka* left in that temple. Like tears into a well, it takes many before there's a bucket full. What magic was there now resides inside *you*."

In this moment, I realized how much it cost Euphronius to be here with me. He could have remained in Egypt, where he was still revered. Instead, he'd followed me to a land where he didn't even have a temple in which he could worship. He'd borne my resentment and coldness for more than a year now, keeping his eyes low and never speaking in my presence unless I spoke to him first. He'd waited upon my every whim without complaint and spent what little magic he had upon my simple request for my daughter. "Forgive me," I said, shamed for the way I'd been treating him. "My mother once said your loyalty was worth more than all the gold in the world. I haven't valued you as I should."

The old man faltered, a tremor in his lower lip. "I'm of no value, Majesty. I've led everyone I've loved to ruin. I know that it's only because of your generosity and sentimental heart that you haven't banished me. I've made too many mistakes in trying to guide you."

"I've made mistakes too," I said, my chest squeezing with emotion. "Too many to count. One of them has been to deny that you're dear to me."

Tears shone in his eyes. "I'd give my life for you, Majesty. You and Philadelphus and this little princess . . ."

People said these things to monarchs. They promised their loyalty and their lives. Yet I knew that Euphronius meant every word. "I'm a most fortunate queen. Can't . . . can't I give you some of my *heka*?"

"Majesty, queens use magic as mothers must, to feed the people and to defend them. Not to murmur little healing spells or help old mages. Remember, the magic inside you came at a costly price."

"Soon my private shrine to Isis will be complete and you can worship here in the palace. But one day, I'll build a temple of Isis. Here, in Mauretania."

"There's no need," Euphronius replied. "For I've foreseen that you'll leave this place soon."

WHEN the first ships arrived that spring, my royal entourage was moored in the marketplace near the stall of rug merchants because Chryssa insisted on interrogating them about dye making. She'd already learned that the Gaetulian tribes manufactured purple long ago. I remained dubious that such an industry were even possible. Given the words of the rug merchant, however, I was starting to wonder. "We need two kinds of snails. We have snails with red dye in Mauretania too. Perhaps not the same as in Tyre, but it's a good fast-setting dye that deepens over time. Yet what good is this to us? We have no Roman senators to wear the purple stripe on their togas."

And if I had my way, we never would.

"Majesty," a courier called for me in the crowd. "You're needed at the palace. A dispatch from Augustus awaits you!"

My blood ran cold. Juba regularly received instructions from Rome, but I'd received only silence. It would be bad news, I thought as we hurried back to the palace. Perhaps something had happened to Philadelphus . . .

"Get the queen something to drink," Chryssa snapped at a servant girl when we burst into my apartments. "She's deathly pale."

"I don't think I can read it," I said, handing the emperor's missive to Euphronius.

He broke the wax seal, read the contents, and announced, "The emperor is gravely ill."

My shoulders sagged in relief. "The emperor is *always* ill. How many times has he thrown Rome into a panic?"

"There's more," Euphronius continued, breathless. "You're summoned to Rome. You and your daughter both. Augustus says that he wants to make peace with you before he dies."

I clutched the arms of my chair, realizing how glad I'd been for the ocean separating me from the emperor. Chryssa hugged herself, her posture an echo of my inner torment. To see Augustus, to be at his mercy again . . . "I won't go, and if I must go, I won't take Isidora with me. She's not even a year old!"

"Majesty," Euphronius said, his voice moderated to soothe me. "Have you considered that the emperor may wish to restore you to the throne of Egypt?"

It could happen like that. On his deathbed. A grand dying gesture, like in all of the emperor's favorite plays. On the other hand, he could execute me. That would also be a dramatic end. Augustus thought he'd rid himself of Helios. Now he only had to do away with Philadelphus, me, and my daughter to make an end of the Ptolemies. But my deeper instincts told me this wasn't his intent. The Romans had rules for how to do away with foreign monarchs— even the ones they created—and Augustus loved to be seen following the rules. "You must be right, Euphronius. He must plan to restore me to Egypt, and my daughter after me. Is that what you've foreseen?"

"I've seen only possibilities, Majesty. Not certainties. The Rivers of Time show all possible futures. In some currents, Augustus restores you to Egypt. I just can't be sure if *our* River of Time flows in that direction."

In spite of this, I dared to hope. As Queen of Egypt, I could make a place for Helios. I could rebuild Thebes and unite North Africa, and revive the worship of Isis. But first I had to return to Rome.

Sixteen

CHRYSSA insisted on packing my trunks for the journey, gathering up combs, polished mirrors, and pots of cosmetics while I dithered over which gowns to take. When I dismissed her to pack her own things, I caught a fleeting look of anxiety that she sought to hide from me. I remembered how she'd never wanted to return to Rome and how sick she'd been on the ship. "Chryssa, if you want to stay in Mauretania, you can stay."

She snapped my strongbox shut. "I belong to you. Where you go, I must follow."

A shaft of sunlight cut through the open terrace doors, illuminating the fabric that curtained my luxurious bed, a bed that would find no equal in Rome. I wanted her with me, but I wouldn't force her. "I'll need someone to stay here with Euphronius. King Juba seems fond of him, and he can look after my interests in the royal council, but I need someone to see that my estates are well managed. To watch over my treasures."

"I can't let you face the emperor alone," she said quietly. "Besides, who would reassure my sister that I'm happy here? Who will make sure that Phoebe is well?"

"I will," I told her. "You needn't return with me, Chryssa. I won't be there long."

She gave me a sidelong glance as if to test my resolve. "Who would tend to your hair and clothing?"

"I'll take Tala with me. She's been a good nurse to Isidora. I've come to rely upon her."

Chryssa scoffed. "You can't trust that Berber woman to make you look like the Queen of Egypt."

I'd been called the Queen of Egypt more times in the past few days than in all the years before, and I worried it would tempt the fates. "We'll manage without you, Chryssa. It isn't certain that Augustus means to restore my mother's throne to me. Even if he intended to do it, he's very ill. He might be dead before I even arrive in Rome."

Her chest rising and falling with emotion, she dared a glance at me. "Isis, forgive me, I wish he already were."

ON the morning of my departure, Juba was drunk. *Frightfully* drunk. Though he had a reputation for being a mild-mannered king, today he was snappish, hurling a finely wrought glass pitcher after a slave boy who displeased him. It had been a rare piece, but Juba didn't seem to care, and he forbade anyone to sweep up the shards. Stepping over the mess, I found him staring out over the harbor where my baggage was being loaded onto the ship. His long body slumped so far over the balustrade that I worried he might fall. When he saw me, he rose back up and took another gulp from his goblet, then let it fall. It rolled off the marble edge of the terrace to tumble down the rocks to the sea. "*Vale*, Selene. Farewell to you and tell Augustus that everything I've done is for his vision of peace, for his glory, and his Golden Age . . . Through all things, I shall always honor him."

I'd never thought to feel pity for Juba, but the pain in his eyes rendered me speechless. In his way, Juba had always been the devoted son the emperor wished for, a son completely blind to his faults. Juba *loved* Augustus and everything my husband did, every stroke of his pen, every slash of his sword, and every breath he took, was a plea for the emperor's approval and acceptance. And yet on his deathbed, Augustus hadn't summoned Juba. He'd summoned me.

Wishing to say something, do something, to ease Juba's pain, I reached for his cheek, but he stopped my hand and gave it a gentle squeeze. "He'll want to see his child. Of course he will. It only makes sense."

"Isidora isn't the emperor's child. She's *mine*."

It was so often our habit to speak past one another that he went on as if he hadn't heard me. "The divine Julius summoned your mother to Rome. Now another Caesar calls for another Cleopatra to join him. And you look so pretty, flush with young motherhood, perfect for the part."

"You're terribly drunk," I said, inhaling the wine on his breath. "You're going to be sick in the morning."

"I'm already sick. I wonder if your mother's Egyptian husbands felt this way. Her brothers. She married them, but it was Caesar she wanted. You've made a brother of me. You've come to think of me like that, haven't you?"

Oh, irony. He thought it was the emperor that stood between us, but it was Helios. It had always been Helios. Still, I didn't like to see Juba in pain and regretted being any part of its cause. "Juba . . . I've come to think of you as a king."

"But not your king." For a moment, I thought Juba might ask me to delay the trip, but I couldn't have stayed. I had a daughter to think of now. A daughter with a proud ancestry who had only me to champion her. I'd stop at nothing to claim our right to Egypt now. Not for Juba or anyone else.

THE winds were against us. In the sleek-oared galley I'd hired to speed us on our way, it still took us much longer to return to Rome than it had taken to leave. Waiting to spot land, my future seemed as fathomless as the blue sea. I didn't know what awaited me; I didn't even know if the emperor would still be alive when we anchored at port. I only knew that if there were any opportunity of winning Egypt, I must seize it.

Our captain spoke Greek, wore an Egyptian amulet at his

throat, and introduced himself as Kabyle, which was a Berber name. Memnon assured me that the skipper was of good reputation, and a few days into the trip Captain Kabyle called upon me in my berth, which had been his. Tala kept near, clutching her babe and mine.

"Captain Kabyle," I said by way of greeting. "You wear an *ankh*. Are you an Isiac?"

"Isn't every sailor, Majesty?" I suppose he had a point. Once, the seas had belonged to Poseidon and Neptune, but those gods seemed to offer only a watery death to those they despised, whereas Isis offered the magic of good winds and salvation of souls. It was the sailors who spread her worship, and every sailing season was marked by a festival in her honor, the Navigium Isidis. But I quickly gathered that the captain hadn't called upon me to discuss a fellowship of faith. His stance was tense, his tone firm. "You and your women need to get belowdecks with the rowers."

Over his shoulder, through the open curtain, he barked something to an officer, and I thought I heard the word *pirates*. I stood and Tala followed me, clutching both children. We'd scarcely taken a few steps onto the deck before I spotted three black ships in our wake. "Are you sure they're pirates?" I asked, my pulse quickening. It hardly seemed possible. Hadn't Augustus boasted that he'd smashed the forces of Sextus Pompey and rid the world of piracy? "There must be a thousand ships that use these shipping lanes."

"And some of them are pirates, Majesty," the captain explained. "They travel together and it's a lean year. There'll be famine in Rome and they know it. If they can seize a ship filled with grain, they can demand a steep price."

"But this isn't a grain ship," I said as the sail snapped and the ship turned sharply at the captain's orders.

"They don't know that, Majesty, and royal hostages are valuable for ransom. Please go belowdecks with the rowers."

Ransom. For the love of Isis, what would become of my daughter and me if we were seized for ransom? Would Juba pay? Would the emperor? My bodyguards tried to hurry me belowdecks as the captain had commanded, but I couldn't make myself move, and Memnon looked ready to carry me off on his shoulder.

"Row!" the captain shouted as the ship bucked over the waves. "Row harder!"

The pirate ships gained on us, and as the ocean spray swept over the deck I wondered how long we could flee, how long before our oarsmen tired. It was Isidora's cry that finally roused me to action. I pried her from Tala's arms.

"We aren't going to outrun them," the Berber woman cried, and I could see that she was right. Our panicked rowers had lost their rhythm, oars wild, the ocean frothing beneath us. As our pursuers closed in, I could see the pirates themselves, hard-looking men. A grappling hook landed on our deck, but it wasn't encased in metal the way that Admiral Agrippa's always were, and the sailors quickly cut the line.

"Majesty, we're going to be taken," Memnon said, grimly drawing his blade. "But it will cost them dearly."

No. We weren't going to be *taken*. I'd been *taken* from Egypt and *taken* by the emperor, but I would never be *taken* again. I cursed myself for being too proud to learn from Euphronius. Holding Isidora in one arm, it was instinct alone that made me raise my free hand, palm toward our outstretched sail. "In the name of Isis," I chanted, drawing from the well of *heka* inside me, and the magic leapt to my command. In Egypt, my goddess is painted with colored wings. She's Isis, she's Hathor, she's Ma'at. Now, like a bird in flight, I heard her flapping wings as a dry gust of air swirled over the birthmark on my arm, then blew clean from my fingertips. Up, up into the sky it went. I tasted sand on my tongue and the scents of the desert filled my nostrils. I'd swallowed the sirocco and now breathed some of it out again, careful not to let it ravage me or topple our craft.

The winds coalesced above us, and I released the *heka* at their core, willing them to blow into our sail. The ship rocked forward with sudden force and I clutched Isidora, who wailed in fear. I wanted to hush her, to tell her that my winds would carry us to safety, but with my hair whipping round my face I could barely hear my own thoughts. Then a *huzzah* went up from everyone as we broke away from the pirate pack, our sail full.

The distance between us and the pirates opened to a wide expanse of ocean. But I was in a fury that these men put us in danger. There was more wind inside me. There was a whole storm. If I could use it to speed our ship over these waters, surely I could use it to swamp the pirate ships and send them to the bottom of the sea. I summoned another breath, the smoky grit of wrath inside my mouth. "Majesty," Tala said, her eyes narrowed. "We're away now . . . we're away."

She was right. I didn't have to harm the pirates; I just *wanted* to. I trembled with the effort to restrain myself, but Isis had given me this power. I couldn't dishonor her by using it in vengeance. There'd be justice for these pirates, I told myself. In this life or the next.

When I lowered my arm, one of the sailors said, "*Sweet Isis*, it was the queen that saved us!"

"*Sorceress,*" someone else muttered in fear.

The Alexandrians aboard rejoiced in it. "Yes. Sorceress! She's the Sorceress of the Nile. Cleopatra Selene is the New Isis!"

Seventeen

WE docked in Ostia in the morning and sent a rider ahead of us. No sooner did we come ashore than we heard the gossip of the citizenry as they muttered blackly about the emperor's health. Mourners wailed at the foot of one of his statues, claiming that he'd perished. I saw in their faces a collective fear that the civil wars would begin again and Roman blood would flow. Memnon commandeered the first carriage for hire and we set off straight away down the Via Ostiensis. Unaware of the danger, my daughter was delighted by the jostling of the coach as we raced down the road under umbrella pines. She giggled while Tala hushed her son, Ziri, and worried at the blue creases of her hands. "I'll look so strange to them."

"You won't shock the Romans," I said absently. "The more exotic you are, the more prestigious you'll make me seem."

Meanwhile, my thoughts raced ahead of our carriage. What if the emperor really *was* dead? Would I grieve? *Should* I grieve? I pushed these thoughts away and tried to guess where the power would go. I'd be fortunate if Marcellus became the next great man in Rome with his wife, Julia, at his side. I might be restored to Egypt yet.

It was dark by the time we reached the gates of Rome, and as we made our way up the Palatine Hill, I felt my chest tighten. I'd never wanted to return, but here I was. The guards at the gate knew me, and the imperial family came flying out into the torch-lit night. I scarcely recognized Philadelphus. He was almost thirteen now, no longer the baby brother I'd left behind, but he threw his arms around me, crying, "Selene!"

I was so happy to see him, so eager to hold him against me, that I went weak in the knees. Julia was next to greet me, dressed in a fashionable gown and dripping with jewels. She was attended by a group of ladies, including Chryssa's sister, Phoebe, who scurried after her mistress to no avail. The emperor's daughter embraced me with such wild abandon that several curls escaped her complicated hairstyle and her bright yellow *palla* slipped from her slender shoulders to the ground.

"Oh, Julia," I said, reaching for her. "Is your father . . . is he . . . ?"

"He lives," she said, her eyes filled with tears. "But for how long? They say I'll be First Woman in Rome, and yet . . ." She suddenly laughed through her tears. "Just look at us. You still found a way to outshine me as a glamorous queen all covered in pearls. Let's see this daughter you've already managed to have for Juba."

Little Isidora emerged from the carriage to a chorus of gasps and sighs. "Oh, just look at your beautiful baby girl," Lady Octavia gushed, taking my child from Tala. I thought it might pain me to see my child in Octavia's fleshy arms, those same arms that had claimed my mother's children as her own. But my daughter would never know her true grandmother. Octavia was the closest thing. "Selene, she's as precious a child as anyone could ask for. Let's get her inside and out of the night air!"

In spite of the strange warmth of this homecoming, this wasn't a happy time in the imperial household. When we went inside, the slaves were huddled in corners, fear and uncertainty in their eyes. Livia was pale and distraught, her hair unkempt, and if I believed she was capable of shedding tears, I'd have sworn she'd been crying. "He's waiting for you, Selene."

It almost gratified me to see her like this, but even a humbled Livia unnerved me. "I'll call upon him in the morning."

"He may not have that long!" Livia snapped, and I was immediately brought back to the night she'd taken me to him. But there was no look of triumph on her face now. She'd been wrong about everything. She'd delivered me to her husband's bed, all to no advantage. If Augustus died now, she'd lose everything and it would serve her right.

"Please, Selene," Octavia said, her own expression grave. "My brother is so *very* ill. He's asking for you. You should go to him while the slaves unpack your belongings."

"We can't stay here," I said, regretting the way Octavia's face fell at my words. She'd missed me, that was plain, but I couldn't lodge in my old childhood room. "I have retainers and no king or queen may properly reside within the sacred boundaries of Rome. I'll take a house outside the *pomerium*."

This appeal to old Roman values softened the blow. Octavia nodded. "Of course. It's good of you to remember our laws."

"You taught me well," I replied, giving her hand a squeeze and hoping she understood that I was entrusting the safety of my daughter to her. I kissed Isidora's forehead, then, leaving my guards behind, I made my way to the emperor's rooms at the top of the stairs.

In the outer chamber, Admiral Agrippa sat with his big arms folded over his chest, jaw clenched, eyes focused somewhere far away. Marcellus was there too, and he brightened to see me, as if I'd alleviated some tension in the room.

Agrippa stood with stiff formality. "You had good speed on the seas, Selene. I was afraid you wouldn't make it . . ."

"Is he *really* that sick?" I asked, for it wasn't beyond Augustus to feign illness.

"Musa says he's suffering," Agrippa said mournfully. Antonius Musa was the emperor's physician, one of my father's freedmen, and the finest doctor in Rome. His word carried much weight and I heard myself sigh with pity. After all the emperor had done, didn't he *deserve* to suffer? And yet maybe calling me to his bedside was evidence of remorse. Of regret. Why else would he say that he wanted to make peace with me?

I found that I was trembling. Marcellus took this for a chill, and gallantly removed his cloak, spreading it on my shoulders.

"Selene, Musa says the time may be short. That's why Augustus called for us. You, me, Agrippa, and Piso."

"Piso?" I asked, confused. "His fellow consul this year?" That the emperor had a colleague under Roman law was only a fiction to protect him from the accusation that he was a tyrannical monarch in deed if not name. It surprised me that he made this pretense even now, on his deathbed.

Marcellus straightened. "I think Augustus is going to name me heir. He wants Piso to witness it."

Agrippa bristled. "You'd better hope not, boy! The emperor's enemies call themselves Republicans and spread word that he's setting up a dynasty for you to inherit. Isn't the memory of Julius Caesar's fate enough to frighten you?" I winced to hear Agrippa speak to Marcellus this way. Marcellus was only a young *aedile*, it was true, but the emperor's nephew had served in the legions already in Spain. He was no *boy* and he might well be the next ruler of Rome.

Musa stepped out of the emperor's chamber and gave a small bow. "Majesty, Augustus is ready to see you. Please go in."

THAT I floated through the doorway with an aura of calm was more of a testament to my skills of deception than my steady nerves. I'd practiced the way I'd walk into his room, the exact expression, bracing for anything.

"Cleopatra," the emperor wheezed, lifting his head. The features of his face had hollowed, but his gray eyes were manic. Was he seeing me now, or my mother? How was I to know? "I told them you'd come."

With difficulty, I hid my distaste for the putrid smell of the room and smiled. "How should I not come, when summoned by Caesar?"

"I'm dying, you know."

"We're all dying," I replied. "Or so the philosophers say."

A fit of coughing shook his frame. "It's the curse you put on me . . . it's killing me."

My hands began to sweat. "Isis cursed you, not I, and she didn't condemn you to an early death."

"Come closer," he whispered, crooking a finger at me. Oh, the strength it took to make my feet move toward that bed. I managed it, one foot after the other, reassuring myself that my body was filled with *heka*, and if I could fight pirates, I could fight him too. "By Apollo," he said when I was fully illuminated by his bedside lamp. "You are a veritable Cyrene. How fair you've become."

I kept my chin high. If he wanted to play at myths, I wouldn't stop him. Apollo had raped Cyrene, but he'd also made her a queen, and that's why I'd come. I'd come for Egypt. My mother's grandest passion and my daughter's birthright. He reached out a hand for mine. His palm felt like paper, and it was everything I could do not to flinch away. To feel his touch again, to be alone with him again, was a trial nearly beyond endurance.

"I wronged you," he rasped. "I want your forgiveness."

There were so many crimes the emperor had committed that I couldn't begin to list them all, much less find any forgiveness for him in my heart, so I asked, "Why should you want my forgiveness?"

He captured my gaze, his mouth working slowly. "I wasn't myself the night I forced you . . ."

He admitted it. Just like that. I hadn't ever expected to hear such a confession from him. It didn't change what had transpired between us, but my throat closed and my eyes dropped to the floor as I fought back tears. He'd told me to cry when he rutted above me, but he'd have no more tears from me unless they were artifice. If I must drive nails into my hands to teach myself to hold in my pain, then I'd do it. And if a glimmer of pity for him should rise up inside me at the memory of how Livia had dosed him, I'd shove it back again, knowing that I wasn't the first girl he forced in his bed.

"You've had your revenge now, haven't you, Selene?" He reached up with shaky fingers to brush my cheek. "You bore me a child, and yet how do I hear about your daughter? Not from you, no. From Juba." A surge of nausea rose in my throat at the thought that Juba committed such things to paper. Did he have no care for discretion? If his letters had been read by others, all the Roman world could be whispering that I was the emperor's lover! "Why do you keep her from me when I've always kept my promises to you?" I don't even think he knew he was lying. "I've treated Philadelphus kindly and I made you a queen."

"You also promised to spare Helios," I said bitterly. "Egypt too. Now Thebes is gone."

He groaned, a sound of disgust in his throat. "I punished Cornelius Gallus for that. You should be grateful to me instead of keeping a dying man from his own daughter."

"Isidora isn't your daughter," I hissed, wondering how I hadn't considered before that he might take her from me. The emperor had taken Julia away from *her* mother the day she was born. Was it possible he'd summoned me to rip my child from my arms? I'd die before I let that happen. Or kill. My eyes drifted to one of the many cushions on his bed. Sick as he was, weak with fever, how hard would it be to smother him?

He didn't seem to sense his peril. "Stop scheming, Selene. She *is* my daughter. Juba swears he hasn't touched you and you think too highly of yourself to surrender to an adulterous affair with some low-bred man. Admit it. I'm not long for this world, so you needn't fear me now."

I'd fear him until the last breath rattled from his chest. "You *cannot* have Isidora. You cannot even claim her."

"Of course not." He coughed again. "It would reflect poorly on my reputation, and as I see the end of my life near, I'm concerned with how I'll be remembered."

"Then be remembered for doing the decent thing! Restore Egypt as an independent nation."

Though he seemed too weak to do it, he managed to pull a hairpin from my coiffure. A dark curl fell over my shoulder. "You're the same ambitious girl you always were." I wanted to wrench away from him, but I'd just asked him to free Egypt and *he hadn't refused.* "You're fertile, just like your mother. You gave me a child. They tell me you even named a city after me."

"Iol-Caesaria," I confirmed, glancing up to meet his eyes.

He chuckled. "Clever girl. You've driven Herod mad. He's promised to name *two* cities after me, and now every petty king in the East thinks to do the same. Ah, think what we could've done together, *my Cleopatra*, but now my tomb is nearly finished and I won't live long."

"You've cheated death before."

He swallowed, his eyes closing. "I've never been so ill before. I haven't slept well since we parted. Until you give me your forgiveness, I shall not even sleep well in my tomb."

My forgiveness. Surely it must come with a price. "Then put me on the throne of Egypt and my daughter after me."

"*My* daughter," the emperor said. "I got a child on you and I'd like to see her before I die."

At this very moment, a shadow passed in the doorway and we both looked up to see Agrippa. I choked on air, the emperor stiffened, and Agrippa looked like a gladiator who had just apprehended a fatal wound—as if someone had plunged a dagger into his chest. I knew, without question, that he'd overheard the last few words, and my blood went to water. Agrippa's gaze slid over me, then back to the emperor, then back to me again. My hair was loose over one shoulder, my hand still in the emperor's grasp, and I couldn't seem to pull away. Agrippa cleared his throat. More than once. Then, slowly, he seemed to come into possession of himself. "Piso is here. I thought you'd want to know."

THE emperor loved theater and he was the world's greatest actor. I might have known that he wouldn't permit himself to die without an audience. We all crowded into his sickroom. Livia took a place beside the emperor's bed, her expression haunted. Julia was there too, clutching Marcellus's hand, though it broke all rules of propriety for a Roman husband and wife to cleave to one another. Then there was Agrippa, ramrod straight, his eyes cutting me with every glance.

None of us spoke, and in the tension it was difficult not to jump every time the fire sparked in the brazier. "Piso," the emperor said, breaking the silence. "You'll find my papers in order on my desk. They detail the finances of Rome and our military situation. I entrust them into your care and commend them to the Senate." Piso stammered, as if he'd never expected to have any official duties, and the emperor wheezed. "Contrary to the slander hurled against me, I don't fancy myself King of Rome, nor will I name a successor to the honors I've *earned* under Roman law."

Then Augustus held out his shaking hand where we could all see it and worked at pulling the golden signet ring from his finger. "This is the seal I've taken as my own. It stands as testimony to my authority."

We all stared at the glittering ring in his palm, the one etched with a sphinx, an apt symbol for the man who even now, in his last acts, was a riddle. Lady Octavia nudged her son forward to take the ring, but the emperor motioned to his most trusted soldier. "*Agrippa.* I'm leaving my seal to Marcus Vipsanius Agrippa. I want everyone here to witness that until I recover, or until the Senate chooses someone to replace me, Agrippa shall have my authority. Even my bitterest enemies must admit that he's qualified, experienced, and competent. I recommend that when I am dead, Rome choose him to rule in my stead."

We dared not speak, and yet the room seemed to erupt. There were sighs, sharp intakes of breath, and a hostile sound came from the emperor's sister. Marcellus shot his mother a warning look. Octavia's son wasn't such a crassly ambitious young man that he'd have demanded to know why he'd been passed over, yet the question still floated in the air. Agrippa took the ring, his expression unreadable, well-practiced stoicism.

The emperor glanced to his daughter. "I'm leaving my *personal* property to my son-in-law Marcellus and my daughter Julia. Let there be no more talk about how I mean to make a dynasty."

Oh, it was a masterful performance! If he died, he didn't want to be remembered for having tried and *failed* to make himself absolute ruler. Better that he pretend it was never his aim at all. Piso was entirely taken in. He clutched the papers against his chest and breathed with heavy emotion. "They're *jackals* who say you mean to make yourself King of Rome. They don't know what a great man you really are, Augustus. You've given us back the Republic. You've ended the civil wars. That's what you'll be remembered for."

My fingernails dug into my palms as I awaited the next pronouncement. My throat swelled with emotion as I willed him to speak of my fate. But though he'd summoned me from across the sea to attend this grand deathbed drama, he made no reference to me at all. "I'm tired," the emperor said. "I bid you all farewell."

The officials hurried for the door and his wife went with them. Livia wasn't one of the *Julii* and she'd given him no children. He'd made no provision for her or her sons, Tiberius and Drusus. He hadn't even encouraged that honors be voted for her after his death. In humiliation, she couldn't retreat swiftly enough. Only the emperor's sister and I were bold enough to stay.

"I don't understand," Octavia said to the emperor. "I thought we agreed that Marcellus—"

"I saved your son's life just now," Augustus said. "Do you think I got where I am because Julius Caesar announced I was the successor to his reign as dictator? No! He gave me all his money and I inherited the loyalty of his soldiers. I made *myself* the ruler of Rome, and so shall Marcellus."

That was all very fine and well for Marcellus, but what of me and my daughter? My mind reeled with a thousand schemes. It wasn't in me to give up. When Octavia stormed out of the room, I said, "Call them back. Call them back and ask them to witness that you're naming me Queen of Egypt!"

Augustus sighed. "Selene, didn't you hear what I just said about Marcellus? If I named you Queen of Egypt now, I might as well order your execution. If I were alive to support your bid, you might reclaim your throne. But without me? Egypt is too wealthy a province to surrender without a fight. If I cede it to you on my deathbed, the Senate would deny it or try to make war on you. You're not strong enough to hold Egypt. Not by yourself and not with Juba. Especially not when you've given me only a girl child."

Curse him. I wanted to shriek and throw things. With his final breaths, he was content to betray those he loved and those from whom he'd asked forgiveness. When I whirled for the door, he called after me. "Be content! You have Mauretania. I've done right by you, and you'll realize that one day. But if I ever wake up again, I want to see our daughter."

UPON leaving the emperor's chambers, I was overtaken on the stairs by the enormous shadow of Agrippa. As he stepped toward me, his eyes burned with dark emotion. "I've defended you," he said, voice low and filled with pain, as if he'd been the victim of treachery. "I sat idly by while Octavia took you to her breast as a daughter. I let you be a sister to my own wife. Even though I knew you for a witch, Marcella and I were *happy* when you became Queen of Mauretania. Now I see how blind I've been. You're a poison, like your mother. No, you're far worse! At least your mother never made any pretense about being a *virtuous* girl."

It'd been a long time since anyone had spoken to me this way and I bristled. "Just what have I done to deserve your insults? When I lived in this house, I offered only love and companionship to Octavia and Marcella."

"You offered a great deal more to the emperor, didn't you?" Agrippa's expression was all fury. "How could you have done it to him?" That's how it was with the men who loved Augustus. First Juba, now Agrippa. Neither of them would see that Augustus was a lecherous tyrant who abused *all* those in his care with neglect, casual cruelty, or betrayal. They refused to see the master they served as he was, so they saw him as a victim. *My* victim. "To take him to your bed," Agrippa growled low with disgust. "To seduce him while betrothed to Juba . . ."

"I didn't *seduce* him. Why don't you go back into his room and ask him? Be a man and not a loyal dog!"

The grizzled soldier's mouth fell open. "You want me to think that he attacked you?"

Why was it so hard to believe? "That's just what he did, but you won't ask him, will you?"

Agrippa looked back up the stairs as if considering it. Then the moment passed. "We all saw you at your wedding, Selene. If he—if he did such a thing—it would only be because you bewitched him. Just like your mother bewitched Caesar and then Antony. It had to have happened more than once for him to get a bastard whelp on you."

I hadn't hated Agrippa for a long time, not even though he'd made possible every bad thing that had ever happened to me. This, however, was a step too far. "Never call my daughter that again." As if seeing a vengeful flash of *heka* in my eyes, Agrippa actually took a step back. Still, I was keenly aware of the emperor's signet ring on Agrippa's finger and knew this balance of power wouldn't last. By morning, Agrippa would be the most powerful man in Rome. Then who would challenge him? Oh, the patricians would back Marcellus against a new man like Agrippa, but I couldn't know who would win that power struggle or what it would mean for my future. Agrippa wasn't the kind of man I wanted for an enemy, so I moderated my tone. "Agrippa, I know disillusionment, so I won't hold your words against you. But whatever you heard, whatever you *think* you know about my daughter, you must never repeat."

"Repeat it?" He looked at me as if beholding a lunatic. "To my dying breath, I'd deny that I heard Augustus claim your child! Thank Jupiter it's a girl, or we'd have another Caesarion to deal with all over again. Whatever he promised you about Egypt, I'll use this signet ring to make sure it doesn't happen. If you expect him to play Caesar to your Cleopatra, put it out of your mind, because tomorrow he'll be dead."

Eighteen

BUT the emperor didn't die. Not the next day or the day after that. Augustus lingered in some place between life and death, neither fully awake nor fully asleep, gasping so shallowly that it seemed as if all Rome held its breath to listen. Beneath the window to his sickroom, Livia sat in the courtyard, her eyes vacant, like a hunted animal unsure of what move to make next. I felt the same way. With the emperor would perish my hopes of winning back Egypt, unless Rome fell into complete chaos—which even I couldn't hope for. My mind spun wildly as I tried to fasten upon a plan . . .

I wanted to side with Marcellus, but there wasn't a ruthless bone in his body. Octavia's good-natured son couldn't stand against Agrippa without that signet ring. Even if he did, it would mean another civil war. Perhaps with Rome at war with itself again, the Parthians would seize the opportunity to expand their empire at Egypt's expense. I couldn't let that happen.

Agrippa had complained about Republican factions in Rome. Those were likely my father's old partisans. The emperor liked to claim that Antony and Cleopatra would have destroyed the Republic to rule as monarchs, but during the civil war, half the Senate—including the staunchest Republicans—had fled to my father's side. They'd feared the young Caesar was the greater threat and they'd been right. Maybe some of those same senators had survived the wars. Maybe one of them would come to power, someone who would favor my claim to rule my mother's kingdom. But who? Pacing back and forth beneath the columns holding up the emperor's house, I came full circle to the very same realization I'd made as a girl. Augustus was my enemy, but he was also my savior. He'd taken my birthright away from me and was the only one who could give it back. I *needed* him. I needed him to live. I needed him alive and indebted to me. For the love of Isis, I needed to find some way to forgive him, at least long enough to nurse him back to health!

Stiffening my resolve with a cup of unwatered wine, I called for a slave to find a *kithara* and climbed the stairs to the emperor's rooms. Musa hovered by the door, tight-lipped and nervous. "I give him cold baths to keep his fever down. He has lucid moments, but he's frail. Nothing else can be done."

"I'll try to soothe him." I took the cushioned stool and positioned the *kithara* on my knees. Dampening the unwanted notes with the palm of my left hand, I used my other hand to pluck at the strings with a little wooden pick. I thought of Mauretania and the unusual melodies I heard in the streets there, until I found myself making music. Augustus opened his eyes, murmuring, "Now she comes to me as Sappho serenading Apollo in his darkened cave . . ."

"Is that what you want?" I smiled softly. "To see Sappho in the afterlife?"

"I won't see anything," he croaked. "I don't hold with that mummery about the Elysian Fields. When I close my eyes the last time, there'll be only blackness. Death is the end of all things."

He said it boldly, but I could see that he was afraid. After all the lives he'd snuffed out, now he was afraid for his own. Somehow Isis allowed me to feel compassion. "My goddess promises salvation. To venerate her is to find our way to the afterlife, reunited with all those we've loved, reunited with the parts of ourselves that we've left behind. In the Nile of Eternity, we live forever. This is why it's so wrong of you to deny the people Isis. Why it's wrong to close her temples and deprive people of the faith that sustains them through this life and into the next."

His dry lips cracked into a near smile. "I'm dying and you torment me like a harpy. You defy me as well. I told you that I want to see our daughter before I die."

I stopped myself from shuddering. "And you *will* see her, for I believe you'll live a long while yet."

Lifting a trembling hand to point in my direction, he said, "More the fool, you. If you were wise, you'd give me your forgiveness and hurry back to Mauretania before the vultures pick over my corpse. Rome isn't a safe place for royalty."

As always, he tested me. "You're not dying and I'm going to stay until you're well."

"If I weren't dying, I wouldn't feel so wretched."

"To make the bread, the wheat must first suffer beneath the sickle. Maybe you feel so wretched because you're becoming something new."

He turned his head, gray eyes meeting mine. "What new thing would you have me become?"

Hope stirred in my breast that even someone like the emperor could change. "I'd have you become a more just and merciful ruler. A man who would rather be remembered for securing the peace than for triumphing over his enemies."

"Ah, Selene," he said. "You're still so pitifully young."

LEAVING the emperor's sickroom, I came upon Philadelphus throwing dice in the courtyard so that Bast could scamper after them. "Oh, Bast!" I cried, stopping to stroke her and scratch behind her ears. It was the first time I'd seen our cat since my return and the first moment Philadelphus and I had been alone. It was an opportunity, at last, to speak without censure or spies. I went to my knees beside him, wrapping my arms around his shoulders. "I've seen him," I whispered. "He's alive, Philadelphus."

My little brother looked over his shoulder at the house, where I'd left the emperor wheezing upon his bed. "He's sicker than before, but he's always managed to claw his way back to health. If I see truly, I think he'll do it again this time."

"Not *him*," I said, shocked both at my brother's prediction and that he'd mistaken my words. "I speak of my twin."

Philadelphus slowly lifted his eyes to mine, his slim shoulders tensing, his mouth forming words of grief and denial that his voice wouldn't sound. Then he leaned closer, as if afraid to even whisper my twin's name. "You've seen Helios? Alive?"

I smiled over the sob in my throat. "Yes. Oh, yes. I thought you'd know it because of your sight. I wanted to tell you before now, but I couldn't think of a way."

Bewilderment clouded his eyes. "But I thought . . . in the Rivers of Time, I so often saw him dead . . ."

I gave him a little shake. If he denied it the way Euphronius denied it, I'd go mad. "Helios came to me in Mauretania in an ancient temple. I felt his touch as real as you feel mine now."

"He came to you. He found you . . ." Philadelphus's eyes glistened, and then he smiled as if it suddenly made sense. "I suppose that he would."

I didn't have to tell him that no one else must know. He'd lived too long in this Roman court of intrigue not to know how to keep secrets. "Now he calls himself Horus the Avenger."

Philadelphus smiled wider, as if overawed. "Just as they named him at our mother's funeral." His smile turned to that characteristic roguish grin. "If he's become Horus, and you're the New Isis, what does that leave for me? Surely, I must be a god too."

It made me laugh. "We Ptolemies are never humble, are we?"

I played the *kithara* again for Augustus the next day. Musa had propped him up in a chair so that his feet could soak in a wooden tub of seawater. Beneath the cold poultice on his forehead, the emperor's complexion was ashen, as if his illness were burning some part of him away; I hoped it was the cruelest part. "I'm so weary of baths," Augustus said irascibly, pointing an accusing finger at Musa. "He made me soak in cold waters at Baiae until I couldn't bear it. 'Just let me die in Rome,' I told him. Still he leaves me wet and shivering."

"We'll have the slaves carry you back to your warm bed soon enough," the long-suffering physician replied, leaning over the emperor to put an ear to his chest. "Or would you be more comfortable at the home of Maecenas?"

"It's too late for comfort," the emperor wheezed, and then his eyes fell on me. "Physicians are torturers, you know. I'm told you have one at your court in Mauretania. This Euphorbus, who hails from Alexandria. What are his credentials, Selene?"

My fingers stilled on the harp, the music dying away. The emperor's question seemed casually posed, but his gaze was intent. It was a potent reminder that even now, even so near to death, he was a danger. He'd been spying on me and I didn't know how much he'd learned; I had to spin a convincing lie without falling into a trap. My hesitation went on too long, and not wanting the emperor to see my rising panic, I averted my eyes.

It was Musa whose voice pierced the uncomfortable silence. "Euphorbus is my brother, Augustus. We parted when Lord Antony gave us our freedom, but everything he knows, he learned from me."

I stared at Musa in surprise, as the emperor was wracked with an interminable cough. He convulsed, one of his feet sloshing water on the floor, and Musa called for slaves to carry the emperor to his bed. They hurried in, taking the emperor by his pale arms and lifting him from the chair. "Come," Musa said to me. "He asked me not to let you see him like this."

I followed the physician on unsteady legs. We stopped in the corridor beneath the painted garlands, vibrant green on the wall, and I leaned back against the plaster. The question that burned in my throat went unspoken, but Musa must have seen it in my eyes. "I hope I didn't just make a terrible mistake, Majesty, but you seemed in need of my help."

My wariness still made me choose my words carefully. "Euphorbus is your brother?"

"No," Musa admitted. "But when I was in Alexandria with your father, I knew a Euphronius. He was a priest. A good man. Your tutor if I'm not mistaken . . ."

A hand to my cheek, I gaped at him. "Why would you take such a risk for me?"

"I've told you before that your father was a good master to me and that I was grateful to him for giving me my freedom. I'm a friend to you and your brothers, Majesty. You have many friends, though you may not know it. If ever I can help you, I will. As for risk, well, whatever we say in front of Augustus now may be denied and blamed upon the fever if he lives."

"If he lives," I whispered. "And he must live. He *must* live."

ONCE Augustus was abed, I returned to the sickroom, taking up my harp again. I thought the emperor had drifted to sleep, but he turned rheumy eyes my way and murmured, "The divine Julius had the falling sickness. He was afraid that anyone should know. Once, I saw him froth at the mouth like a dog, and I drew the curtains and let no one see."

Plucking a soft melody, I said, "He must have been grateful to you."

"I thought I was the only one who knew of his illness, Selene." He winced with pain. "But *Cleopatra* knew too. It was hinted at in your mother's letters, the personal ones that she kept and showed to me to soften my heart toward her. She tended Caesar whenever he fell, just as you're tending me now."

He was still trying to live another man's story, and here I was to complete the illusion. To see the hunger for me in his eyes was no less disturbing than it had ever been, but would my mother have flinched from it? She'd always done everything for Egypt and would expect the same from me. I gritted my teeth beneath a serene smile, knowing that I must stay by him and stoke this fantasy.

THE surest way to re-create the emperor's fantasy would have been to stay in my mother's old residence, the one she lived in as a guest of Julius Caesar. But if I were to relive my mother's life—if I were to succeed where she'd failed—my story must not end with *my* little girl delivering to me a deadly basket of figs. So I bought a house across the river with ample room for my courtiers and an excellent view of the boat-shaped Tiber Island, the center of which was adorned by an obelisk resembling a ship's mast. It was in my new house that my daughter first learned to walk, falling to her knees countless times upon the black and white tiled floor. When she cried, I'd take her to the terrace to watch young waterfowl test their wings while fishermen pulled in their nets.

My days were devoted to nursing the emperor, but entertaining consumed my evenings. My royal retinue was delighted to receive important guests and I was grateful for the tasteful entertainments of my poet and pretty Ecloga, my young mime. My house was a veritable embassy of Mauretania where Roman luminaries and foreign ambassadors came to call.

This house was, I realized, the first place in which I'd ever been my own mistress. It wasn't my mother's home, nor the emperor's, and though it paled beside my beautiful palace in Mauretania, I didn't even have to share this house with Juba. Not yet. I did write him a letter, apprising him of the emperor's health and beseeching him to empty our storehouses and send more grain as proof against the coming famine.

Juba didn't reply. I received word only from Euphronius: *The king cares nothing for matters of state. He ignores dispatches, doesn't meet with his council, and spends his time in the stables. Several Berber girls have been offered as concubines to comfort the king, but you've no cause to worry on that account as he refuses them, saying that he doesn't want to favor one tribe over the other. We should, however, fear the influence of a Greek* hetaera *who has come to court as a gift from Herod.*

Juba's disinterest in the coming famine disturbed me even more than the fact that my enemy was providing my husband with female companions. To my immense irritation, I could do nothing about *either* as long as I was obliged to stay at the emperor's side. One morning, as I prepared to make my daily pilgrimage up the

Palatine, Tala said, "It's shameful that you tend Augustus like a humble nursemaid. He doesn't need you there *every day.*"

She made a good point and not just because the emperor's health was improving. In spite of his drama with the signet ring, almost everyone still believed that he intended to rule Rome as a monarch. I feared they would blame his ambitions upon me and didn't wish to give rise to gossip that I hosted lavish feasts while the Romans went hungry. Nor did I want to be seen as closeting myself away from Rome's plainer citizens. I had my own reputation to protect, so I decided to take Philadelphus for a day at the races.

THE Circus Maximus was politically neutral. Patricians, plebeians, equites, freedmen, and slaves were all equally passionate about the races, and the enormous stadium was an excellent place to be seen. *How Roman he's become*, I thought as Philadelphus excitedly rattled off the names of the best charioteers. I couldn't help but be a little excited too.

Julia and Marcellus joined us at the arena, which turned my royal processional into an even grander thing, prompting trumpeters to announce our presence to the crowd. As we took our seats in the imperial box, the Romans cheered for the beautiful young married couple, and Marcellus glanced at the chair usually reserved for the emperor, laughing. "I could get used to this!" I must have looked appalled because Marcellus turned to Julia and said, "I see the sunny shores of Mauretania have done nothing to improve Selene's sense of humor."

"Don't taunt her," Julia said, waving to the crowd. "We'd hardly recognize Selene if she weren't fretting about *something!*"

"It's just that you shouldn't jest about taking the emperor's place," I said. "People might think that you wished him dead."

Below us, in the arena, charioteers rode into view, flying their colors. Red, white, blue, and green. Four matched white horses in golden harnesses trotted at the command of one of the circus stars, and from the crowd, rose petals fell like rain. The lash of a whip sent the stallions into a gallop and over the thunder of horse hooves, Julia said, "Don't be so *dramatic*, Selene. Of course we don't wish my father dead. Besides, everyone knows he's getting better. I sense that it's your doing, but they're going to erect a statue to Musa in the temple of Aesculapius for saving my father's life."

"Musa is a fine physician," I said. "I don't begrudge him."

Julia plucked grapes from a platter and wiggled her toes in her sandals. "Neither do we. Like I said, we don't wish my father dead, but he *will* die sometime, and when he does, Marcellus and I will change everything in Rome."

Philadelphus had been counting coins to make his bets, but this made him look up. "What will you change?"

Marcellus waved his hand with a carefree patrician air. "I'd pack up Livia's things and throw her out onto the street. What's more, I think she knows it!" Marcellus and Julia both laughed, but I worried that they were overly sure of themselves, grown wild and careless after a few months of relative freedom. Rome was filled with Livia's powerful Claudian family, and their clients numbered in the thousands. Some of them were probably in the stands even now. Such words, cast so casually about, could get back to her. "Tiberius and Drusus can stay," Marcellus added, motioning to a vendor who poured us some very fine wine. "Livia's sons may be Claudians, but they aren't *evil*."

"Tiberius is a boor," Julia told me. "The only one who ever seems to make him smile is Agrippa's daughter. If I thought Tiberius actually had a heart, I'd swear he was sweet on her." By *Agrippa's daughter* Julia meant Vipsania, of course, not little Marcellina, Agrippa's youngest, born to him by the emperor's niece. But someone outside the family might be forgiven the confusion. The Romans mocked my family for our brother-sister marriages, but they wound their own families almost as tightly. "Every young aristocrat in the city wants to entertain us," Julia continued. "We all go. Drusus, Minora, Philadelphus. Even Marcella and Antonia can sometimes be persuaded to abandon their dour old husbands for a good party. But Tiberius claims that he's too busy counting money in the treasury and advancing his career as *quaestor* to be out gallivanting with the smart set."

My, how things had changed since I'd been gone. "Your father lets you go to parties?"

Julia smirked. "I'm a married woman now. My father says it's my husband's burden to rule me."

"And I'm a tyrant over her," Marcellus reassured me with a wink. "When Julia misbehaves, I threaten to take her to Greece."

Julia sighed happily. "I *so* want to go to Greece and Egypt and Spain and everywhere! But mostly Greece. My friends tell me about the Mysteries at Eleusis. Some of them have been initiated and they had visions. Even those who believe in *your* goddess take part."

"Isis isn't only my goddess," I said. "She's all goddesses."

"How very convenient!" Julia laughed then clutched my hands to soften the sting of her mockery. "We should do it together, Selene. Go to Athens and take part in the Mysteries. You can work your magic. The kind with the wind, though, not the bloody hieroglyphics. That always ruins your gowns."

"Julia," I began, exasperation all too evident in my voice. "You're—"

"A wicked, shallow girl," she finished. "Yes, I know. Livia tells me all the time. You love me anyway!"

I did love her and somehow knew, even then, that this time with my loved ones was precious.

Philadelphus placed his bets on the blues. I bet on the greens because the horses were Barbary steeds, bred in Mauretania. "You're going to lose your money," Marcellus told me. "If Philadelphus bets on blue, we all do. He has a knack for gambling. He beats Augustus at dice all the time."

Was Philadelphus so foolish as to use his powers of sight for sport? My littlest brother didn't seem to notice my glare, and then the horses were off. While the chariots roared around the treacherous circuit below, Iullus and some of his friends dashed up the stairs to join us. Like Marcellus and Tiberius, Iullus had also started upon the so-called *cursus honorum* in which young Roman men took on a succession of public offices with the intention of reaching the pinnacle of power. I knew he was campaigning for office and had wondered how he afforded it. Seeing the way Julia greeted him with a kiss upon both cheeks, I wondered no more. Iullus smiled at Julia, eyes smoldering, and she turned pink from head to toe. If her husband hadn't been seated between them, so untroubled, all of Rome would have known they were lovers. "Iullus Antonius," Marcellus said, raising a cup. "We've chosen the wrong profession, campaigning for office like common drudges. If we took up racing, we'd be able to hire our own armies. Have you heard the absurd sums charioteers take home?"

"Only if they live to collect their prize money," Iullus replied. The two young men laughed together and I realized how comfortable they were with their arrangement. Though I tried to fight it, I envied them. It had been here, in this very arena, where Helios had won the crowd's adulation in the Trojan Games by rescuing Drusus from being trampled. That was the very same day the emperor tried to give him a new name, the day that Helios ran away . . . now I despaired of ever seeing him again.

"HOW can you waste your gift on gambling?" I cried.

Seated by my hearth with Bast purring contentedly in his lap, Philadelphus only shrugged. "Should I use my sight to help Augustus plan his war on Parthia? At least gambling doesn't hurt anyone."

I shouldn't chastise him. He was only doing as I'd commanded him. Finding a way to survive in this Roman world. Though he would soon don the *toga virilis* of manhood, Philadelphus had managed not to draw too much notice to himself as one of the children in the emperor's household. His relative obscurity might protect him. Even so, I couldn't help but wonder what I might do if I had his gifts. "I wish I could see into the Rivers of Time . . ."

Now he looked very grave. "You wouldn't like it. I see horrible things, like starving people . . ."

Juba and I had been sent to Mauretania to stave off famine, but it was coming anyway. "It's a late harvest in Mauretania. I worry that the next shipments of grain won't be ready before the sea closes. To get more, Juba will have to coerce ship captains into risking the winter journey and some won't go at any price."

"Write him a letter," Philadelphus suggested. "With Augustus so ill, maybe no one has."

"I have! Juba doesn't reply."

Philadelphus glanced at me, alarmed by my distress. "Is he a bad king? A bad husband?"

I told only the plain truth. "He's well intentioned, but I fear neither kingship nor marriage has turned out the way he expected . . ."

"Is it what you expected? To hear some tell it, Mauretania is an unforgiving land filled with howling savages."

"Oh no. Mauretania is beautiful. The sea is so blue, and the harbor looks like the gods created it to be Alexandria in miniature. In the market people speak a thousand tongues. Desert merchants on camels bargain with wealthy shipping magnates. Bankers and financiers shop alongside silversmiths and stoneworkers and slaves. One day, I'll take you into the wheat fields where the farmers drive oxen behind their plows. I can't wait for you to see it all."

"I *can* see it," Philadelphus whispered.

"With your *eyes*. I want to take you there."

"I always stay in Rome, Selene."

He'd said that before, when he was ill. I liked hearing it even less now. "You don't know that. You've said yourself that the Rivers of Time can shift course."

"I don't mind," he said. "Our family is in Rome."

Philadelphus had lived fully half his life in Rome and our half sisters had become his siblings in truth. It broke my heart that he should forget what brought us here, but he was young. Perhaps it was a blessing for him to forget what I never could. I knelt beside him. "Philadelphus, when you look into the Rivers of Time, does the emperor make me Queen of Egypt?"

"Sometimes."

Sometimes. A frustrating answer. "When you see me become Queen of Egypt, *how* does it happen?"

He closed his eyes. "Augustus opens an engraved box of silver and gold, bearing the Ptolemy Eagle, then places our mother's diadem on your brow and her scepter in your trembling hands."

It was a tantalizing image, one that seared itself into my soul like destiny. "How? What leads to that moment?"

Philadelphus flinched and his eyes flew open. "You don't need to know."

"Tell me."

"No." Suddenly, he leapt to his feet, making ready to leave. "Telling you won't help make you queen. I've never seen it happen because I told you anything!"

What had happened to the pliant boy I'd left behind? I had to take him by both arms to make him stay. That's when I realized he was shaking. "You're upset."

"I don't want to talk about my sight," Philadelphus said.

"All right," I said, eager to calm him.

"I don't want to talk about it, Selene. We don't have much time together. We have to talk about something else. Ask me about the chariot races, or let me tell you how I bested Drusus in the gymnasium, but you mustn't ask me what comes next, because I won't answer and I can't bear it."

Nineteen

❧

IT'D been another hot summer, tempers on edge, and not enough food. Riots weren't uncommon in Rome, but the increase in gang fighting and public unrest worried me. I sent letters to Euphronius, commanding him to find some way of sending more grain, no matter what the risk, no matter what the cost. Bribes. Magic. It didn't matter. We needed more grain.

When the emperor was well enough to get out of bed, I could put off a dreaded task no longer. Carrying Isidora in my arms, I knocked softly on the door to his study. "Leave the door open for a breeze," Augustus said, rising gingerly from his couch. "I'm still feverish, but I think Virgil will have no cause to write mournful funeral poetry on my account."

"I'm glad." He searched my face for a lie, but he wouldn't find a trace. I needed him to live, at least until he made me Queen of Egypt. "Caesar, this is my daughter." There are no words to explain how difficult it was for me to close the distance between us, bringing my child near enough that he could touch her.

"Is she ill tempered?" he asked, taking her from my arms. "Julia was a very disagreeable child." I didn't answer him, ready to snatch her back at the slightest provocation. He stared at her little face and said, "She's a Ptolemy, that's certain."

It was then that Agrippa happened by and went pale at the sight of my baby kicking her little feet while Augustus held her aloft. "You should be abed, Caesar, not entertaining the queen."

"The queen is entertaining *me*," Augustus said, returning Isidora to my arms. "She's been at my bedside nearly every day."

"Touching," Agrippa said, flatly. "Now that you've recovered, perhaps she can return to Mauretania and help Juba with the task we've set for him. We need grain. Between the mess in Egypt and the imbeciles administering the dole, famine is inevitable. We'd best prepare for it."

I seized my opportunity. "If I were Queen of Egypt, you'd never want for grain."

Agrippa exploded. "How much further will you two play out this farce! What next, Caesar? Will you don red boots and a laurel-leaf crown and cruise down the Nile with her?"

This open insubordination shocked me but shocked the emperor more. "*Remember* yourself, Agrippa."

The admiral worked his square jaw. "I remember that when Rome believed you were dying, they turned to me."

The emperor all but hissed with fury. "Remember also, that you'd be nothing without me."

In truth, the emperor would be nothing without Agrippa. He'd have gone down in defeat at Actium, and my parents would now rule the world. Neither man seemed to realize it. Agrippa dropped his eyes, one meaty hand outstretched in a plea. "Caesar, there are those who plot your death even now. If you even entertain the idea of giving Egypt to Selene, it will inflame your enemies. Make Petronius the Prefect of Egypt. He's a military strategist. He'll crush rebellion and ensure the grain supply."

My mouth went dry when the emperor asked, "And if I don't? If I entertain the idea of giving Egypt to Selene?"

"By the gods!" Agrippa choked, his accusatory glance falling upon me. "She's bewitched you. First Caesar, then Antony. I won't watch it happen to you too." With that, he pried the signet ring from his finger and winged it to the floor near the emperor's feet. That done, the big soldier turned and stomped away, his boots thundering in the hall.

This was disaster. With Isidora in my arms, I gave no thought to my royal dignity but chased after Rome's most fearsome general, my sandals slapping against the tile floor as I hurried. "Agrippa!" I caught up with him on the landing, where a statue of Apollo watched down on us from behind a potted plant. "What do you intend to do?"

He was a simmering pot ready to over boil. "I'm leaving Rome."

It was the last thing I thought he might say. "Wh-where will you go?"

"*East,*" he snapped. "You're every inch your mother's daughter, so I can predict your moves before you make them. You'll try to contact old allies, drum up support for your return to Egypt. Money for bribes, soldiers for your cause. Just know that I'll be there to see that your ambitions are thwarted."

"WELL, good riddance to Agrippa," Julia said as we made our way into the city, rows of Nubian slaves carrying our covered litter. The four of us were often together—Julia, Marcellus, Philadelphus, and me. We traveled everywhere with a large contingent of my courtiers and Julia's new friends. Some of them, like the poet Ovid, were up-and-coming artists, eager for patronage. Others were young patricians who made a competition of outspending one another with entertainments. In their company, Julia had blossomed from a neglected little girl into a vibrant center of attention. She had the glow of a young woman in love and whenever circumstances permitted, she and Iullus met secretly for their trysts. Marcellus cheerfully made excuses for them. In truth, Julia's false marriage seemed a good deal happier than my own, so I set aside my misgivings and enjoyed spending time with friends my own age and the children of my youth.

In the litter, Julia leaned back against her husband and said, "I wonder why Agrippa really left." I knew *exactly* why Agrippa had fled the city, but some secrets were too dangerous to share, even with those I loved. Julia continued, "Marcellus, your sister says that her husband, our good admiral, was in a fit of pique. That he had some falling out with my father."

Marcellus yawned. His face was shadowed and he looked tired. I guessed he'd spent one too many late nights carousing with Virgil, or perhaps he'd been working too hard, trying to impress Augustus. "Who knows what goes on in Agrippa's iron heart. My sister certainly doesn't. As for me, I've no time to pay attention to Agrippa now that the emperor has appointed me to the College of Pontiffs; I'm too busy obeying his commands to chase down and destroy scraps of paper with false prophecies about saviors and sun gods."

Philadelphus and I exchanged a secret glance at the knowledge that even now, the emperor still feared Isiac beliefs. Julia pressed her painted red lips together in thought. "I think Agrippa doesn't approve of my father's theatrics. Have you heard, Selene? My father has given up his consular powers and says he intends to restore the Republic."

Everyone had heard, but Philadelphus said, "Don't believe it." I lifted my eyes to his in warning. But he was right. Even half dead, Augustus had consolidated his power while silencing his enemies. They all accused him of choosing Marcellus to succeed him, so he gave Agrippa his signet ring. He offered to have his Last Will read in the Senate to prove that he'd not given Marcellus anything that wasn't his to give. Now he was orchestrating a bit of stagecraft that would humble the finest playwright in Rome: He'd announced that he wished to become a private citizen.

Marcellus smirked, his eyes still drowsy. "Augustus knows how to put on a good show. It wasn't enough simply to resign the post. Like some musty old forefather, he had to go all the way to the Alban Mount to lay down his office. Do you know he chose Sestius to replace him!"

"You think his resignation is only a performance?" one of Julia's new admirers asked. "It seemed real enough. Sestius is an avowed Republican. Why would Augustus elevate his worst critic unless he meant to give up power?"

Newcomers were so naive about the emperor. I found myself explaining, "He's only given up the consulship. In exchange, he accepted some form of tribunician powers for life." What I didn't say is that he'd made a *pretense* of giving power back to the people, all while gathering new and unorthodox powers. And I couldn't find it within myself to be sorry about it either. It wasn't for the good of Rome, after all, that I'd sat by his bedside, willing the tyrant back to health.

Julia tapped to make the litter bearers set us down. We wanted to walk the rest of the way to the site of the new theater Marcellus was building, but as soon as we climbed out we were mobbed by hungry citizens, begging for food. With the surge of the crowd, Marcellus stumbled. It seemed at first that he'd merely caught his sandal on a stone, but when Julia tried to steady him Marcellus slipped through her hands, drenched in sweat, his eyes glassy. He managed to find his footing and gave a dazzling smile to our entire retinue as if it were all of no consequence.

Then he collapsed.

THE first day, Marcellus burned with fever, quaked with chills, and ended the night in a sweat-soaked bed. By morning, he rallied and summoned Virgil to read to him. But within two days, the cycle started again, this time with headaches that made him groan. Julia stayed with Marcellus as if she were his true wife, tending to him even when he vomited, proving what I'd always known—that her compassion was greater than her vanity.

How swiftly fate turns. When the emperor lay dying, it'd been Livia who haunted the halls, fearful. Now, as summer faded into autumn, it was Octavia who became a shadow of herself, hovering near her son's bed as if she could will him back to health. The Antonias beseeched her to sleep, but she sent them away with angry words. I braved her wrath with a platter of fruit and urged her to eat. "Don't be kind to me right now, Selene," she said. "It galls me."

She was thinking that her son was dying and that as Cleopatra's daughter I ought to take pleasure in it. I didn't. This fever was no divine retribution. Marcellus had nothing to do with the tragedies of my family. He was a beautiful young man, intelligent and good-humored. He was my friend. He was an innocent, and in some ways, so was Octavia. Sitting beside her, I said, "I understand. Your kindness has always been difficult for me to accept, but somehow we both must bear it."

"Oh, my girl." She reached for me, her calloused fingers lacing with mine. Her hands had once seemed stronger than Agrippa's, but now they shook with human frailty and fear. "My other daughters have never known real suffering. But you know. You can tell me. If I made sacrifices to your goddess, would she save my son? Will you ask her to do so?"

"I will," I promised, and that night I burned sage and poured a libation to Isis, asking her to spare the emperor's heir.

Marcellus got no better. Musa feared the air in Rome and suggested that we go to the resort town of Baiae. Thus the imperial family made ready to travel but I was overcome with a feeling of foreboding. I thought to stay in Rome, but Philadelphus said, "You have to come with us. Octavia needs us and I need you!"

So we all went to Baiae. Virgil owned a house near Lake Avernus and opened it for me and the rest of our entourage. The emperor's poet was himself never overly fond of company, but his fondness for Marcellus was never more evident. He would do anything to restore the young man's health. At dusk, before our procession could bed down beneath the shadow of Mount Vesuvius where the air smelled of sulfur and the ground itself was warm, Musa insisted that Marcellus must swim in Lake Avernus. The evening air was frigid, and I was tired from the journey. Even Philadelphus complained of aches and pains resulting from our bumpy carriage ride. He was all out of sorts.

But Marcellus was wild with fever and wouldn't be persuaded to go out into the lake unless we all went. As Bast prowled the shoreline, stalking fallen leaves, Philadelphus shivered beneath his cloak. "Hold my hand, Selene."

He was nearly a man grown now and usually shrugged away from my affection in embarrassment, but now he clutched my hand like a small child. "It's peaceful here," he said, staring at the surface of the water, his eyelids half lowered. But when I looked into the sky and saw its royal purple mantle darken the moon, I feared that the gods were readying a kingly cloak for a dying prince.

"Just a little moonlight swim," Lady Octavia said to encourage Marcellus. Her voice was strung tight with fear. She'd poured all the hopes of her life into her son and if she lost him, I knew it would break her. Still, Marcellus was young and vigorous. The emperor's health had never been robust, yet *he* survived this fever. Surely it would pass over Marcellus too.

"Come now," the emperor said to Marcellus, and began to strip off his clothes. "I'll go in too." I turned my head to dislodge the memories that the emperor's pale torso aroused in me but admired the way he encouraged his nephew by saying, "If I can bear it, you can too. You're a strong Roman boy. It's just a bit of cold water."

While Augustus waded into the lake, Philadelphus let go of my hand and shrugged out of his own clothes. "I'll go with you, Marcellus," he said. I took my brother's cloak, wrapping it over my arm, smiling to find a bag of dates tucked inside it, as Philadelphus braced himself against the cold water, his hand on his amulet as if to give him strength. Then he splashed up to his knees. "It's not so terrible. We can do this together."

At this, Marcellus finally consented, though the physician had to help him into the water, and I felt an unnatural shiver down my spine. While everyone else watched Marcellus, my eyes skimmed over the water to where Philadelphus swam. He looked at me, our eyes locked, then he dipped below the surface. He reemerged a moment later, gasping, then disappeared again. Clutching his clothing, I cried out for him. "Philadelphus!" I called his name again, but all I saw was the surface of the lake. Unreadable black ink.

No, no. My goddess couldn't let my little brother drown! I shouted again, and the emperor hastened to my call. He didn't wait for the guards but swam to where Philadelphus had been. I dropped the garments in my arms and threw off my own cloak, ready to dive into the water myself, when the emperor fished Philadelphus from the depths. Rushing to shore, Augustus carried my brother in his arms. Philadelphus was wet and unmoving, and I died inside to see his foot trailing limply.

"He's breathing," the emperor said, spitting water to the ground, and yet again gratitude made me sink to my knees before him.

I cornered Musa outside the room in which my little brother shivered. "What's wrong with him? He didn't drown. Why hasn't he recovered?"

"I don't think it was the water, Majesty. It's an illness. A fever."

"Or poison." I said aloud that which everyone else was whispering. The emperor's illness had pushed Livia to the edge of desperation. She didn't want to be left at the mercy of those who despised her, so it made sense to strike at Marcellus. But why my poor Philadelphus? Musa stared up at the Doric columns as if their scrolled caps contained the secret to the mystery, but he made no answer. "Maybe the sweet wormwood will help," I suggested. "It helped Philadelphus before!"

Musa bit his lip. "Your brother is much sicker this time. I've felt his spleen and it's swollen—"

"Musa, if you ever loved my father, I call upon your loyalty now. You must heal Philadelphus. You must make him better."

Emotion bobbed at the physician's throat. "My dearest Majesty, Philadelphus is a stouthearted boy and I have much affection for him. He never complains. He never has a harsh word for anyone. He has your father's charm and if there were more that I could do, I'd have done it without your needing to ask. Sit with him. Hearing your voice may help him where medicine cannot."

Later, when Philadelphus and I were alone together in his room, he murmured. "I told you, I stay in Rome."

"Stop saying that! We're not even in Rome now. We're on the Bay of Naples. Can't you smell the sea?"

"I'm dying, Selene," Philadelphus rasped. "I've seen it in the Rivers of Time . . ."

That stilled my heart. "Whatever you've seen can be changed."

"Do you remember our mother's funeral? You were dressed as Isis, Helios as Horus, and I was Osiris."

Osiris, the dead god. I shook my head, vehemently. "You'll outlive me."

"I've never seen it happen that way, Selene. You're the last of us."

This couldn't be happening. I wouldn't let it happen. They all said the emperor would die, but I'd willed him back to health and I'd make Philadelphus better too, somehow. "Not the last," I said, a meaningful look passing between us in which we acknowledged the brother whose name we couldn't say. "And there's Isidora."

He shivered but smiled at the mention of her name. Since the day our mother died, Philadelphus had never been without his shining Collar of Gold amulet. Now he removed it from his neck and held it out for me to take. "Give this to your daughter. You may be tempted to give it to the son you'll bear, but it's meant for her . . ."

I stumbled back. "No. You keep it. It's yours. You'll need it."

Despite his entreaties, I left the gold chain coiled around his fist like a viper. I took it only hours later, when seizures wracked his frame, and it dropped from his hand to the floor. He didn't cry out—not like Marcellus, whose howls echoed through the halls. Philadelphus, my precious little brother, only whispered, *"Isis."*

He died in the depths of the night when the sky was as black as the soil of Egypt. I was with him, clutching his amulet, breathing with him until he breathed no more. I thought I'd cry or sob. Anything to break the unnatural quiet. Instead, I sat stunned, crushed beneath a pain too large to contemplate. How could it be that my Philadelphus would never see another dawn? Somehow I made myself get up. I'd go to Octavia. She'd tell me that Philadelphus was only sleeping. She'd chide me like she did when I was a girl and set the world back to its natural order. But when I stepped into the hallway, I was assaulted by a keening wail.

"Marcellus!" Octavia stumbled out, tearing at her clothes as if some creature were eating her alive. "My boy is dead, my son is dead, my son is dead!"

Twenty

FRESH timber was cut for the enormous funeral pyre and it seemed as if all the city came out into the damp and somber cold to see Marcellus burned. It was a grand state funeral. Augustus himself gave the eulogy. Virgil, grief-stricken and shattered, read a section of his unfinished *Aeneid*, in which the great Roman hero saw the shade of Marcellus in the underworld, lamenting that he was destined to die young, without fulfilling his promise. At hearing this, Lady Octavia collapsed. She'd borne all the other calamities of her life with grace, but this was too much. What's more, the public spectacle of her grief shamed her such that she never allowed another poet to speak her son's name.

Augustus pronounced that he'd finish the theater of Marcellus. Whether this was because the emperor genuinely mourned or because it was the politic thing to do, I'd never know. Those Republicans who'd seen Marcellus as a champion of their cause wondered whether the emperor had poisoned his son-in-law to keep his own power secure. Those who'd seen Marcellus as a threat to Republicanism insisted Livia must have poisoned him to make room for her own sons. Still others gossiped about the conspicuous absence of Admiral Agrippa. The celebrated military commander didn't return for the funeral of his brother-in-law. Not even for the sake of his wife, Marcella, a grieving sister. Not even, I thought, for Octavia, a grieving mother, the woman he loved.

This wasn't because Agrippa was a cruel man but because all his fundamental beliefs, all the ropes that tied him so tight inside, had begun to fray the moment he heard the emperor say that he'd fathered my child. It was somehow my fault, I thought. All my fault. And in all this sorrow of great personages, all this speculation and jockeying for position in the new political landscape, the death of Antony's boy—young Ptolemy Philadelphus—was entirely overshadowed. It was only the smaller people who seemed to remember him. The slaves, the priests, the Alexandrians, and the friends of my parents who'd long since been driven out of public life.

And the Antonias, of course. Both my half sisters came to help me prepare his body, but I'd let no one else touch him. I brushed a ringlet of auburn hair back from my little brother's dead face, knowing that I'd never see a flush upon those once-rosy cheeks again. He was in danger from the moment he was born, a living token of my father's break from Rome. He'd been born a prince of Egypt and made a crowned king, but he'd never dwelled upon that. He'd been a thirteen-year-old boy whose greatest joy had been betting on chariots and throwing dice. Philadelphus found pleasure in simple things, like eating and playing with our cat, as if he'd known all along that his time in this world would be brief. Why hadn't I listened? Why hadn't I understood when he told me that we didn't have long together . . .

He wouldn't be burned like Marcellus but embalmed according to Egyptian custom, let no one try to stop me! I'd have his organs preserved in canopic jars, his body mummified, protective amulets wrapped in the bandages to ward off dark magic. It would take seventy days to do it properly, which meant I'd have to stay in Rome until the seas opened again in the spring. I didn't care. Time had lost all meaning. I'd lost my mother, my father, my older brothers—all cut down violently or forced to suicide. Only Philadelphus had been taken from me for no reason I could discern, and I desperately wanted someone to blame.

IT was the saddest Saturnalia. The grimmest holiday in memory. Like mimes, we went through the motions of the festivities but took no joy. Octavia didn't want music, poetry, or games. She purged the household of everything that reminded her of Marcellus and took personal affront to any show of merriment. But with the death of Marcellus, Octavia's influence was waning and the emperor's wife was once again the most powerful woman in Rome.

Livia made no secret of the fact that she thought our grief was excessive. Un-Roman. Since Virgil couldn't be persuaded to celebrate, she hired minstrels and invited King Herod's young sons, who had lately come to the city, as honored royal guests. When Terentilla, the beautiful wife of Maecenas, fawned over Augustus so scandalously that guests openly acknowledged her as the emperor's mistress, Livia revealed not the slightest tremor of jealousy.

Livia's game was transparent to me. She was making new allies in the emperor's circle who could be counted upon to support her. She was recruiting royals to lessen my prestige and encouraging promiscuous women to turn the emperor's eye away from me. For all that she was my enemy, I didn't care. I only knew that if I found any evidence that she'd poisoned my brother, I'd have vengeance.

Beneath the frescoes in the dining hall, Terentilla's high-pitched laughter echoed and I sat staring into my goblet of wine. It was a sweet Falernian that had gone dark with age, so strong that it bit the tip of my tongue. I wondered how many cups I'd have to drain before I no longer felt the bite. The Herodian princes presented Livia with a pair of emerald earrings as a Saturnalia gift and she made much of them, even as she demurred, "Perhaps you'd better give these gems to my stepdaughter, as Julia so loves to ornament herself. As for me, my children are my jewels."

Julia took no notice of this. "Marcellus and Philadelphus both loved the Saturnalia," she murmured, and I remembered the long ago Saturnalia, when Philadelphus chose the pastry with the bean and was proclaimed the Lord of Misrule. I remembered too how delighted he'd been when we were given a gray kitten . . . and now Bast curled up in my lap, her chin low and ears back as if she also mourned for him.

"The pine wreaths," Julia continued, stammering and sniffling.

"The r-red berries, the gilded candles and spiced w-w-ine . . . Marcellus loved it all." She dissolved into a gale of sobs. Iullus rose to comfort her and she buried her face in his toga while he stroked her hair. He risked much by revealing his tender feelings, and for the first time, I thought to myself, *He truly loves her.*

The same thought must have occurred to the emperor because he disentangled himself from Terentilla and called Julia to him. Then he dismissed the rest of the family and our guests to exchange gifts elsewhere. I stayed behind with Julia, hoping to defend her. Or perhaps I was simply too drunk to stand. Facing the emperor, Julia whispered, "I want my mother."

At this, Augustus rocked back in his seat. "Your *mother!* You dare mention her to me?" Whatever Julia's mother had done to merit her virtual exile from Rome I'd never learned, but we all knew better than to mention Scribonia. With bleary eyes, I watched the emperor lean forward and say, "You're an embarrassment, Julia."

Julia dabbed at her eyes, losing a battle to still her trembling lips. "I'm a *widow.*"

"What do you have to show for it?" Augustus snapped. "Are you with child?" Julia shook her head, crossing her arms over her empty womb. Then the emperor turned on me. "Her moods are your bad influence, Selene. When are you going to give your brother a funeral? You can't keep his sarcophagus in your house forever."

What a silly thing to say. Nothing was forever. Not Philadelphus. Not my house on the other side of the Tiber. Not even Rome itself. In this life, everything would someday turn to ash. Bereft, I took another fortifying swallow and let the wine burn all the way down. "Let me see him safely to Egypt and put him in my mother's crypt."

Augustus rubbed his face, eyes upon the ceiling as if begging Jupiter's indulgence. "Don't try my patience, Selene."

Perhaps he thought it was a ploy, a desperate gambit. This time he was wrong. I set down my goblet to plead with him. "Caesar, I'll go secretly to Egypt and I won't stay. I'll perform the proper ceremonies. No more than that. Just let me see to it that Philadelphus rests with our mother and father. That's all I ask."

"*All you ask?* You're a Ptolemy, Selene. You can't step foot in Alexandria without being proclaimed Queen of Egypt."

"Why would that be so terrible?" Laid bare, I pressed with both palms to my cheeks to hold back the grief. "I've done everything you've ever asked of me. Let us go home. Can't you, for the sake of mercy, at long last, *just let us go home?*"

He just stared at me, then stood up and walked out of the room, his toga trailing after him. Even after he was gone, his footsteps still echoed in my mind, and I drank deeply, chasing after the drunken state of oblivion my father had so often sought for himself.

"How do you do it?" Julia asked. "How can you not weep?"

Because I'd spent my youth swallowing my grief like it was mother's milk. Because I'd learned to mask my pain. Because I was bleeding inside and dared not pull away the bandage to inspect the wound and because—

"If she starts weeping, she'll never stop," Octavia said from the doorway. Though some Roman women wore white in mourning, she wore a *stola pulla*, all in black. Sadness had etched itself into the very lines of her face and I wondered at my own reflection on the surface of the wine. How was there color on my lips? How had that comb come to be in my hair? Tala must have dressed me, but I could scarcely remember.

Slaves had been dismissed from work on account of the Saturnalia, so Octavia took it upon herself to start cleaning up the meal. I should rise to help her, but I glanced over to see Julia fiddling with something in her lap. When she saw me looking, she held up little vials. "Perfumed oils. A gift from Tiberius. I fear he means to begin a courtship."

Perhaps if I'd been sober, I wouldn't have said, "Anything Tiberius gives you comes straight from his mother, and Livia is nothing but poison to you."

I'd only meant to point out Livia's all-too-obvious campaign to marry one of her sons to the emperor's now-widowed daughter. Octavia fastened on a different meaning to my words. She never looked up, never changed expression as she gathered up plates from the feast. She only asked, "Do you think Livia works in poisons?"

We shouldn't have this conversation. Not here in the emperor's household where Livia's spies lurked behind every pillar. Certainly not with Octavia half mad from grief. Even though my lips had gone numb, I was still wary enough to say, "I don't know."

"My son was healthy," Octavia said, her lips pinched tight. "His brilliant future was cut short at the moment, *the very moment*, Livia saw her fortunes dwindling. Do you think it's coincidence?"

Livia was known to prepare tonics for the emperor. Only *I* knew that she'd dosed him with something the night he took me to his bed. Only I knew that she'd offered me poisoned wine the next morning. And that was nothing I could share. I wanted to blame Livia for Philadelphus's death; I wanted to punish her for it, but what proof did I have? Surely if Livia had hated anyone enough to poison them, it would have been *me*. Yet here I was, alive.

Octavia grabbed up a napkin and shook it free of crumbs. "There is one thing that's certain. I'll never let Livia benefit from the death of my son, even if that means Julia never remarries."

At this, Julia flinched. She'd done her duty to her family; she deserved some reward, some hope . . . "Julia will *have* to remarry," I said. "She's sixteen and hasn't any children yet. Marcellus wouldn't have wanted her to live as a widow forever, and the emperor will insist that she take another husband. So why not Iullus? He's twenty-one, another son of your household, and a *quaestor* with great potential—"

"He's Antony's son." Octavia shook her head. "For the emperor to give Julia to Iullus would be like allowing Antony to bed his daughter. It would humiliate him. Don't you know that Augustus would see them both dead before he allowed such a match?" I'd warned Julia that a future with Iullus was impossible, but Octavia's words rang down like unshakable prophecy and there was nothing I could say to lessen the blow.

Julia's expression fractured. "But Iullus is loyal to us," she cried. "He isn't Antony."

As if she hadn't heard Julia, Octavia reached for my goblet. I held it fast. I thought she'd lecture me on the disgrace of inebriation and almost welcomed the argument that would follow, but she only said, "I'd like you to lay Philadelphus beside Marcellus in the family mausoleum."

In the tomb of Augustus, she meant. She'd loved Philadelphus and wanted to honor my brother as if he were her son, but how could I allow Philadelphus to rest eternally beside the emperor?

WITH a jar of wine and a basket of barley cakes, I went to the old Temple of Isis. With Saturnalia celebrants still stumbling drunk about the city, there was no one to stop me. The temple was dark and the gate was closed, but Memnon broke the chains and pulled the overgrown vines away so that I could slip inside. The potted trees were now nothing but desiccated stalks, dead and brown. This place had once been a sunlit sanctuary for me, where my blood blossomed into flowers. Where magic flowed and crocodiles defended me. Now the inner sanctum was shadowy and filled with a vile stench. The pools were clogged with muck. Following a chain on the ground, I found the rotted skeleton of a crocodile with spears in its remains. I couldn't say if the magnificent beast had been killed for sport or mercy, but I grieved for him too. Everything I touched, everything I loved, I seemed destined to lose. Perhaps it was my punishment for allowing this to happen to the temple. Philadelphus once told me that I'd save the goddess, but I looked up at her statue to see the damage I'd wrought. Though moss had grown in the folds of her stone garments and all her finery had been stripped away, that perfect compassionate expression hadn't lost its power. This was Isis in her own guise. A sistrum rattle in one hand and the sacred knot between her breasts.

"Oh," someone whispered. "Isis is beautiful."

I turned to see Julia standing with the Antonias amidst the debris. "What are you doing here?" I asked.

"We followed you," Minora said.

"You shouldn't risk yourselves! Augustus has ordered this temple closed . . ."

Julia held up the hem of her expensive silk gown, stepping over a fallen chunk of marble. "Yet here you are, Selene, in defiance."

I didn't want them here. I wanted to fling stones at them and drive them away. "Will you just go? Leave me!"

As a queen, I was becoming accustomed to obedience, but Antonia put a stubborn hand on her hip. "No." With that firm-set jaw, she was her mother in miniature. She adjusted her *stola* as if afraid to touch anything. "We want to know where you're going to entomb Philadelphus."

"In Mauretania." I'd built a tomb there for one brother; it would have to shelter another.

"Please don't take him," Minora said. "Philadelphus would be a stranger in Mauretania. Leave him with us."

I gasped. "With *you*?"

"We're his sisters too," Antonia replied. "If you won't put him in the tomb of Augustus, give him his own place here in Rome."

I always stay in Rome, Philadelphus had insisted. Had he foreseen that he'd remain behind, even in death? What was I to do? He *would* be a stranger in Mauretania, alone in an empty tomb. Was I to risk his earthly body, his *khat*, to a voyage across the sea? "He was a child of Isis. Who would invoke the goddess over his remains?"

"We will," Julia said, her tone brooking no argument, and the Antonias nodded their agreement. "Teach us to honor Isis and the rites he should have and we'll perform them."

They left me quite speechless. If the women in the emperor's own family came to love Isis, would it not soften hard Roman hearts to my faith? How I wished that Isis would guide me, engrave her words on my hands. I held my palms up now, as if summoning her, but there'd been no Isiac blood spilled to work that magic.

"We'll help you, Selene," Minora said, taking up the jug to pour libations. "We're not going to leave you alone."

I'd never wanted sisters; it had upset my sense of place in the world where I had thought myself my father's only princess. Still, as the Antonias laid out offerings to a forbidden goddess I knew I'd never be able to hold myself aloof from them again. I must love the Antonias because Philadelphus had loved them. And though I was heartsick, I resolved to entrust my youngest brother to their care.

WE sealed Philadelphus in a tomb that I commissioned, knowing it wouldn't be complete for months. The funeral was small. Though Crinagoras offered to compose poetry, I refused. No grand orations would accompany Philadelphus from this life to the next. Teeming crowds of professional mourners and curious onlookers would not pass by to lay flowers upon his bier. I allowed none but those who'd actually loved him. I did for Philadelphus what I couldn't do for Caesarion—I touched the lips of his sarcophagus with the iron wand and performed the Opening of the Mouth ceremony that would allow him to eat and breathe and speak in the afterlife. Beyond that, I won't describe the funeral; I cannot, for it hollows me to think of it. And once it was done, I retreated to my house on the Tiber and shut myself in.

In my grief, it seemed only natural that the fields should be fallow. As if my sorrow had sent the whole world into a dark time of famine and ill omens. A wolf was caught in the forum and the river rose, flooding the city. Whereas the Tiber was usually unnavigable, it now ran swift and deep enough to accommodate small galleys filled with grain . . . if only there'd been any grain to be had. The wheat and barley in Rome had been spoiled by mice and other vermin; the people starved. Whenever I went out onto my terrace, my eyes were drawn to the Temple of Aesculapius, where the sick and hungry thronged for help and every wind carried the moans of the dying. Slaves had once sought sanctuary with Isis for compassion, healing, and scraps of bread. Her temples were all closed, but there were more Isiacs in the city than ever. Many of her followers had taken to wearing *pileus* caps, like the ones Romans wore during the Saturnalia, so that they might recognize one another and promote the cause of liberty. They called openly for reform.

At the same time, a different impulse was taking hold. Some said, "We were well fed until Augustus gave up the consulship." They were wrong. The roots of this famine could be found in the emperor's policies, but this didn't stop the Senate from meeting with the express intention of asking Augustus to take up his mantle of power again.

This must have been his plan all along.

From the relative safety of my balcony across the river, I watched the angry mob gather, fists raised and shouts carried on the frigid morning winds. I had no idea what would happen next. If the mobs turned on Augustus and his family, I'd have to leave by carriage in the dead of night—fleeing Rome as my mother once did, and with even less to show for it. I *would* leave. I wouldn't risk my daughter's life, even for the throne of Egypt. Shivering with cold, I went back inside. Retrieving her from the nursery, I grabbed Isidora into my arms and pressed my lips to her temple, where her hairline was downy soft. Though the city was in an uproar, I could think of nothing more important than the way her little fingers curled around mine.

A few hours later, Julia and Iullus called upon me. I should have discouraged them from using my home as a clandestine meeting place, but how could I deny them even a moment's happiness? Besides, no one raised an eyebrow at Julia's arrival, for it was well known in Rome that the daughter of Augustus had befriended the daughter of Cleopatra. Likewise, because I was Iullus's half sister, there was no scandal associated with his visits. My servants brought out modest refreshments. A silver pitcher of wine and a matching platter of olives, nuts, and cheese. Meanwhile, Iullus shrugged out of his bulky toga and tossed it over the back of one of my couches. It was an unwieldy outer garment that he was required to wear to official functions and he looked relieved to be free of it. "A motion just carried to make Augustus dictator for life," he said.

Julia threw up her hands. "*Dictator for life?* After all the controversy about how my father intended to make himself king, now they offer him a lifetime dictatorship!"

Iullus took a handful of olives. "He refused it. You should've

seen him. He dropped to his knees and rent his clothes like a grieving woman, begging the Senate not to put this burden upon him.
He accepted responsibility for the grain supply—said he'd send
Tiberius to Ostia to help oversee everything—but he wouldn't
accept a dictatorship. He told the Senate that he desired nothing
more than to settle outstanding business and retire to private life."

I knew him too well to believe that. "He's afraid. Dictator for
life is the authority they offered Julius Caesar before they plunged
their knives into him. Augustus either fears he's being offered a
death sentence or he simply wants to be seen to refuse so that no
one can accuse him of ambition."

Julia bit her lower lip. "He *is* afraid. Without Agrippa here to
protect him, he's vulnerable." Which made all of us vulnerable. How
must my mother have felt here in Rome with little Caesarion in her
arms, wondering if *her* Caesar would triumph or fall? I thanked Isis
for the thousandth time that I'd never claimed my child was the
emperor's, or Isidora's fortunes would be tied to his even more surely
than mine were.

"How can you both be so cynical about Augustus?" Iullus
asked.

I'd learned from long experience that arguing with men who admired
the emperor was fruitless, so I didn't bother. Julia and I knew the truth
of it. This was the emperor's mad gambit. It was risky. It could all go
wrong. The mob could tear him limb from limb, or the senators might
turn their knives on him, then come to murder his family. We'd be next,
my daughter and me. I was trapped in this dangerous situation, in this
hateful city! As I paced, Iullus tried to comfort us, but some curious
activity on the Tiber caught my attention.

I went to the balcony, where I looked down at teams of oxen on
the towpaths alongside the river, hauling barges through the frigid
water. It was an otherwise ordinary sight, but people flocked to the
shore, swarming the bridges, pushing and shoving their way. That's
when I recognized the cargo. *Grain sacks.* Heaps and heaps of them,
all stamped not with the emblems of Egypt—but of *Mauretania*.
My Mauretania!

Twenty-one

SOMEHOW, Euphronius had done it. Perhaps he'd enchanted the sailors or bankrupted the treasury to bribe them. Either way, I was sure that it had cost us dearly. I stood watching barge after barge make its way up the Tiber. A man climbed atop the sacks of grain and lifted one hand in the direction of my house. He might've said anything in that moment, and the people would have cheered, but he cried, "Thank the Queen of Mauretania!"

I stood dressed only in a gown of mourning. I wore neither a diadem nor a circlet crown upon my head. My lack of queenly adornment seemed to win the crowd. This year had been one of grief and misery; they knew that I'd lost a brother and shared in their pain. "All hail to the queen!" someone cried. "All hail, to the *good* Queen Cleopatra!"

The crowd roared their approval and my guards pushed their way out onto the balcony. It seemed as if my entire household rushed out with them—only Julia and Iullus remained in the house. The people continued to cheer. "Thank Selene of Mauretania, blessed of Isis! Thank Selene of Egypt, last of the Ptolemies!"

"Not the last," I murmured. "Not the *last* of the Ptolemies."

Crinagoras rubbed his hands together against the chill. "Majesty, have you learned nothing about the allure of tragedy? Let them forget Princess Isidora for the moment. Let them think you're the last of a noble line. It's the sorrow of your story that'll win their love and send you back to Egypt."

He spoke openly this way because my aims were no secret to any of my courtiers, many of whom seemed more ambitious for my success than I was. "Who is that man standing atop the grain, proclaiming my largesse?"

"It's Captain Kabyle!" Until that moment, I'd never believed the stories about Cupid and his bow, but watching the flush that stained Tala's cheeks, no one could doubt that the Berber woman been pierced by an arrow of desire. Given that he'd just delivered food to a starving city, I wanted to kiss the captain myself, but Tala was breathless. Had she conceived her affection for the man on our journey from Mauretania?

Not wanting to question her, I said, "Tala, go down to the river and tell Captain Kabyle that I'll receive him and hear what news he brings from King Juba."

But moments after Tala rushed away, I received a summons from the emperor.

THE Temple of Apollo was a magnificent structure, a monument to the emperor's victory over my parents. Each sculpture wrought with symbolism, every gilded adornment chosen with care, every cornice framing priceless artwork. Not for his *own* glory, Augustus would say, but for the glory of Apollo. As I passed through the giant bronze doors, which were carved in relief with the story of proud Niobe and all her slaughtered children, I shivered. As far as the emperor knew, all of my mother's children had been struck down too. All except me.

Though it was a temple, it was also a massive governmental office. Amidst scrolls and various secretaries who hurried to do his bidding, Augustus was to be found in an antechamber not far from where he'd later lock up what remained of the Sibylline Books after he'd purged them of prophecies he feared. When I reached the entryway, his *lictors* tilted their ceremonial axes to either side of the entryway to let me pass. Alone behind closed doors, the emperor lowered his hood and pinned me in place with his icy eyes. "I suppose you expect me to thank you for your shipment of grain. It's changed the mood in the city. A nice bit of sorcery . . ."

I thought he'd be glad, but I detected an edge in his voice. Was he actually displeased while all the city rejoiced? "It wasn't sorcery, Caesar. I simply sent word when you were too ill to do it yourself."

He pushed papers across the table in annoyance. "You conjured grain out of the air."

"I conjured grain from Mauretania, where farmers worked the land and Isis rewarded them with a harvest, so that a fleet of sailors could risk their lives to bring it across the winter sea."

"No," he said. "There was magic in how it happened. The crowd threatened to burn down the Curia until I promised to take control of the grain. Mere hours later, your sacks of grain were ferried up the river."

I realized he *was* displeased, as if he suspected me of something. "It was fortuitous timing."

"Fortuitous?" he snapped. "Do you know what my enemies say? They say I feigned my illness and engineered the famine. They say that your *fortuitously* timed shipment was positioned to make me look like a savior."

I myself might have wondered if he'd purposefully brought this famine down upon Rome, but there were some things not even Augustus could control. Something else had him agitated, and I couldn't guess at what. "It's the fate of a ruler to do good for his subjects and be ill spoken of by them in return," I said, quoting Alexander. "Our enemies will always have something to say against us, Caesar. The important thing is that the hungry have a little more food."

He tilted his head, appraising me. "Do you know what I think? I think you held the grain back to please me. To glorify me. Is that what you did?"

I'd never hold back food from starving people, but that wasn't the answer he wanted. "I might have done it had it occurred to me. I'll find a thousand ways to glorify you if only you restore me to my mother's kingdom."

"I can't," he said, simply. "There's war in Egypt."

I was taken entirely off guard. "War? In Egypt?"

"The Kushites took advantage of Gallus's disastrous campaign in Arabia." He leaned forward, so wasted by his recent fever that his gaunt face took on a serpentine edge. "The temples at Aswan have been captured by a Kushite force from Meroë."

I blinked. I couldn't help it. Meroë was to the southern border of Egypt, a land of ebony people who shared many of our customs and gods, but they'd been friendly during my mother's reign. "Why should they attack Egypt?"

The emperor steepled fingers beneath his chin. "The Kandake of Meroë claims she's a pharaoh. She's seized the temples in the name of Isis. She's *routed* Roman forces."

Impossible. I hadn't believed any force in the world could rout the Romans, and yet, somehow, this queen had done what I couldn't! "I never thought . . ."

"There are rumors that the Kandake is served by a fearsome wizard who can throw fire with his bare hands. Do you know what the small people call this mage? They call him Horus the Avenger."

Oh heart, be still. *Helios.* This was his doing. I'd thought the Romans were invincible; Helios had himself said that he couldn't beat them, not with swords or magic. But he'd done it again. He'd *routed* them and I hoped that my exultation wouldn't show. All the lies I'd ever told, all the practice I'd had at hiding my true feelings, every lesson in deception I'd ever learned had all been to prepare me for this moment. I forced every muscle of my face to an appearance of bewilderment. Not so much as a tremor shook my innocent facade. "Horus the Avenger? This legend often rises up in Egypt. It's an imaginary hope."

The emperor's quiet rage would have sent a shiver through me if I hadn't been prepared for it. "Those weren't imaginary wounds my soldiers suffered. I wonder . . ." The emperor's eyes scrutinized me. He was a shrewd judge of character and he was judging me now, but I was nothing if not a fine actress.

"Caesar, I'm not surprised that Roman soldiers made up stories to explain their defeat. Haven't they always done so? Your forces suffered a humiliating defeat at the hands of a woman. Is it possible the Kandake has a magician who fights for her? Yes. Did falcon-eyed Horus drop from the sky to smite Roman soldiers? I think not."

He ground his teeth. "Her warriors cut off the head of a bronze statue that had been erected in my likeness."

So Augustus had put a statue of himself in the holy precinct of Isis? I imagined Helios swinging his sword, decapitating a statue of the emperor, then burying it somewhere in the sands. My twin had pushed the Romans from the sacred temples and he'd done it with this foreign queen, this Kandake, and not with me. Still, I betrayed nothing. "What can the Kushites want?"

"I think you *know* what they want, Selene. I want you to tell me why they captured the Isle of Philae. There's nothing there. No stronghold. No lands to settle. The temple treasures have already been seized. Why would the Kandake attack us here?"

"Because it's the holiest place for Isiacs," I said, emboldened by the idea that Helios might yet wrest Egypt away from the Romans. "They're making war for religious reasons and you have only your-self to blame. All through the empire, the Romans let people wor-ship whatever god or goddess they wish. Yet you've singled out Isis for unique suppression—"

"Did she not single me out?" He pressed his hands to the table. "Or did you lie when you said that Isis cursed me? Why shouldn't I retaliate?"

"Retaliate against a goddess? Hubris is a Greek idea, but I thought even Romans understood it."

His lips thinned at my boldness. "If the followers of Isis were content to make sacrifices at her altar, I'd have no cause to com-plain, but the priests are influential with the people. They involve themselves in politics. They speak out against war and slavery and the proper relations of the sexes. Isis worship undermines the state and leads the small people to think that they have as much worth as those who rule over them."

I couldn't deny this, for I'd heard such sermons. "So you'll suffer because you think yourself too great to bend to the will of a goddess?"

"Perhaps it pleases you to see me suffer, Selene." He stood, very composed. Very angry. "I remember that on the edge of death, I asked for your forgiveness. You wouldn't give it."

Some of my smugness drained away. "Why should Caesar need my forgiveness?"

"I don't need it," he said with a curl of his lips. "I *wanted* it and you refused me."

Augustus always wants what he cannot have. When had this interview slipped from my control? The emperor's fascination with me was all that kept my daughter safe, and I must foster it. "Caesar, if I withheld my forgiveness, it's only because I didn't want to give you an excuse to die."

"You say this because you want to be Queen of Egypt. Not because you care for me." He said the last petulantly, like a spoiled child.

I swallowed, reaching out for him. "My mother forgave Caesar many things. For burning her books, for his dalliance with Queen Eunoe. How could she not forgive him? Don't I walk in her footsteps?"

"You swore to be my Cleopatra," he muttered. "You *vowed* it."

I might've known that my *kithara* harp wouldn't satisfy him. "How have I failed you?"

He came round the table, drawing so close that his breath warmed my shoulder. "You know exactly how you've failed me. You gave me only a girl. Not a *son*. Not the heir that I need."

The words he'd whispered came back in rush. Hateful words. Vile words. Sickening words about how I was his Egyptian whore and would bear his child. Had I sat by his bedside, nursing him back to health, only so that he could be the same monster as before? I straightened to my full height and I was now taller than most women. "Did you think you could force yourself upon me and stand to gain from it? Isis would never allow it."

Color returned to his face, as if this old game between us invigorated him, and he reached to brush hair back from my cheek. When I turned away, he caught my pearl earring and rolled it between his thumb and forefinger. Then he asked the question that seems so inevitable now but which shook me to my foundations. "What if you came to me willingly, Selene? Could you give me a son?"

The suffocating weight of his proposal settled over the room and my mouth went dry. It made me want to retch. In his death throes, Philadelphus had murmured something about the son I might bear. Could he have seen this in the Rivers of Time? I'd endured much for the sake of my brothers and to defend my faith. But to give myself to the man who raped me? There were no words for such an *abomination*. "You're a Roman," I said hoarsely. "You make too much of your need for a son of your own bloodline. You can simply adopt the way Caesar adopted you."

"I mean to rule more than Rome. War with Parthia nips at my heels and Alexander's name still strikes fear into their hearts. You alone can give me a son that joins the blood of the Caesars with Alexander's divine ichor."

Perhaps this was what my father had asked of my mother too. Perhaps it was the reason that my mother named my twin Alexander Helios. I always thought of my mother and the emperor as two very different kinds of people, but maybe they'd always been very much alike. And maybe I wasn't enough like either of them.

"You want Egypt," the emperor said flatly. "Well, I want you to give me a son."

Twenty-two

MY mother had known when to retreat and where to regroup her strength. As a young queen, betrayed by her mentors and driven from her throne, she fled to the city of Ashkelon to gather an army. I was seventeen now. I didn't have an army, but I was no less under siege. I too would flee, for the emperor had confessed to me a crucial bit of information: The Romans in Egypt were under attack. Helios might win our throne without my having to surrender to the emperor's twisted desires. I went straight to my house across the Tiber, sweeping through the atrium and throwing open the doors to the receiving room. The ship's captain was waiting and dipped low in a bow to me. "Majesty."

I had quite forgotten I'd sent Tala to retrieve him. He expected pleasantries, no doubt. Perhaps a well-deserved thanks and a decent night's sleep. I would disappoint him. "Captain, I want to return to Mauretania tonight."

Captain Kabyle's smile faltered. "It's better to wait until March—"

I couldn't wait until March. I couldn't wait even one more day. "We need to leave now. You've seen me call the winds to my command. There'll be no danger to us so long as I'm aboard your ship."

He puffed up, affronted. "I fought winter storms to bring grain to Rome without any such assurance of safety. It's not a lack of courage that gives me pause. What of your retinue? Your baggage? Does it not take time—"

"I must leave tonight!" I wound my fingers in my pearls. "Can the arrangements be made?"

His brow furrowed. "We can be to Ostia by morning, certainly, but it may take a day to round up my lads and set sail again."

Tala's tattooed hands clasped the high arm of a couch. "Are we in danger, Majesty?"

I gave the only explanation I could. "There's war in Egypt. As Cleopatra's daughter, I don't want to be in Rome for the inevitable recriminations." Thereafter, I alerted the servants and made quick decisions about what to leave behind. I'd abandon the statuary and the furnishings. I'd abandon all of it but for the cat. As servants hurried to gather the barest necessities, Tala and the others complained that many of my retainers weren't ready to travel. My mime wasn't even in the city, as I'd granted Ecloga permission to visit a school in Baiae. If we set out tonight, we'd have to leave her behind. The mime wasn't the only one, but like an animal cornered in the arena, I tore into anyone who tried to delay my escape. "Then I'll do without them!"

Crinagoras lifted a wry eyebrow. "Why, you half persuade me to stay in Rome."

"I'm sorry," I said, for I didn't need more enemies. "If you aren't ready to travel, you can follow on another ship, at my expense, but I must go."

My power, my only refuge, was in Mauretania.

I sent no word to Augustus because any pretext I made for my swift departure would have been insultingly flimsy. He'd be furious, but his hold over me had loosened the moment Philadelphus breathed his last. Augustus could no longer threaten my little brother to make me obey and I wouldn't let him use my daughter. Besides, if Egypt threw off Rome's yoke, I didn't want to be a hostage to compel their surrender. These are the things I told myself only after our frantic night escape from Rome. Only after we reached the port of Ostia, once the sails had been hoisted, did my blind animal instinct to flee abate.

It was the salt spray on my cheeks that awakened me to the reality of what I'd done. The emperor told me he wanted to get a son on me and I'd run from him. It was my first true rebellion. I wasn't afraid of the repercussions; he couldn't afford to preoccupy himself with punishing me. Not when his power was uncertain, while Egypt was under invasion and tensions were mounting with Parthia. A calculating man like Augustus wouldn't jeopardize everything for the sake of spite. He needed grain, so he needed me. He needed a stable and prosperous Mauretania at his back, a place where he could settle his veterans as he'd promised, so as to maintain the support of his legions. For once, I understood my own power.

On the third day of our chilly but uneventful journey, I asked Captain Kabyle, "When the pirates attacked us, why weren't they stopped by Roman vessels? Agrippa has an enormous fleet. Why isn't it guarding the shipping lanes?"

"The sea is vast," the captain said. "The Romans spend most of their time protecting the grain ships from Egypt and harrying pirates in Crete and Delos. Otherwise, scouring the coasts for pirate lairs is left to local authorities."

The Romans were still trying to subdue the Cantabri in Spain. The proconsul of Africa Nova was busy trying to rebuild old Carthage in the midst of hostile Numidian tribesmen. These Roman authorities were too preoccupied to concern themselves with the sea. That left only one local authority to deal with piracy. *Ours.* "What resources would we need to guard the shipping lanes?"

The captain's eyes flicked over to me. "You need only call down a swirling maelstrom upon those criminals and send them to the bottom of the sea."

"I can't be everywhere at once," I said, as if considering using my sorcery for such a thing.

"Majesty, it would only take once."

I was mindful of what the old mage had always said about spending my *heka* wisely, and I didn't relish the idea of drowning men, not with the memory of Philadelphus slipping beneath the waters so fresh in my mind.

* * *

ARRIVING in Iol-Caesaria, I saw a half-built lighthouse jutting up from the harbor. Beyond the rocky shore, marbled stairs led up to our splendid palace. It was more beautiful than I remembered it, ethereal beside the sparkling blue waters, like some fabled residence in old Homeric tales. Beside me, Bast yowled, her tail swishing furiously at the sight of land. This would be a new home for her, and in my hand I gripped Philadelphus's amulet, hoping that his spirit, his *ba*, was nearby. I wished that he'd seen this place with his own eyes, but few of my wishes had ever come true. Crowds came running to see our ship, since we were the only one that had dared to cross the ocean in winter. We made our way down the gang-plank and tension knotted my shoulders. There'd been some expec-tation that if I returned, it would be with the crown of Egypt.

If the Mauretanians were disappointed, they didn't let it show. Some followed, joining the processional, and when I looked behind me I saw a sea of people. Men in turbans and women wearing brightly colored scarves, silver jewelry, and henna tattoos. Even bare-legged children with sticks cried, "It's the queen and our little princess!"

I'd been gone almost a year—a *miserable* year—and it light-ened my heart to return to my very own kingdom, where the peo-ple seemed so happy to see me. This place was untouched by Augustus. He'd sworn to me that he'd never step foot in Maureta-nia, and I told myself that I'd be safe here. Safe, for now. Even if he sent some furious letter demanding that I be punished, his orders would be unlikely to arrive before spring.

With the crowds still cheering, we passed through the gates into the royal enclosure, where officials rushed out into the bright sun-light to greet me on the stairs. "Majesty!" Euphronius cried. "We had no word that you were coming. No time to prepare." He was a strange sight. In the Egyptian tradition of mourning, he'd ceased to shave. Gray hair adorned his once-bald head. A beard covered his chin. I realized that he knew Philadelphus was dead. Perhaps news had reached him or perhaps he'd seen it in the Rivers of Time, but he knew. I wanted to run to him as I'd done as a little girl and weep.

Instead, I swallowed my sadness and said, "I'm glad to see you again, old friend."

"The sight of you is the only thing that can brighten the dark days of my grief," he replied.

I turned away lest I lose my composure. A contingent of Juba's Roman advisers gathered around Balbus. He gave me a very slight bow, and they all mimicked him. Then I noticed the tall Berber chieftain. "Welcome back, Majesty," Maysar said, jingling as he bowed, for he seemed to have acquired an impressive silver chain belt. "You've been missed."

I'd missed them too. Climbing the marble stairs, I was even eager to see Juba. "Where's the king?"

Did I imagine the sidelong glances and low murmurs?

It was Maysar who finally spoke. "King Juba is gone on expedition."

"I'm sure he'll be back soon," Balbus said, but the Roman veteran seemed to lack his usual blustery confidence.

This awkward exchange made me happy to go inside, away from public scrutiny, where I was reunited with my slave girl. We embraced, but when she saw Bast, Chryssa choked back a sob. "Oh, his little cat . . ."

"No tears, Chryssa. I can't bear it. Today I just want to rejoice in coming home."

Euphronius leaned on his divination staff, stroking it as if to conjure memories. "Majesty, *Egypt* is your home."

Did he think I'd forgotten? Tala whisked the children off to the nursery and I retired with Chryssa and the mage. I sought out the sanctuary of my rooms, the ones with windows overlooking the ocean. I threw back the silky curtains to let in more light and it seemed as if every winter blossom turned its face to me; the perfume of the sweet alyssum in my gardens beckoned, clean and welcoming. Chryssa put my things away, taking careful inventory of each new acquisition, and I found myself comforted by the familiarity of her service. Yet something niggled at me. "Why did no one want to speak of King Juba?"

"He went on a journey with Circe, his Greek *hetaera*," Euphronius said. "I think she's Herod's spy."

If I'd known Juba's head could be turned by a *hetaera*, I might've hired one for him myself. "*Circe?* That can't be her real name."

"Of course not," Chryssa snorted. "She's a professional, and everything you might expect from such a woman. She's talented in a variety of arts. There are rumors he's settled her into a palace in Volubilis where he treats her like its queen."

No bitter reply escaped my clenched jaw. Harem intrigue had long been a part of my family's history and I knew better than to permit a genuine rival in my own kingdom. "Are the rumors true?"

Euphronius rubbed his chin. "I don't think so. The king's missives are long accounts of his travels, detailing everything from the behavior of elephants to his theory about the source of the Nile. Sometimes he sends plants for me to catalog and other times he sends maps for Rome. He couldn't do all this if he were indolent with pleasure in a palace with a prostitute. But he seems in no hurry to return, no matter how we beseech him. He's been gone for months."

Was I fascinated or appalled? "*Months?* Who has been ruling the kingdom?"

Euphronius shrugged. "The council, Majesty. With much disagreement. I can't count the number of times that Balbus and Maysar have nearly come to blows."

With a critical eye, Chryssa examined a set of engraved ink pots I'd acquired in Rome. "I think the Berber would gut Balbus like a fish if he weren't mindful of the trust you placed in him. It's only by some miracle of Isis that blood hasn't yet been spilled."

"What are they fighting about?" I asked, realizing that I'd been gone too long and had much to catch up on.

"What *don't* they fight about?" Euphronius snorted. "The slaves, the raising of troops, war with the Garamantes, the endless stream of veterans needing to be settled, the treasury—" He broke off, exchanging a guilty look with Chryssa.

"The treasury? No, don't tell me. Not now." I didn't want to hear any more bad news. I would learn it all tomorrow in the council chamber. Right now, I just wanted to sleep peacefully in my own bed.

IT wasn't until I'd changed gowns for the third time that I admitted to myself I was anxious. When I left for Rome, it was barely acknowledged that I *had* a place on the council as Mauretania's queen. What political dynamics might I face now, after having been away? To be sure, I had my partisans, but Juba's Roman advisers still made up the bulk of the government, and they'd been hostile to me. I dreaded the inevitable clash.

When I pushed aside the fringed draperies and passed beneath the archway into the council chamber, the herald announced me and the assemblage stood. I wore a splendid emerald-colored gown held in place with a long rope of pearls that looped round my waist three times, then crisscrossed my breasts before encircling my neck. In my hair, I wore a decorative diadem, likewise studded with pearls. On my shoulders, the royal purple cloak that Balbus had given me.

I forced my countenance to one of confidence. An expression that said this was my council, my palace, and my kingdom. I swept up the stairs of the dais and seated myself on the throne. Then I lifted my eyes to see the most astonishing thing. Juba's Roman advisers looked *relieved*. "Majesty," Balbus said, as if speaking for them all. "We welcome you home and wonder what news you bring."

I reported everything hurriedly: The Kandake of Meroë had invaded Egypt. Admiral Agrippa was in self-imposed exile in the East. The emperor had survived his illness. Marcellus and my little brother had not. To keep the grief from my voice, I turned quickly to matters that concerned Mauretania directly. Our grain shipments helped ease the famine, but Rome would need more wheat and barley. "I must extend my thanks to Euphorbus and the rest of you for ensuring that grain arrived, even in winter. I know it was difficult. Perhaps near impossible. Yet I must ask, how much more can we send and by when?"

Maysar rose to his feet. His ornamented slippers swept softly against the marble as he took a few steps. "Majesty, Mauretania is a land of fruit and honey. We send the bulk of our grain to Rome, and for ourselves we eat fish and olives and the flesh of animals that roam in abundance. But those last shipments of grain cost us dear. We made no profit."

I expected this and feared the worst. "So our treasury is empty . . ."

Maysar gave an uneasy smile. "Empty? No. Our treasury is growing. With the new seaport, we're doing brisk trade. Lumber, carpets, animals for the arena. These things are all in high demand. But . . ."

"But?" I leaned forward, preparing myself for bad news.

"While you were away . . ." He cleared his throat and swept a hand in the direction of Chryssa, who skulked by the entryway, a bundle in her arms. "At the insistence of your rapacious slave girl, we started a dye works off the coast."

Chryssa came forward, bowed deeply before my throne, then snapped open a voluminous garment before me. It was a purple cloak, a nearly exact duplicate of the one that I wore. "The sea snails? Juba gave permission for this?"

"Yes, Majesty," Chryssa said, then climbed the marble dais and held the new cloak against the old. "It isn't exactly the same shade as the Tyrian but very close. A little bluer. Prettier, I think."

"And there's demand for it?" I asked. Nervously, she looked to the others, and I sighed in exasperation. "Oh, will one of you please tell me!"

Chryssa was the brave one. "We call it Gaetulian purple. We put out that *this* is the color *you* favor. As you were born to the purple, the only remaining Ptolemaic queen, it's become fashionable. We've received orders from all over the world. But we did this without your permission, Majesty. We beg your forgiveness . . ."

The council chamber was silent, everyone straining for my reaction. Since my mother's death, I could scarcely count the days upon one hand that I hadn't lied about something. Yet they all stood in mute terror over their harmless deception. "Well, I *do* favor Gaetulian purple, and I hope Lucius Cornelius won't be offended, but I don't think I'll ever wear the Tyrian again!"

Balbus laughed, and as sighs of relief filled the chamber I removed the older cloak and fastened the new one on my shoulders. It was very fine indeed! If this new dye sold for even half that of its Tyrian counterpart, I'd have gold aplenty to send to Helios and his Meroite armies . . . if only I could find him. I'd never worry about how to fund a Temple of Isis or any other project. Sweet Isis, we were going to be *rich*.

Apparently, Chryssa already was. Presenting me with a note that detailed her share of the dye works investment, she lowered her eyes. "This is my *peculium* and I submit to you my request for liberty."

This formality was unnecessary, but I knew how much it meant to her that we observe the official forms as nearly as we could. Though it would be expected of me, I wasn't obliged to grant her freedom, and with the whole council looking on, her eyes met mine in silent plea. In truth, I'd never wanted to own another human being; I'd always intended to free her. Yet the fear that she might leave me made me hesitate. To sever this bond was to risk losing my closest companion.

This was, I thought, why love was so dangerous. I searched for the right words, when a certain warmth stole over me at the realization that her happiness was more important than my fear. Even if she left me, I'd never regret speaking the words, "My council may serve as witness that I gladly grant your freedom and will enroll you in the census. You'll be known hereafter for official purposes as Cleopatra Antonianus."

As I had received citizenship through my father, she'd bear his name and mine. In this way, even if no other, we would always be connected. She seemed to know it too and her eyes glistened as she took the new name to herself, bowing before me as a free woman.

EARLY the next morning, my courtiers and I boarded a small ship that ferried us out to an island upon which fishermen hauled in large wicker baskets filled with murex. It was the smallest of the dye factories and touring it was an otherwise idyllic adventure but for the stench. Going ashore, I nearly gagged. "What is that vile smell?"

Chryssa grinned, inhaling rather dramatically. "Learn to love it, Majesty. It's the smell of profit!"

"It's the dead snails, fermenting in the sun," Maysar said with a grouchy roll of his eyes. "You'll grow accustomed to it."

I somehow doubted that. We tread a footpath between mountains of crushed shells. Muscular men stirred giant pots from which putrid plumes of steam rose up to sting our eyes. The workers wore veils to cover their mouths and noses. Even with such coverings, they must have had very strong constitutions. Much stronger than those of my courtiers; Lady Lasthenia pinched her nose shut and before Crinagoras could utter a witty word he rushed back to shore to vomit. With my own stomach churning in disgust, I asked, "Must the dead snails be fermented *and* boiled to get the color?"

The Berber chieftain and Chryssa answered me at the same time. She said yes. He said no. Then they grinned at one another as if they'd argued about it before and had enjoyed doing so. Maysar kicked at a little pile of shells, saying, "The sea snails need not be crushed up and turned into pulp. As I've told your greedy little freedwoman, the snails can be milked for pigment. When you poke them, they secrete mucus. Alone, it smells nothing so offensive as rotting shellfish. If we kept the snails as Romans keep lampreys, we wouldn't have to keep dredging the sea for more."

This seemed like a much more agreeable way of making the purple dye, but Chryssa argued, "As I've told this uncivilized Berber, milking the snails would require staggering amounts of labor. We'd need a legion of slaves."

Too many slaves had already come with us from Rome. More arrived every day. I didn't like the stench of this dye factory, but when I considered the alternative, it wasn't difficult to decide against the snails.

Twenty-three

A few days after my return, Lady Lasthenia took me on a tour of the unfinished lighthouse. She and her students had employed mathematics to design new mirrors that better reflected the light. Now those enormous silver mirrors dangled at the ends of ropes as men used cranes and pulleys to haul them up. Someday, a fire would burn in that lighthouse, blazing as an eternal beacon of welcome to Iol-Caesaria. It was a thing of wonder to me and a great source of pride.

As we stared together up at the lighthouse, Lasthenia said, "We all share your sorrow for Philadelphus, Majesty. Pythagoreans believe the soul is indestructible and that he'll be born again. In this, we aren't so different from your Isiacs."

I'd run from Augustus's grotesque proposal like a hare from a hunter, only fearing that I'd be captured. I'd failed my Alexandrians, but my flight from the emperor was only a temporary setback. I hadn't forgotten Egypt or the war happening there. "I wonder what your eyes and ears in Egypt have told you about the Kandake of Meroë?"

Lady Lasthenia crossed her arms over herself and adopted a scholarly tone of voice. "She's a powerful queen who calls herself a pharaoh. I'm told she's very majestic. She has a high proud forehead and wears thick gold bracelets on both arms. Her lips are very lush, very full, and they say that her skin is like polished onyx—"

"Enough." I closed my eyes, hand over my heart. Until that moment, I hadn't known that jealousy could cause such excruciating physical pain. Helios had found a warrior queen to fight where he had not found one in me. Why did I insist on torturing myself by hearing it again? "And the wizard in her service?"

Lady Lasthenia's expression turned cool and haughty; she enjoyed being in the know. "She claims Horus comes to her in the form of a young mage, but this is likely meant to demoralize the Romans. You shouldn't worry so much about her. The Kandake of Meroë won't rule Egypt in your stead." This hadn't been my worry until she said it. "None of the other monarchs in the East would stand for it. The Kandake isn't part of the civilized Greek-speaking world. She's an outsider. She's not a Ptolemy."

"As much good as that name has done me," I said, staring out over the sea, my cloak threatening to fly away in the wind.

"Majesty, your name holds such power that even here, exiled to this outpost, you've aroused the envy of other monarchs. King Herod of Judea starts construction on his own harbor city this year. He calls it Caesarea-Maritima."

It made me smirk. "How original." Herod was emptying his treasury to imitate me. I could at least take pleasure in that!

Several weeks passed and Iol-Caesaria became my city in truth. I was the highest authority in residence and didn't need to ask permission for anything from anyone. Why should I care if the king brooded in some far-off city with some other woman? For the first time in my life, no man ruled me. And I ruled a kingdom.

The first thing I discovered is that Juba had been right to chastise me for my arrogance. I knew next to nothing about the day-to-day administration of Mauretania. It wasn't as simple as weighing options and saying that this or that must be done. Though I had an aptitude for it, I still had much to learn about governing my kingdom and I swiftly came to appreciate our advisers—even the Roman ones—for their knowledge of law and finance.

As part of my new education, I took my courtiers on an inspection of the city. Everywhere we went, crowds hailed me by name. My advisers said that the people loved me and I came to believe it. Perhaps they loved me because I was a sorceress. Maybe I'd won them over with my eagerness to include Berber chieftains in the

royal council or because they thought I was the last of the Ptolemies. I didn't know the reason; I only found myself profoundly
grateful. They would be my protection against the emperor's wrath.

"They love you because of *me*," Crinagoras said. "My poems
remind them that you're a vibrant young queen with a babe at her
breast. I quite fear for your reign should you ever allow me to leave
your service."

He may have been right, but the people also seemed pleased
with the new cisterns for drinking water. The new markets for trad-
ing. The bathhouses and paved roads. These things made their lives
better. I took pride in that, but when we came upon an elongated
oval structure I was less proud. "Someone tell me this isn't going to
be an amphitheater! Juba means to bring gladiators here?"

"The king and the council thought gladiator games a good
idea," Chryssa said, fanning herself, sharp eyes alert for pickpock-
ets. I hardly thought she needed to worry with surly Memnon and
his men guarding us. "Maysar is the only one with sense. He
believes the influx of criminals to fight in the arena will disgust the
Berbers and goad the Garamantes, specifically."

I shielded my eyes from the hot African sun. "That's the second
time you've spoken of Maysar approvingly."

A blush reached to the tips of Chryssa's ears. "For a barbarian,
he's quite sensible."

"Then maybe he'll know how to put a stop to this. I don't want
Mauretania stained with gladiator blood."

We returned to the palace. The scent of roasted kid and spiced
vegetables drew us to the banquet hall, where my court assembled for
our evening meal. Servants removed my sandals, bathing my feet in
rose-scented water, and I summoned Maysar and Balbus to join me.
The two men glared and, situated between them, I half feared they'd
draw knives on one another. I hoped the servants would *heavily* water
their wine, and only after the meal had been served did I broach the
subject. "I'd like to stop work on the amphitheater."

Balbus paused midbite, nearly choking on a bit of grilled meat.
"Stop work?"

Finding my courage, I swirled a lump of root vegetable in the thick yogurt sauce. "I don't approve of gladiator games. Egyptians would never tolerate any monarch who asked her subjects to fight to the death."

"This isn't Egypt," Balbus said, lamplight illuminating his reddening jowls.

Taking a deep breath of the rose-scented air, I said, "Nor is this Rome."

Balbus wiped his mouth with the back of his hand. "The people must have entertainment."

"Then let's give them a hillside theater." The suggestion came from Leonteus of Argos, our court tragedian.

"Yes," I decided. "We'll have plays, comedies, and tragedies."

Several Romans groaned, bloodthirsty lot that they were. Balbus clenched his teeth, something he often did when he was about to flatter me. "Majesty, your beauty startles all who set eyes upon you and it does credit to your sex that you concern yourself with the gentler arts. If it's a theater you want, finance one, but work on the arena has already begun. You cannot countermand the orders of the king."

My temper rising, I sipped my wine to consider a politic answer. "I'm certain the king would approve. He's actually started writing a history of theatrics, did you know?"

Balbus protested, "Madam, you cannot simply turn an arena into a theater!"

The entire court watched us. The Alexandrians, the Romans, and the Mauretanians. Important ministers and servants all listened with rapt attention, straining to hear what I'd say next. This was a confrontation that I must win or fight to a draw. "I propose only that work stop on the amphitheater for the time being."

Balbus snorted. "But King Juba—"

"Isn't here," I interrupted, an edge to my voice, one that the emperor used when he was vexed. "He's *not here* and I am. I'm not questioned in Rome and I won't be questioned in my own kingdom."

Balbus slammed down his cup. "You're only a woman!"

"I'm your queen." Only the flickering torches were brave enough to crackle. Everyone else was silent. Balbus stewed, his face redder than ever, and I knew I'd let it go too far to be mended. I must cut him down hard and not show the uncertainty that made me wring my hands underneath the table. "I'm your queen and so long as you remain in Mauretania, you *will* submit to my rule."

His proud eyes burned black. "Then perhaps I should seek my fortune elsewhere."

"Perhaps you should."

"Madam," he said, rising to his full blustery height. "You go too far."

I hadn't studied at the knee of Augustus to be cowed by a man such as this. *Always know the most important person in the room,* Augustus had told me. This time it wasn't Balbus. It was *me.* I didn't blink. I stood to face him and my Macedonian guards flanked me. Memnon's hand must have gone to his sword, because the crowd gasped. Lifting a hand to calm them, I said, "Lucius Cornelius, like so many Roman veterans here, you fought for Julius Caesar. You were with him in Alexandria when he fell in love with my mother. And after he died, you joined King Bogud to fight for my father." Oh, yes, I'd studied Balbus, but this speech was for the other veterans of Actium who had loved my father and could still love me. "I honor your service, Balbus, so if you leave me, let's not part on bad terms. Let me buy your plantations at double their value."

Balbus's piggy eyes grew wide, his rage half forgotten. "Double?"

Thank Isis for the purple dye that would fund such an extravagant gesture. "I'm not stingy with friends, even when we must disagree or part ways."

"I shall consider your offer," he said, as his scarlet rage paled to the mere pink of pique. He realized that he was being banished in the gentlest possible way and that I'd won the day.

"HOW proud your mother would've been to see that," Euphronius said as we picked through the scroll racks lining the walls of Juba's study.

I unfurled some sketches, determined not to be caught unawares by anything else that Juba had put into motion while I was away. "I doubt that. I don't remember my mother's council ever questioning her."

"Oh, they did. When she was your age, the eunuch Pothinus and General Achillas tried to drive her from power."

"Let's hope Balbus isn't planning to do the same." As I made sense of the sketches, I sat in Juba's chair, suddenly light-headed. "This is ghastly! It's a cult for the emperor. Juba means for us to build a temple for Augustus as if he were a god."

Euphronius peered over my shoulder, one eyebrow raised. "Chryssa tells me you proclaimed yourself a goddess at your wedding."

"That's different," I insisted, glad he didn't press me to explain why. This sketch of the cult statue was no accurate representation of Augustus but some idealized version of the emperor, with bare feet, like some Homeric war hero. I might have laughed were it not for the carved cuirass. There, meant in clear relief, would be a celebration of the emperor's victory over my parents at Actium. As a child, I'd been forced to endure nightly lectures about the failings of my family. I thought I'd left all of that in Rome. Now Juba wanted to bring it to Mauretania? Lucky that he was away!

Perhaps I should have trembled to do it, but I took the sketch and all the accompanying scrolls and threw them into the fire. Euphronius watched them burn. "You're changed, Majesty."

He remembered me as a frightened princess. As the girl who refused to run away from Augustus to pursue an uncertain destiny. But now I *had* run away and I must make myself so powerful that even the emperor couldn't punish me for it.

BLOSSOMING springtime flowers meant that dispatches from Rome would soon arrive and I'd be held to account. I felt as if I must do everything before the emperor could act against me. With the help of several of my father's veterans, we recruited and trained marines to guard our ships from pirates—a move that was quite popular with the businessmen in Mauretania. Always, wherever I went in the city, my eyes sought out a place for a temple to Isis. I never forgot her; never forgot that she was the throne upon which I sat. I owed everything to her. *Everything*. But to build an Iseum would require the services of skilled architects, almost all of whom were Roman and already hard at work. I couldn't hire more.

As it happened, the King of Judea's new cities were effectively monopolizing most of the talent in the empire. There was one talent, however, whose artistry I was particularly fortunate to have. Master Gnaios was the only artist at my disposal who had known my brothers. Here in my own kingdom, at long last, I could memorialize them. I commissioned a statue for each of them. Caesarion, Antyllus, Helios, and Philadelphus. I even commissioned a statue of Petubastes, my cousin, the priest of Ptah. "Do you remember him, Gnaios?"

"Yes, Majesty," the gem cutter said, bowing. "But I'm surprised that *you* do. You were only a little child."

Sudden emotion made my voice thick. "I forget *nothing*."

Poor Petubastes. What had he done but breathe air with a claim to the throne of Egypt? I never knew how he died, but now I wondered if the emperor had ever intended to leave any male claimant to the throne of Egypt alive. When Augustus fished Philadelphus out of the lake, my gratitude made me forget how deadly he could be. Is that why I'd suspected only Livia of poisoning my brother? Why had it never occurred to me that the emperor would prevent my mother's son from taking the *toga virilis* and becoming a man? As this thought occurred to me, the raucous bray of trumpets punctuated some commotion outside the palace. I was so conditioned to the unhappiness of Rome that I asked, "Is there a riot?"

"It's the king's caravan," a breathless Tala answered. "King Juba has returned!"

Twenty-four

✿

WAGONS rolled into the city carrying caged exotic animals. Others were piled high with ivory tusks, minerals, and lumber. Most of the men rode camels, but a team of wild-looking horses galloped at the back of the royal procession and I didn't see what happened to them after they rode by. A fancifully embroidered palanquin was lowered to the ground by its bearers, and when the curtains parted, a lovely woman stepped out. She was dressed exquisitely in the Greek fashion, her dark hair curled in lustrous ringlets and her shoulders draped with a patterned shawl. "Good greetings, Majesty," she said, with a grace at once natural and practiced. "I am—"

"I know who you are." I gave a false smile that could have rivaled Livia's. It wouldn't do to let my husband's whore think that I resented her. For that matter, it wouldn't strengthen my hand with the royal court if I seemed threatened, so I extended my hands. "We welcome you most gladly, Lady Circe. Where is the king?"

She almost faltered but recovered quickly enough, lowering to kiss my fingertips. "King Juba has gone hunting for hippopotami."

It surprised me to learn that there were hippopotami in Mauretania. I knew them to be dangerous creatures and would have warned Juba against hunting them, but I doubted he'd welcome my counsel in any matter. "Come into the palace, Lady Circe. The sun grows too hot for your fair skin."

She gave the impression of delicacy, but I was cautious; I knew that creatures weren't always what they seemed. Once inside, the *hetaera* delivered a few messages from Juba—hastily scribbled instructions to his advisers, reminders to do this or that. Several sealed letters addressed to old friends in Rome also featured Juba's florid script. None were addressed to me. If my husband was even aware that I'd returned from Rome, there was nothing to indicate it. He'd filled scroll after scroll with details about our new kingdom. There were maps too, all of them meant to be sent on to Agrippa, who collected such things. I immediately set about having these copied so that we'd have the originals for our own library when it was built.

When all this was sorted out, I found myself alone in the receiving room with Lady Circe. Quite suddenly, she sputtered with tinkling laughter. "Juba says you're a temptress who guards her chastity at knifepoint. I thought you'd be a pitiless Artemis, but you're just a tall, gangly girl!"

It was brazen of her to speak this way to me; I nearly slapped her. "And you're just King Herod's spy."

Circe gave a little shrug of her pretty shoulders. "Herod said that he'd pay me as long as I pleased King Juba. Now that your husband has sent me away, I'm without a contract."

So, Juba had *sent her away*. Why was I glad to hear it? With Juba, I never understood myself. "I'm sure there are other wealthy clients for you. Especially in the East. Far away from here."

Circe smirked. "The wealthiest is currently amusing himself with Terentilla. Is the wife of Maecenas as pretty as they say? Do you think I could compete with her for the emperor's attention?"

Greek *hetaeras* were more than simple prostitutes. As educated women of high status, they were allowed access to the most powerful men. It didn't surprise me that she knew about the emperor's affair with Terentilla. I said only, "You aim high."

"So do you," she said, and this *did* surprise me. I wondered how much she really knew. Did she receive her information from Herod? If so, how would he know anything about me? Then I remembered his sons, Alexander and Aristobulus. Livia had favored them and they were still in Rome even now.

Circe took one of the incense burners from my table and sniffed at it. "I think we could learn much from one another."

"I'm a royal queen. There's nothing for me to learn from a prostitute who befriends King Herod."

At that, her mask of unaffected glamour fell away. "I'm no friend to King Herod. I *hate* Herod. He's mad and I don't want to return to his service. I'd rather stay here in Iol-Caesaria."

I was shocked at her nerve. "So that you can reconcile with King Juba when he returns?"

She laughed. "Your husband is an agreeable lover, but like all men, he likes a challenge. Unfortunately, there's little challenge for him in a woman whose companionship can be purchased."

I was astonished at her candor, if it *was* candor and not some ruse. "If not for Juba, why would you want to stay in Mauretania? Go home to Greece."

"I've reached the level of wealth and prominence to which the greatest *hetaeras* aspire but also the age at which we must compensate for fading beauty. There's a fortune to be made here in Mauretania."

"I think you mistake me," I said, snatching the incense dish from her hands. "I won't suffer a spy. The moment I catch you corresponding with Herod, I'll have you put to death. Don't think I can't do it. Even if my husband returns to defend you, I'll make sure some tragic accident befalls you."

She looked into my eyes as if measuring me, but I'd been measured before. There was a catch in her breath, and then I heard her swallow. "Majesty, I vow never to correspond with King Herod and to make myself useful if you'll only allow me to stay."

I wanted her gone, but how would it look if I banished *all* Juba's favorites? Besides, I'd learned from the tension between Augustus and Agrippa that it wasn't always better to have your detractors in some remote part of the world, outside of your reach. At least here in Mauretania, I held power over the *hetaera*. "You may stay, but you will be watched."

* * *

FOR weeks I'd dreaded the angry letter from Augustus that I'd thought inevitable. I had run from him. He'd be furious. But I should have remembered that Augustus burned cold. Now I worried at his silence. I sent grain, emptying our warehouses and filling the hulls of ships bound for Rome, but still he said nothing. Perhaps he knew—as I knew—that famine still lingered, and if we didn't have spectacular rains, our next harvest would be a disaster. Adding to my worries, Lucius Cornelius Balbus sold me all of his holdings in Mauretania and accepted a military appointment in the province of Africa Nova. I feared that I'd been prideful and mistaken to make him leave. Thankfully, the exorbitant profit he'd made in our exchange seemed to have sweetened his disposition considerably, and he gave me lengthy advice on how best to profit from his plantations. Still, the king would likely be livid that I'd driven away his most able soldier . . . if Juba ever returned, that is.

As for the Greek *hetaera*, Memnon reported back to me on all her doings. She didn't take a new client, but I couldn't count that against her. As the king's acknowledged mistress, there was no other man in Mauretania willing to claim her. Besides, she seemed like a vain woman, unlikely to accept *less* than a king for a lover now. Instead, she made a business of teaching Greek and earned a reputation as a talented grammarian. She was charming, made friends easily with the Alexandrians, and I found myself studying her. She wasn't the beauty I originally supposed, but skillful cosmetics enhanced her best features. She carried herself *as if* she were a great beauty, and the act made people believe. She'd said that we could learn from one another, and I began to suspect that was true.

Meanwhile, in Juba's absence, it became easy to believe that Mauretania was my kingdom alone. Juba's Roman advisers treated me with a new deference. Work on the amphitheater ceased. Work on a theater commenced and I put Maysar in charge of the project even though the Berber chieftain protested that he wasn't a builder.

To convince him, I said, "You're the only one I can trust to take into account the concerns of my subjects and not simply knock everything down in Roman fashion."

He gave a wolfish grin at my praise. "This will be costly. I'll need the help of someone with a keen sense of finance. Perhaps you can lend me the services of your freedwoman, Cleopatra Antonianus."

"*Chryssa?*" Perhaps a swarthy desert warrior like Maysar was incapable of embarrassment. He showed me a flash of teeth and I realized that he fancied her! First Julia and Iullus. Then Tala and her ship's captain. Now Chryssa and the widowed Berber chieftain. It seemed as if all my intimates were involved in amorous affairs whereas I . . . Oh, yes. I was *pitiless Artemis, guarding her chastity at knifepoint.* It wasn't the worst thing that could be said of me. My mother's reputation for promiscuity had been her undoing. Perhaps I'd do well to follow the example of Artemis and surround myself with loyal maidens, forgetting men altogether.

BY summer, my daughter was talking in complete sentences. Not just incoherent baby babble but real expressions of wants and needs. Tala taught her some Berber words too. She'd become the delight of my life and the adored princess of my court. Beekeepers gifted her with honeycombs. Cooks gave her pastries hot from the kitchens. Dairy maids let her sip the cream from their buckets. I indulged her in everything.

Though the Berbers didn't count the years of their birth and seemed to have some superstition against doing so, on the occasion of Isidora's second birthday, I hosted athletic games in her honor. Memnon wasn't in his prime anymore, but the captain of my Macedonian guard was still strong, and his tolerance for pain allowed him to prevail over a younger opponent in the wrestling event. With his sinewy muscles oiled and gleaming in the sun, Memnon beamed with pride when I awarded him the victor's wreath. And I thought to myself, *He must have looked at my mother this way. He sees in me a true Ptolemaic queen and I must never disappoint him.*

I hosted games for the Berbers too—contests for the finest woven textiles, competitions for the best-looking camel, and equestrian events in which they proved their superb horsemanship. The winning stallion might have been sacrificed if this were Rome, for their October Horse was always given to the gods, but my daughter's birthday games were bloodless. Greeks, Romans, Alexandrians, and Berbers had all competed and now shared fond memories. I took it as proof that we had no need of gladiator games!

After the final wreath was awarded to the last winner, I saw to it that trays of saffron-sprinkled cakes were adorned with edible blossoms from the garden. I hired a group of minstrels to make music and invited the young children of all my courtiers to spend that summer day at play. While the children splashed in the shallow palace pools, I sipped at watered wine that had been chilled with snow from the Atlas Mountains. My ladies and I lounged beneath an enormous canopy of ostrich feathers to protect us from the summer sun. It was hot. Too hot. Summer scorched the land, and if the rains did not come early this year, we'd have famine even in Mauretania. This weighed on my mind as I read a missive from Julia:

To My Friend, the Most Royal Queen of Mauretania,

Even though you are a wretched friend to leave me without so much as a good-bye, I hope this letter finds you well. I suppose you abandoned Rome just in time, because the city is a nest of vipers all hissing and striking at one another. Some blame everything upon my father, who they still say means to do away with the Republic. Others say that it's because we've offended Isis. Since you're so well loved in Rome, the Isiacs are emboldened. They demand that their temples be restored and claim that it's the evil of slavery that has turned the city into a mob of idlers on the dole. They risk much in light of my father's hostility. He won't hear their grievances—as if Isis had herself personally offended him. Or perhaps you have.

Your sudden departure from Rome seems to have vexed him even more than it has vexed me. The Antonias and I have faithfully performed the rites for Philadelphus that you taught us, but none of us can pretend to understand why you'd run off in the middle of the night. I can only surmise that Livia must have said or done something to make you go. With Octavia broken by grief, Livia has all the power again, but if only you'd waited, you could've enjoyed Rome without her. When my father refused the consulship, he left the city. He's gone east—to reconcile with Agrippa, I think—and has decided to winter on the Isle of Samos in Greece. Livia went with him. Tiberius too. Also, Maecenas and his wife. Their departure makes Rome a less disagreeable place for me, but I worry that I've been left behind yet again. How is it my father is master of an empire and I've never been farther away from Rome than the Isle of Capri?

Marcellus and I used to talk of how we'd travel, but now Octavia would have me mourn the rest of my life. Even so, I'd prefer it to marrying Tiberius. How grimly he climbs the ladder to power just for his mother's approval. He hasn't yet realized that no one can ever please Livia. Not truly.

Julia's letter went on to detail her exploits with Ovid and the other young aristocrats of her social circle, but she never mentioned Iullus—not even to reassure me that my half brother was still alive and well—which is how I knew that their love affair continued. Julia gave the impression of being careless, but what she cared about most, she guarded.

I looked up to hear Isidora cry with gladness, clapping her hands when presented with a basket of mewling kittens. "Baby Basts!" My daughter laughed the way Philadelphus had laughed, with unreserved joy. In my rooms, at the bottom of an iron-banded strongbox, his amulet rested beneath my other treasures and I remembered how he'd wanted her to have it. Perhaps, someday . . .

Setting Julia's letter aside, I turned to Juba's writings with surprising enthusiasm. My husband appeared to be making a complete accounting of this part of the world. His words brought a new landscape to life for me. He claimed to have found the source of the Nile; he said it flowed underground for several miles in the desert before reappearing again. I devoured every detail as he described finding the flora and fauna of Egypt here in Mauretania. This was as much a surprise to me as my own delight in Juba's prose. Every time I thought I understood the man, I discovered a new side of him. In person, he could be bloodless. Pedantic. Suffocating and frustrating and lacking all vision. But his writing voice was somehow more passionate than the one I heard when he spoke. And when I finished reading the last scroll, I longed for more.

When I looked up, my daughter was covered in kittens, squirming things that snuffled under her chin and made her giggle. As if to express her regal indifference to these interloping youngsters, Bast curled up by my feet, tucking her paws under and purring. I wondered, fleetingly, traitorously, what it might be like to give up all my other ambitions and embrace moments like these.

Chryssa ducked under the ostrich feathers to join me. "That's a strange smile you wear, Majesty. I think it's happiness. It becomes you."

Happiness. A word that all but forced the lips into a delighted shape to speak aloud. It spoke of pleasures, of blissful decadence, both of which were easily found in Mauretania. No sooner had I taken the word into myself and considered it, than guilt consumed me. By what right had I survived to feel such a thing? What would my mother, my father, and all my dead brothers think of me relaxing here in the sun while they languished in the shadows of the underworld? "It can't be right to enjoy happiness when so many suffer."

Chryssa's smile fell away. "Majesty, happiness and sorrow change partners in the dance of life. On the same day you've wept with loss, someone else has wept with joy. It can't be wrong to feel gladness. Isn't it a gift of Isis?"

I eyed her suspiciously. "You sound like a philosopher. Have you been attending Lady Lasthenia's lectures?"

"Bah, the wealth of this life is lost on the Pythagoreans. There has been much on my mind, though . . . The Berber chieftain desires to wed." My eyes must have flown wide because she hurried to say, "It's the custom of his people to ask the bride's family, so he might ask you. I won't consider his suit unless he learns Greek and unless you give your blessing, of course."

"You're a free woman, Chryssa. You don't need my blessing, but you have it if you want it. I only ask you to consider how you'll feel if Maysar takes a second wife, or a third."

"Maysar swears he'll only have one," she said, pressing her lips together. "He says that while some of the tribesmen treat their women badly, his own reveres women. Do you think he can be trusted?"

I wasn't optimistic when it came to the trustworthiness of men. "I suppose a good test is whether or not he learns Greek."

"He's taking lessons from Juba's pretty *hetaera*. We'll see if Circe turns his head as well as trains his tongue to a civilized language." She threw her feet up onto the pillows. "If he disappoints me, well, there's always the future, for it's said you'll bring about a Golden Age."

"Is that what you believe?" I asked, watching a lizard sun itself beneath a potted citron tree. "That I can make everyone happy and end all suffering with a wave of my hand?"

"I used to believe it, but even Isis couldn't deliver her son, Horus, into a world of complete happiness. The dark god Set was always there, lurking. If Isis cannot do it, how can you?"

I arched a brow. "Should I be pleased or disappointed that I've somehow broken your faith in me?"

"Oh, I still believe in you and the Golden Age. It's too important an idea. Everyone believes in it. The Easterners, the Asiatics, the Jews, and even the Romans pine for a time that's more just, more peaceful, and more enlightened."

That's because everyone is looking for a savior, I thought. *Some extraordinary person who will rescue them from all their cares.* "No one person can be all things to all people."

"That's why the idea of twins is compelling," Chryssa said. "It isn't just *one* extraordinary person. It's the idea of a partnership. Symbolic for the notion that a Golden Age can only be attained by combined effort."

There was something vitally important in what Chryssa had said, but I was distracted by my child, who squealed when Euphronius showed her the trinkets in his magician's box. Alabaster lamps and magic wands and little bowls for mixing potions. She was enraptured by all of it, a pampered princess who knew only the delights of the world, and while it could never be that way for me, I wanted it to always be that way for her. I marveled at the way sunlight made her hair a golden halo and couldn't help but see Helios in her profile. My ache for him was only made worse every time I thought of him battling in the sands of Egypt, making war at the side of a mysterious queen. I imagined the Kandake as an ebony beauty with gleaming skin and a long neck that bent gracefully when Helios stooped to kiss her ear. I shook my head, trying to dislodge the image, for it wounded me. It wasn't only a stab of jealousy but some deeper despair.

When my mother was my age, she'd only just met Caesar. Her love for him would be the beginning of her journey as a lover, not the end. My romantic future, by contrast, seemed bleak. Even if I could find it within myself to have feelings for Juba, he seemed to have abandoned our false marriage at long last.

That night, music awakened me, the soft strum of lute strings, the mournful longing of the double-reed pipe serenading me. I'd heard this song before, this Song of the Nile, and knew Egypt was calling me. Half asleep I sighed at the soft breath upon the nape of my neck. Strong wet hands caressing my shoulders, thumbs tracing down my spine. It was the god, come to me again, and need flowed hot through my body. I tasted the silted water of the Nile as it kissed my lips. And with damp bed linens clenched between my knees, I wanted . . . I wanted . . .

But I was alone. Rising from my bed, I went to the terrace where the full moon lit the sky and glinted silver off the sea. The roar of the ocean, waves folding over waves, didn't drown the music out.

At my throat, my frog amulet seemed to vibrate with *heka*, as if it had leeched from my body. *I am the Resurrection*, the engraved stone said, and I ran my fingers over the etching as if to remind myself. Was I meant to be the resurrection of my mother's spirit or was I meant to resurrect the goddess in a hostile Roman world? By dawn, having dressed and wandered into my gardens on the far side of the palace, I realized that the melody echoed from the sunlit mountains of the Atlas to the south. And why not? If Juba was right, then that was the source of the Nile, the sacred river.

I couldn't go to Egypt. I couldn't fight with Helios. But perhaps I could go to Osiris; I must find the source of the Nile.

Twenty-five

IVORY wands from Egypt adorned my wizard's lair, but new instruments found their place here too. Bundles of dried herbs hung from the walls, mortars and pestles littered a workbench, and baskets spilled forth green plants of every variety. Like me, Euphronius had learned to keep himself busy in exile, but when I told him my plans he forgot about all else. "Majesty, no one knows the source of the Nile. It's a question that has plagued geographers for centuries. Your husband the king is an eager theorist; you ought not take everything he says as fact!"

I was nearly eighteen years old now and disliked it immensely when people lectured me. "What am I to make of you, old man? You always caution me not to forget Egypt. Now I want to journey to the highlands of Mauretania to find the very source of Egypt's Nile and you discourage me."

He furrowed his bushy white eyebrows. "I'm only concerned at the way you busy yourself. Since your return from Rome, you sleep very little and you eat even less. Except for Isidora's birthday, I don't think I've seen you take your leisure for a moment."

"I feel too guilty to eat much," I confessed. "There wasn't enough food in Rome. I saw people starving. We must have early rains here in Mauretania to prepare the soil for the winter sowing if we're to have more grain in the next harvest."

And I must have grain. What Augustus needed from me—what he had always needed from me—was grain. If Helios should fail in

Egypt, grain would be my last political leverage. "Euphronius, when I was a little girl, my mother brought me to the Isle of Philae, where she gave herself to the Nile. It was the first time I watched her work *heka*. The first time I ever knew that there were things queens could do that kings couldn't. The Nile rose. The crops were bountiful. Now she's gone and famine stalks the lands. She gave me this amulet and said that I was the Resurrection. Why can't I make the land fertile the way she did?"

"Majesty, as Queen of Egypt, you'd have already made that journey down the Nile. Should I live long enough to see you on your rightful throne, I predict the most bountiful harvest that Egypt has ever known."

But that wouldn't come soon enough. "You taught us that Isis is a goddess of a thousand names," I argued. "I found Isis in the temple of Carthaginian Tanit. Crinagoras compares her to Kore. Are we to believe that her story is only an Egyptian story? That the great god who is her lover can find her *only in Egypt*? The Nile sings to me, as Osiris sings to Isis. I must go to him."

Even after I'd convinced the mage, my plans met with almost universal opposition. The Berbers argued that in my absence Juba's Roman advisers would wrest away control of the country. The Romans didn't want me to go either. Without Balbus, no clear leader stood out amongst them. They disliked taking orders from a female monarch, but there was something in the Roman psyche that preferred *order* above all else and my presence provided a reassuring hierarchy. They feared that my journey would plunge the government into chaos. I assured them that given the new roads and an accompaniment of soldiers, I'd be gone no more than a few weeks. A month at most.

I had no idea how arduous the journey was going to be.

Camels travel swiftly over great distances without food or water, but that doesn't mean that their riders don't fatigue. The scorching sun forced us to slow our pace and there were days, thirsty and dispirited, the stink of camel in my nostrils, that I considered turning back. Yet the parched land still called to me.

I'll never be able to capture the beauty of that journey the way Crinagoras did in the poems he later read at court; I am, nonetheless, compelled to try. As our expedition rode southwest, expanses of shimmering fields gave way to the vast steppes upon which the Berber tribes grazed their animals. I gasped with delight when our camels carried us past a family of African wildcats playing in the brittle grasses and thought how Isidora would have clapped her little hands to see them. Many days later, ascending from the steppes into the cedar-forested mountains where wild boars rustled in the green foliage, we looked down upon a rippling sea of sand. I knew the stark desert and its deadly beauty. Still, the cold mountains seemed even more intimidating.

Crinagoras had always indulged me with flattering verse, but I knew he took me for an eccentric queen and this trip a bizarre divergence. Swatting a fly that plagued him, he called to me, "We're on a fool's errand, Majesty. My hands are almost as blistered as yours and you'd cry if you could see how the sun has ruined your skin." Then he leaned forward on his mount. "Besides, I think you're killing your mage."

At the sight of Euphronius slumped on his camel, huddled beneath his white robes as if in a trance, I wondered what price we all might pay for my folly. I pressed my chapped lips together, considering a retreat. But no sooner had my confidence wavered than a lone jackal appeared atop a rock outcropping. *Anubis,* I thought, as the jackal howled, and my resolve was renewed.

We didn't climb to the snowy summits but hugged the edges of the mountains where fruit-laden trees and freshwater oases offered respite. It seemed hardly possible that the source of the Nile was to be found so far from Egypt, but I followed Juba's maps and his exacting descriptions, relying upon my husband in absence as I'd never relied upon him when he was near.

The deeper into the wilds we traveled, the more familiar our surroundings became; I didn't even have to close my eyes to imagine myself in Egypt. When at last we reached the banks of a river, I spied a hippo spouting a mist of water from its gaping nostrils! At the marshy scent of the river, Euphronius came awake. "Egyptian lotus," he whispered, captivated by the floating water lilies.

"Look, Majesty, all the gods of Egypt have come to do you homage," Crinagoras teased, pointing at the far bank where a crocodile sunned himself, vicious jaws cracked in a toothy smile. "First Anubis, then Hapi, now Sobek too."

I ignored my poet's irreverence. "What do you think, Euphorbus? Can the great god be found here? Is this the source of the Nile?" I urged my camel to kneel, unwrapping the shawl from my shoulders as my guards helped me down. I needed only a steadying hand from Memnon, but Euphronius had to be lifted from his mount. I didn't like to see my mage so stiff and frail, as if his bones creaked when he moved, but his awed expression told me that his spirits had been lifted along with mine.

Holding his divination staff in one hand, and his rattle in the other, he stepped onto the low rocks on the shore and stooped to touch the water. His eyes were damp when he said, "Maybe it *is* the Nile . . ."

Inside my hastily erected tent, Chryssa undressed me and brushed my hair until it gleamed. "I never thought to prepare you for another wedding," she said. "But if Osiris is here, you must come to him as a bride, divine wife to divine husband."

Though she was Greek, she'd studied well under the priests and priestesses of Egypt. I closed my eyes, surrendering to her ministrations, listening to Euphronius chant prayers and hoping the river god awaited me. I'd come to him once as a lover in the arms of Helios, so I told myself that we weren't strangers. For a thousand years, queens of Egypt had met him on the Isle of Philae, where Isis first wept for her murdered husband. Where she brought him back to life with her magic, where he waited for his love. I couldn't go to him in Philae, where the warrior queen, the Kandake, now ruled. Was it foolish to think he'd come to me here?

I emerged from my tent accompanied by a chorus of frogs. Adorned in the pure white robe of an Isiac devotee, I carried a bouquet of wildflowers. My hair was loose about my shoulders and my amulet throbbed at my throat with a heartbeat of its own. I stepped into the shallows. Close behind me, Chryssa held my robe so that I slipped naked into the murky water without revealing myself to onlookers. The mud of the riverbed sucked at my feet and warm water caressed my skin. I remembered Helios as he'd been that night in the storm, when the god had first taken me. Now I felt certain he'd been waiting, pining for me all along. "I'm the queen of this land," I said quietly. "I call upon you, Lord of the Rebirth, to bring us water for the crops. To bring us grain."

Memnon shouted in alarm as the crocodile on the far shore roused from its stupor and slid into the river with me. I wasn't afraid. Isis was in me; I had nothing to fear from crocodiles. Already, the green waves were lapping at my consciousness, drawing me into the marshy reeds of a waking dream where life teemed. And I realized that I'd seen this all before. The moment my mother put my amulet around my neck, I'd seen myself surrender to the river. Not in Egypt. Here.

It had always been *here.*

"She is the Resurrection," Euphronius chanted. *"She brings life from death. She gives to her kingdom an heir, she gives to her people their daily sustenance, and she gives Isis an embodiment on earth for Osiris to love."*

Closing my eyes, I drew the *heka* inside me, releasing it like a kiss. The wind was soft at my neck and I flushed hot all over. My nipples tightened and I felt the river swell for me. The god had come! The sweet rush of heat between my legs made me moan, a rapturous sound so foreign that I knew it belonged to the goddess. Not to me. My skin expanded to accommodate Isis. She smiled a seductive smile with my mouth. She opened her legs to the water and my thighs trembled. She panted, beckoning her paramour, and through her, I learned how it was that a woman might tease a man and make him want her.

With *heka* swirling warm in my womb, I opened like the petals of a flower. I hadn't known before that I could use magic upon my own body, to make myself ready for a child. Tentatively, I pulled at the *heka* inside me so that my womb closed again, then allowed all the wonderful sensations to come rushing back. With a wild toss of my head, I laughed. All my life, my body had been at the mercy of others. The flesh of my arms had been a canvas for my goddess to paint with blood. My breasts and the tender flesh between my legs had been in the emperor's possession, to give away to Juba or plunder for himself. Mastery over myself, over my body, over my fertility itself, was a triumphant thrill.

"Now," Euphronius said, somewhere in the distance. "Work your magic *now!*"

Controlling *heka* the way he'd taught me, I found the core, the hopes and fears and dreams, and I let it flow out of my fingertips into the river. I let it go. Sweet release! I saw the frog and the minnows, the life-giving silt settling onto the fields beyond and everywhere I turned in the water, the birds flocked and water lilies blossomed. I traced lazy circles into the river, bringing fish leaping to the surface. I passed dried brown foliage as I made my way to shore, and it sprouted green with life again. I gazed upon the washed-up carcass of a viper and it arose, swollen and shimmering like the phallus of a lover. My mother had surrendered to his venomous love bite, but I wasn't ready to pass into the afterlife.

I rose up, gloriously naked, glistening rivulets of river water flowing over my bare belly, hips, and thighs. With the flush of divine lovemaking on my body, I knew that I radiated beauty. I was beautiful at last. Filled with promise. An overflowing cornucopia.

None dared to look upon my nudity. Chryssa seemed lost in reverie as she enveloped me in my white robe. Poor Memnon trembled. Crinagoras stood speechless, the papyrus he'd been writing upon lost to the breeze. Others joined Euphronius in prayer, and he led them, though his voice was hoarse.

And then it rained.

RETURNING to Iol-Caesaria, I spread my arms and lifted my face to welcome each raindrop. I was no longer a stranger here. I felt connected to the camel, to every brown rock and green blade of grass. These were *my* juniper bushes that hugged the mountainside, *my* antelopes that danced across the steppes of the Maghreb, and *my* people who waved to us from passing caravans. This was *my* Mauretania and love swelled in my breast as if I were seeing it for the first time.

When we reached the palace, riding through the gates and giving our weary animals over to the stable, Isidora ran out to welcome me home. I swung my daughter up into my arms and spun her in the rain.

Twenty-six

MY servants prepared a bath of milk and honey to treat my sun-burned skin. Once I was bathed, and perfumed with rose water, and wearing clean clothes again, I took supper in my rooms. Eggs and olives. Grilled flat bread and seasoned lamb. A creamy pudding made of goat's milk, dotted with raisins and dates. All to be washed down with a pot of hot mint tisane. I enjoyed it as I'd never enjoyed food and drink before, certain that a bountiful harvest was to come.

As I made to sink down with Bast into my indulgently soft mat-tress for a well-deserved rest, Memnon knocked at the door. "The king has returned," he said.

Stroking my cat's fur, I didn't even stir. "It's just another cara-van with all his scrolls and hunting trophies, and possibly some other woman he's discarded."

Memnon gave a quick shake of his head. "Majesty, Tala *saw* King Juba dismount from his horse and says he's now coming in from the rain."

TOO late, the trumpeters rushed to announce the king's arrival. He waved them away. I wasn't sure I'd have heard them anyway, over the thunder of my heartbeat. Juba stood under an awning that shielded him from the downpour and nodded to me in stiff, formal greeting. A circlet of gold made him appear to be the king that he was, and such adornments finally seemed to rest easy upon his brow. It'd been almost two years since I'd seen him and I'd forgotten his good looks. I was momentarily captivated.

Whether it was the stuporous rain or the late hour, we were quite alone in the cavernous throne room and Juba said, "*Salve*, Selene." He often retreated to Latin when distressed, and truly, Juba did look pained.

"Are you ill?" I asked.

He laughed, sweeping his hand through his wet hair. "It's just that nothing here looks quite like I left it. Even *you* are changed. A woman now."

Why should I want for him to look at me and find me beautiful? What I wanted—what I *truly* wanted, I reminded myself—was to ensure that all my hard-won gains wouldn't be spoiled by Juba's return. "Perhaps you're just looking at it all with new eyes . . ."

Juba shook the rain off and looked abashed when it puddled on our mosaic floors. "I wanted to see you, Selene."

"That's why you've come home?" I asked, not ready to believe it.

"Perhaps it was the rain." It was autumn. A year since Philadelphus's death. I wasn't the only one counting months. Juba's gaze traveled down to the flat expanse of my belly. He didn't allow his eyes to linger on my empty womb, but Juba wasn't a practiced liar. That single glance told me his fears. That glance told me that he still thought of me as a wicked seductress and feared that I'd brought home another bastard child. If I told him, *This time I ran from him. He told me what he wanted from me, and I ran,* Juba wouldn't believe me. Perhaps he'd even tell me that I shouldn't have run.

With that horrible thought, I said, "I'll summon Lady Circe for you."

JUBA'S arrival wasn't the only thing to ruin the evening. While we were gone to the river, war in Egypt raged on. News arrived that the latest Roman prefect had launched a counterattack, destroying the Meroite city of Napata. I held my breath, terrified that I should read that the so-called Horus the Avenger had been captured or killed in the fighting. Instead of total Roman victory, however, I read of Rome's failure to make substantial gains against the formidable Kandake of Meroë and her war elephants.

Still, this news shattered me. In searching for the Nile, I told myself that if I could make the land fertile again, a burden would be lifted from Egypt. Now I worried that I'd simply fallen too much in love with Mauretania and the comforts it afforded me. No one else might ever know it, but *I* knew Helios was fighting the Romans. I should be with him, helping to free Egypt from Roman tyranny, trying to win back my mother's throne. She'd entrusted to me her legacy, but I let the Queen of Meroë fight my battles. And she was losing them.

JUBA had returned from his expedition with a caravan of precious salt from the marshes, spectacular hunting trophies, and a variety of exotic animals, including a Barbary macaque. The king came to my apartments with the furry monkey on his arm. "I've heard tell that the Princess Isidora likes animals," Juba said. "I brought this little creature back for her as an early Saturnalia gift."

Juba was a stranger to my daughter, but far from being afraid of him, she was delighted. She lowered to him in deference, a baby's imitation of the other ladies in the palace, and her bright eyes glittered as she reached out for her new pet. I was wary of the monkey's mischievous little hands. My Berber woman nodded a warning to me when the creature yawned, pointing out the sharp teeth. What kind of gift was this for a young child? I wanted to refuse it but didn't like to refuse my daughter anything. Moreover, I regretted the churlish way I'd left Juba the night before. "You're not to play with the monkey unless Tala is watching," I said to my daughter, then thanked Juba politely.

He was also polite, commenting approvingly on the artwork I'd chosen for this part of the palace and admiring the carved gemstones I'd brought back from Rome, for he collected them, and was a great connoisseur of beautiful things.

Then we had nothing to say.

The next day, letters arrived from Rome. Two were from my

half sisters, the Antonias, telling me that the tomb for Philadelphus was now complete. Minora's letter was dreamy and idealistic, and she confessed to me an abiding affection for young Drusus, whom I remembered fondly even if he was Livia's son. By contrast, the elder Antonia's letter was stiff and stilted, expressing a deep sadness that she'd yet to give her husband a child.

While I was occupied with these letters, Isidora disappeared from under Tala's watchful eye and sent the palace into an uproar. After hunting for her behind statuary and potted palms, we found her in Juba's study, sitting on his lap. "North African elephants assist one another when they're hunted," he said, reading to her from his latest treatise, "and will defend one that is exhausted. And if they can remove him out of danger, they anoint his wounds with the tears of the aloe tree, standing round him like physicians."

I was in no mood for fanciful talk of elephants. "Isidora, you're not to run off from Tala!"

"It's all right," Juba said, cradling her. "Every writer needs an appreciative audience once in a while." Nevertheless, I pried her out of his arms and sent her off. As I turned to follow, Juba stopped me. "Stay awhile, Selene . . ." He motioned me into a seat that had ornate, talon-shaped feet that reminded me of a Ptolemy Eagle. When I was seated, Juba said, "I should have said this before now. I was saddened to hear the news from Rome. Marcellus and Philadelphus were fine young men. I can't imagine how you must have grieved for them."

No, he couldn't imagine it, and I could barely speak of it. "I *still* grieve for them."

"As do I," Juba said, then paused a moment before adding, "You were gone a long time in Rome."

"You were gone longer, Juba. Our advisers despaired of your return."

"My absence didn't grieve *you*, though," he said, amber eyes alight. "Did it?"

I flushed. "It gave me a chance to prove myself. To prove that I can rule—"

"Without me," Juba interrupted, shaking his head, though he didn't seem angry. In truth, his journey seemed to have rejuvenated him. He seemed somehow more at ease with himself and with me. "You're almost eighteen years old now and just *look* at you." I was wearing nothing scandalous—a white Grecian dress with a thick collar of aquamarine gemstones around my neck. My hair fell in a single braid down my back and I wasn't even wearing cosmetics. Nonetheless, Juba said, "You're tall as a goddess and just as assured. I suppose Augustus can't be blamed for keeping you in Rome so long."

Not this conversation again. I rose to my feet. "He didn't *keep* me and I'm sorry that Isidora disturbed you. She's normally a well-behaved child. I'll make sure she doesn't bother you again."

Juba lifted a hand, a gesture of apology. "She's not a bother. She's my daughter."

Because we were alone, I dared to say, "We both know she's not."

"Has Augustus claimed her?" With silence as my answer, Juba leaned back. "Then I'm her father in every way that matters and I'd like to know her." It gave me pause. I had loving memories of my father whereas Juba had none. Perhaps he took pity on Isidora. "Selene, I promised that no one would ever have cause to believe that she's not mine."

That statement forced two years of pent-up fury out of me. "A promise you broke! You wrote to Augustus about her."

"Gods!" Juba slammed his palm on the desk. "Do you think I wanted to tell him? Do you think I enjoyed the humiliation?"

To see Juba behave as if this tortured *him* was too much. "Then why didn't you *lie*? Why confess to him that you'd never laid a hand on me as a husband?"

His lips tightened. "Because I'm not a Ptolemy, Selene. Intrigue isn't bred into my bones."

I clasped my hands beneath my chin in a gesture of mockery. "How could I forget? You're the noble savage. The scholarly king. *Rex Literatissimus.* Too busy with your studies to worry about keeping your word."

"I thought you *wanted* Augustus to know," he said, rising to face me.

"Why would you think such a thing?" Had he believed I'd force the emperor to acknowledge my child and willingly make myself the most notorious woman in the empire? It's what my mother would have done. What she *did* do. But Isidora was a girl. There could be nothing gained from using her in such a way. "What gives you the impression that I wanted to reveal *my* humiliations?"

Juba came closer, as if to unsettle me. "Am I to believe, in the years we've been apart, that you've stopped scheming to reclaim what your mother lost?"

"Oh, Juba." I made a sound of disgust. "Have you returned only to rejoin our tedious circle of recriminations?"

"No." He held up his hands in surrender. "I'm sorry. This isn't how I envisioned our reunion."

"Then just how *did* you envision it?"

"Like this," he said, darting forward to fasten his lips upon mine. It was a sudden, unexpected kiss, and my hands flailed behind me, finding purchase on the edge of his writing table. He'd taken me entirely by surprise, but he didn't force his kiss upon me beyond that first shocking sensation. It was my own nature—awakened by the god in the river—that allowed me to give myself over to him, like some common doxy.

In Juba's kiss, I detected the hint of sandalwood and cinnamon, the scents of the desert that always seemed to cling to him. A scent I'd mistaken for *heka*, and perhaps Juba did work some small magic on me, because I didn't pull away even when I felt his hand press at the small of my back. Instead, I wrapped my arms about his shoulders and he rained kisses down the column of my neck, until I realized how very much I wanted him to kiss my mouth again. When he did, the brush of his lips against mine was electric. I kissed him back. I kissed him again and again, until my bosom rose and fell with desperate little breaths.

It wasn't until Juba pushed his knee between mine that I became a frightened girl again and the shuttered doors rattled open with a gust of wind. "Let me go."

Juba whispered, "Selene, I'll be gentle with you . . ."

"Let me go before the servants see us together this way."

He withdrew, blinking in bewilderment. "You're my wife. There's no shame in this."

"To the contrary. I've never done anything so shameful in my life."

* * *

IN my chambers, I threw myself down on the bed, burying my face in the pillows, smothered with self-loathing. What had I done? What had I allowed to be done *to me*. Always before, desire was the goddess in me. Not my needs, but *hers*. Desire had always been something *holy*. Something sacred—no, that wasn't true. My body had responded to Juba on our wedding night. Of course, that was before he'd given me over to the emperor's bed. Before he'd betrayed me and accused me and threatened me . . . what excuse did I have now? Juba had kissed me and I'd kissed back. I'd kissed a man I *knew* I couldn't trust. Agrippa, Livia, and Augustus had all accused me of being a wanton. I'd always denied it. Now I wondered if I knew myself at all. Perhaps I *was* a faithless whore. All my family was dead, or presumed to be. My twin brother was fighting a war. Egypt was suffering. And I? I'd survived all so that I could kiss a man I didn't love. If I'd known I was capable of prostituting myself, perhaps I wouldn't have run from the emperor. What difference did the man make if the shame was all alike? In Rome, I'd had the emperor in my hand and the double crown of Egypt poised above my head. But I'd fled, all so that I could offer myself to a man who had no higher ambition than writing his next treatise on geography!

"Majesty?" Chryssa entered the room. "The king told me that you were upset . . ."

"Of course he did. The king has no sense of discretion whatsoever."

She sat on the edge of my bed, unbidden. "I think that he cares for you."

I turned to glare. "Chryssa, you have little idea the myriad ways in which he's betrayed me."

She knew more than anyone not to argue in Juba's defense, but she asked, "Doesn't Isis ask us to forgive?"

I didn't want to listen. Her eyes were bright with love for her widowed Berber chieftain and I knew that love made women foolish. She probably envisioned that Juba and I could find the same companionship she'd found with Maysar. She simply didn't understand. "There are some things that are unforgivable. And I was born with my mother's hard, unforgiving heart."

Chryssa had the temerity to laugh at me. "You couldn't even make your heart hard enough to throw your husband's whore out into the street! And when you finally banished that odious Balbus, you sent him off with a ransom."

"Those were matters of political expedience. The king . . . my husband . . . Juba is another matter."

Chryssa rose to extinguish the candles in the sconces on the wall, plunging our talk into darker, deeper intimacy. "You think your mother wouldn't have forgiven him."

"She wouldn't have."

"Didn't your father break with your mother to marry Octavia?" Chryssa asked, snuffing out another candle. "Yet Cleopatra forgave Antony, didn't she? She took him back."

I'd been only a little child when that happened. Isidora's age. Even so, I'd known of my mother's distress. Her tears. Her passionate vows that she'd have nothing to do with my father again. How had I forgotten that? Shaking the memory away, I said, "My mother must've forgiven him because it was in the interests of Egypt to do so."

I smoothed my hair back, returning myself to composure. From now on, I'd learn more control. I already knew how to mask my face; I could master the rest of me too. No one would see my cheeks flush with humiliation unless I allowed it. And no one would kiss me and feel my body quicken with desire unless it was for political gain.

EUPHRONIUS hunched over his table, sniffing something that looked like a cactus. "Your cat nibbled upon this plant and vomited it up with no ill effects. The local tribesmen say that it has a purgative effect and the king has promised to name it after me if I discover it's useful as an herbal remedy."

I rolled my eyes. "Is Juba afraid he'll need it as an antidote to poison?"

"You don't seem pleased that he's returned."

"Why should I be?" I asked, watching him work. Trying to learn. "Juba is ruining everything!"

"How so?" the mage asked. "Lady Lasthenia tells me that the king has acquired an interest in Pythagorean philosophy."

"What of it? Juba has an interest in *everything* and a commitment to nothing."

Euphronius cut the plant with a sharp knife, exposing a milky substance. "Our little princess seems quite taken with him."

"My daughter is a small child and she's excited about the monkey Juba gave her for the Saturnalia. She doesn't know better. Now that the holiday season is past, Juba's ordered that work start again on that horrid gladiatorial arena. What's more, he's countermanded my orders that Maysar invite ambassadors from the Garamantes for a hearing of their grievances. Worse, he recommended to the Roman Senate that Lucius Cornelius Balbus be made proconsul of Africa Nova. Just as I thought I was rid of that man!"

"Majesty," Euphronius interrupted. "You summoned the rains; it's going to be a very good harvest. You'll provide Augustus with a veritable mountain of grain. He'll see, he *must* see, that you're meant to rule Egypt, so why concern yourself with a husband that you may not have for long?"

His question startled me. "You think I'll be able to divorce Juba . . . or . . ." I eyed the plant.

Euphronius scowled at my implication. "If Augustus sets you on the throne of Egypt, I think you'll be forced to divorce and compelled to give up all claim to Mauretania. It's one thing to restore Cleopatra's daughter to power. Quite another to expand her territory beyond the farthest reaches of the Ptolemaic Empire."

The vapors from the plant stung my eyes and I was suddenly eager to be done with this conversation. "It's useless to speculate," I finally said. "Augustus hasn't had a word for me since last winter."

Euphronius was uncharacteristically frank. "Your paths to rule Egypt *do* narrow, Majesty."

"WHY must we visit Master Gnaios?" Isidora asked, swinging like her monkey at the end of my arm. She didn't even notice the palace guards who followed us down the corridor; she took them as her due. "I want you to take me to see the lambs."

Now that it was lambing season, I had promised to take her to watch the ewes giving birth, but it would have to wait. "First, we're going to see Master Gnaios because he's made some statues for us."

"Why?"

"Because I asked him to."

"Why?" she asked again. This had apparently become her favorite question.

Fortunately, Gnaios relieved me of an exasperated reply when he cried, "Majesty!" Hurriedly grabbing up his tools when we were announced, he warned, "This is no place for a child. There are bits of stone and dust and sharp instruments—"

"She likes to be with me." I'd never deny her that, and whenever Isidora's tantrums strained my nerves, I reminded myself of all the dark nights I'd longed for my own mother, never to find her there.

Without fanfare, Gnaios pulled a curtain aside to reveal the first statue, and my hands went to my mouth. "It—it hasn't been painted yet," Gnaios said quickly, to fend off criticism. "It's only pale marble."

It was a ghost of Caesarion, features waxy, like they must have been after he was strangled. "I think you've captured his *ka*. This is what my brother looked like."

"It's what *my* brother looks like," my daughter said, spouting nonsense just to vex me.

"Isidora, behave!" I recovered from the surprise of seeing Caesarion, only to be saddened by the likeness of Philadelphus, with its cherubic cheeks and pudgy fingers. "Oh no. But you've made him look so young . . ."

Gnaios hung his head. "He was only six years old when last I saw him, Majesty." And when I nodded my understanding, he went on to say, "For Petubastes, I adopted the Egyptian style, in basalt. Only proper for an Egyptian priest."

"Selene?" I turned to see Juba in the doorway with an official dispatch in his hand. A purple cape trailed from his shoulders, and he looked kingly and resplendent. Yet his face was grim as death. "We've received word from the emperor. You've been summoned to the Isle of Samos."

IN Juba's study I read the missive twice; then, as I dizzied, the lettering ran together like spilled ink. It wasn't the emperor's handwriting. Nor was it an expression of imperial fury. It was a formal and official document penned by Maecenas that summoned me to Greece. A broken water clock perched precariously at the edge of Juba's writing table and he tinkered with its decorated parts, intent upon repairing it. "Why do you seem so stunned, Selene?"

Because the reckoning is finally at hand, I thought. More than a year had passed since I'd fled Rome. Plenty of time for the emperor's cool anger to rise to a roiling boil. I'd used the time to make myself a capable queen; the reports he'd receive from legionaries and plantation owners should convince him I was a useful, if not essential, part of his plans. I'd gambled that his ambition was stronger than his vindictiveness. How anxious I was not to lose that gamble. "Why am *I* stunned, Juba? Why aren't *you*? What have you heard? What does the emperor intend?"

Juba carefully removed the little chime from the water clock, inspecting it for rust. "I'm not surprised that you've been summoned because all the Eastern royalty are being called to Samos. Archelaus of Cappadocia and Iamblichus of Emesa are both seeking to be reaffirmed to their kingdoms. I'm told that Augustus will restore Tarcondimotus to his ancestral lands. He might do the same for Mithridates III of Commagene." In short, there wasn't a petty prince in the Mediterranean world who wouldn't be there, currying the emperor's favor in the hopes of retaining or regaining his patrimony. I was only different because I was a woman and because I was Cleopatra's daughter. Augustus had gone to the East to play kingmaker, and he was summoning *me*.

Juba leaned back, jingling the bell in his hand, avoiding my eyes, but his concentration on the water clock couldn't disguise the bitterness in his voice. "If I had to guess, Selene, I would say that at long last the emperor plans to give you your heart's desire."

At the word *desire*, an arrow of shame pinned me to my seat as I remembered my lust-soaked lips pressed against Juba's mouth. In Rome, I'd given no consideration to the emperor's proposal to bear him a son, though it may have granted me everything. Then I'd kissed Juba for no advantage whatsoever. Regrettably, he had plainly read something into that kiss. Taken some sign from it. "I'm sorry," I whispered with genuine sorrow, for it seemed as if I were destined always to disappoint him.

"Augustus will expect tribute," Juba said, stoutly. He was right. From the other princes, the emperor would demand monuments and oaths of loyalty. From me, the emperor would demand grain, but I couldn't lie to myself. Augustus might demand much more. *You want Egypt*, he'd said. *Well, I want you to give me a son.* Inwardly, I flailed like a bird in a net. Could I actually *let* Augustus put his defiling hands on me? Even for the throne of Egypt, could I open my legs for the same man who had forced them apart?

Augustus had wanted me to be his Cleopatra, his lover, the mother of his son. Perhaps that was what he still wanted. Or perhaps his single objective was now to punish me. If that was the case, my only defense would be to enchant him, drawing his fascination tight as a bowstring until he'd risk anything to have me and do anything to please me. Digging my fingernails into my palms as if to raise blood, I reminded myself that I'd endured worse than a rutting man inside me. What right did I have to hold my body somehow sacred while others suffered? Hadn't Isis herself written that I was more than flesh?

Juba interrupted my thoughts, a look of melancholy settling on his features. "Are you going to go?"

I let the summons fall from my lax grip. "What choice do I have?"

Twenty-seven

DESPITE the king's distress, the mood in the palace was festive. Crinagoras lifted his wine cup in yet another toast to himself. "Such good fortune for Alexandria! Not only will Egypt be blessed with her rightful queen, but that fair city will soon be the home of the greatest court poet ever known."

Lady Lasthenia sighed with sentiment. "Oh, I *have* missed the Museum. All that we've learned here will generate much interest as a series of lectures."

Even Memnon, usually so professionally distant, quietly observed, "We'll be exiles no more."

I was struck by the red-rimmed emotion in his eyes. Had none of my courtiers come to love Mauretania as I had? Or was it simply that none of them knew the price I might have to pay? Unutterably selfish ideas crowded my thoughts. I flirted with the idea of refusing the summons. Of staying here in Mauretania, where I might live in defiance. I fantasized about building something new, something untouched by the emperor . . . but I was a Ptolemy and these people, these Alexandrians, had been my mother's subjects. Now they were mine. I must fight for them. I must fight for my heritage. I must fight for Egypt.

At the start of their romance, my father had famously summoned my mother. At Tarsus, she'd come to him as Aphrodite. She'd come to seduce him, and no one who saw her gilded barge with its perfumed grottoes could've mistaken her intentions. Was that part of the grand drama that the emperor felt compelled to re-create? I wasn't the only one to wonder. "He expects you to make a spectacle of yourself, doesn't he?" Chryssa asked, as if calculating how this journey might drain the treasury.

"Why *wouldn't* she make a spectacle?" Lady Lasthenia asked. "She's good at it. Our queen has theatrical sensibilities. If she's to be the Queen of Egypt, isn't it appropriate to show that she's wealthy, powerful, and beloved of the gods? How else will people understand the import?"

She wasn't wrong. Before the other royalty of the world, it must never seem that I was just a minor queen of an unimportant Western kingdom. I'd have to bring lavish gifts that wouldn't laden down our ship—smaller things of value, made of pearls and ivory. I'd need extravagant royal costumes and even the sails of my ship ought to be dyed in Gaetulian purple. Every prince in the world must see me as a worthy heir to my mother's legacy.

It would all play out on the world stage, so I must consider the symbolism behind every choice. With the emperor, everything was a game, a test. This one might well be the most important of my life. So how was I to make my entrance? Was I to dock the ship and invite Augustus and his men to join me for a feast? To flaunt my wealth, should I, like my mother before me, dissolve my pearl earrings in a glass of strong wine vinegar and drink it down? *No*, I thought. Augustus might have claimed my father's place, but he didn't see himself as *Antony*. He was *Caesar*. If I went to him, better to be rolled out at his feet in secret than come to him in open invitation.

If I went to him . . . How was there any other choice?

I might finally be going home to Egypt, so why did I feel so melancholy? Perhaps it was my maudlin tendencies or perhaps it was because I might never see Mauretania again. The cream and yellow marble of our palace, the green columns, the blue Berber carpets, the tapestries and statuary, the aloe plants beneath the almond and olive trees, and the glittering fountains in which my daughter loved to play. Without remembering how I got there, I found myself standing in the gardens, amidst the ocean of lavender that swayed in the breeze. When Euphronius came upon me, the sun was setting into the glow of dusk; I hadn't noticed the lateness of the hour. "Majesty, you'll send for me, won't you?"

It was understood that he couldn't come with me to Greece, where he might be recognized as a mischief maker. "I'll send for you the moment I step foot in Egypt . . . *if* I do."

"This may be your last opportunity, Majesty."

One didn't need to see into the Rivers of Time to know that. Lifting my arms, I hoped to catch sight of symbols carved there, red and vivid, serpents and sails, ropes and staves, papyrus reeds and boats. There was nothing. No hieroglyphs to guide me. "Isis used to speak to me. She used to etch her words in my skin. If she'd only show me the way . . ."

"I'll find a blade," Euphronius said. "If she's called by the blood of her followers, I'll spill my blood for you."

His offer, so earnestly made, so faithful, touched me. Once, Philadelphus had given his blood for just such a purpose, but now it seemed wrong to call upon my goddess by making someone else suffer. "No, Euphronius. I suspect Isis isn't to be summoned to account like some client queen." When the old man's face fell, I took his hands. "There's a story about Isis in Tyre. To protect her child and all of Egypt from the dark god, she lay down as a prostitute, did she not?"

"So some stories say," the old man admitted.

I fingered the jade amulet at my throat. "And I am the Resurrection . . ."

IN the days leading to my departure the Alexandrians weren't just festive but jubilant. By contrast, the Mauretanians were dispirited and, in Maysar's case, *insolent*. Hastily announcing his resignation in the empty audience room, the Berber chieftain gave no hint of that flashing white smile I'd come to appreciate. "I wish you luck, madam. If it's time for you to return to Egypt, then it's time for me to return to my tribe. I wasn't meant for city living and can no longer be of use."

"That isn't true," I argued. "Without me here, Juba will need your advice more than ever."

Maysar snorted, his dark eyes boring into mine. "The Garamantes are a people much like the Egyptians. For months now, I've been extolling your virtues to their emissaries, making it known that you're a queen who honors the same things they do. Can I say the same of King Juba? Once you leave, it isn't difficult to predict what will happen. Within a year, Lucius Cornelius Balbus will use the legions of Africa Nova to crush these tribes and there'll be no sanctuary for them in Mauretania."

"Perhaps they deserve to be crushed," I said with a nonchalance I didn't feel. "They're rebels. The Romans aren't *always* wrong in all things. Perhaps the Garamantes will only respond to a show of violent force."

"You don't believe that," he said sadly.

I rubbed my forefingers over the pearled arms of my throne chair. "And you're not resigning because of the Garamantes. You're leaving because you're angry with me."

He shrugged his shoulders, throwing his blue-stained hands to the sides. "You're right. I *am* angry with you."

"Why? How have I offended you?"

An indignant puff of air burst from his lips. "You're abandoning Mauretania, madam, where you're needed. Where you're loved."

There was no pretense to be made about my ambitions, so I said, "I'm loved in Egypt too."

He gave a stubborn shake of his head. "Your mother is loved in Egypt. You are merely *remembered*. Mauretania is the land where the people have turned to you with hope. This is the city you've built. The city in which you rear your daughter, our beloved princess. But it isn't enough for you."

What did he want me to do? Who did he think I was? "I belong in Egypt. I'm a Ptolemy."

"Yes," he said, staring more boldly than a subject had a right to. "The *last* of the Ptolemies; I've heard it said. You've never forgiven yourself for it. Do you think you can bring your dead to life?"

"Yes, I do!" Was I not the Resurrection? "My family is dead and I must walk the steps they can't walk. I must breathe the breath that was stolen from their lungs. Speak the words their silenced tongues can't speak. It's a sacred thing. Berbers honor their ancestors, why shouldn't I?"

My words changed his expression and for a moment he bowed his head. When he lifted it again, he said, "Because you let yourself enjoy nothing that your mother didn't enjoy. Love nothing that she didn't love. You refuse to be content where she couldn't be content. I think you punish yourself for being *alive*. That is not sacred."

This was too much, and I rose to my feet. "I should have you flogged for speaking to me this way."

Contemptuously, he threw the end of his woolen burnoose over one shoulder. "You wouldn't even trouble yourself, madam. Your mind is on Egypt. You wish for Augustus to make you queen and Pharaoh. If he grants your wish, you'll live in Alexandria and we'll never see you again. It's understood by all. So I bid you farewell."

I was appalled. "I haven't dismissed you. Will you leave Chryssa too? Didn't you ask her to wed?"

He paused only long enough to say, "Cleopatra Antonianus has chosen to be at *your* side, not *mine*, so I cannot marry her. I'm not so well mannered as our king to sit at the shore and watch my bride go."

I sought Chryssa in my rooms but found only a horde of servants packing up clothing, jewels, furnishings, and artwork—all my belongings, as if they too, didn't expect me to return. In all this bedlam, Tala's little son, Ziri, and my Isidora ran riot. To their great delight, the yellowish brown monkey was pelting the children with dates. Tala sat nearby, mixing a henna paste for her tattoos, raising no objection whatsoever. When I complained, she gave me a cool stare such as she hadn't done since I first arrived in Mauretania. "Your brother has already given me an earful of contempt today, Tala. If you plan to do the same, please let it wait until tomorrow."

She pounded the mortar down into the henna paste and a headache began to pound behind my eyes. "Perhaps it's better that we not speak of things upon which we'll never agree, Majesty."

"I have no choice but to go. You were with me in Rome. You *know*."

She stopped stirring the paste. "I know that you suffered in Rome as I've never seen you suffer. You were so sad and afraid. I can't be glad that you'll return to those people. I go with you only because Isidora must go."

Chryssa appeared in my doorway, giving a delicate snort. "Tala's going with us so she can spend time with her ship's captain. Hope she doesn't shame you with scandalous behavior."

Tala glared at Chryssa, but as it happened, I cared nothing about scandals with ship's captains. "Chryssa, you've made a place for yourself here as a freedwoman. You have a chance at happiness with Maysar. You don't have to go with me to Greece."

"I've always wanted to visit Greece," she said, checking my strongboxes to make sure they were locked. "Besides, you have too many young, inexperienced girls tending to you. I don't trust any of them to style you properly."

I rubbed at my temples. "You're not an *ornatrix* anymore. You preside over a royal monopoly. What you've done with the Gaetulian purple makes you as important as any minister in any other royal court."

Chryssa's voice changed then. It went deeper and filled with emotion. "I want them to see me. Livia. Augustus. I want them to see me standing upright and not cowering. I want them to see me wearing jewels that I *own*. I want them to see me as a freedwoman. *Cleopatra Antonianus.*"

I wanted her with me, so why did I discourage her? "Even the well-born cower before Augustus. Slave, freedwoman, or queen, remember that the emperor and his wife can do us harm."

But Chryssa wouldn't be dissuaded. She'd come with me, and Tala would come too. Next, I sent for the *hetaera* and she dipped gracefully before me. "Lady Circe," I said, pinching the bridge of my nose, for my headache had only worsened, "I'd like for you to accompany me to Greece."

This seemed to have surprised her as much as it did my other servants. Her painted eyes went wide, and for a moment, I thought she'd refuse. "Will you leave the king no comfort at all?"

If she were still my husband's lover, she'd been remarkably discreet. I dared not leave her behind. "The king's comfort isn't my foremost concern. Furthermore, I was led to understand that you'd taken up a vocation as an academic. Will you travel with me or no?"

We both pretended she had a choice. "Are you sure you wish to have a *hetaera* in your retinue, Majesty?"

"I won't. I'll have a grammarian. Princess Isidora needs a teacher."

"She's still a very little girl," Circe said.

"But already speaking three languages. Ptolemies are educated at the youngest possible age."

This was all true, but subterfuge, and Circe wasn't fooled. "Ah, *education*. I suppose one can never be too young, or too old, to learn."

The pain in my head made me impatient. "I'm going to be the Queen of Egypt."

"So everyone says," she replied. "But very little in life is without a price."

So, we understood one another, and I found myself grateful not to have to spell it out. She'd told me that we could learn from one another. Hopefully, in Greece, I wouldn't be required to put this to the test.

ON the morning of our leave-taking, I went to my private shrine to pray for a safe journey. Euphronius had taught me to kiss the back of my hand and display it to Isis as a gesture of welcome and to burn sage in offering. I did these things and lit candles too, so absorbed in my devotions I was startled to look up and find Juba standing in the doorway. He never came here, never even acknowledged the shrine—whether it was to forestall criticism from Rome or to leave me a sanctuary, I never knew. Now here he stood, shoulders slumped, head low, his hair unbarbered. "Don't go, Selene."

My senses were still hazy with ritual devotion. "What?"

"Don't go," Juba repeated, coming to my side. "Stay here, in Mauretania."

I swallowed. "You, of all people, can't expect me to defy Augustus."

Dark circles under his eyes told me he hadn't slept. "You're the only one who *can* defy him, Selene. *Delay.* Wait until autumn, when the sea closes, and we'll say the dispatch arrived too late for travel." Such deception wasn't beyond me, but it shocked me that Juba should suggest it, and here in this sacred space no less. I'm afraid my mouth hung open. "Listen to me, Selene. I have a plan. If you were with child, he wouldn't make you go. If you were with child . . . with *my* child . . . he might not *want* you anymore."

I remembered the emperor's reaction to my maidenhead and how much pleasure it gave him to know he was the only man to have me. If I were to give myself to Juba, it might break the emperor's fascination, and a part of me seized upon this as the solution to everything. Then I thought of those statues I'd commissioned, my mother, my brothers, all those who'd died, and I came to my senses. "It would ruin everything, Juba. I'd lose *everything.*"

His head fell back and he closed his eyes. "Don't tell me that you haven't come to love Mauretania. Can't your ambitions be satisfied with this new kingdom we're building? That's all that drives you. *Ambition.* You can't have conceived a true passion for Augustus, so why can't you stay? Tell me what stands between me and your heart, and I'll conquer it."

This kind of talk frightened me. "I cannot abandon Egypt. Especially not when she is at war!"

"You worry needlessly for Egypt. I have it on the best authority that the Kandake of Meroë will send ambassadors to negotiate a peace treaty with Augustus."

This news was a lightning bolt, electrifying my blood until every hair stood on end. Tingling everywhere, I scarcely trusted myself to speak. "Meroë will send a delegation to Augustus? To the Isle of Samos?"

Juba tilted his head, eyes wide with confusion. "So I'm told. The Kandake herself may go."

Any hesitation, any doubt, that I might answer the emperor's summons vanished. For Isidora's sake, I might embrace a life with Juba, but Egypt and Helios stood between us. If the warrior queen of Meroë was to join Augustus, so must I. I must see her with my own eyes. I must search her retainers for even a glimpse of my twin. I'd leave for Greece today and not all the sincerity in Juba's eyes would stop me.

Twenty-eight

EXCEPT for the billowing purple sails on my ship, my arrival on the Isle of Samos was without fanfare. No cherubic children threw flower petals from the prow. No harpists played at the rail. My ladies were all well turned out and sweet-smelling but eschewed the more exotic perfumes. I scandalized no one with my dress, for my voluminous purple cloak covered me from shoulder to ankle. Let no one claim that I'd answered the summons of Augustus with a notorious campaign to seduce him, even if it was the truth.

Captain Kabyle dropped anchor and my guards escorted me to shore. A deep breath assured me that this place wasn't like Rome or Egypt or Mauretania. Peeking out between the foliage were beach houses, shops and villas, some painted in washed-out pastels, accented with the occasional blue or terra-cotta. Samos was the birthplace of Pythagoras, that great philosopher and mathematician. There was even a school here to honor him and a contingent of Lady Lasthenia's colleagues stumbled over themselves to make me feel welcome. They weren't my subjects, but I was Cleopatra's daughter. My mother and father visited this island before the Battle of Actium. They feasted and entertained so lavishly on the eve of battle that the people anticipated a great victory. Now I had returned to wage a war of my own. "Great Queen Cleopatra! New Isis, New Isis!" the people cried.

Could the emperor hear them chant? Would it please him or harden his heart against me?

As a girl in Rome, my survival had depended upon my ability to predict his moods and guess at his next moves, but my time in Mauretania had obviously dulled my skills, for I certainly never anticipated that he'd send Livia to fetch me. "Welcome to the Isle of Samos, Queen Selene," she said with her least genuine smile. "I've come to invite you to stay at our villa. You and your darling little daughter."

Livia's pleasantries were meant for our audience—the crowds and curious onlookers who gathered near the docks. Even so, her invitation was an honor that I couldn't refuse, so I took Isidora's hand and we climbed into Livia's litter. The moment the curtains shut, Livia's smile faded. "Listen to them cheer you, the half-wits. *I'm* the one who asked Augustus to restore this island to self-governance, and yet *you* are the darling of the Hellenes."

"Perhaps they cheer me to please you," I remarked as Isidora nestled against my hip, fists curled under her chin as exhaustion closed her little eyes. "We're allegedly family, after all."

Livia stared at my daughter's fair curls, not bothering to hide her scrutiny. "She doesn't even look like him, you know."

My daughter seemed to already be asleep, but I wished to forestall this line of conversation at all costs. "Livia—"

"She's probably a sailor's get." Livia lowered her hands to the crimson cushions beneath us and let her nails dig in. "No matter how modestly you dress, you're still a strumpet, Selene. Still, Augustus will never see it, because men are fools." It reassured me to find her still full of petty insults and animosity, for if Augustus intended to punish me, Livia would have been gleeful. Instead, she was behaving like the woman who had stolen the emperor from Julia's mother and now feared that I'd steal him from her. "Last year, you ran from him, Selene. That was clever. You've learned to tease him but that game cannot go on forever. Eventually, you must surrender, and when you do, what do you think will happen?"

Lifting my chin, I met her gaze. "I think he'll make me Queen of Egypt."

She laughed, throwing her head back. "As if that would be enough for you."

It had never occurred to me to want more. I wasn't like Livia, always jealous of everyone else's success and happiness. Since we were being candid, I asked her the question that had been burning in my soul. "Did you poison Philadelphus?"

Her shoulders lifted in a shrug, her voice bored. Indifferent. "I did nothing but wish him dead. Your brother was a sickly boy. Hope that your daughter doesn't share the same ailments."

This was the woman who had placed a cup of poison beside my bed and urged me to drink it; I knew she was a monster, but she wasn't the only one with a darkly destructive creature inside. At the sound of so casual a threat made against my daughter, molten hatred surged up inside me. My *heka* stewed in rage, and I scented the metallic notes of iron and blood in my nostrils. The litter jostled as if caught by the wind. "Don't you know that I could kill you, Livia?"

She looked up swiftly, head bobbing at the top of her fragile neck. "I'm the emperor's wife. You don't dare harm me, you sorceress, you witch, you *striga!*"

I wrapped one arm around Isidora. "You're right to say that I'm a sorceress. And you've seen only the smallest fraction of my powers. If I want to be rid of you, some late night, you'll stand at the edge of a cliff or at the rail of a ship, and a gust of wind will grab you and drag you down." These things weren't in my power, but I enjoyed the way she went white with fear. "I'm not that little girl you bullied in Rome. I'm not the dazed bride that you betrayed on a rainy night. I'm a nightmare of your own creation, so remember this: If you ever harm my daughter, if you so much as put her in fear, I will make you *disappear.*"

Livia's bony hand fluttered uselessly at her neck. "Augustus will hear of this threat. There'll be consequences!"

"Do you think so?" I was still hot with ire, my fingers tingling with the *heka* that I longed to wield against her. "Years ago Augustus watched me throw you to the floor. How did he retaliate? He made me Queen of Mauretania. This time, he'll give me Egypt." I said this with utter conviction, but it was false bravado on my part;

I had no confidence in my influence over the emperor, and Livia might well be the one to laugh last.

THE emperor received me publicly sitting upon his ivory curule chair in the presence of his *lictors* and various staff members. The villa he'd commandeered as his headquarters was large and luxurious, and I was sure that Maecenas had chosen it. Indeed, the emperor's political adviser was close at hand, scribbling notes. Livia's son Tiberius was also nearby, the very picture of a military tribune, standing straight in his armor, carved greaves accenting his strong legs. I'd expected these men to be here, but I hadn't expected Admiral Agrippa, who stood stony-faced, as if he saw in me a gorgon approaching.

Giving me all the due courtesies of a queen, the emperor greeted me formally. This was to my advantage. It allowed me to measure him before we were alone. I couldn't tell if he was glad to see me or holding back a year's worth of frothing rage, but Augustus looked healthy. Robust. As if he'd spent the past year in the gymnasium every day. When he rose to his feet, he even seemed taller, but it was only his sandals, the soles of which had been built up to give him extra height.

He was a man who meant to make a physical impression on me.

Once the official forms had been observed, I clutched the hand of my tiny princess as she made a very proper bow. Then I followed suit. The emperor didn't smile at either of us, and I was grateful when Tala quickly ushered my daughter away. As I've said, I dressed modestly for the occasion, but beneath my cloak, I wore my mother's serpentine armlet, and when I moved to hand over Juba's correspondence, the emperor must have caught a glimpse of it because a brief spark finally lit behind his otherwise frosty gray eyes. I drew the moment out. I reported in minute detail upon the prosperity of the kingdom he'd given me and gave assurances that there'd be more grain this year. I inquired about the health and well-being of each member of the imperial family.

At last, when the emperor was actually fidgeting, I agreed to retire with him to a more private part of the house. Agrippa and his wife followed, and I was so genuinely happy to see Marcella that I kissed her on both cheeks and held her hands fast. "How does Lady Octavia fare?"

"Not well," Marcella admitted. "Of all the children in her nursery, she has only Minora with her now. My mother wishes to retire from public life." We both sighed together at Octavia's fall. Then Marcella said, "I'm so sorry, Selene. For Philadelphus. He was always the sweetest little boy."

She didn't acknowledge Helios and, given our present company, I didn't blame her. The emperor pretended that Helios simply never existed, and so we must all do the same. "I grieved for Marcellus too, but let's not speak of sad things." I made myself smile. "Your little Marcellina must be growing fast. Perhaps she and my Isidora can play together."

"I don't think that's a good idea," Agrippa said, muttering to himself as if he were stunned to see me in the flesh.

As a servant poured my wine, I asked, "Didn't you know I was coming, Admiral? I *was* summoned."

Agrippa glowered. "Not by me."

"Enough, Agrippa," the emperor snapped. That they'd quarreled again was made plain by the emperor's guarded posture. "Don't you have something else to do?"

"My wife wished to visit with the queen," Agrippa said. "I wouldn't trust any *decent* woman in Selene's presence unsupervised. I'm sure she has some new scandalous surprise for us, no?"

"I do not," I said, more irritated on behalf of Marcella than myself. She didn't need supervision, like a child.

"You see, Selene?" Augustus said, making notes on a wax tablet. "Your dignified arrival has disappointed those who'd expected to see a seductress upon her pleasure barge."

My heart sank. Perhaps he *had* wanted me to answer his summons in ostentatious fashion, to remind all the world of my mother and set the stage for this latest drama. Had I failed this first, vital test? "My mother went to Tarsus on a pleasure barge to please my father, a man of exotic tastes, but I wish to please only *Caesar*, who is an entirely different sort of man."

It was my opening salvo, and the corners of the emperor's mouth twitched as if he were considering a smile. "If you wished to please me, then why did you leave Rome without my permission?"

With Agrippa and Marcella looking on, I could hardly remind him that he'd demanded a son from me. "I was mad with grief for my dead brother, Caesar, and your poor nephew. I beg your forgiveness."

He cast a baleful look my way. "Why should I forgive you?"

"Because I've come swiftly to submit to your will," I said. "May I ask for what purpose you've summoned me?"

The emperor removed a crown of oak leaves from his brow. In Rome, he normally hung the *corona civica* on his doorpost. Here in Greece he wore it to give the semblance of royalty, but I gathered from the way he tore it from his head that it wasn't as comfortable as a crown might be. "I've summoned you to help with negotiations, Selene. This Kandake of Meroë may respect your authority as a nominal Queen of Egypt."

About to gulp his wine, Agrippa stopped and his hand tightened around the goblet. "Since when is Selene *any* kind of Queen of Egypt?"

The emperor snapped, "She is whatever I say she is."

Marcella put a calming hand on her husband's wrist, and Agrippa fell silent. I tried to pretend his silence wasn't dangerous and I asked, "When will we meet with the Kandake?"

"Her emissaries should arrive shortly," Augustus said. "I want you to convince them to deal fairly with me. Soften them, so that when I give terms, they'll accept them. I don't want to worry about Egypt when we're readying for war on Parthia."

War was certain, then. Once, I might've welcomed the idea of the emperor lying dead in some foreign field, stuck with Parthian arrows, but I still needed him alive. "I'm eager to do all that you ask, Augustus."

I hadn't intended a double meaning, but Agrippa slammed his cup down. "So it begins again!"

The emperor's stormy gray eyes narrowed. "Mind your tone, Admiral."

Ever one to flinch away from conflict, Marcella rose from her chair, giving me an apologetic look before fleeing. No well-bred Roman woman would allow herself to be caught up in a man's quarrel, but I stayed where I was. This seemed to enrage Agrippa even more. "What is it about her, Caesar? Is it the ring?" At that moment, the burly soldier grabbed me to expose the carved amethyst. My betrothal ring. My *mother's* ring. It wasn't the first time Agrippa had grasped me roughly. With painful childhood memories coming fresh to my mind, I lifted my free hand to fend him off. Without my consciously having summoned it, *heka* raced down my arm. The wind ripped past my elbow and slammed into the celebrated general. Agrippa fell back, his chair tipping as he was forced to release me. He clambered for balance, slipped on the tile, and one leg went into the pool. Grasping at the ledge, his big hands too wet to find purchase, Agrippa roared in anger.

To my horror, the emperor laughed. "Maybe a dunk will help you cool off!"

Now was not the time to taunt the man. I rushed to say, "I'm sorry, Agrippa. You startled me. You shouldn't have put your hands on me."

"Why not?" Heaving himself up, Agrippa shook like a wet dog and water sprayed me in the face. "You've come to play the whore, haven't you?"

I let the insult slide off of me. If the price for Egypt was that I must give the emperor a son, I'd do it, though all the world might think me a whore. It's what Egypt would expect from me. But whenever I allowed myself to imagine it, I wanted to throw myself into the sea and drown.

Agrippa turned to leave, puddles on the floor in his wake, and the emperor cried after him, "Where are you going?"

Agrippa turned back only once. "Back to Rome to look after her interests. One of us should."

I was aghast—stunned in the aftermath of Agrippa's fading footfalls. Like my father, Agrippa was popular with the legions. He was a hard soldier and a brilliant tactician. He was the emperor's *might*. "Are you just going to let him leave? Send someone after him!"

The emperor returned to scratching notes into his wax tablet. "Tell me, Selene, *who* should I send to fetch Marcus Vipsanius Agrippa back to me like some errant schoolboy?"

"I don't know, but you need him for your war with Parthia."

"I don't need him. I have Tiberius."

"Tiberius?" Livia's drone of a son could be counted upon to perform his duty competently, but he was still a young man with little fighting experience.

"Yes, *Tiberius*. It's good to have men of your own family at war. Iullus will join us shortly, and I have my legions. Agrippa isn't the only general in the Roman military, you know."

"No, but he's the *best*," I shot back.

At last, he looked up at me. "I hadn't realized you were such an admirer. Agrippa doesn't seem to share the sentiment when it comes to you. It'll be far more comfortable for us to conduct our business here without him."

"And what exactly is our business here?"

"Oh, my Cleopatra. That's entirely up to you."

Twenty-nine

❋

HONEST negotiation was never part of the emperor's game. My mother and Julius Caesar hadn't haggled. She'd rolled herself into his bed. Augustus wanted that same kind of passion and daring from me. I'd have to find a way to give it to him. I must arouse the emperor's interest, awaken memories of my body. And I must do all this without ever giving gossip-mongers cause to condemn me as an Eastern seductress. It was a very fine line. One that I was keenly aware of when my servants dressed me for the evening's entertainment. We weren't in Rome, where a married woman might cause a scandal if she failed to wear a *stola* over her gown. Nor were we in Athens, where women were sometimes sequestered away. We were, however, in the heart of Hellenistic society; some latitude was permitted.

"Not the *chiton*," Lady Circe advised. "Let her wear the Egyptian *kalasiris* so that she might reveal as much, or as little, as she desires."

Chryssa huffed with indignation. However, Lady Circe's recommendation had much merit. This particular *kalasiris*, spun of brilliant white gossamer threads, covered each breast but its wide straps left my arms and breastbone bare. For the sake of modesty, I normally topped the garment with a pearl-studded pectoral necklace and wrapped my arms in a shawl. Tonight I would be less modest. Donning my gown like a suit of armor, I slipped the sheath over my body, knowing how it accentuated the curve of my hips. With eerily steady hands, I fastened earrings, which glittered above my smooth, bare shoulders. Chryssa draped a strand of pearls over me as I adjusted the straps over my chest, knowing that glimpses of my breasts might be seen if I let my shawl slip away. Then, once my hair was brushed to a sheen so that it resembled mahogany silk, Chryssa divided it into ringlets at the back of my neck and drew patterns around my eyes with the scrape of kohl and the powder of malachite in the ancient Egyptian fashion; I intended to put on a performance that would let everyone in attendance know that I'd come to this island for my mother's kingdom.

At the banquet that night, Maecenas was so startled by my dramatic appearance that he rose to his feet. "Ah, Queen Cleopatra Selene of Egypt!" A nervous titter alerted him to his mistake. "I meant to say *Mauretania*, please forgive me."

"All is forgiven," I said, as if forgiveness was mine to give. "After all, I'm Mauretanian by way of Egypt!"

The guests laughed, but the emperor scowled. "Perhaps your latest *costume* confused him."

"Why, I'm dressed to honor the sea," I said, touching my pearls. "Mauretania is rich with oysters, and I'd be a poor queen not to boast of that. In fact, I've a gift for each of your guests."

The room was filled with Easterners, all of whom happily accepted my gifts of pearled jewelry and pearled knives. I was to share my couch with Archelaus of Cappadocia and his daughter, Princess Glaphyra, who fastened a string of Mauretanian pearls around her neck and exclaimed, "Why, they're beautiful. I feared you'd give us *garum* sauce."

We all laughed. Especially Terentilla, whose hyena cackle hurt my ears. In full view of Maecenas, she draped herself over the emperor's knees. I wondered that he allowed his mistress such latitude in public, but with Livia looking on so serenely, who could object?

"Princess Glaphyra, we have more than fish in Mauretania," I said, describing the olive orchards, the vineyards, and the exotic animals.

"It does sound wonderful," the young princess said, her eyes wide with admiration. "If I were you, I'd keep it quiet, though, lest one of your rivals invade your kingdom and steal it all."

I admired her brazen honesty, because she reminded me of

Julia. Sometime after the traditional first course of boiled eggs was served, her father, King Archelaus, leaned toward me, his voice not quite a whisper. "There's something I must say to you, Cleopatra Selene. Your father made me King of Cappadocia. No doubt, you've been told that I abandoned him and took up Octavian's cause. Realize that I did so only *after* Actium. Only when all was lost and to do otherwise would bring ruin to my kingdom. I know you must count as betrayers those who turned against your parents, but I hope you won't count me amongst them. I was your father's true friend."

Archelaus had come to the Isle of Samos to receive official forgiveness for having sided with my father in the first place; he had nothing to gain by saying this to me. In fact, he gambled. He couldn't know that I wasn't every bit as loyal to the emperor as I claimed to be, unless, of course, this was a test. I couldn't risk a sincere answer. "King Archelaus, if I held Actium against the survivors, I'd have scarcely a friend left in the world."

The king's expression hardened, as if he sensed my political artifice. "I support your claim to Egypt, but not every monarch does. You have enemies, and none more implacable than King Herod of Judea."

That hateful man again. "Is Herod here, on the island?"

The King of Cappadocia shook his head. "No. He sent an ambassador, though. Nicholas of Damascus."

At this, I brightened. "I remember Nicholas. He was one of my tutors in Alexandria."

"Don't trust him," Archelaus said. "He's Herod's creature now and will undermine you. Herod would be here to do it himself except that he doesn't like to compete for the emperor's attention."

Neither did I, but I didn't have to glance over my shoulder to know that the emperor's eyes were on me, lustful and contemptuous in equal parts. I shifted, letting my shawl slip over one shoulder so that only he might see bare flesh. But I never looked his way. Instead, I made an excuse and left my dining couch.

"Well done," Lady Circe whispered in my ear. "You have a stillness about you that conveys purity. Even better, because your face is aristocratic rather than beautiful, you bewitch without seeming as if it were your intent. The emperor can't take his eyes off you."

"I begin to regret asking you along, Lady Circe."

If she was wounded by my reproach, her soft smile didn't reveal it. In a flutter of silk, I turned from her and mingled with royalty, including Iamblichus of Emesa, who'd just been restored to his throne. "Queen Cleopatra Selene," he said with a regal dip of his head. "Will you walk with me?" The men were drowsy in their cups and the cooler air of the terrace beckoned, so I followed the swarthy king, my own guards and attendants at a discreet distance. As I made my departure, the emperor's stare was sharp enough to cut me, but I pretended not to notice.

"I think you met my uncle, Alexander," Iamblichus was saying, and my attention fell away from all notion of seducing the emperor to remembering the day he dragged me through Rome in chains.

The memory was still vivid. The flower petals, the trumpets, the roar of the crowd. The baying and the crimson pool of blood at my feet. I had to clear my throat to find my voice. "He—the Prince of Emesa was very kind to me . . ." My peers shouldn't remember me as a humiliated prisoner, so I said nothing more of how Alexander of Emesa marched beside me in the emperor's Triumph. And died for it.

"My father sided with Augustus," the king said. "My uncle Alexander sided with your father. They each had their reasons." It wasn't unlike the kings of Mauretania, Bocchus and Bogud, brothers who'd chosen opposite sides to preserve their dynasty. Exactly the reason that Juba maintained only one man must rule the empire. "Queen Selene, I was hoping you could tell me of my uncle's remains. Emesa is a holy city and my people would like to see Prince Alexander of Emesa honorably buried."

Even now, I could feel the prince's lifeblood as it poured over my sandals. *We fought for the Golden Age, but they fought for an Age of Gold*, he'd said. It all seemed so ludicrous now. "His body wasn't kept," I said, as gently as I could.

Emesa might not practice embalming, but it was the duty of a monarch to bury his predecessors with due honor, and I could see that this weighed upon King Iamblichus. I wished I could say something to comfort him, but he quickly took his leave.

BEFORE the banquet ended, I went to the emperor's rooms, where Strabo stood with spear and crested helmet. Having once seen me bloodied with the ecstasy of Isis, the emperor's praetorian avoided my gaze. He admitted me to the emperor's rooms and I was certain that he'd warned Augustus of my presence, but when the emperor arrived to find me sitting at his desk, his steps stuttered to a halt, as if he'd come upon a hooded cobra. "*What* are you doing here?"

Oh, dear Isis, was I ready to play this game? The bedroom was the battlefield of other women. Women like my mother or Circe or Terentilla. Not women like me. My confidence fled from me like wounded Aphrodite at Troy, but I'd left myself no path for retreat. I glanced up from beneath long lashes. "I'm here to answer your summons, Caesar."

"I didn't summon you to my private rooms," he said, snatching maps and battle plans off the table. Did he suspect me of espionage? He leveled me with a withering gaze. "I thought surely, by this hour, you'd be sharing a bed with Archelaus or Iamblichus or any of the other petty kings you shamelessly enticed this evening."

Sensing that my hands trembled, I tucked them beneath my gown. "I'd never humble myself to bed with men such as those. And if those men are enticed, it's no fault of mine. I'm a vessel of Isis. All men desire *her* and if they see traces of the goddess in me, they must be forgiven their lust."

"Must they?" As if he'd been given permission, Augustus stared openly, his eyes drifting to my breasts, down the flat of my belly, and to the curve of my hip as if he were comparing my womanly figure to the body of the girl he'd taken all those years ago. I half worried that he might not feel desire if I didn't look barely old enough for marriage, but when his lips parted for a deep intake of breath, I knew better. Though he rarely drank after dinner, he turned to fill a silver cup. "You've driven me to wine, Selene. You've driven me to excess. To *drunkenness*, I may even predict." He drained the entire cup and slammed it down on the table with his discarded maps and papers. Thus fortified, he lurched forward as if to ravish me.

I raised my hand.

He knew the defensive gesture that had flung Agrippa into a pool and stopped in his tracks. "Now you toy with me, Selene."

"Because you love games, Caesar."

His eyes narrowed. "I don't enjoy being *taunted*. It seems that I cannot lay a hand upon you without your consent. But you've no right to secrete yourself in my bedchambers, then expect me to resist you from a sense of virtue."

"True," I confessed. "Who knows better than I that you only *pretend* to be a virtuous man."

"Oh, you're a sharp-tongued whore!" he spat. "Your costumes, the way you behaved tonight—you belong in a brothel."

I pressed against the chair to brace myself. "A queen cannot dress as a Roman matron, but there's nothing scandalous about my clothing."

"You're right. It isn't the way you dress. It isn't the things you say. Your manners are perfect. Your words, the plain meaning of them can always be denied." He lectured me as if we were back on the Palatine Hill and I could see it aroused him. "You *play* the irreproachable woman, but everything about you is improper."

I arched a brow. "Did you summon me all the way from Mauretania to discuss propriety?"

"I didn't summon you here to be my mistress!"

"Of course not. You already have Terentilla."

He seethed, teeth snapping together. "You *defied* me, Selene. You left Rome. You ran from me."

"I couldn't have defied you. You never forbade me to go."

He crossed his arms over himself, as if he felt a sudden draft. "I've spent the last year plotting all the ways I could make you *suffer*, but I only wanted to see you again. Agrippa is right. You've ensorcelled me."

"Is that what you wish, Caesar? For me to bewitch you?"

He swallowed and looked away. "I should never have summoned you to this island."

"Then why did you? Why am I here?" I lowered my arm, letting him approach, and his clammy hands fastened on my shoulders. Pushing down the revulsion, I reminded myself that he could only touch my flesh, never more than that.

"I don't know, Selene. I don't know why you're here. Are you a test from the gods? I didn't wish you into existence. You were just there in Egypt when the fighting was done. You and your brothers. What was I to do with you?"

My stomach rolled and heaved, but I showed none of it. "Are these questions meant to seduce me?"

He snorted. "*You* accuse *me* of seduction?"

"Am I only dreaming your hands on me again?"

"Ohhhh." His was a growl of anger. "Who has a better right to you?"

I braved his temper with a determined stare. "The man to whom I give myself freely. Are you going to be that *one* man? For you must know that no other man has ever touched me."

I'd learned how to play the emperor's game, but he hadn't apprehended mine. He jerked back in surprise. "Is that true?"

It wasn't difficult to lie to him. "Once claimed by Caesar, how could I lower myself to bed with a lesser man?"

Such a blatant appeal to his vanity might have roused his suspicion, but this rationale was easier for him to believe than a sudden lust. That I'd conceived a passion for him out of my own arrogance was something far more plausible. He stared, his mouth working slowly. "You and your damnable Ptolemaic pride!"

"You want your own Cleopatra," I said, struggling not to choke on my words. "Well, I want my Caesar. I'll either be as pure as a Vestal or I'll be the mother of Caesar's son."

I'd named his dearest desire and he groaned as if wounded. He pulled me against him, taking in the scent of my hair. He clutched at me, murmuring, "I didn't know *how* you'd come to me, but I knew you'd come. I thought you might disgrace yourself by flaunting our daughter. Yet you knew to come to me in secret."

"What's between us isn't for the eyes of the world," I said, knowing he took sexual satisfaction in clandestine, guilt-ridden, and shameful things.

He reached to yank up my gown, and I caught his hands. "What game now, Selene?"

"Not tonight." For he'd promised me nothing. My mother had been a gambler and Julius Caesar may have let the dice fly high, but I was the *emperor's* apprentice. *I* always proceeded with caution. "Tonight I offer you a kiss."

He recoiled as if the act were some sort of Eastern perversion, and I wouldn't have been surprised if he'd never kissed a woman before. He grabbed at my gown and I feared what would happen next. Would he throw me down again? Would I be forced to use my *heka* to stop him? Both possibilities seemed frighteningly likely. What myth played out in his head? Was he Aeneas, resisting Dido for the good of Rome, Mark Antony falling prey to a corrupt Queen Cleopatra, or a new creature altogether?

He stared and I wet my lips, sensing the tide was turning in my favor. Navigating some sea change with an instinct as old as womankind, I sensed that I was surrendering and conquering at once. He felt it too, and bent to kiss me. I squeezed my eyes shut when his thin lips found mine. The bitter salt of them was horrifically familiar. So much worse than I imagined. Not like the kiss I'd shared with Juba. *This* kiss was revolting for the memories it awakened, but I let it go on until he murmured, "What kind of goddess comes to me?"

"I'm a Child of Isis and will be the Queen of Egypt."

All at once, he let me go. He *pushed* me away as if his fingers were singed by touching me. He retreated several steps behind the table. We were both quiet and my knees went to jelly. Then, as I'd seen him do a hundred times before, he brought his emotions to an unnatural calm. "You may be a Child of Isis, but I am Caesar. I have other choices in allies. I must yet be convinced that you're capable of politicking upon a world stage."

Thirty

CHRYSSA washed the cosmetics from my face, brushed my hair, and helped me into my sleeping gown. I didn't go to bed but knelt beside a strongbox in which I kept expensive gifts and coins. Throwing the top back on its iron hinges, I dug out a small package at the bottom and untied the cords. Inside was a little girl's gown, dirtied and stained brown with old blood. A slave girl had once tried to take it from me and I'd slapped her away. Chryssa had been that slave girl, and when our eyes met, hers glistened with tears.

I'd always kept the dress. Hidden beneath a mattress or buried at the bottom of my traveling satchels, it'd been a talisman of the wounds in me no one could see. A tangible reminder of the dark memories in my *khaibit* that held my rage. "I have to get free of this," I said, fingering the cloth. "The hatred. Do you know how deeply I hate him? How long I've kept it hidden?" We'd each been taken to the emperor's bed, but we never spoke of it. Now I would. "He wants a son from me," I said flatly.

She made a strangled sound. "Tonight . . . ?"

"No," I whispered. "It seems that we both require certain proofs from one another."

THE next day, I called upon an unsuspecting King Iamblichus in his apartments. Crinagoras announced me with all my titles, real and honorary: "Queen Cleopatra Selene of Mauretania, of Cyrenaica, Libya and Numidia, Princess of Egypt, and the eighth Cleopatra of the illustrious House Ptolemy."

"I'm glad that you've come," the King of Emesa said, but the lines around his eyes told me otherwise. He'd thought better of asking after the remains of his dead uncle. Or perhaps he worried that I'd come to ask him to join some intrigue or to support my claim to Egypt. Perhaps Nicholas of Damascus, on Herod's behalf, had already been here to blacken my name.

In spite of the chilly reception, I went directly to the issue. "I've come with a gift," I said, and Chryssa came forward to place the package on the low table between the king and me. "This is the gown I wore on the occasion of Octavian's Triumph . . ." My voice quavered and I was tempted to snatch the dress back, so precious was it to me. Instead, I forced myself to say, "The bloodstains are all that remain of your uncle, Alexander of Emesa. I hope that you can use this to help him find his final rest." The king stared at me as if he thought I were lying. Then he unwound the twine on the package and examined the old, tattered cloth. I felt suddenly, unbearably, foolish. "I know it must seem macabre . . ."

King Iamblichus brushed the fabric, his eyes filled with an emotion that may have been outrage. He snapped his gaze to mine and pointed one shaky finger at me, as if in accusation. "It's true what they say about you. You *are* a holy person. This is a sacred thing you've done, one that will bind our families together in friendship."

I exhaled, fearing to speak, swallowing back emotion as I realized that a burden had been lifted from me. One less dead spirit to haunt me. One less broken piece of my life that I must mend. Perhaps, having let go of the dress, I could release the sorrow and hatred too.

IN the weeks that followed, I wasn't alone with Augustus again. The business of the empire beckoned and he made me wait. This came as no surprise to me. When the emperor wanted something, he made a slow and unrelenting advance. So when he gifted me with caged songbirds, I understood that it was more than a token of his favor. It was a message, that even my bold offer couldn't distract him from the work at hand. Nor could I fly free.

His latest preoccupation was the news from Rome. As Augustus had refused to be elected to the office of *consul*, the people refused to elect anyone else. Whether this was driven by popular will or by fawning allies, I couldn't say. Casting about for someone else capable of feeding them, the Romans granted Agrippa *independent imperium*. I shuddered when I heard this, for it meant that Agrippa was now a virtual coemperor. He had his own *lictors* and had redoubled efforts to purge Rome of Isiacs. Agrippa forbade the worship of Isis not just within the *pomerium* but anywhere in the city, and he actively hunted down Isiacs for punishment, claiming that this was necessary to put down an insurrection.

It was everything I'd tried to prevent and yet had somehow brought about. All these years, Agrippa had contented himself to be second man in Rome. No longer. Now he was making audacious moves fueled, at least in part, by his enmity for me. And I had no idea how to stop it short of my campaign to take back my mother's throne.

Each day, on some pretext, I went down the stepped streets to the harbor in the hopes of news from Egypt or a delegation from Meroë. Each day, I was disappointed. My ship, with its beautiful purple sails, was at anchor, and I struggled against my instinct to climb aboard and sail away. Always, my ambition won out. I'd come for power, and this island was now the center of the world. There was nowhere else I should be.

For allies, I could count upon many of the Eastern kings, but it wasn't only royalty who offered their support. I also received a most unexpected visit from the very wealthy widow of a Greek magnate, wife of the late Pythodoros of Tralles. The heavyset woman claimed to be my half sister and when she introduced herself as Antonia, Chryssa murmured, "Not *another* Antonia. Just how many children did your father have?"

I elbowed Chryssa sharply, then smiled at my guest. "I'm at a terrible disadvantage, Lady Antonia. I'm afraid I hadn't known of your existence . . ."

The wealthy widow was at least thirty years old and she wore a jeweled ring on every finger of every hand, an ostentation that would have marked her as my father's daughter even without the family resemblance. She also had a booming laugh. "You've never heard of me because I'm pitied in Rome. *Poor Antonia, married off to some foreigner,* they say. I'm told Octavian, that limp little prick, used my marriage as another way to prove that our father had quite lost his mind."

The vulgar way in which she insulted the emperor left me speechless. When I struggled for reply, she only laughed louder. "Don't fret, little sister. I've come to tell you that you have a friend in me. You seem rich enough, but one can never have enough money, and I have more gold than I can count. I pledge to use it to put you back on the throne of Egypt."

Chryssa made a noise, a grunt of suspicion, but I tried to be gracious. "Lady Antonia, you needn't feel obliged to empty your treasury because we share blood."

"Call me Hybrida, after my mother," the fleshy woman said. "In truth, my offer has only a little to do with our shared blood. Though I'm the daughter of a Roman triumvir and richer than Midas, Roman society shuns me. They think I'm tainted. I can find no good husband for my daughter, Pythodorida. I believe her marriage prospects would improve if we were to move to Alexandria and join your court as kinswomen to the Queen of Egypt."

If I were in Hybrida's position, the same thoughts would have occurred to me. It was entirely sensible. Moreover, her frankness appealed to me. "We welcome your friendship, Lady Hybrida. And I applaud your ambitions for your daughter, who is, if nothing else, my niece, a kinswoman to the Queen of *Mauretania*."

Hybrida spent the rest of the afternoon regaling me with tales of my father. Because she was older, she remembered him as none of my other half siblings did, and her stories were a gift to me that I treasured. As it turned out, my niece Pythodorida was a charming little thing—a few years older than Isidora—but the two girls enjoyed one another's company. It gladdened my heart that my daughter should have a cousin to play with, and I imagined the two of them growing up together in my mother's palace in Alexandria. If I needed another reason to win back Egypt, this reminded me how many other people depended upon me to do it.

A few days after Hybrida's visit, two hulking slaves whose muscles had been oiled to a high sheen knocked upon my chamber door. They presented me with a chest of priceless frankincense and myrrh, a gift from the emperor. I used it as an excuse to call upon him where he was closeted with Maecenas, Tiberius, and a number of other officials whose names I no longer recall. Strabo was on duty, which was fortunate, because the emperor's praetorian had become accustomed to admitting me without question. When I thanked Augustus for the expensive gifts, the emperor didn't even glance up from the pile of papyrus and vellum and other scraps of paper. "I'm glad the gifts pleased you, Queen Selene. Now please absent yourself, as I'm busy."

"Perhaps I can help," I said, slipping into a chair. "I can translate in several languages."

If he planned to banish me, the emperor forgot it when whatever he read sent him into a scarlet rage. "Opportunistic cur!" Augustus tossed the letter to the middle of the table and announced, "Agrippa has divorced Marcella. He's divorced my niece. Without any good cause. Without leave from me!"

I was very glad that I was already sitting down. "*Divorced* her . . ." It had to be some cruel hoax. We'd just seen them together. What could biddable Marcella have possibly done to make Agrippa abandon her? No, it was nothing Marcella had done, I realized. It was what the emperor and I had done. What we might still do. What we *planned* to do. Recent Roman history was filled with episodes of colleagues falling out and fighting wars for supremacy. Marius, Sulla, Pompey, Caesar, Octavian, and Antony—that wasn't even the complete list. Now history was folding back upon itself. When my father divorced Octavia, it had led to war. Agrippa's divorce of Marcella might start the fighting again.

It was like one of the ingenious grappling hooks Agrippa had invented for sea battles. He shot this insult across the bow and now it would dig in. It was a rebellion that couldn't be ignored or cut away. Augustus knew it too. "There's more. Having divorced my niece, Agrippa now wishes to marry my *daughter*."

Aghast, I nearly shot out of my chair. This was Agrippa's counteroffer. Augustus could save face by marrying his rebellious general even more closely into his family. By giving Julia to Agrippa, he would be declaring the old soldier his heir. It would seem as if the whole thing—even the divorce—had been the emperor's own idea. It was brilliant. I would never, *never* underestimate Agrippa again.

"The admiral aims too high!" Tiberius cried.

No higher than you, I thought. Livia had planted the idea that *Tiberius* was a viable candidate for Julia's hand. That *he* could inherit the empire. Neither of them had counted upon Agrippa's ambitions. Nor had I. But perhaps wily Maecenas had seen it coming, because he leaned back, adjusting a gold ring upon his finger, and said, "Augustus, I think you must allow it."

"Why must I?" the emperor asked. "Agrippa is my creature. I've made him everything he is."

"It's *because* you've made Agrippa so great," Maecenas said. "You must now either kill him or let him marry your daughter."

Augustus circled the table, catching us all in the eye of his storm. That's when he noticed me sitting there. "And you, Selene, what do you advise? You know the women of my family."

I sickened at the idea that somewhere in Rome, my dearest friend sat unaware that her future was being decided right here in this room. Clever, beautiful, warmhearted Julia. The last time I'd seen her, she was more in love with Iullus than ever before. Agrippa would never stand for it. He would make her life a misery. What was I to say? Was I to encourage the emperor to murder or to war?

You should kill Agrippa. The words were in my mouth but wouldn't pass my lips. The admiral stood in my way and I should be glad to be rid of him, but I couldn't make myself say it. "Shame on Agrippa. Find a way to tell him no. Julia isn't a war prize to be passed out to your victorious general. She wasn't born to give you an heir. She's a grown woman with desires of her own."

These bold words should never have been spoken in front of these men, but now I couldn't take them back, and Augustus stared pointedly. "Tell me, Selene, about these desires my daughter has."

Julia's secrets weren't mine to tell, and I shrugged, knowing it would make no difference in the outcome anyway. "She desires to be consulted in matters of her own future."

The emperor shook his head, then read Agrippa's letter again. "Apparently, my sister supports the idea. Why would Octavia be well disposed to this match between Agrippa and my daughter if it means that her own daughter must be divorced and discarded?"

To spite Livia, I thought. Octavia swore that she'd never allow the emperor's wife to profit from Marcellus's death. This was one way to keep Livia's sons from climbing any higher. "Why don't you ask your daughter what *she* wants?"

Augustus wiped at his face with his hand. "Selene, it doesn't matter what Julia wants if her happiness leads to war. We must all make sacrifices for the greater good. Don't you agree?" How could I argue? If I'd made only the choices that would lead to my own personal happiness, I wouldn't be here at all. "Maecenas is right," Augustus said, his mind made up. "I've let Agrippa rise too high. I must either destroy him or let him marry Julia. Or both."

Or *both*. I should have thought of that, but the emperor's mind always worked faster when it came to treachery. A marriage to Julia would advance Agrippa politically, but it would also tie his hands. The admiral couldn't divorce or offend *Julia* without giving the emperor an excuse to destroy him.

Having secured the emperor's permission, Agrippa wasted no time. Before winter we learned of two weddings in Rome. In a hastily arranged ceremony, Agrippa married Julia and in the most perverse twist I could imagine, the discarded wife, Marcella, was married off to Julia's secret lover.

WAITING for the delegation from Meroë, months passed. At the back of the emperor's magnificent villa on the Isle of Samos, I'd been apportioned my own private beach, accessible only from the terrace outside of my rooms, closed off from outsiders by tall green hedges and a rock wall. It was the perfect place to avoid Livia.

While I stretched out beneath a palm tree, Isidora splashed in the ocean with Tala's boy. The winter sun on my arms and legs was warm, not hot, and my ladies and I could be at our ease, but I was restless. In Mauretania, there'd be a hundred petitions to read, a thousand decisions to make. It wasn't in my nature to be at leisure and I worried that precious few messages came to me from Mauretania. As I brooded upon this regrettable fact, Isidora squatted in the surf, using her hair ornament to dig into the wet sand, the Isle of Samos itself a canvas for her imagination. "She's going to lose that expensive silver circlet," Chryssa warned. "Surely your mother didn't allow *you* to run loose like a wildling child!"

I don't think my mother ever allowed me to be a child at all. Playful by nature, my father had indulged us, but all my mother's amusements had some political purpose. Everything in her life was calculated to Egypt's advantage—every burst of laughter and perhaps even every sigh of pleasure. I was becoming just like her, but I didn't want Isidora to become just like me. "Let her play."

That evening the delegation from Meroë finally arrived. Wild with anticipation, every sense heightened with hope that Helios might be with the delegation, I berated servants who weren't swift enough to make ready. On the emperor's behalf, I went to greet the Meroites, my litter accompanied by torchbearers and a small cavalcade of mounted guards, commanded by Tiberius. So anxious was I to see this Kandake of Meroë that my first steps upon the creaking wooden dock were unsteady, and not even a deep breath of night air could calm me. Pearls and jewels and purple cloak all weighed me down, but the dazzle of my finery was swallowed in the dim light. I'd come all this way for a chance to reunite with my twin and wondered if he'd know me in the dark.

As they disembarked from the ship, I saw that Meroë's emissaries were few in number. All men with long limbs displaying every manner of decoration in the old Egyptian style. Thick gold bracelets at their wrists. Jeweled trinkets on their strong ankles. Carnelian amulets about their necks. Lines of kohl and blue azurite around their eyes. They looked as if they'd stepped off the wall of an Egyptian tomb, but they weren't a honey brown like native Egyptians. Their skin was dark. Luxurious. Black as night. No pale Macedonian Greek could have hidden himself amongst them and I didn't sense Helios near.

Though I should have felt nothing but relief that my twin hadn't been foolish enough to come to this island with his warrior queen, I despaired. That gaping maw of misery gnashed in the pit of my stomach. I was so stricken that it took me a moment to realize Tiberius had introduced me in surprisingly majestic terms, using the full panoply of my titles. I'd have thought he ridiculed me, but Livia's eldest son didn't have *any* sense of humor, not even a cruel one.

The Kandake's ambassador said, "Greetings, Queen Cleopatra Selene. We come on behalf of Queen Amanirenas, the Kandake of Meroë, Priestess of Isis and Pharaoh of the Kushites." He'd been chosen as a diplomat, I thought, because he spoke passable Greek.

That wasn't the language I wanted to use. I addressed him in Egyptian. "And we," I began, using the royal *we*, "were sent by Augustus to encourage you to make a peace treaty. We can tell you from personal experience that it's the more customary practice of the Romans to invade places, steal everything, enslave the populace, and expand the boundaries of the empire so that a general can be granted a giant victory parade. Take advantage of this rare opportunity to negotiate, since Romans don't normally offer terms."

The ambassador grinned, agile in switching to the Egyptian tongue. "The Romans don't normally find themselves fought to a standstill either."

So, they were proud, these Meroites. I had nothing else to say.

In my chambers that night, I let my fingers play over the oil lamp, flirting with the flame. Chryssa watched me. "That seemed a rather feeble effort at diplomacy, Majesty."

"What do you expect from me? If I mean to help Helios, I doubt very much he wants me to negotiate on behalf of the Romans."

She glanced at me sharply, alarmed. Her voice lowered to a whisper. "After all these years, you cannot still think he lives."

I didn't answer. I *knew* Helios was still alive, but perhaps it was a secret best kept by me alone.

IF the emperor required proof that I was capable of politicking on a world stage, I'd given him no evidence of it. That the delegation from Meroë included neither Helios nor his warrior queen had rocked me; I'd allowed my bitterness to show, and by the next morning I knew I must make up for a poor first impression.

I invited the ambassador to call upon me aboard my ship. Captain Kabyle was charming and gracious to the Meroites, and the Kandake's ambassador lunched with me on the deck beneath my purple sails. The ship was the only place on the island that belonged to me, where I could be reasonably certain that no spies would report our conversation. "Ambassador, I'd like very much to know about your Kandake."

The ambassador smiled, brilliant white teeth against his ebony lips. "Our pharaoh is the most beautiful woman yet born. Blessed of the gods. She doesn't bow to the Romans or to any man. A fierce fighter, radiant of spirit and beloved of our people."

I put down my spoon, suddenly quite without appetite. Would it have been better to hear that she was ugly and hated? "And the Kandake thinks she can beat the Romans? Drive them from Egypt?"

"I've heard tale of you, Queen Selene, so you'll hear only the truth. The Kandake didn't fight this war to conquer Egypt. Like you, the Kandake considers herself to be a daughter of Isis."

Perhaps a truer daughter than I had been. "So, she wants the temples."

"She makes war to *protect* the temples, but our mother Isis doesn't like war. As Pharaoh of Meroë, she speaks to the gods. Horus told her to make peace. He also told her that *you* would be here and that you'd do everything in your power to see this war end to our advantage."

I hoped the sound of waves below disguised the fluttering of my heart. "*Horus* told her?"

"He comes to the Kandake as a young man with golden hair and eyes as green as the Nile. A young warrior who wields a sword with ten times the strength of any other man. A desert soldier who shares the privations of men under his command. He fought beside us in battle and the men all love him. The women too."

I closed my eyes as if the sun reflecting off the water were too bright, but it was only to hide the searing longing inside . . . "The Romans will want to know where to find him, this Horus the Avenger. Will you tell me where he is?"

"Where Horus is now, I cannot guess."

"He's left Meroë?" My voice rose in pitch. "He's left the Kandake?"

"He's with us always in spirit, Majesty, but gods go where they're needed."

I was crestfallen. For almost four years now, I'd yearned for Helios. Now he was gone again like a shadow. Still, he'd somehow guessed that *I* would be here. He'd promised the Kandake that I'd help her, and I would. I said, "When the negotiations begin, remember that Rome is poised to make war on Parthia. Augustus is capable of fighting more than one war at a time, but the battles aren't finished in Spain either. Roman generals celebrate as if they've returned victorious over the Cantabri tribes, but then have to fight again. The Cantabri don't stay conquered."

"None of us do," the ambassador said softly. "Every great power eventually tumbles down."

Once, I'd said something similar to Maysar. I had believed it then. Now, I was less certain. "I fear that Rome is like Augustus, always at the edge of death, coming back stronger. You have an ally in me, even if it may not seem that way. The mask I wear for the Romans isn't a true reflection of my heart."

I only hoped that I hadn't worn the mask so long that I forgot my own face.

Thirty-one

PINCHING my cheeks to make them appear pink with offense, I reported to the emperor. "The Meroites are insufferable. They call the Kandake a *pharaoh*, even in my presence!"

"That pricks at your Ptolemaic pride, does it?" the emperor asked, amused. "Does the ambassador know how resentful it makes you?"

"I'm not a fool, Caesar. You asked me to make them amenable to a peace treaty, so I did."

He stroked at his chin and I could see that he was enjoying this immensely. "Tonight I'll allow you to be present during the negotiations for peace in Egypt. You may have Livia's place at the banquet."

I bristled but not for his wife's sake. "I don't wish to give rise to gossip."

"I assure you, Livia will endure it silently, as she must."

This would only be to my detriment. Octavia had once played the silently suffering wife with my father. Caesar's wife Calpurnia had endured with dignity his open association with my mother, engendering a hatred for Cleopatra in the hearts of sympathetic Romans. If I allowed Livia to cast herself in the role of the wronged wife, it would ruin me as it had ruined my mother. "I won't be paraded about like Terentilla, just another mistress."

He stared, much unspoken between us. "I assure you that you'll be shown all due honor."

"Not when your wife is here. I want her gone. Send Livia away."

The request had seemed natural, inevitable, but his eyes narrowed and my stomach fell away. I'd gone too far. My mother had been young, overawed by Caesar; she made requests of him, not demands. Augustus wanted that same humility from me. I had blundered.

"Go to your rooms, Selene," he said, his voice icy. "You're banished to your rooms like the child you still are. I'm no longer certain that you can conduct yourself properly at tonight's negotiations."

This condescension made me hot all over, but he was right. I'd pushed too hard for something I *wanted* at the expense of something I *needed*. To be present at these negotiations would signal my restoration. Other leaders would come to think of me as the Queen-in-Waiting of Egypt. I *needed* to be there. "I beg your forgiveness, Caesar. It's only that so much time has passed since the night we were alone together. I worry—"

"That I've forgotten?" The icy tone gave way to something else. "No, Selene. I've accepted that to beget my son upon you, you must come to my bed willingly. But *you* must accept that you belong to me; you're as much mine as the chair I sit upon, in all its silken cushions and gilded finery."

Now it was my turn to narrow my eyes. "I'm not a piece of furniture. I don't sit silently in a room as adornment to be used by whomever I'm offered. I'm a woman and a queen."

He leaned back, a finger caressing the curved edge of his chair as if it were my flesh. "And I have made you both. Only *my* hands have taken pleasure of you. Only *my* seed has taken root in your womb. I *made* you bear a child and your body is changed because of it." His eyes swept over my high, rounded breasts, and the swell of my hips, as if he were an artist who'd carved me from stone. "You're *mine* and you'll be the Queen of Egypt only when you accept my mastery. Not before."

I lowered my eyes in feigned submission. "If it pleases you to have me at the negotiations, I'll be glad to attend."

I hoped that having made his point, he wouldn't deny me. But later that night, I wasn't invited to the banquet at all, much less given Livia's position.

In my apartments, Crinagoras babbled some verse to entertain me. I paid no attention until the poet asked, "Majesty, why do you refuse yourself the enlightenment of my breathtaking prose?"

Pinching the bridge of my nose did little to alleviate the newest ache behind my eyes. "Leave me."

Crinagoras rose to obey, stopping at the door to ask, "Augustus *is* like Hades, isn't he? He's rolled out the pomegranate of Egypt to tempt you."

My poet seldom spoke about anything without allusion, but we understood one another. "Right now, he's punishing me. At this very moment, he could be negotiating with the Meroites for Egypt and I've been banished."

Crinagoras nodded slowly. "I'm sure you'll find a way back into his favor. As I recall, Hades had a singular obsession with Kore. He let her go, but always he'd send for her again . . . If you wish to be the Queen of Hades, you must partake of the fruit, no matter how bitter."

LATER that evening, the emperor finally relented and I received a summons. Augustus sat at one end of the hall, flanked by Maecenas and Tiberius. And though Livia's son had never been my enemy, his dour presence here was a reminder to me that it would take more than sending Livia away to diminish her influence over the emperor.

At the other end of the hall was the ambassador from Meroë, leaving me to find an unobtrusive place in the middle with the scribes and minor officials. My presence wasn't even acknowledged, whether to prevent awkward questions or because Augustus was still angry, I didn't know.

Since the Kandake hadn't come in person, the emperor allowed Maecenas to do the talking, ambassador to ambassador. The balding man began with, "The situation as it stands is this: The Kandake of Meroë has unlawfully invaded Egypt, seized control of the Isle of Philae, defiling the statues of Augustus and taking booty and Roman prisoners. In retaliation, Rome's Prefect of Egypt has razed Napata and is now besieged in Primis."

"Your Prefect of Egypt, this Petronius, can leave our lands

anytime he likes," the ebony ambassador said with a good deal more hubris than was wise. "But he will not leave with treasure nor will he keep the city."

"Tell the Kandake that the city of Primis is lost to her," Maecenas said with a flick of his bejeweled hand. "She may consider the loss of this city to be the price for her ill-advised adventure in Egypt. However, if she agrees to our terms, we'll tread no farther into her kingdom."

"Yet it was Rome who offended first," the ambassador insisted. "The temples at Philae may be situated in Egypt, but the gods belong to us. If Egypt cannot be a throne for Isis, then it's the Kandake's sacred duty as Pharaoh to make Isis a home in Meroë."

I let my fists clench at the word *Pharaoh*, and the emperor saw it. "Have you something to add, Queen Selene?"

Spreading my arms wide, I let them see the sacred knot of Isis between my breasts, my own declaration of devotion to the goddess. "The Kandake must give up all religious claim to the temples in Egypt. If Meroë honors Isis, then build your own holy places for her."

In saying this, I hoped to give the ambassador from Meroë something to bargain with that he may not have realized he had. The Romans only cared about claims to land. They didn't care if the Kandake maintained a *spiritual* claim to the temples, but perhaps the emperor could be made to care for my sake. The ambassador seized the opportunity at once. "How can she give up her claim when the Romans show nothing but contempt for Isis? Egyptian priests have fled to our country to escape persecution."

Maecenas was a shrewd man when it came to temporal things. He owned luxurious houses, wore the finest clothes, and patronized the most talented artists. Spiritual matters, however, were entirely out of his grasp. He pounced on what he believed to be an advantage. "If amnesty were given to Isis worshippers in Egypt, would Meroë then give up all claim to the temples and retreat from Egypt?"

I held my breath steady, waiting for an outburst from the emperor that never came. Augustus sat impassive as a statue, his glacial eyes inscrutable. Was it possible, at long last, that he would make peace with my goddess and her worshippers? The Meroite ambassador paused before saying, "If such amnesty were granted, the Kandake would give up her claim. And if—*if*—the Romans will withdraw from Primis, back to our original borders, I'm authorized to sign this peace treaty and end our hostilities."

Maecenas would have it done, but the emperor said, "No. We cannot simply return things to their original borders." I thought that he'd demand tribute from the Meroites, or say that Primis was not negotiable, or baldly proclaim that he'd continue to persecute the Isiacs until the religion was destroyed. Instead, Augustus said, "There will have to be some sort of guarded neutral area to serve as a buffer between both kingdoms and to ensure that this never happens again."

He made it sound like a point of contention, but I realized the emperor's offer was startlingly generous. Too generous. I couldn't believe that he meant it. The ambassador recognized favorable terms and quickly agreed. Then, assuring his guests that Maecenas would see to the details, Augustus dismissed everyone in the room but me.

EVEN after all the officials had shuffled out, I continued to play my role. "Do you mean to honor that treaty? You gave her more than fair terms. The Kandake will continue to call herself Pharaoh and no one will gainsay her."

"Don't be petty, Selene. You got what you really wanted. The Isiacs can practice their witchery; the priests and priestesses will be safe too. Perhaps I'll make a donation and they'll carve my likeness on some stone tablet in honor of my largesse."

Now I was more than astonished. "You'd acknowledge Isis?"

"That depends upon you," he said and motioned with his fingers for me to come closer. "I've taught you patience as a virtue, have I not?"

Patience. Caution. Incrementalism. How many times Augustus had been at the brink of failure, clawing his way out of one perilous situation after another, always stronger, his eyes implacably upon his prize. He plotted, he planned, but he never wavered. I was becoming very much like him. "Yes, Caesar. I've learned from you."

"Then you'll understand when I say that I cannot yet make you the Queen of Egypt."

Oh, bitter words! "Why not? How many petty princes have you restored to their little kingdoms? Archelaus, Iamblichus . . ." I went on to list them all. "Why can't you do the same for me?"

"Because Egypt isn't a little kingdom and you aren't a petty prince. Egypt is still the wealthiest, most productive nation in the world. I cannot even allow senators to visit without my permission. It's that vital. Until Mauretania and Africa Nova produce enough grain, he who controls Egypt can starve the world."

"But *she* who controls Egypt can feed the world. I've already shown you that Mauretania can produce grain. Combined with the wheat from Africa Nova, you'll have enough. What you pretend to wait for has already come to pass. When you were ill, you said that you couldn't support my claim to Egypt in death. Now you're very much alive and I'm offering you the son and heir that you need. I'm offering—"

"For your sake, I'm faced with the rebellion of Agrippa!" he shouted. "I cannot now offer him another weapon to wield against me. If I make you Queen of Egypt, he'll break with me. As it stands, he has my daughter hostage against your interests." I bit my lower lip. *Julia.* I loved her as much as I resented that she too was now in my way. "Selene, everyone thinks my military victories are not mine. They give all the credit to Agrippa. It makes me look like a man of straw. It *invites* him to defy me."

"So what are you saying? That Agrippa must be destroyed before I can have Egypt?"

"I'm saying that I must win my *own* war. I must return victorious from Parthia, and when I do I'll then be in a position to give you what you want." This was why he'd waited to take me to his bed. Also, why he'd dealt so fairly with the delegation from Meroë. He merely wanted to be rid of distractions so that he could effectively pursue *his* war. "Selene, if I'm successful against the Parths,

I'll have the power to give you Egypt. I'll have the power to do *anything.*"

How many times had my mother heard these words and hung her hopes on them? Caesar had said this to her. My father had said it too. But Caesar had been assassinated for his ambition, and my father had gone down in defeat. As far as I was concerned, Parthia was the battlefield upon which all hopes and dreams were slain. "*Must* there be war? Romans want a Golden Age too. Maybe you can give it to them." How bitter it was to stoke a desire in him to accomplish what Helios and I had been prophesied to bring about. "After your Triumph, you closed the doors of the Temple of Janus, a sign that Rome was no longer at war. What a legacy you could leave if you became the man who keeps those doors closed!"

"Do you think I haven't thought of that? Ever since the Battle of Carrhae when Marcus Crassus lost Roman battle standards to the Parthians, we've tried to avenge the loss. Your father tried too, and he failed, losing his own eagles. I need to win those standards back. Are you so naive as to believe the Parths will allow me to wipe this stain from Roman honor without a fight?"

"Why not? Surely there's something the Parths want that you can offer in exchange for Roman eagles."

Like me, Augustus was a born schemer, and the machinations of some plot turned behind his eyes. Whatever it was, he didn't share it with me. In the end, he only said, "I must lay the groundwork for war. I'm leaving the island for a time. When I return, I expect you to be here. No sailing off into the night as you did before."

So this was to be another test. "Where are you going?"

"I have matters to settle in Bithynia, Syria, Commagene, and so on."

He had people to punish, cities to tax, and territorial boundaries to redraw. That was why we'd all been summoned here, wasn't it? "And you want me to *wait* for you?"

"I will want a good deal more from you than that."

Thirty-two

THE delegation from Meroë sailed away without giving me an opportunity to say farewell, as if they knew the terms they'd reached with the Romans were altogether too favorable. There was no reason to risk Augustus changing his mind. Or perhaps the emperor had told them to go. He didn't like to leave things to chance.

Overlooking the courtyard where Augustus readied for his expedition, there was a balcony. It wasn't nearly as pleasant a perch as the terrace at the back of my rooms overlooking my private beach, but from this vantage point my ladies and I watched the Romans rush back and forth readying for Augustus's journey. We sat there painfully idle, a lute player making music for us.

"You won't travel with Augustus?" Circe asked, a well-plucked eyebrow raised.

"I've no desire to be in the company of Livia."

"I think you're relieved to see him go," Circe said quietly. I turned my head to the side, as if I hadn't heard her, but she only drew closer. "Majesty, you think that he'll never notice your contempt, that you can lie to him, and you can. But you'll never reconcile yourself to this if it is *only* a lie."

"What do you know of it?" I whispered.

"I know it's a mistake to feign desire. You must feel it. If it is a fat man, you must glory in the size of him. If it is a cold man, you must admire the way his ruthlessness has made him rich. If it is a man you *hate*," she said, meeting my eyes, "you must find something in him to *love*."

"I am no *hetaera*. Remember that I'm the queen and you are my daughter's grammarian."

How unworthy of me to reprimand her for advising me when it was precisely the reason I kept her near, but the ease with which she'd deduced my true feelings for the emperor left me unsteady. Unnerved. What expression had betrayed me? What words had slipped? Were she an intimate like Chryssa or Tala or even Crinagoras, I might have expected her to read my heart, but if I couldn't fool Circe, how was I to deceive Augustus?

On the day of the emperor's own departure, Isidora and I went to the docks to see him off and before he climbed the gangplank to join Livia and his courtiers aboard the ship, he asked for a private moment. He smiled down at Isidora and murmured, "Queen Selene, I bid you and your daughter a fond farewell."

My voice was soft, a bare whisper. "I beg you to reconsider, Caesar. It will cause gossip if I'm penned up here like a harem girl."

Crinagoras and Lady Lasthenia were already prone to exchanging knowing looks with my Alexandrian courtiers. They remembered my mother, and no matter how properly I might behave before the royalty of the world, those closest to me had noticed the emperor's fascination. But Augustus was unconcerned. "You aren't penned up. The entire island is at your command and I leave you the highest-ranking official here."

"What am I to do here but wait for you?"

"Do as you wish, Selene! It's springtime and you're in the heart of the Hellenistic world. Visit Ephesus if it amuses you."

Ephesus was one of the largest cities in the world and I should have liked to see it, except that it was also where my mother's sister, Princess Arsinoe, had conspired against the throne of Egypt and been killed at my father's command. Given that history, I wasn't sure of my reception. Still, it would be something new to see. Some distraction to keep me from missing Mauretania . . . *No*, I told myself. I could not go to Ephesus, Athens, or anywhere else. Wherever *Augustus* went, the business of governance followed, but I didn't have a squadron of ships to carry my messages. Few enough missives arrived from my kingdom as it was and it pained me to think I might miss one. Moreover, it vexed me that I should be marooned here as an object lesson. He wanted to prove to me that I was just like that damnable chair, a piece of property he could leave where it was and return to find it in the same spot. And I had no choice but to let him believe he was right.

WITH Augustus gone, the client kings slowly began to abandon the island. Some of them had been restored to their thrones or seen their territories expanded. Others left empty-handed. Only my status remained in question, so I was grateful for those who supported my claims to Egypt and was obliged to see them off. I'd grown especially fond of Iamblichus, the King of Emesa, and the Cappadocians, King Archelaus and his daughter, Princess Glaphyra. My other friends included the Bosporans, King Asander and his queen, Dynamis, who, with a sly grin, kissed me on both cheeks before setting sail.

I was glad that at least Lady Hybrida and my niece Pythodorida remained on Samos with us because I'd come to enjoy my older half sister's garishness and boisterous good humor. On our way back from the docks, we joined her in an oversized covered palanquin, framed in gilded wood and encrusted with jewels. "You've started a disastrously expensive trend with your purple sails, little sister. Your freedwoman must have taken a hundred orders for Gaetulian purple."

Chryssa shrugged at Hybrida's words. "For all the good it will do us without the Berber chieftain to oversee the dye works."

She didn't have to say Maysar's name for me to know that her mind was on the love she'd left behind. As our litter was swarmed with merchants hawking their wares, my guards keeping them at bay with their ceremonial shields, I wondered what I was doing here on this island, filling my days with useless entertainments. *Don't go*, Juba had said, but I couldn't have stayed for his sake alone. For my crown, for Maure-tania, for the people, for my retainers, perhaps I could have made a different choice. Perhaps if I had been heavy with Juba's child, Augustus may have broken free of his obsession . . . and perhaps I could have broken free of my own. For all that I loved my mother's kingdom, I hadn't set foot on Egyptian soil since her death. If my life was my own, perhaps I could have forgotten Egypt and let it pass through my fingers like the silken sands of the desert. But my life was not my own. My family had died for Egypt; I must live for them.

Chryssa had no such obligation. She'd spent most of her life in bondage to others and now I'd see to it that she was truly free. I put my hand on hers. "You've done everything here you set out to do. Go back to him."

Chryssa shook her head. "The emperor looked at me only once, during a meal, as if he couldn't place me."

"Be glad of it! Go back to Maysar and find happiness."

If I'd ever thought that the beatings she'd suffered as a slave had broken her, now I realized that they'd only served to infuse Chryssa with a stubborn streak of iron. She shook her head so sharply that the garnet beads of her dangling earrings rattled. "No. Maysar could have accompanied us on this trip. He was too proud. Either I was to stay behind as his wife or he would resign from your council. Am I to reward him by running back to his arms?"

"Don't go back for him, then. Go back for *me*. I need someone in Iol-Caesaria to write regular letters to me. Euphronius grows older, his handwriting ever more cramped. Be my eyes in Mauretania. I need you to go. As your queen, I *command* you to go."

WE found passage for her on a merchant ship, and Chryssa came to the back of the house on the little beach to say farewell. We embraced as if we might never see one another again. When we drew apart, Isidora hugged her about the knees, and Chryssa told my daughter, "You be good for Tala, even if she *is* our dear uncivilized barbarian."

The big Berber woman bit her lip, blinking rapidly.

"Tala, are you *crying*?" Chryssa asked.

"It is only the sun in my eyes, *Cleopatra Antonianus*," Tala said, fanning away the evidence of her bald-faced lie with one hand. "If you lower that fine Greek nose of yours long enough to reunite with my brother, tell him I wish you both well."

THE months passed slowly after the emperor's departure. To pass the time, I visited the Temple of Hera. I also purchased expensive Samian wines and red Ionian pottery. To win friends, I funded theater performances of a number of beloved plays, most of which were spoiled for me by Lady Hybrida's loud running commentary. Excepting her, the island seemed quiet—almost deserted—and it wasn't until autumn that a small detachment of Romans made landfall.

As Augustus had said, the Isle of Samos was at my command, so I received the unexpected visitors in the courtyard. Decked out in parade uniform, complete with shiny helmet, my half brother Iullus stepped forward to greet me and we exchanged formal pleasantries. All the while, I kept hoping his wife would appear behind him. The companionship of my stepsister would have been a welcome change, so when we were finally alone in the courtyard, I asked, "Is Marcella with you?"

Iullus removed his helmet and shook his head. "Selene, you look very well."

"You don't," I replied, noting the dark circles under his eyes. "Are you ill?"

"I'm sickened. When you write to Julia, tell her so. She refuses all missives from me."

I winced at the stab of guilt his words dealt me. I hadn't received a letter from Julia since she'd been wed to Agrippa and I hadn't sent one for fear that her new husband might punish her for it. Now I wondered if it might have been better to risk Agrippa's wrath. "How does she fare?"

"How do you think she fares? She's hurt and humiliated and angry. Especially at me." Sitting down, he leaned back and squeezed his eyes shut. "I couldn't refuse to marry your stepsister. Marcella is the emperor's niece. I could no more refuse than *Julia* could refuse."

"I'm sure Julia knows that—"

"But *you!*" His eyes opened again. "For all the influence you have over the emperor, you couldn't dissuade him from marrying Julia to Agrippa? I'm sure you'll tell me that you tried, but you didn't try hard enough. Agrippa wasted no time in putting his filthy hands on Julia. She's with child, you know."

My blood went to water. I didn't know what appalled me more—that Julia should be forced to carry Agrippa's child or that my dearest friend might soon become my greatest rival. If she *did* manage to have a son, would the emperor still have a need for me? I'd been wary of Livia, but after all the lies I'd told and the predations I'd endured, would it be *Julia* who finally broke my spell over her father? Stunned, all I could manage to utter was, "Julia? Pregnant? By Agrippa?"

Iullus caught me with a sideways glance. "Congratulate me. I'm to be a father soon."

Examining each word, I dared not ask the questions they raised. Was Julia pregnant with his child, or did he mean that Marcella was pregnant too? "You have my felicitations."

He nodded, eyes still locked on mine. "Our sisters speak of you often, Selene. They've even expressed a desire to visit."

"I hope they do visit!" I said, my spirits brightening. "Did you know that we have another sister? Antonia, the wife of the Greek magnate. She calls herself Hybrida, after her mother."

He showed no sign of surprise. "I'm told she's a vulgar woman. She shouldn't be here. For that matter, neither should you be. Augustus left for Syria at the opening of the sea, but the sea is nearly closed now. It's been months since he left. What are you still doing here?"

"Augustus asked me to wait for him." I almost winced at the reminder. I'd left Mauretania knowing that I might never return, but now I felt something akin to homesickness. I missed the loamy scent of the fields and the songs the Berber women sang round the fires. I even missed the taste of the wind. The sirocco. I would much rather have waited for the emperor *there* than here. In Iol-Caesaria, it would be time to start planning the winter banquets and the palace would be a bustle of activity while servants scurried to adorn the doorways with candles and garlands. "Will you stay through winter? Until the Saturnalia?"

My Roman half brother's lips tightened in grim military style. "No. I'm to join up with Tiberius outside Armenia. The Armenians no longer wish to be ruled by King Artaxias, so we're going to replace him with Tigranes."

"They no longer *wish* . . ." It was a strange idea that the people should choose their rulers but not *entirely* foreign. Riots in the streets of Alexandria had settled matters of succession in Egypt more than once. But that was Egyptians fighting Egyptians. This was Rome interfering. "I suppose it has nothing to do with the fact that King Artaxias executed every single Roman citizen he could find within his borders."

"That was a long time ago," Iullus said.

"Not so long ago. It happened when our father was alive. Your father and mine. Artaxias executed the Romans to settle a score with Mark Antony. Rome doesn't forget and neither do I. Neither should you."

He rolled his shoulders, his eyes on the floor. Iullus never liked to be reminded of his patrimony and let out a mirthless chuckle. "If I do battle in Armenia it will be for Augustus and for Rome, not to avenge Antony. Your twin brother was his defender, not me . . . Why do you still concern yourself with politics? You're a mother now."

As far as the world knew, Iullus was my only living brother. How was it that he still knew me so little? "Yes, I am a mother and that is precisely why I am so concerned."

IULLUS didn't stay long. He and his cadre of young Roman officers shipped off to join Tiberius and the legions. As soon as they left I was again mistress of the dull island and its servile inhabitants. My Mauretanian subjects were respectful but seldom afraid to approach me. By contrast, Easterners were flatterers who abased themselves before the powerful with fluttering fingers and quaking knees. They embroidered their words with long, colorful phrases, not only for the sake of form. They were in terror of me, clearing wide swaths through the streets whenever I traveled. Some of them even bowed to my cat, knowing how highly we regarded creatures like Bast in Egypt.

"That's right, look away, for you are in the presence of greatness!" Crinagoras teased upon our return from a lecture at the Pythagorean School. "And of course, Her Majesty the Queen of Mauretania and future Queen of Egypt."

"Have a care!" I chided him. "I don't need Augustus to hear that I've crowned myself in his absence."

Crinagoras huffed. "Perhaps my humor would be better appreciated in Mytilene."

"You may visit your birthplace whenever you like," I told him, imperiously.

My unwillingness to be threatened with abandonment, even in jest, seemed to sober the poet.

"Well, it's only a stone's throw away and I could be back at your side within days," he said quietly. And I knew there would be no more talk of leaving me.

When we'd returned to the emperor's villa, Circe suggested, "Forget Mytilene, we should all go to Athens. The Athenians loved your father. They would actually *worship* you there."

I was keenly aware of my daughter's stare. What was I teaching her here on this island, I wondered. When she looked at me, waiting upon the emperor, what would she remember? The truth was, I'd accomplished nothing worthy of worship. Until the emperor returned, I'd stay where he left me, like his accursed chair. Though my rule in Iol-Caesaria had been a maelstrom of projects and politicking, magic and magistracy, now I was restless, a Ptolemy Eagle with clipped wings. My work in Mauretania had warmed my heart with a sense of pride. Here I'd been reduced to a secret *hetaera*, and I was reminded of that whenever Circe was near. "If you want to go to Athens, I won't stop you."

"A woman traveling alone?" Circe asked, as if scandalized. "Perhaps you could send Memnon to watch over me. Who knows what trouble I might find without his strong sword-arm to protect me."

I should scold her for such comments, for as long as she remained in my retinue, her conduct reflected upon me, but I feared I might choke on my own hypocrisy. Besides, my stiff-necked Macedonian guard didn't so much as acknowledge the flirtatious comment.

Calling for some sheets of papyrus, I sat down to write Julia a letter. My pen hesitated over each word, and I ended up committing it to the fire. I'd had no messages from her since her remarriage. She was being closely watched; I was sure of it. Besides, even if I could slip a letter past Agrippa's censorious eye, what could I say to her? My ambitions had driven a wedge between her father and her husband. I loved her, but we were now, she and I, kept women in enemy camps.

ON a brisk morning, Memnon knocked softly on my door to wake me. "The emperor's ship has been spotted."

I roused myself, intent upon racing to the shore to greet him with the pomp and circumstance to which he'd no doubt grown accustomed, but he hadn't sent word ahead or given us time to prepare. Indeed, as would later become his habit when entering Rome, he'd arrived swiftly and secretly to forestall any grandiose welcome.

I hurriedly dressed and rushed down the stairs. Augustus was already in the courtyard before my sandal left the last step. The folds of my *chiton* swayed behind me, and I quite feared that my diadem was askew. "Welcome back, Caesar!"

Holding his arms out so that a slave could relieve him of his dress armor, he seemed almost amused at my breathlessness. "You seem altogether too surprised by my arrival."

"Iullus said there was to be military action in Armenia. I thought you'd be there with Tiberius, to fight King Artaxias."

"As it turns out," he began flatly, "King Artaxias is dead."

I swallowed. "You had him executed? A sovereign king?"

"It wasn't my doing. By the time our forces arrived in Armenia, the king's relatives had already assassinated him. So we were able to install the newly made king Tigranes of Armenia unopposed. Tiberius put the crown on his head."

"That ought to please Livia," I said, regaining my bearings. "Her taciturn son is now a kingmaker."

"It ought to please you too. For this clears the way for our campaign in Parthia. Armenia is now an ally, and I can amass my legions there."

All very tidy. I could never fault Augustus for poor planning. His game was expansive and deep whereas mine was of a single, narrow purpose. But I still remembered my father's tales of arrows launched upon him in Parthia like a plague of insects that darkened the sky. The Romans were infantry fighters, foremost and always; they'd never fared well against Parthia's mounted archers. "If Agrippa were with you, he'd have some new invention, some new technique to frustrate the Parths."

"I have something better than Agrippa and his strategies," Augustus said, those gray eyes fastening on me. "I have a sorceress who can summon the winds with an upraised hand and knock hardened warriors like Agrippa to their knees. I have *you*, Selene."

When everything we think we know about the world fractures in an instant, we don't hear the shattering. We feel it in our bodies as if we were all dry brittle bone instead of flesh. "*Me?* You expect me to—to do what? To call down a storm upon the Parthian army and bury them in sand?"

He answered only after he'd waved all the slaves and attendants out of the courtyard. "Is that within your power?"

"No!" Were it in my power, it wouldn't be Parths buried under sand but Roman legions.

"I've had you *watched*, Selene. I've had reports that you swallowed a storm whole. That you swam in a Mauretanian river and brought dead animals to life. That you nearly swamped a pirate ship with your magic. You've grown stronger."

"So that I could give you grain. I've asked Isis to bring her blessings to the soil of Africa, and she's done it for my sake. To feed people, to nourish people, to protect people—those are the purposes for which I can use her magic. She didn't give me these powers to make war."

"Why not? Your mother made war."

"And you condemned her for it!"

"Quite so," the emperor mused. "But she commanded Antony. You will be commanded by me. The Kandake and the rumors of her fire mage demoralized my Roman legions; I can play the same trick on the Parths." So that is why he kept me on this island—so that I would be near enough to send for if I was needed at the scene of a battle. He motioned me into the seat beside him, and I sank down into it in shock. "Together, Selene, we can avenge your father's ignoble defeat."

My father had been defeated in Parthia, but it had been anything but ignoble. It had been a disastrous campaign, but my father had bravely led a retreat through the Parthian snows. He inspired his soldiers by example, eating grass and insects to survive. His bravery in the face of relentless pursuit by Parthian forces was a thing of wonder. He'd lost his battle standards, he'd lost most of his men, and he'd lost the fight, but he hadn't lost honor, and even if he had, the emperor was the last man who could have restored it. "No, Caesar. I've never wanted to go to war; I've never wanted to kill anyone."

"That's a lie," Augustus said, leaning close. "When you were a frightened little girl, your face would go pale as the moon. When you were angry, your cheeks burned scarlet. Now your skin betrays nothing. But there is a flutter, right here, at the base of your throat, just beneath your amulet . . ." He tapped his forefinger against the very spot. "This shows me when you lie and when you're afraid."

Heart, be still. I measured my breaths, slowing them, allowing a tiny stream of *heka* to thicken my blood, willing the rest of my body to mold itself to my artifice. He would find no satisfaction in feeling my heartbeat quiver beneath his thumb. No corpse has ever been as still as I. "Is there something I should fear?"

"I've sent Livia away," he replied, leaning a little closer, his lips brushing my cheek.

"And Terentilla?"

"She is Maecenas's wife, not mine. You and I shall winter together here on the Isle of Samos. It will be enough time to conceive another child, I should think. The price of your throne has come due, Selene. I will come to you this night."

Thirty-three

✿

SOMEHOW I wasn't ready. I'd come to this island to make myself the mistress of Augustus more than a year before, and still I hadn't reconciled myself to it. I should have listened to Circe, but I'd been a fool. I was *still* a fool. When the door swung open to reveal Augustus on the threshold, torchlight blazing behind him, I propped myself up on my pillows, unsteady, unsure. Then he disarmed me completely by saying, "It seems that I have a grandson."

A grandson. Dismay hollowed out my belly. Oh, *Julia*. She'd had a *boy*. Instead of rejoicing for my friend, I could only grind my teeth with bitter frustration that her otherwise rebellious loins could not have defied her father in this one thing. Augustus had his heir now. He wouldn't need me. All of this for nothing! But the emperor didn't look nearly as pleased as he should have been. "Is it not what you hoped for, Caesar?"

"It is not," he said, closing the door behind him. "The baby's name is Gaius Vipsanius Agrippa. Moreover, Livia writes that Julia's child is fast fading. She doubts he'll live past winter."

It wasn't an uncommon fate for babies born into a loving family, much less for a child with an unhappy mother and murderous step-grandmother. Julia's son weakened my position but destroyed Livia's hopes for her sons. Another woman might have been content to be married to the ruler of the world, but no Claudian had ever been satisfied with less than total victory. If the opportunity presented itself, Livia would kill Julia's son without hesitation. That my own interests would also benefit from the little boy's death made me sick at heart. If I were like Livia, I'd wish the child dead. But I *wasn't* like her and I vowed that not for Egypt, not for anything, would I wish harm to come to Julia's child. "I'll pray for his recovery."

"You should." Augustus came to the side of my bed and yanked the coverlet away. "My grandson's illness is your doing. You and this curse you've put upon me that I shall outlive all my heirs. You and your witchery. What are you doing to the boy?"

I forced myself to take a breath. "I've done nothing. Truly, I *am* sorry that he's sickly. Not only for you or little Gaius, but for Julia, who doesn't deserve more unhappiness in her life. I pray that Isis—"

"Isis is a faithless whore of a goddess!"

My eyes went wide and round at this blasphemy. "You tempt her."

"I've done everything to *appease* her. I've granted amnesty to the Isiacs in Egypt. I've sent gold to the temples in Philae. So, tell me, Selene, Isis would not make *your* son sicken and die, would she?"

"No," I said, making a wild gambit. "But I don't have a son and you won't give one to me."

He grabbed at my arm. "Oh, I would give you a son."

"No," I said, yanking away. "You would give me a *bastard* and then leave for a war from which you may never return. You'll go off to die on some foreign field and leave me alone with your son to defend, just as Caesar's death left my mother desperate, thrashing about for a new defender."

He didn't like to be reminded of Caesarion. "What new game is this?"

"It's only the plain truth of it," I said, leaning forward so that my dark hair cascaded loose over one shoulder. "When you're gone, Agrippa will point to me and say, 'There goes the great Egyptian whore who stole our good Octavian away from us.' Then what fate for your children?" Genuine emotion swelled in my breast because it could all play out again in just such a fashion.

As he watched me all atremble in my bedclothes, his gaze softened. "You *do* fear for me . . ."

"Of course I do. When you were so very ill and all Rome said you were dying, Livia couldn't bring herself to sit beside you. Agrippa and Marcellus vied for power outside your door. Even Octavia and Julia, for all that they love you, were paralyzed. But *I* sat beside you, willing you to live. Now you accuse me of cursing Agrippa's infant son and insult me by allowing yourself to be surprised at my concern for your well-being."

He sat on the edge of my bed and the anger went out of him. "Insult is not what I wish to offer you."

He wished so badly to believe me that he had allowed this to become a lover's spat. I pressed forward. "Then why have you humiliated me by summoning me to this island and denying me my mother's throne?"

"My dear girl, I have not denied you. I've merely asked you to wait."

"As I'm asking you to wait."

His eyes slid to mine. "Your mother didn't make Caesar wait."

I tilted my chin and said, "My mother was already the Queen of Egypt."

He would not have satisfaction this night. I knew it because of the stillness of his hand in mine. The lustful monster inside him was safely chained for now, perhaps because the news of Julia's son had shaken him. He would leave without touching me. Perhaps I shouldn't let him go. Perhaps it would be safer to seduce him before he had a chance to ponder whether or not he still needed a son from me at all. But I knew one thing about him as I knew nothing else.

Augustus always wants most what he cannot have.

IT had been a year since the negotiations with the Kandake's ambassador from Meroë. Now the weather turned cold again, and a delegation purporting to come from King Pandion of faraway India arrived to meet with Augustus. The delegation carried with them credentials written in Greek, alleging that King Pandion was an overlord of six hundred vassal kings. His eagerness to open diplomatic relations was a matter of great import and the entire court of Augustus was obliged to welcome the Indians in celebration of the winter solstice.

I was grateful for the cloying presence of Terentilla, because she disguised my status. Whereas she draped her beauty in gaudy jewels and little else, taking no pains to hide her adultery, I maintained the very image of maternal virtue, wearing gowns that Octavia would have approved and keeping my daughter close so that few might guess the true reason for my extended sojourn at the emperor's side.

Keenly aware that Nicholas of Damascus, Herod's ambassador, was always watching me, ready to report all my doings back to my enemy in Judea, I made subtle inquiries about him too. He maintained frequent contact with Livia. I hadn't forgotten how she'd feted Herod's sons during the Saturnalia in Rome. Herod and Livia. That was a dangerous alliance that I must not underestimate.

When the feasting began, the Indian embassy presented Augustus with exotic gifts. Slaves rolled huge cages into the room inside of which were enormous striped cats. And when the animals roared, all the feasters gasped. *"Tigers."* Augustus tested the word with great pleasure. "I've never seen such a creature before. They will make for excellent entertainment in the arena. Look at their teeth, almost four inches long!"

My daughter, who seemed intent on forming her very own menagerie, wanted one for a pet, but I told her that these tigers would eat the rest of her little animals in one gulp. Nonetheless, the great cats were beautiful and I was no less amazed by the rest of the curiosities. The Indians also presented Augustus with a giant river tortoise, a very long python, and an enormous partridge with a red beak. In addition to the animals was human merchandise. At the emperor's feet, eight naked slaves prostrated themselves, one of whom was a boy named Hermes, whose arms had been amputated at the shoulder.

The armless boy demonstrated that he could perform tasks with his feet, bending a bow, throwing a javelin, and even playing a trumpet with his toes. When the boy glanced up at me as if sensing that I might have some power over the new life he'd find as property of the emperor, I had to look away.

We learned that a much larger Indian contingent had set out to reach a treaty with Augustus in support of his quickly approaching war with Parthia but that a great many of them perished on the way. One of the survivors was a holy man named Zarmanochegas, who said, "We're told that you have a powerful sorceress to aid you in battle."

All eyes turned to me for there were some rumors I couldn't squelch. My congress with the emperor was a well-guarded secret, but my magic was not, so I allowed a smile to touch my lips. "Caesar doesn't need a woman to fight his battles."

My words only echoed the very Roman ideals Augustus strove to embody, but he recognized my political volley. The more this line was repeated, the less likely he could make use of me in wartime without losing face. Irritation twitched at his brow, just beneath his oak-leaf crown. "The Queen of Mauretania speaks truly," he said. "But perhaps there will be no battle. Rome seeks to fight only *just* wars. Parthia must surrender to us our lost battle standards and make tribute for their offenses. If they refuse, they'll be crushed by the legions I've amassed near Armenia. But if they *can* be persuaded, the Parths may recover something *they* want."

I doubted my words alone had convinced him but found myself strangely delighted by this apparent change of heart. The Indian ambassador seemed pleased as well. "We'd be happy to travel with you, Augustus, to serve as intermediaries."

I could see it now. All the emperor's actions here on the Isle of Samos had taken on a shape of the same character. From his willingness to negotiate a peace with the Kandake to his toppling of Artaxias . . . he was, step by step, ensuring a stable stage upon which to perform his next act. Marcus Crassus failed to conquer Parthia because he was a fool. Caesar failed because he was assassinated before he could try. My father failed because he left diplomatic instability in his wake. Augustus had studied; he'd learned from these men. Now he approached his attack on Parthia in slow crawling steps, just as he'd approached everything he wanted, including me.

HE summoned me to his rooms that night. I waited until the oil lamps burned low, half dazed by my unexpected admiration for his thoroughness. When I entered, Augustus wasn't abed but throwing dice upon a table. *"Caesar doesn't need a woman to fight his battles for him,"* he mimicked, shaking the *tali* bones in his cup. "You think you're very clever, don't you?"

"Not as clever as you are," I admitted without prevarication. Circe had advised me to find something in the emperor to love; his cunning, his persistence, his plodding determination all resonated deep inside me. We were alike in so many ways that it ought to have disturbed me. "I begin to sense that you may actually prevail with Parthia."

"I'm touched by your confidence."

The blood of the Ptolemies ran in my veins; Alexander's ambitions were a siren call to me too. Much as I might will it away, the desire to be near the center of the political world was as real for me as the pull of the moon. That was something else to appreciate when in the presence of Augustus. "I shouldn't have doubted you, Caesar. Agrippa may have formulated a genius battle plan, but you . . . While Agrippa is off battling Cantabri hillsmen in Gaul, you're here threading each kingdom into your alliance like so many disparate beads on a single string."

The emperor had been the subject of much praise in his life. But what he had wanted—what my mother deprived him of—was her *appreciation*. She'd died before he could make her look upon his brilliance and recognize it. Now he wanted that recognition from me. My words changed his posture. He preened at my praise, like Bast sometimes did when I told her she was a good kitty. My genuine appreciation of his talents also aroused him. Instantly. Powerfully. He took no pains to hide it, his face flushed, a rising bulge between his legs. "Selene, the Indians bring me creatures large and small for my amusement. What will you offer me? Surely I've earned some reward beyond a kiss." I'd known from the start that he wouldn't be forever content to plunder my mouth with lips and tongue, so I braced myself for his approach as he rose to his feet. "I must leave soon for Parthia, but I *will* make you Queen of Egypt once the Parthian matter is decided. Trust in Caesar. Do not refuse me."

"I only refuse to be bedded as a prostitute," I said as he circled me, his breath lifting the downy hairs at the back of my neck. "My mother did what she liked with shameless disregard for the judgment of good Romans. I'll never allow myself to be dishonored, even by you, because it would taint your honor and that of your son."

His hands went to my hair, roughly. "No more games. Tell me what you want."

"I want to give you a son. A *legitimate* son and heir. Make it possible for me to give myself over to Caesar's hands, body and soul."

That stopped him. "You wish—you wish to be my *wife*?" The idea of marrying the emperor was revolting in every possible way, but he wanted to possess me. He'd *always* wanted that. Let him believe that I wanted it just as much. He stammered with astonishment. "I'm married to Livia."

"I know it all too well. And I wonder if it was this way with your father, Julius Caesar, whining about Calpurnia. Do you think he skulked about in the middle of the night, pretending he didn't summon my mother to his bed? He took her to bed and to wed, his Roman wife be damned."

"I'm not—"

"Caesar?" The word echoed through the room, and the oil lamps flickered, as if we'd summoned his spirit. The emperor now stood taller, strength regained. He *was* Caesar; he'd never admit otherwise.

"I'll consider it," he said, and I was stunned into silence. I'd just asked him to make me Empress of the Empire. He should have slapped me for the suggestion. He should have cursed me or banished me to my rooms the way he had the day I demanded he send Livia away. "I'll consider it, and you'll allow me liberties this night," he said, his lips capturing mine. The acrid tang of his kiss burned like poison. It made me want to spit, but I commanded my lips to receive it as honey.

Every princeling in Asia Minor would have eagerly lain beneath the emperor, so why should I flinch from it? But Augustus took pleasure in the despoilment of virtue. Not the lack of it. So I wouldn't allow him to ravish me. I broke away from his kiss and said, "We won't make a child this night." He must have heard me, but his mouth fastened on the hollow at my throat. Then he yanked the front of my gown open, mauling me with both hands. To my surprise and relief, this was less intimate than kissing. Easier to pretend that I wasn't inside my own body and that my *ba* was floating somewhere near, somewhere apart. "Gentle," I scolded as his fingernails raked at me. "I'm not some Gallic girl you captured in a field."

"You're as tall as one," he said, and I knew that displeased him, but I could feel his arousal pressed against me. "You're my Cleopatra. More like her every day. I didn't think it would be better with you willing, but perhaps it will be."

With that, he lowered his head to capture one of my pink nipples between his lips. I hadn't expected this because suckling was the kind of hedonistic, pleasure-giving, pleasure-taking indulgence that he viewed as oriental deviance. Yet he gloried in it. I arched my back, pushing upon his shoulders to encourage him. In so doing, I forced him down to one knee. A worshipful pose.

A thrill went through me. *He was kneeling before me.* I'd brought the ruler of Rome to his knees, and I wanted to make a fistful of his hair and revel in my triumph. I wanted to force his head back and make him beg, as he'd made me beg. I wanted to strike him across the face as I'd done when he raped me, but it had excited him then. Now, it might break the spell, and I was almost as bound by it as he. It was the feel of his hand moving up my leg that brought me back to my senses. "I've allowed you liberties, Caesar, but I warned that we'd make no child."

He didn't hide his annoyance but pushed no further. "As you wish, Selene, but this will be the last time you refuse me. When I return victorious from Parthia, you'll be the one to kneel."

THINGS happened swiftly after that as the grand machinery of the empire rolled into place. Preparations for the emperor's departure were made with military precision. He readied for a campaign. He wouldn't be delayed even by the news that the Romans had again refused to elect a new consul, hoping Augustus would relent and take up the office again. The Romans had clearly not realized what the rest of the world already knew—if Augustus succeeded in Parthia, the highest office in Rome would be too small for him.

And I—what part would I play in making him a giant? Since the night he told me that he might call me to his side on the battlefield to use my sorcery for war, I'd dreamed of battle and blood. Horrible dreams. My mother had been a warrior, but she'd given that strength to Helios, not to me. Like the emperor, my weapons were treachery and guile, and I doubted that either of us would fare well in open warfare. Still, the emperor pressed on with his plans.

In the absence of an elected consul, a man named Rufus had claimed the office for himself and created some sort of minor rebellion in Rome that was swiftly put down. Along with this news came a cadre of men accompanying a boy. "Who is he?" I asked as we loitered on the balcony.

"A Parthian prisoner," Lady Lasthenia said. "Tragic, really."

"A pretty boy, though. He'd fetch a fortune in certain Greek quarters," Lady Hybrida said.

I glanced down again at the boy with his dark ringlets, all gleaming with oil. He wore gold bands about his neck and an expression upon his face that I recognized, for I too had once been a chained captive. "How dear is he to the Parthians?"

"He's the son of the Parthian king," Lady Lasthenia replied. "He was kidnapped."

I closed my eyes. *Surely there is something the Parths want that you can offer in exchange for Roman battle standards*, I had said. Now I must earnestly hope that the King of Parthia would bargain for the life of his son. "A package, Your Majesty," someone said, and I opened my eyes to see it was Captain Kabyle, who was so restless with his ship always at anchor that he'd taken it upon himself to bring the first news from the docks every day. Or perhaps it was only his excuse to see Tala.

It was winter; I hadn't expected letters until spring, but Chryssa must have believed it urgent, for she'd sent me a letter along with a tiny pouch. I opened the letter first.

Beloved Queen,

I write to inform you that as the Proconsul of Africa Nova, Lucius Cornelius Balbus has begun a campaign against the Garamantes on the eastern frontier of your kingdom. King Juba has not committed Mauretanian soldiers to the cause, but neither will he hear the appeals of the Berber tribesmen who want the king to negotiate a truce. In truth, the king will hear nothing at all on any subject but his horses. He's out riding all morning, at the stables all afternoon, and in the evenings he shuts himself up in his study. Only one command the king has given—to strike a coin. I thought you might like to see it.

It had all unfolded just as Maysar predicted, only made worse by the fact that my husband had somehow transformed from a competent monarch into a brooding malcontent. I opened the little pouch and reached in for the coin, with its new portraiture of Juba. But when I turned the little gold disk over, I startled to see my own face. It was an engraved image of me in profile, a diadem in my hair, my cloak fastened over one shoulder. I traced the lettering. Juba's side was engraved in Latin. Mine was in Greek. Moved beyond words, my throat tightened. I, Cleopatra Selene of House Ptolemy, was no petty plaything for an unimportant princeling. Here was proof. I was queen. Queen of Mauretania. Writ there on enduring metal for all the world to see. It wasn't the best likeness of me, my nose too long, my chin too short, but I imagined that all that I'd suffered, all that I'd survived, was somehow captured in my expression.

"Is it bad news?" Circe asked.

I clutched the coin, but only said, "There's war on the boundary of Mauretania. We must return."

Tala, making eyes like a moon calf at the ship's captain, seemed pleased by this statement, but my Alexandrians were stricken. Lady

Lasthenia actually grasped the hem of my shawl. "Your Majesty, Mauretania is *behind* you. *Alexandria* is before you. *Egypt* is in your grasp."

She couldn't know how truly she spoke. Euphronius would have told me to forget Mauretania if he were here, but he was not. He was safely ensconced in my palace by the sea. *My* palace, which I had helped design in every particular and which might almost be finished now. And this coin, this *coin!*

Below, the emperor was finishing his business and preparing to depart. Smartly dressed in his military garb—a blue tunic layered over a red one, all worn beneath a colorfully enameled breastplate—he removed his oak-leaf crown and made to leave.

I swept down the stairs and stopped him before his procession reached the gates. In a rush, I said, "Balbus is making war on the Garamantes in Africa Nova."

Augustus nodded. "They are just tribesmen, no? In his dispatches to me, Balbus claims he can defeat them handily."

"Send me back to Mauretania," I said in some fit of madness. "To help end the conflict. Surely you don't wish to leave such instability in the empire while you fight the Parthians."

Augustus tilted his head as he regarded me. "Mauretania is a half world away. Let Balbus handle matters. I need you here and you know why. There's a chance I must send for you." As his sorceress. His secret war weapon. Here waiting in the East where stormy seas couldn't prevent my journey to the battlefield. It'd been foolish to ask, but if I hadn't tried, how could I call myself queen?

When I bowed my head, Augustus said, "You will stay here. Or do I need to leave soldiers behind to guard you?"

"I'll stay," I promised. "Memnon and my Macedonians will be sufficient protection."

"Good. I'll either call for you to serve on the battlefield or return to you victorious, Queen Cleopatra Selene. Either way, there shall then be a reckoning between us."

With that and a red swirl of his cape, he took his leave of me.

Thirty-four

AT the edge of the sand, I watched the emperor's ship go. I'd come to this island for Egypt—I might well come away with the world. I might have *everything*. My daughter, a queen of Egypt. My son, the Emperor of Rome. That had been my mother's dream when she came to this island. She'd given me her *ba* and so now it must be my dream too. It wasn't my *only* dream, though.

There were darker ones that called to me like a siren from the sea. I'd made myself endure the emperor's groping. Reveled even, in the way I forced him to his knees. I'd made him *desperate* to have me. So desperate that he might well make me his wife. It would be a stunning triumph, one that repaid Livia for her crimes against me and mine. So why did I wish to throw myself beneath the waves?

Mine was a dark, soul-spearing despair, like a bony hand closing upon my throat. Did I need to breathe? My expressions were carefully composed works of art. My blood now stilled and slowed at my command. For my survival and my ambitions, I'd mastered myself. When Augustus returned to me, he would find a body flushed with arousal for him. A body that molded itself to his comfort, just like his gilded chair.

At this thought, my chest rose, fell, then did not rise again. How heavy my limbs felt without breath. How long was it before sound rushed in upon me with a strange quality and numbness crept into my extremities? I stood there, swaying, my white gown flapping in the wind, until I became aware of something soft against my thigh. I looked down to see Isidora clutching at my leg, her warm cheek pressed against me . . . In her strange blue eyes, all possibilities unfolded and I sputtered for air.

MY father was a man who allowed the darkness to crowd him in. One extreme or the other—wild parties or hermetic seclusion, raucous laughter or bitter recriminations. My mother, by contrast, kept the darkness at bay by never allowing herself to be idle. In this, I followed her example. When I wasn't writing correspondence, I enrolled in a series of lectures at the Pythagorean School. I purchased art from traveling merchants and entertained aboard my ship. I even prepared for my reign as Egypt's queen. When my mother was defeated, the emperor had issued a coin depicting the crocodile of Egypt in chains. My first coin as Queen of Egypt would show an unchained crocodile, a signal to the world that I was free. That Egypt was free. This and other plans I made as winter became spring and the whole world awaited news from Parthia.

"How much longer do you think we must wait?" Tala asked, feeding seeds to my little caged birds. "The sea is open once again, and our good captain grows restless."

"*Our* captain, is he?" I asked with an arched brow.

"He's loyal to my queen," she said, then grinned a little. "But she's not the only moon in his sky."

"Will you marry?" I wondered aloud.

Tala sobered, shaking her head. "To be a sailor's wife is a misery. You never know where he is, when he'll return, or what battles he must fight on the sea. To be tied to such a man is to have a phantom husband, only real for those few nights he returns."

"Aren't those few nights better than none at all?"

Tala shrugged. "I loved a husband and lost him. I grieved him and wove in his honor. I have my son now, my Ziri, and no other man can have my whole heart."

Long after Tala drifted away, I watched the songbirds in their cage, thinking of what she'd said. I too loved a husband and lost him, though we never spoke vows. I'd loved Helios and I'd loved Egypt, and no other man and no other land could have my whole heart. Wasn't it better to forget about Mauretania and its rains, to forget about Juba and the coin he'd made with my face on it?

I *must* forget.

Visitors crowded the Isle of Samos to gloat in the aftermath of the emperor's defeat or to celebrate his victory, whichever might come. Thankfully, most of the guests called upon Maecenas and Terentilla at their exquisitely luxurious villa. There was *one* visitor I was happy to see at my gate, however. "Virgil!" I cried, eschewing all formality when the poet presented himself. "How unlike you to travel so far."

"The emperor commanded me to be here when he returns," he said. Three years of grief had robbed him of his vigor so that his smile was barely visible beneath heavily lidded eyes. "I accused Crinagoras of flattery when I read his verse about you, but to see you now, Cleopatra Selene . . . you've become all your mother could've wished."

I wanted very badly to believe that. "That's kind of you to say and I'm so pleased to see you. You must tell me of Lady Julia. How fares her son?"

"Little Gaius is sickly and small, but he still lives."

Be glad or damn your soul, I told myself. "There must be something I can do for Julia, some gift I can send her."

"I doubt she'd receive it," Virgil said. "You should know that she's been forbidden to write to you. Agrippa believes that you've been a corrupting influence. He packed her off to Gaul to join him and his legions, and allows nothing to pass into her hands that hasn't been seen by him first."

Oh, Agrippa could be so arbitrary and unreasonable! My heart ached for my friend. Why hadn't I pushed the emperor to kill the man when I had the chance? That Agrippa wasn't truly a bad man, but a misguided one, should have no place in my decisions; sentimentality didn't suit rulers. Such concerns were not for poets, however, so I said only, "How fares this grand *Aeneid*, which will declare Augustus our savior, our messiah, the bringer of the Golden Age?"

He knew how I felt about his work. "Oh, Gracious Majesty, please don't take me to task again . . ."

The days when I'd been young and idealistic enough to protest the emperor's propaganda seemed long past. Virgil would write the story and now it seemed that I would do everything in my power to make it true. "I only ask that you not use your work to vilify African queens."

"Ah, you are no Dido of Carthage." Virgil laughed. "You're beloved in Rome, in spite of your sorcery. They call you a goddess of grain, a maiden and mother. You're no temptress to lure good men from their duty and you have no fear of comparison in my work."

Even Virgil didn't know me. He knew only the masks that I wore. "Is the poem finished?"

"No, which vexes the emperor. He's given me a deadline and I fear that meeting it may kill me." Now he leaned forward to whisper. "But you needn't worry. I've instructed my slaves to burn the rotted thing when I perish."

"Burn the *Aeneid*?" I sputtered.

"It isn't very good," Virgil said, though I thought he was wrong. "And I don't expect to live long."

I frowned, examining his pallor, looking for telltale signs of fever. "Are you unwell?"

His smile was tight. "Not with anything but a longing to be with a young man who is lost to me."

I should have chided him for this morbidity, but it resonated too closely with my own.

CIRCE licked her lower lip as she gazed through the gauzy curtains of our enormous litter. "Gods be good, Hercules has returned to walk amongst the mortals. That man must be a rower to have arms like that."

She always noticed handsome men so I paid no attention until

Lady Lasthenia also leaned out to look. "With those scars? I think he must be a gladiator! A most dangerous man."

Hybrida sighed. "I'd happily risk that danger to press up against him."

Now I too lifted myself off the cushions, straining to see. In truth, I never knew if the man my eyes fastened upon was the same one my ladies had singled out for admiration. The man that captured *my* attention hefted a wooden chest onto his shoulders, the glistening muscles of his back rippling with the effort. He was broad as a bull, and as he turned, I glimpsed a flash of golden hair. Our eyes met and the whole world went still.

Helios. I wanted to call out his name, but the breath went out of me. If I hadn't known him soul to soul, I might never have recognized him, for there were no traces left of the fair-skinned prince with whom I'd shared a childhood. Beneath that tawny mane of hair, the boyish softness in his face had burned away. He was all man now, sweating in the sun like a dock laborer and not a prince of Egypt.

"Stop the litter!" My shout caught the bearers midstride so there was a great deal of confusion as they attempted to bring the massive carrier to a halt. I didn't wait, but leapt out. The moment my sandals struck the ground Memnon announced, "All hail, Queen Cleopatra Selene of Mauretania!" Beggars surged forth with outstretched hands and merchants crowded round with baskets of trinkets, amphorae of wine, and carts filled with fleece; I couldn't get past. Had there ever been a moment I wished more to be unimportant and obscure?

My eyes searched the crowd, desperate for another glimpse of my twin, but he'd disappeared, as if he'd never been there at all. I trembled all over and my entourage stared at me as if I'd gone mad. Perhaps I had. Lady Lasthenia tried to draw me back inside the litter. "Majesty, the heat—"

"That man. I must find that man," I sputtered. Only after Memnon promised to make inquiries did I curse myself for a reckless fool. If Helios was here on the Isle of Samos—and how could he be?—calling attention to him put him in jeopardy. And yet, and yet . . . the need to find him was sharp and urgent. Unrelenting.

We returned to the emperor's villa and I paced my rooms, *waiting*. It can't have been more than a few hours before Memnon returned, but it seemed as if I aged years in that time. "Majesty, there is no man on the island that meets the description you gave," he said, concern etched onto his scarred face. "Your ladies say he had dark hair, but you say he was golden. The only fair-haired man the merchants can think of is a mercenary man, a ship's captain."

"What ship?" I whispered, knowing that I sounded half deranged. "Where is the ship? Where is it now?"

"Anchored offshore . . . Is this man some kind of danger to you?"

"No," I said, my throat closing, and because I was too shaken to concoct a better lie, I said, "I thought he may have been from Mauretania, come with news."

Memnon didn't question me further; he had a tendency to accept everything I said without reservation, a quality in a guard both valuable and alarming. I dismissed him and the rest of my servants too. I didn't want anyone to see me like this.

Helios. The presence of him like a whisper, luring me to stumble across him, as if I might open the patio doors to the terrace and find him sitting there. On my secluded beach, I held my hand over my brow, squinting against the sun as I considered each of the boats at anchor, wondering which one might be his and whether or not he was staring back. Caught in some kind of madness now, walking back and forth in the surf, letting it wet the hem of my gown, my mind raced through possibilities. Had he come to find me? Ought I be seen in public where he might approach me? I'd decided upon that course, climbed the stairs up from the beach, when I heard a song, a prayer.

I call you to me.
I call you by the breath of your body.
I call you by the truth of your soul.
I call you by the spark of your mind.
I call you by the light of your spirit.

There. One ship anchored not far offshore, ghostly on the horizon, bobbing in the sea as if it was waiting for me . . . as if *he* waited for me. I needed to go to that ship, but how? I could call the winds to my hands, but I couldn't fly across the water. I could ask my own ship's captain to take me out to sea, but this would be noticed and remarked upon—witnessed by a crew loyal to me, but insensible to the danger of this thing I would ask them to do.

I stared until the sun set and the moon was full and low in the sky, its silver light illuminating the mast of that ship. My hands clenched and unclenched as I felt the pull of *heka* drawing me to the ocean. As the waves lapped at my feet, I was at last seized with an inspiration that overcame all reason. I'd *swim* to the ship. Yes, why not? It was the only way I might go anywhere without an armed and gossiping retinue of attendants. Casting my shoes aside and hoisting my gown up, I walked into the water. The sea foam hissed around my waist before I plunged all the way in. I worked my arms, my legs, going with the current. It seemed easy, effortless. Euphoric, even.

I kept swimming until the first telltale signs of fatigue made themselves known in my arms. What if I tired? No, there was no room for exhaustion now. Not after all these years of separation. I don't know how long I swam. My arms and legs churned in the water until I felt myself being tugged by some treacherous current. Salt water flooded my mouth and I spit it out again, realizing that my arms and legs burned. This had been an impetuous thing I'd done. A desperate thing. A thing lacking in all sanity. But then, how many times since coming to the Isle of Samos had I been tempted to throw myself beneath the waves? Speckles danced before my eyes and, exhausted, I let myself drift in the bright moonlight, rising upon each wave, sinking back down again. Had it been this way for Philadelphus, I wondered? What if I were caught in a current and dragged out to sea? Would I even care?

Her mother chose an asp, they would say. *But Selene chose the sea.*

I slipped beneath the surface of the black water once, twice, three times, closing my eyes. Then I thought of my daughter. *I'll never leave you*, I'd promised her. But hadn't Helios and I made promises to one another too? I broke the surface for a gasp of air, unsure if I drew breath in this life or the next.

What would happen to Isidora if I died? The emperor would take her, I thought, and I gulped down another mouthful of precious air. It was the thought of her in his clutches that made me fill my lungs. I cried out for help, though I doubted anyone could hear me over the sounds of the ocean, and the ship still seemed very far away. I'd have to turn back and swim to shore. It was my only choice. Drawing upon my *heka* for a surge of strength, I fought the current. I'd drifted too far away to even make out the contours of my beach. The taste of salt water flooded my senses as I swam, buffeted by the waves. I heard men shout—sailors perhaps—and again cried out for help but dared not hope. My legs cramped painfully, toes curling in protest, and again, I sank beneath the water, squeezing my eyes shut tight. It was as if I swam through honey; my limbs were dead weight.

As I sank, something struck the side of my head, hard. The shooting pain warred for my attention with the ringing in my ears. It hit me again, and this time I clung to it. A stick? A tree branch? Something wooden. An oar. Moments later, I came up choking, gasping, spitting out seawater. A hand reached for mine, an iron grip on my forearm that battled the pull of the ocean itself.

I knew this hand at once and I had no fear, for the hand that held me now was the same one that had steadied me as a chained prisoner. The same hand that had reached through a small hole in the wall when I was a lonely child in Rome. He hoisted me onto the edge of the rowboat, where stunned sailors cried out as if they'd captured a mermaid. With my hair in wet tendrils, seaweed wrapped round one ankle, and my sodden white gown clinging to me, I may have looked like an exotic creature from the deep, but it was all I could do to keep from retching into the bottom of the boat like a pitiful mortal.

Strong hands clutched me and I found myself staring into that beloved face. So much the same, and yet so much changed. I flung my arms around his neck with a sob of gladness. "Helios!"

"Is it you, Selene?" Helios shook me. Literally, shook me. "Are you mad? You must be mad!"

"Yes," I whispered, shivering with cold and horror at my near-suicidal folly. "But you saved me."

No one else could have. Not with magic or moonlight. Only Helios could have found me in the water, sensing me as one senses a breath in the dark. I clutched at him while men rowed the little craft back to the ship, oars dipping into the water, flashes of pale wood in the moonlight. And a strange sensation rushed through me, something I could only think was exhilaration.

The watchman on the ship cried out and there was some commotion on deck before a ladder was lowered down for us. Once aboard, Helios said, "Take her to my berth. Get her something dry, some blankets . . ."

A salty-looking sailor snapped to attention. "Aye, Captain."

Captain. So he was the skipper of this vessel.

"Go with him, Selene," Helios said, in a coaxing tone, prying himself away. "I'll join you shortly."

My gown felt as if it had been woven from snow, so I allowed myself to be led inside his berth. Once inside, I didn't wait for the sailor to return with a blanket but snatched one off the bed. I wrapped it around myself, then groaned at the familiar scent. It struck me at my core, the overwhelming recognition driving me to my knees. This was *his* blanket. This was *his* bed. Cautiously, I opened a bronze-studded wooden chest. It was filled with mismatched armor. A desert cloak. And there, his vulture amulet, wrapped carefully and stashed beneath the rest of his things. All these years, I'd tried to picture where he might sleep, what things he might have kept near him, but I'd never imagined this. It was agony to see how simply he lived while I spent my days in lavish palaces and ostentatious villas.

At last, Helios parted the curtains. Alone in the flickering lamplight, we stared. We'd been not quite fifteen years old the last time we were alone together. How must I look to him now at more than twenty? I noticed a scar on his chin that hadn't been there before and another one on his forearm, the pale traces of what must have been a terrible gash. I wondered what flaws he saw in me that made him ask, "What happened to you?"

How I wished to reach up and straighten my bedraggled hair, but my fingers were clamped too tightly around the blanket for warmth. "I thought I could swim to your ship—"

"You're mad!" he said again, drawing me to my feet. "To attempt such a thing . . ."

"Well, if you hadn't disappeared on the docks, I wouldn't have had to attempt it."

He winced. "I thought perhaps you hadn't recognized me—"

"Then you're the one who is mad, Helios. I'd know you anywhere. Anywhere!"

His throat worked and his voice was hoarse. "Sweet Isis, Selene. Can you be real?"

"I should ask the same of you," I whispered, hugging myself. "I thought I'd never see you again in this life."

His head jerked up, wild grief in his eyes. "Philadelphus. Was it fever? They say it was fever, but I won't believe it unless you say so."

"Malaria," I said, though I'd never be certain. "I was with him." Helios squeezed his eyes shut and didn't open them again until I let out a sob. "How can you be here on the Isle of Samos, Helios? How can you risk it?"

Removing his cloak, he wrapped it around me. "There's no risk for me, Selene." My knees threatened to buckle again at the sensation of his body's warmth so close to mine. "Remember that I've been dead for five years now. No one knows me here."

"Augustus winters on this island! What if Maecenas had seen you?"

"I'm much changed," Helios said. "He wouldn't know me."

"You cannot be sure of that. Virgil is here too. When the emperor returns from Parthia, he'll have Iullus and Tiberius with him. They all know you. And I know you. *I* know you."

He hushed me, drawing me close. The heart in my chest leapt free of my iron control and my pulse thundered in my ears. He took my face in his hands and all my practiced defenses fell away, leaving me raw. I turned my head and he cupped my cheek in his large, warm palm. Oh, familiar ache. In the more than five years we'd been separated, it was like learning to know myself all over again. "Where are your guards, Selene? Who knows that you're here?"

"No one."

"What if someone looks for you and finds that you're not in your rooms?"

"They'll find my shoes in the sand and assume I've drowned." *And I would be free.* It was a siren's song, but I must resist. "We haven't much time. It will be light soon. I have to get back. But tonight, I'll build a fire on the beach outside the emperor's villa when it's safe. Come to me and I'll explain everything."

"It's too dangerous," he said.

That he should be the one to say such a thing to me! "You must come, Helios. If you disappear into the night again, I really will go mad. You *must* come. *You must come.*" Hysteria seized me. "Swear it. Swear that you'll come to me tonight or else I'll never be able to leave you again."

"I swear it by Isis," he said, and I believed him.

Thirty-five

THE first rays of dawn broke over the sea just as the rowboat was within swimming distance to shore. I held tearfully to Helios's neck, made him promise again that he would return that night, then lowered myself back into the water. If questioned upon my return, I'd say that I'd gone swimming, got caught in the current, and was unable to get back to shore until now. I concocted the harrowing tale, ready for a dramatic performance, but by the time my bare feet touched bottom in the shallows, I saw no one combing the beach for me. The light was faintly golden now, and my sandals were still in the sand where I'd left them. I gathered them up, then, dripping water on the stairs, made my way up to the terrace and slipped into my rooms.

Tonight Helios will come to me.

I laughed with the elation of it all. I'd done it, and none were the wiser! I should have been exhausted. Unable to keep my eyes open. Yet the certainty that Helios would come left me as alert as a sentinel. I was careful to observe my daily routine, dressing for the day, playing with Isidora, reading correspondence, receiving visitors, and taking my meals in the main dining room. I did nothing to call attention to myself. I'd always been of the opinion that Maecenas could smell secrets in the wind, which was one of the reasons Augustus kept him close. Fortunately, the emperor's political adviser didn't come calling. Moreover, Virgil and Crinagoras were too delighted to fall back into one another's company to worry themselves over me.

"I want a ship," Isidora announced at dinner, giving me a look that stopped my heart.

"You shall have one, Princess," Lady Lasthenia announced, hastily creating one from folded papyrus, pressing angles into angles. Fortunately, this bit of mundane magic made Isidora drowsy and good-humored by bedtime.

Tonight Helios will come to me. With my hair oiled and gleaming and my skin freshly softened with aloe, I donned my best cloak, the one dyed in Gaetulian purple. Then I waited until dark, until the sounds of life within the villa quieted and most of the island was asleep. Taking a torch, I slipped from my bedroom down to the beach, a canopy of stars overhead. In my queen's finery, I collected driftwood and pulled it into a pile, using my torch to set it alight. Then I waited.

Straining to hear the sound of the oars over the crackling fire, I stood in a pool of moonlight. I wanted Helios to see me illuminated by silver light. I didn't want to appear to him as a shaking, traumatized girl but the goddess he'd known. How long must I wait? Five years might as well have been a lifetime, but these few hours had been agony and a tiny thread of worry tugged inside me. What if he didn't come? More time passed and the fire burned low. Worry became a deadening weight. How many other women had waited, abandoned at the edge of the sea? He'd promised. He'd *promised* me. He'd vowed it by Isis!

Perhaps he couldn't see the fire from his ship. I'd add more driftwood. Yes. And if I couldn't find any, I'd throw my cloak into the fire, though it could buy a fleet of ships. Just as I reached for the clasp, I heard a faint splash. Maybe a fish jumping. Maybe a small boat. It was too dark to see. My breath caught, my muscles rigid as I leaned toward the water. The faint glow of a torch swayed. Then I saw a big man at the oars, alone, and it was everything I could do not to rush into the waves. I forced myself to stay by the dying embers of my fire, smoothing my gown while he pulled his small craft ashore and secreted it in the brush. At last, he emerged like a tall dark shadow, coming to a halt some feet away.

I nearly sobbed. "I feared you wouldn't come."

"Selene, I'm bound to you in life and death, for always. Don't you know it?" He took a few steps closer and a look of awe passed over his features. "You've become a queen in truth."

"Your queen," I said, because even in the guise of a mercenary he would always be Egypt's king.

"Yes," he admitted, finally close enough to take my face in his hands. "You've always been that."

"I've looked for you, worried that you'd die somewhere far away and I'd never know. Tell me everything."

Talking wasn't foremost on his mind; he leaned forward to kiss me. I thought to turn away, so he wouldn't taste the poison of the emperor in my treasonous mouth. I thought to turn away, because I must know what had passed between him and the Kandake of Meroë. I thought to turn away because I was—at least in the eyes of the world—married to another man. But there could be no turning away from Helios. He kissed me with such ferocity that all my questions flew away, any desire to speak extinguished. His flesh and blood, warm and alive, was such a miracle to me that I forgot all else. I wanted only this—a kiss as familiar to me as my own soul but as mysterious as the afterlife.

In all the years we'd been apart, and all the ways I'd imagined kissing him again, I couldn't have predicted the way it would strip me bare. I'd taken such pride in mastering my every reaction that I'd forgotten entirely what it was to feel something with my whole body, without restraint. "Selene . . ." They say the gods can call you by your true name and hold you in their thrall; I believe it, because when Helios said my name, I'd have done anything for him. Anything. Since my marriage to Juba, whatever tentative passions I experienced were always tempered by darker realities. Even my first time with Helios had been tainted by grief and pain, all mixed up with the *heka* and the desire of an eternal goddess for her god. Now I claimed a lust that was mine alone. I didn't want Helios because he was the god or because he was the husband I should have married or because I needed his kisses to wash the emperor away. I wanted him because I *wanted* him, a deep, defiant desire. Kissing him boldly, I bunched his tunic in my fists, trying to yank it off. My eagerness made amusement rumble in his chest. "Selene, wait . . ."

"I don't want to wait," I said, trying to pull him down, but that was like trying to move a colossus.

He held me against his chest where his heartbeat galloped against my ear. "I just thought you'd like to do this somewhere warm and dry this time."

I glanced to the terrace where my oil lamps still burned and he swept me up into his arms. Kissing my cheeks, my shoulders, my neck, my mouth . . . he carried me up the stairs and through the open doors. He didn't look upon the riches of the room with avarice—he didn't seem to notice the priceless statues and vast mosaic floor. His eyes were on my face. The whole bed, heaped with pillows, creaked with his bulk as he climbed atop me. "Selene, are you sure?"

"I'll die if you don't." I knew that I should be thinking of the consequences, weighing the risks, plotting what lies I must tell in the aftermath, but my need for him had become such a torment that I truly believed it would kill me to deny it.

I believe it still.

AFTERWARD, we lay tangled together, damp and breathless. Whereas I'd gone limp, too weak to lift my head from the pillow, his hand still caressed me, tracing the pale lines on my belly. They weren't so prominent as when Isidora was first born, but it vexed me that his fingers should worry over them. "I have a daughter."

His hand went still. For a moment, he didn't breathe. Then, finally, "Her name?"

"Cleopatra Isidora."

"A good name," he allowed, teeth clenched. "Does she look much like Juba?"

I tensed, clasping his hand to make him listen. "She's not Juba's daughter."

A flash of jealousy sparked behind his eyes. Was he imagining me frolicking with some nubile slave? Whatever emotion tormented him, he reined it in. "It doesn't matter who her father is. She's yours. She's a Ptolemy."

"Helios, you misunderstand. She's nearly five years old . . ." A pause. An unspoken question. Then he squeezed his eyes shut and made a sound that broke my heart. He clasped his head in his hands, then pressed his palms to his face. I touched his shoulder, trying to comfort him. "Oh, Helios, be glad—"

"Glad that monster forced a child on you?" he snapped. "Or glad that I have a daughter I've never known and can never see?" I felt his anguish deep in my soul and was now sorry for having told him. Sorry for having added to his misery. He'd lost so much. His throne. His family. His name. Now this.

"But you *can* see her. She's sleeping not far from here. I'll fetch her."

He sat up, abruptly, then his shoulders sagged. "No, we can't do that. If I were to meet her, we'd have to ask her to keep it a secret. That's a terrible thing to do to a child. Even a royal child."

We'd both been forced to keep secrets since we were children. All the secrets I'd held and the lies that I'd told had transformed me into someone I wouldn't wish my daughter to become. "You're right. I'm sorry. But there must be some way that you can see her."

"Bring her to the market," he said. "In the daylight. In a crowd. Where I can see her from afar."

This was easily arranged but raised new questions. "When? You can't mean to stay here. If Augustus is victorious in Parthia, he'll return to this island."

"And when he arrives, I'll be waiting for him," Helios rasped, eyes bloodshot with emotion.

Dread coiled in my heart. "To what end?"

"You know it already, so why do you ask?" He found his tunic in the pile of pillows and pulled it over his head. "I've spent all these years fighting the Romans. In Arabia. In Egypt. In Meroë. Wherever I could fight them. But now I'm here to fight for *you* . . ."

"Don't say it's for me," I said, wrapping the bedsheet around me.

"I've come to kill him, Selene," Helios said with a fearsome stare. "I'm going to kill Octavian. I'm going to kill him for all the wrongs he's done. Win or lose in Parthia, he'll return to the Isle of Samos. When he does, I'll make an end to him. But *you* . . . you must be away. Go back to Mauretania."

How I wished that I could. "That isn't possible."

Helios had grown from an impetuous boy to a man who gathered all the facts. He paused in dressing, tilting his head to ask, "Why? Is Juba a danger to you? Is that why you've stayed so long?"

"Of course not." *Juba is only a danger to himself*, I thought.

"Then why are you here on the Isle of Samos? It's almost summer. Your business with the Kandake is long done and Octavian has refused to make you Queen of Egypt. Why have you lingered?"

My heart could only bear to give the simplest answer. "Because the emperor asked it of me."

It wasn't simple enough to deceive him. The blood drained from his face, leaving him pale to the tip of his nose, a white-faced fury that was terrifying to behold. He shuddered and I thought he might break something, smash aside the lamps and pretty bottles and little adornments by the side of my bed. "It isn't bad enough that he violated you all those years ago? Now he keeps you as his . . . his . . ."

Afraid of what word he might settle upon, I hastened to say, "He hasn't taken me to his bed again."

"Nor will he," Helios vowed, turning to grab hold of my arms. "I'll see to that. I'll avenge you."

He couldn't know that I'd resolved to give myself to the emperor and that I needed Augustus alive. There must be more to this conversation between us, but I couldn't bear to have it now. Not *now*. Not when there were so few precious moments until the sunrise. I clung to him as long as I could, and when he finally readied to leave, he promised, "Sleep a little. I'll come again tonight, when it's dark."

IN the weeks that followed, I lived for nightfall. Helios was the only sun in my sky. I walked about dazed, counting the hours until

I could be rid of my servants and make my way to the water's edge. You must understand that Helios was my brother no more—if he'd ever been. He'd grown to be a large man, his hardened body a specimen of devastating masculinity. It was as if he'd been carved like one of those great cult statues, and there wasn't a woman alive who wouldn't have stopped in her tracks for a worshipful glimpse of him. There was no woman he couldn't have seduced—from the lowest slave to the highest queen. For him, they'd have all thrown their bedroom doors wide. But at night, he came for *me*.

We always made love in twos. The first time, he'd descend upon me like an invading army, yanking at my clothes, tearing the fabric if need be. I never resisted or even feigned struggle, but as swiftly as I'd spread my thighs to welcome him, it never seemed quick enough. His heart thundered in his chest loud enough for me to hear it and he'd clutch at my hips as if he were frantic to feel skin against skin. My own need matched his so precisely that we often cried out together.

Yet it was always the second time that left me annihilated. The second time, sheepish and between kisses, he'd murmur apologies for his barbarism. Then he'd lay me gently on pillows and navigate the sensitive spots of my body without hesitation—as if he'd memorized a secret map of my skin. He knew just where to kiss the places that made me burn. He knew just how to capture me beneath his sweat-slick limbs so that the air ignited in my lungs. Trapped between him and my own desire, I was defenseless. He wielded my arousal against me like a weapon he'd mastered, thrusting, parrying, exhausting me until I begged for quarter. Then and only then, when I was scarcely coherent, he'd bury himself inside me and we'd become one.

There was never a time he didn't make me burn with desire. Never a time he tired before I did. Never a time that he didn't leave me storm swept and shaking. It was an art, what he did to me. A practiced talent. "You've been with other women."

"Yes." He let his broad palm rest on the expanse of my belly. "I wanted to be good at it." He didn't need to say why. He was Antony's son. *Antony*, as famous a lover as he was a fighter. But when Helios saw my expression, his eyes lowered. "But now, I swear, there will never be another."

Who was I to insist upon fidelity, having married one man and now seducing another? "I can't ask that of you."

"You didn't," Helios said, rough hands kneading the fleshiest parts of me. It didn't matter that I was tall; he was taller. He made me feel delicate in his solid arms, fragile and safe all at once. And though it was selfish and petty, I hated to think he'd made some other woman feel this way too. "I want to know about your lovers. Like this Kandake of Meroë."

I didn't expect him to laugh.

"Don't mock me, Helios. You have no idea how it pained me to hear about her. How she's a fierce fighter, beautiful and—"

"She *is* beautiful," he said, his golden hair upon my pillow, a playful smile on his lips as if in fond remembrance. "Her spirit is beautiful. Though she lost one eye in battle, she's majestic. A true embodiment of Isis."

These words were soured milk in my belly. "I've changed my mind. I can't bear to hear."

"Selene, she's nearly fifty years old. Devoted to her people, to her son, and to her *husband*."

Though I'd long since learned to keep blood from rushing to my face, I flushed like an unpracticed girl. "Do you think I'm a fool?"

"You are," he said, forcing me to look at him. "My relations with the Kandake have been entirely chaste, but it wouldn't have mattered anyway. *You* are the magic in my soul that keeps me alive. *You* are as constant in my heart as the moon in the night. *You* are my other half and I'll always seek you out somehow, even though it puts you in danger, and that is my shame."

His words melted my anger away and filled my veins with sweet honey. "You should never be ashamed for returning to me. I need to know where you've been and what you've done and where you've triumphed and who has hurt you!"

"Then I'll tell you," he said, soothing me like a falconer smoothes ruffled feathers. "I'll tell you anything."

In the next hours, we exchanged five years' worth of tales. I told him of how I'd helped poison the emperor against the first Gallus. He told me of Arabia, where he led the second Gallus into a trap. I learned of Helios's ships—yes, he'd had more than one. And I traced each scar on his body and listened to him tell me how he got it. When he was done, I told him about Mauretania—about the crops and the lavender, the harbor and the lighthouse, and about the wondrous purple that the royals all clamored to have. I told him about the crocodiles and my visit to the river. And even about the tomb I'd built for him. The only thing I didn't tell him was about my bargain with the emperor, and whenever his questions tread too closely to that subject, I distracted him with tales of Isidora. Her first steps. Her first words. "I want to see her *tomorrow*," he said. "Take her to the market. I'll watch for her from afar."

THAT day, in the market, I feared to look up into the crowd. Were I to somehow find Helios in daylight and lock eyes with him again, it would remind my servants of the day I leapt out of the litter and raved like a madwoman, so I instructed Tala to take the children amidst the merchant awnings and let my daughter spend what she would on any trinkets that pleased her.

While the common folk fawned over my little princess, I remained in my litter with a package newly arrived from Mauretania. It bore a wax seal pressed with a lion signet, the mark Juba had taken as his own. After all my complaints about the scarcity of word from Mauretania, now I didn't want to break the seal. Juba and Augustus were a world away, but Helios was here, with me. My skin still tingled from his touch, and the tender places he'd left sore now ached so pleasantly I might have sighed or laughed or even sang with the joy of it. And I did not care for Augustus or Juba or what either of them represented.

But I did care about Mauretania. I broke the seal. Inside was a letter all smudged and wrinkled as if it'd been worked beneath perspiring hands or spotted with a pale wine. *Selene*, it began. So it was to be informal.

> Selene, I write to you from Spain where I have joined with Agrippa and received an appointment as a *duovir* in Gades. We've received word that Lucius Cornelius Balbus has crushed the Garamantes and been hailed as imperator. He's asked to be granted a Triumph in Rome. No mercy was given to the combatants. Perhaps this will be a lesson to our own rebellious tribesmen, the Gaetulians, who show little respect to our throne since your departure.
>
> Of course, I write as if this were still of some consequence to you. I blame myself for your leave-taking. But whatever holds you on that island is illusion. What you want cannot be. It is not real, whereas you and Isidora are very much real and very much alive. I had hoped the anniversary coin I struck would prove to you that I would care for and protect you both, so what compels you to place yourself and the little princess in such peril? You throw away what you have to grasp hold of what you cannot. Is this the way of the Ptolemies?

I crumpled the paper. The nerve of the man to write these things to me! Juba, who could not be bothered to rule Mauretania, was now across the strait in Spain as a *duovir*, an honorary magistrate? If I could have reached him, I might have struck him. The show of Roman might against the Garamantes would do nothing but stir up rebellion amongst our fiercely independent tribesmen. And he had the temerity to lecture *me* about illusion?

His bitterness and condemnation astonished me. As if I hadn't been *summoned* by the emperor. As if I hadn't been *commanded* to stay here in case the emperor wished to use my powers against his enemies. I had no choice! Then, calming myself, I muttered at the absurdity of a man like Lucius Cornelius Balbus holding a Triumph. I knew Augustus. He was the imperator, the emperor. He would never sanction another of equal status. How would they dare arrange such a thing so hastily while he was away? I sensed Agrippa's hands on this . . .

I read the last lines of Juba's letter again, still seething. *You throw away what you have to grasp hold of what you cannot. Is this the way of the Ptolemies?* Perhaps it was. I didn't care. Helios was here and would come again to me, this very night.

"Look!" Isidora cried, waving a little wooden tiger in my direction. "It's like the ones the Indians brought in the cage. I want a lion and a falcon too."

"Let her buy what she wants," I told Tala, who surrendered the coin. "She is a Ptolemy. She can have *anything* she wants."

"DID you see her?" I asked Helios when he came to me that night.

He nodded, as if he scarcely trusted himself to speak, and a needle of doubt pierced me. Helios was quiet. Somber. With a brooding expression that left me half to wonder if he was going to build some cabin by the sea and waste away. In silence, we listened to the waves as I wondered if he saw the emperor's features on Isidora's face where I could never see them. "Aren't you going to say something about her? Can you not love my daughter because—"

"Not love her?" He rounded on me, his voice rising. "She's a *miracle!*"

I knew she was a miracle and not simply in the sense that every mother knows her child is a gift. Isidora represented the survival of the Ptolemies. She embodied my desperate attempts to preserve our dynasty and all the dreams my mother had ever dreamed. And yet miracle that she was, she seemed to have put Helios in agony. "I only meant to ease your pain. I didn't think that seeing her would make it worse."

"She looked at me," he finally said. "I was so far away. She shouldn't have even glanced in my direction, but she did. She looked up from her wooden toys, stared through the crowd, and found my eyes. It was like looking into a River of Time. Like everything I'd ever done or wanted to do or dreamed is all inside of her. And she'll never know me. She'll never know me."

I wanted to promise him that I'd tell her tales of Horus the Avenger. That one day, when the world was different, we could all be together. Maybe I could make it so. Even if the emperor returned from Parthia victorious, even if I gave him a son and he made me his wife, he couldn't live forever. Helios and I were young, we were—

I froze at the sound of rustling in the shrubbery and Helios had the presence of mind to crouch low. A small sword was in his hand as swiftly as if he'd conjured it, and the quick spark of *heka* snapped in the air to his command. Dear Isis, I didn't know whether to hope our intruder was Memnon or not, given Helios's deadly intent. To be caught here, even by my own guards, alone with a man . . . Just then, Helios loosened the grip on his weapon. "Is that *Bast?*" he asked, a small smile upon his lips as the cat pushed leaves aside to emerge with glowing eyes.

"Wretched cat!" I said, gasping for breath. I'd gone weak all over with relief.

Helios stooped to pick the cat up, and she knew him, purring in his hands. "Not such a sleek huntress anymore, are you?"

"She's old and pampered and well fed," I assured him, grateful that Bast was one courtier who could keep our secrets.

TWO pieces of news arrived almost simultaneously. The first was a missive from Rome stating that Lucius Cornelius Balbus would celebrate his Triumph. The second missive was from Armenia, stating that the Parthians had negotiated for their kidnapped prince. They agreed to return the lost battle standards and what captured Roman prisoners they still held.

Augustus had done it. Once again, he'd prevailed. And he'd done it without Agrippa. He'd done it without me. *It must be some trick, some charade, some farce*, I thought while the island celebrated around me. "Oh, Virgil, how I envy you." Crinagoras laughed.

"The poetry you'll write in honor of this *New Alexander* who needs not even command his armies in battle to return with victory!"

Virgil smiled. "We'll have to make much of this if we're to compete with Agrippa's bloody slaughter in Spain. He's all but extincted the Cantabri tribes, something the citizens will admire. They aren't accustomed to celebrating such an occasion as the emperor's latest victory. Maecenas will want to mint coins, showing the king of the Parthians kneeling in supplication to Rome."

I pressed my lips together. "Won't that offend Phraates and start the war up again?"

"Augustus has been generous," Lady Lasthenia replied. "He gave the Parths back their prince and made gifts to the king. An Italian girl he admired. An acknowledgment of his territorial boundaries and hegemony over Armenia. It's a good bargain."

A good bargain, indeed. What wouldn't I give to have Isidora back in my arms if someone kidnapped her? The thought agitated me such that I needed to remind myself of my good fortune. I wouldn't be needed to work magic for war. Augustus hadn't won a military victory for himself, but in retaking those battle standards, he could claim to have restored Roman honor. Only one question plagued me. "When will he return?"

"There are still matters to resolve," Lady Lasthenia said. "A few weeks? A month at the outside."

Thirty-six

I prayed that my idyllic nights with Helios would stretch on for-ever. Let a storm delay Augustus's triumphant return. Let him stop in some city to be feted and worshipped as a god. My distress about the emperor's return must have been obvious, because even Circe felt the need to reassure me. "Majesty, you must have taken my advice to heart. No one will ever doubt your love for Augustus. Every day now, you're flushed, like a lily about to bloom."

Yes, I thought. But I blossomed only when the moon was high in the sky and my lover came to me. Afterward, I folded in upon myself as if to protect the sacred places where he'd explored me. Everything he touched became sacred. The oil lamp he'd snuffed out. The pillow upon which he'd rested his head. Even the ashes of the fires he lit on the beach to keep us warm. I was in love—yes, I was finally bold enough to name it to myself. This was nothing I could hide within the dark shadow of my soul with the rage and the hatred and the grief. It was an emotion stronger than all my artifice, and I laughed at the thought that even my own courtiers were convinced by it. They might tell Augustus how I asked after him every day, how I so carefully dressed as if to welcome him home. How I sat in dreamy contemplation, my cheeks pink with passion. And I didn't care. I didn't care! These days of happiness were mine to treasure, even if they must soon come to an end.

That night, Helios stroked the purple silk of my cloak, our

makeshift bed on the sand. "Have you any idea how many ships I could buy with this?" he asked.

The nights were warmer now, and I liked the smell of his sweat on me. "Take it. Sell it. Do with it as you will. I deny you nothing."

He tugged me closer and the waves tickled our bare toes. "Even a talented pirate would have to explain how he acquired a cloak like that one, Selene, and I'm not a talented pirate."

"Good," I said burrowing my nose beneath his chin. "Because I'm training a fleet to capture pirates off the coast of Mauretania. At least, I ordered such a thing be done." Juba's new authority in Spain may well have been part of that effort, but it was now all very far away across the sea.

Helios nuzzled against my hair. "You must be something to see. Commanding that this or that be done. Hearing petitioners. Presiding over a council. It's a proud thing to be a queen's lover."

I'd always wondered what my mother must have felt like to carry on an affair with men even before she'd taken them to wed. I wished it was in me not to care what anyone might think, but I couldn't stop fretting. "What must your sailors think of your late-night liaisons?"

"They think it's none of their concern," Helios said. "They also know that I'd cut the tongue out of any man foolish enough to speak about my doings. I love you, Selene. I would die for you. Or kill for you. For you or for Isidora. You must know it."

"Let there be no talk of dying," I whispered. "Or killing."

Helios paused. "You say this, but what if you're with child? I must kill Augustus before he—"

"I'm not with child," I said, suddenly guilty for the way I'd used my *heka* to close my womb to him. "The goddess must be inside me for that to happen now, but here, with you, I wanted to be mortal."

Helios sat up, drawing me with him. "She was inside you the night I came to you in the storm . . ."

"Yes. I think Isidora is yours. I *wanted* her to be yours. To keep some part of you with me always."

"When I kill Augustus, Isidora can know of me. It'll be safe to tell her, then."

"What she'll know," I said, blinking back sudden tears, "is the world that we make for her. Which is why you can't kill the emperor."

Helios growled his frustration. "How can you still defend him?"

"I'm not defending him. I only ask you to consider what you hope to accomplish. Do you think killing him will free Egypt?"

"It will free *you*."

I reached out and touched his face. "Do you think I haven't wished him dead a thousand times? Do you think I've never been tempted to poison his food or slip a dagger between his ribs or use my winds to blow him into the sea? Helios, when he lay dying of fever in Rome, it would've been so easy to smother him while he slept."

"So why didn't you?"

"Because Rome isn't one man. Because we didn't lose Egypt in one battle. Because when we were born, people looked to us to bring them a Golden Age and I don't want to bring them war and chaos and pain! Especially not when I can get back everything we've lost by giving Augustus what he wants."

Helios's gaze snapped to me and the fire crackled. "What have you promised him?"

This moment was infinitely worse than I had imagined it would be. "A son."

Those eyes of his were as eternal as the Nile and now they narrowed with anger. I thought he'd rage at me, but he didn't. He didn't reel back in fury or call me a harlot or accuse me of treachery or infidelity or otherwise decry my lack of morals. Instead, Helios took me by the arms and steadied me as if forbidding a small child from dangerous play. "You can't do that."

"I have to."

"No," he said.

"You didn't forbid me from Juba's bed."

He looked away, as if slapped. "But you didn't go, did you?"

"I might have, were the circumstances different." What was one more ugly confession now, added to all the rest? I'd tell him that Juba was a decent man. A man who wanted to be a good husband. A good father to a child he knew wasn't his own. A man who had begged me, pleaded with me, not to go. And that I felt something stir inside me at Juba's kiss.

Before I could tell him any of this, Helios said, "I'd rather you *did* go to Juba. If he gives you some small happiness, then return to him. Become his wife in truth if you must. If it will keep you from this folly with the emperor."

I cried out, my nails digging into his arms. "If you loved me, you'd never say such a thing."

"I say it *because* I love you. I could haul you over my shoulder and carry you away, right now. I could take you. Were it not for Isidora I *would* take you but she deserves more. If you came with me, it would be an end to everything our parents wanted for us and perhaps an end to Isis too."

All this was true. I couldn't go with him. As long as Augustus breathed, as long as Rome stood, we couldn't be together. Still, his heartbeat had been next to mine in the womb, and I would listen for it my whole life. "But I love you."

Love. We'd both spoken of it now. We both felt it. We both knew how real and dangerous it was. We knew better than anyone. Our mother and father had loved one another so desperately that they set the world aflame and let it burn. Their love, timeless and enduring as it was, had known no reason. No caution. No limits. Their love had eventually defied political sense and self-preservation. Their love had killed them and set in motion all the things that had led to the abuse and torment that shattered me and destroyed Helios. All the things that had twisted us inside so that we could never love anyone the way we loved each other.

"Would you have us be just like them?" Helios asked, reading my thoughts. "Gamble everything, bold and reckless and defiant? Shall we risk your daughter? Egypt? Isis? The world? You cannot be mine." His lips pressed to my cheek, the stubble of his beard scratching my chin. "So let it be Juba. Let it be any man but Octavian. You cannot give yourself to your own rapist. To do so would be to spit in the face of our goddess."

I shuddered, then shook my head in denial. "Isis will forgive me. You must let Augustus live and this is how this game must play out. If I cannot have you, then I will have the world, and this is the only way to get it."

"Isis *will* forgive you," Helios agreed. "But will you forgive yourself?"

For months now, I'd lived with the self-loathing of knowing I was making true everything my enemies said about me. That I'd set myself upon a course of action in which my ambitions ruled me. In which I'd even pit the interests of my child against Julia's infant son. I'd convinced myself that I must push aside that guilt. "I'm a queen. What does it matter how I regard myself?"

"You're not a crown," Helios said, kissing my brow. "You're not a scepter. You're a queen but a woman too. Haven't I proved that to you again and again?"

My cheeks heated at the reminder, but I had to make him understand. "When we were young, I was afraid of everything but you were always brave. Well, I'm not that frightened girl anymore. I'm Cleopatra's daughter. I've clawed my way to the pinnacle of power. How can you ask me to back away?"

"I've lost everything for my recklessness. Why would you follow my example?"

Because I'll triumph where you failed, I thought, the blood of my ancestors singing proud in my veins. My mother and father had made battle plans upon this very island and now I would triumph where they had failed too. I would even triumph over the emperor and Alexander too, for I, Cleopatra Selene, will have won the world without ever having wielded a sword. And the only blood I'd spilled was my own. Down my arms in the holy words of Isis and between my legs on the emperor's sheets.

"I won't let you do it," Helios said.

"This is what our mother would have done. What she *did* do.

She offered herself to Caesar, even though she didn't know what manner of man he might be—"

"She knew he wasn't a perverse fiend!"

I winced, silent tears now flowing down my cheeks. "Helios, when she died, our mother gave Philadelphus her sight. She gave you her strength. But she gave *me* her spirit. She told me not to forget, and I never have. When I'm unquestioned ruler of Egypt and all North Africa, when my daughter has her birthright, when the emperor is burned to ash, you'll see it's all been worth it."

"I won't let you do it," he said, again, his fingers digging into my arms.

I put my palms flat on his chest. "It's my *choice*. Should I let anyone take that from me again?"

He released me, then fell silent, staring into the black ocean. "If it's your choice, then *change your mind*."

"There are people who depend on me. Given the way I feel about you, it doesn't seem possible, but I don't belong only to you—or even only to myself."

"You don't belong to Octavian either. You owe him nothing more."

How like Helios to know what no one else did. That in spite of my hatred for the emperor, I'd always felt grateful for his mercy. In his debt. When he made me a queen, I felt that was part of his largesse too. When he told me that he had every right to take my body—that it was no more than he had paid for, hadn't some part of me believed it? "If I have his son, Helios, he'll belong to *me*."

"This conversation isn't done," he said, but dawn, accursed dawn, was here, and I had to let him go.

NOT since old King Aegeus saw the black sails of his son Theseus's ships and threw himself into the sea has anyone reacted to the sight of sails with such despair as I did now. The vision of the emperor's flagship, emblazoned in red and gold, made my hands tighten on the terrace rail for balance. The whole world had tilted, realigned itself, and put me at its middle.

I wouldn't have been the only one to have realized it. Out there, somewhere on that sea, with all the other merchant ships, was Helios. Squinting into the sun, I surveyed the horizon for a glimpse of his ship, but in the bustle of the harbor only the Roman flotilla announced itself like the trumpet of a new god. Then the whole island erupted at once, word passed from merchant to servant, from slave to master, from soldier to commander, "Augustus has returned! Make ready!"

I hurried back to my chambers to check my hair, my face, my jewelry. *How had my mother rushed to greet her Romans?* I wondered. Or had she tarried, waiting in the palace, forcing them to come to *her* . . . but this wasn't Egypt. This wasn't even Mauretania. The gown I chose was a bright saffron that set off my features dramatically. I opted for a bun at the nape of my neck, studded with pearls, and just over the white peak of my diadem, the front of my coiffure raised like the *uraeus* of Egypt. Finally, I grabbed up Isidora and was borne to the docks, where the gathering crowd chanted, "Triumphator! Io Triumphe!"

This was entirely inappropriate. Augustus hadn't defeated any new foe in battle. The Senate hadn't voted a Triumph for him, and this was certainly not its appointed day. Moreover, we weren't in Rome, and oh, the calamity my father had suffered when *he* dared to celebrate his victories in Egypt instead of Rome!

From between the parted curtains of my litter, I glimpsed Augustus on the deck of his ship. He was in his military cuirass, one arm upraised in a pose that has now become famous in so many of his statues, all of which depict a more flattering, never-aging version of the man. *He looks as satisfied as Apollo*, I thought, giving Isidora's little hand a squeeze. Then we stepped out of the litter to greet him.

But he didn't come ashore; his ship remained far out in the sparkling sea. A small group of his soldiers rowed in. Iullus was with them, and when my Roman half brother approached me, his prominent chin jutted proudly beneath his helmet as if he'd conquered Parthia himself. He snapped his feet together and executed a curt bow. "Queen Cleopatra Selene, Augustus requires your presence aboard his flagship."

A trill of fear echoed in my ears. "For what purpose?"

"I didn't question him, Majesty," he said, offering his arm with great formality.

Myriad possibilities swarmed my mind, stinging flies all. The emperor would have some dramatic gesture planned. He might make me Queen of Egypt here and now. It had all been settled aboard ships at Actium, so perhaps it was only right to do it this way. Why couldn't I be glad of it? Why should I dread the very thing I'd struggled all my life to reclaim? Why should I, on the brink of victory, turn away my prize? Perhaps it was some wary instinct that warned me of the emperor's treachery. Perhaps, just as he'd made an end to my father's forces in Actium, he would now make an end to me.

No. I could defend myself and Isidora with my magic. And even if I couldn't, some deeper part of me understood that he would never kill me. The emperor might torment me every day for the rest of my life, but he would want me alive.

I fixed my most gracious smile upon my face and allowed myself to be brought aboard the emperor's craft. He greeted us with all the correct and public decorum one might expect. He looked unchanged by battle, for there had been none. Still, I couldn't help but be affected by the stance he took, the hard, shrewd aura of command that surrounded him now. He drew me aside into the awning erected to protect him from the heat. "Queen Cleopatra Selene, I return to you triumphant. The whole world has surrendered to me."

I lowered my lashes. "As do my daughter and I, Caesar."

A degenerate expression of pleasure spread over his features such that I wished Isidora weren't staring up at him with her steady gaze. Augustus tilted his head back and made a sound not unlike carnal release, and for a moment I wondered if the force of his obsession shook the ship. The deck lurched beneath my feet, and I heard the commands below to the rowers.

"Why are we moving?" Isidora asked, ignoring the squeeze of my hand that should have silenced her.

Augustus smiled. "We're en route to Athens, my dear child. I stopped here only to retrieve you."

Seldom did I allow a gasp of surprise to escape my lips, but now I did as the ship steered for open water. *Sweet Isis*, where was Helios? Was it not bad enough that my twin may have watched me board the emperor's vessel? Must he now also watch me sail away without a word? I wondered if, like my father chased after my mother's ship at Actium, Helios would rush after me. I prayed that he didn't! I needed to get word to him. I needed to return to the Isle of Samos, just long enough to somehow leave a message. "Caesar, what of my clothing, my servants, my guards, my courtiers, and my *ship*?"

"They'll all follow," Augustus said, taking a seat upon his folding curule chair as if he intended to dispense judgment, or perhaps he now found it more comfortable than all other chairs. "And if they don't follow, what need have you for them? I can afford you with anything you desire . . ."

He was carrying me off! He'd tricked me into boarding this ship and now I was being born away as a captive again. "But surely we can go back, long enough for you to fetch Terentilla, and Virgil. He traveled all this way to greet you—"

"My poet can travel a little farther, to Athens. Come, Selene, let's play a game. Why would I take you to Athens?"

To make me miserable, I thought. *To tear me away from Helios and my happy stolen nights. To ruin me. To again strip from me all that I have and drag me behind some chariot in chains!* These fears weren't mature or reasoned but came from the desperate part of me I thought I'd cut away. "I don't know," I whispered.

"Yes, you do," the emperor said. "What begins in Athens?"

I made my heart match the slow and steady drumbeat of the rowers and commanded myself not to fly to the rail with my daughter and leap into the water to escape. Augustus looked at me expectantly, as if I should enjoy this game, as if my distress were a puzzle to him. *What begins in Athens? Think. Think. Think!* Athens was one of the oldest cities in the world, home of the Parthenon, of democracy . . . "The Panathenaic Games?"

How irritated my unsuccessful guess made him. "What else?"

"I don't . . . Forgive me, I'm so overcome with joy at your return I can't think clearly."

He stood and offered me his hand. "Come." I took it, understanding that I must leave Isidora behind. I tried to tell her with my eyes that she must be very well behaved and wait right where I left her, and this helped to steady me as he led me into the dimly lit berth that was his own. I didn't know what he would do then. Rush upon me? Grab me in his bony little hands and trail his curiously cold kisses down my neck? Instead, he pulled back a draping and revealed the tattered battle standards of Roman legions.

I'd known that he recovered them; all the world knew. But somehow I hadn't expected him to keep them so near. And oh, Helios might condemn me for it, but I felt a certain reverence for these Roman symbols too. I went to my father's—I recognized their insignias. These sticks of his legions, the loss of which had been his descent, his end. These standards that had been borne by men who fought for him, who had died for him, and had known him at his best. There *was* something sacred in them and Augustus laid his hand upon the battle standards, worshipfully. "My enemies will put out that I'm a coward, that I resorted to trickery, but I've conquered Parthia without blood. Is it not a fine thing that I've done?"

"Yes," I admitted, surprised to hear the emotion in my voice. "It may be the finest thing you've *ever* done."

"Worthy even of you, my arrogant little Ptolemy?"

I didn't want to say it, not with my skin still tender from Helios's touch. It broke my heart to say it, but show me any woman who says she feels no compulsion to surrender to a man who has just prevented the deaths of hundreds of thousands, and I'll show you a liar. "Worthy even of the Queen of Egypt."

"Ah," he said, moving behind me so that my shoulder blades came to rest upon the hard and unyielding surface of his breastplate. "That is what you want, still?"

"Always," I said with a lift of my chin. "At last, you're in a position to give it to me."

"And I shall." Three dizzying words. "Give me a son, Selene."

Lady Circe had known what I hadn't. What he'd done in Parthia, I could admire. The thought that perhaps he would become a more peaceful ruler was a hope I could reward and nurture. And though every moment I'd spent with Helios turned this into treachery, I reached for the clasp of my bright saffron gown. "No, don't take it off." Augustus stopped me, his hand closing upon mine. "I like this color on you. It's the color a Roman bride wears and I'd like for you to wear it the day we make our son."

My heart leapt to my throat. "Is that not today?"

He eyed me smugly. "You said that you'd give me an heir, not a bastard. So, first, I must take you as my bride . . ."

My throat seemed to swell shut. Though it had been my own suggestion, I'd never wanted to be his bride. I'd only thrown up that condition to delay his passions and to ensure that he could not promise me Egypt and then go back on his word. To ensure that whatever censure and scandal touched me would touch him too, in equal measure. "How can I be a true wife to you?"

"Ah, my African queen, my sorceress and temptress . . . I'll take you in a ceremonial rite that will appease your vanity and your religious fervor too. I've made arrangements for us to go to Eleusis, where we'll be initiated."

What begins in Athens? The Eleusinian Mysteries. This was his grand dramatic gesture. "But it isn't the season—"

"They'll *make* it the season. As I've said, the whole world now surrenders to me. Even Demeter and Kore . . . That is what they call you now, don't they? The New Kore? Another name for your Isis. You warned me once that my name would fade to dust if I denied her. Well, in this ritual, I will acknowledge her. In her Greek guise, I will honor her before all the world. Isn't it appropriate that I take you as my own during this initiation?" It seemed as if sawdust had filled my mouth. When I could make no reply, he continued, "Back in Rome, I've ordered that they prepare for a great celebration of the Mother Goddess. The Secular Games come about every hundred and ten years, so this too is out of season, but my astronomers have found a way to argue otherwise."

I didn't know if he'd done all this to please me or to help lift the curse that Isis had laid upon him, but these were well-calculated moves in every respect. I felt shamefully dispirited, as if I'd never wanted him to be true to his word, as if I'd never wanted to be Queen of Egypt. Had I secretly hoped to fail? To break faith with my dead family and turn away from the legacy that they'd fought and died for?

Augustus saw my hesitation and said, very simply, "Once my son is safely born, I intend to divorce Livia."

It was the last thing I expected; I choked on my reply. "You'll make an enemy of the Claudians!"

"They're nothing to me now," he said, with a note in his voice that alarmed me.

The Romans always claimed that the East changed their generals. That the luxury, the indulgences, the older practicalities, and the corruption and religion and complicated cultures all warped simpler Roman virtues, twisting men into something other than they were. Now I wondered if it were true. All the East might glory in a battle won without bloodshed, but how would the emperor's victory be perceived in Rome? "Y-you will cause great offense . . ."

"I don't care. I'm the one who should be offended. A Triumph was allowed for Lucius Cornelius Balbus though he fought with legions I gave him. These kinds of insults must be met with confidence." I actually feared for Balbus at that moment. For Balbus and Agrippa and Livia and all those who stood in the way of anything Augustus wanted for himself. "Your marriage to Juba must be annulled. I'll not let the world think I'm taking *the leavings* of a king. I'll have it known that you're *mine*. That you've always been *only mine*."

"Then you would make my daughter a bastard," I said, stomach roiling.

"As your father did to you. It hasn't hurt your prospects, has it? You stand poised to rule at my side."

Here it was then, the world glittering at my feet. To grasp it, all I had to do was abandon and betray everyone who had ever loved me. Were the emperor to divorce Livia and marry me, it would hurt nearly everyone . . . "You will turn Agrippa against us *completely*."

"If he lives long enough," Augustus said. He meant to make Julia a widow for the second time. "And he's not my only ally. I'm told you like coins. Consider this one. A gift from Herod in contemplation of what comes next."

Digging into a small pouch on a table, he pulled out a coin and pressed it into my hand. A gift from Herod? I shuddered to think what I might see. Wetting my dry lips, I turned my palm and opened it. What I saw was a shocking surprise but not so pleasant as the one I'd experienced in seeing Juba's coin.

What must Nicholas of Damascus have reported to Herod to make him mint such a coin? This coin celebrated Kore. A veiled representation of the goddess with some of my features, for I was the New Kore. Herod had always scented the winds of political change and calibrated his moves to survive the oncoming storms. The Judean king who was my enemy had studiously avoided human imagery on his money until now, out of fear that his Jewish subjects would protest. Herod could say that it was meant only to commemorate his new city of Sebaste. That it was meant to glorify Augustus on the occasion of his impending initiation into the Eleusinian Mysteries. But for Herod to take such a risk as to honor me and my goddess, even in her Greek guise, he must have believed that it was in his interest to swallow his hatred and ally with me.

The very idea of such an alliance was repugnant. Apparently, I'd finally mastered all the lessons the emperor had to teach me. I'd turned my friends into enemies and my enemies into friends. *Change your mind,* Helios had said. Now I shook my head, trying to dislodge his words from my thoughts.

Augustus took the coin from my cold fingers. "You fear another civil war, Selene. But I say, let it come. For once, like my father, the divine Julius, I'll let the dice fly high!"

It was with the darkest, most treacherous satisfaction that I realized I was destroying him. As a girl, I'd sworn to become whatever I must become to fight the emperor. When he raped me, I vowed that I would make him rue the day. Now I could make good on those promises. He wanted to believe that having negotiated a settlement with Parthia, he could now do *anything*, but I knew better. By divorcing Livia and marrying me, he'd lose his allies. He'd open himself up to the very same charges the assassins made against Julius Caesar. And I, if I was willing to eschew my mantle of respectability, if I behaved high-handedly, demanding not just Egypt but Judea as well, and all the territories my mother had claimed, I could reignite the flames that brought down my father.

Laughing, I turned my eyes to the emperor with a sense of mad power. I had his life in my hands. Not just his life but his reputation. His legacy. His entire empire. I could *ruin* him . . . as long as I was willing to destroy myself in the process. So long as he was alive and obsessed with me, I could have *anything* from him. Even his downfall.

I could have my mother's kingdom and all her glory. Nay, more than that. I could have anything but my heart's desire. Of what consequence was it, then, that I loved another man or loathed this one? For so many years my *khaibit* held my ugliest thoughts, my deepest pain, kept them safely away from me. Now my *khaibit* flew free. It ruled me like an avenging specter and I said, "Let it all be done as you wish, Caesar."

Thirty-seven

THE first thing I saw in Athens was the first thing anyone sees—the Parthenon, that most perfect building, high above the city. There it was, that temple to the city's patron goddess, shining white in the sun like an ethereal palace against the blue sky. "Is that Mount Olympus?" little Isidora asked, staring up at the fortified acropolis.

"Maybe it is," I admitted, more than a bit thunderstruck.

The city couldn't have greeted Zeus himself with more enthusiasm. Athens is very old, and very flat, so the claustrophobic aspect of a roaring crowd wasn't even alleviated by hills or high spots upon which the people could view our procession. Instead, the press of humanity mingled with the blare of trumpets, the cheers, and the flower petals that rained down before us. The ground itself trembled beneath marching feet and the roar of the chariot wheels. If I closed my eyes, I could still feel the clasp of my golden manacles at my wrists, the tight collar at my throat pulling me forward. But this was no Triumph and I was no prisoner. My daughter wasn't chained to a wax effigy of me all covered in spit, enduring the venomous curses of her enemies. She was at my side, a celebrated little princess, and I blinked back tears. I could give her this. I could give her all this.

Or I could smash everything.

"You *are* the darling of the Hellenes," the emperor said, for no secret was made of the people's adoration. I was the last Ptolemaic queen, Cleopatra's daughter, the pride of Greece. And if they guessed that I had seduced the emperor away from his wife, what of it? They would be proud of my wit, of my ambition.

My courtiers followed me to Athens, and at night we stayed as the guests of a very rich government official. When the roosters crowed the morning, the priests of Athens shouted their invitation to join in the Mysteries. Ours was a great procession, not just the emperor and his secretaries and soldiers and attendants but a whole great horde of religious pilgrims, who seemed delighted to embark on this journey with such great personages. Anyone who spoke Greek could participate in the rites—men, women, and even slaves. And so the proclamation was spread by the heralds calling all who were pure of soul, who'd lived a life of justice and righteousness, and did not have blood-guilt on their hands.

Augustus surely didn't fit this description, and neither did I, *khaibit*-ruled creature I'd become. Yet this pageant had been arranged for our convenience, so we prepared to go from Athens to the sacred spot in Eleusis where the goddess Demeter was said to have mourned for her daughter, Kore. Many of my courtiers, including Lady Lasthenia, had decided to be initiated with the rest. But whereas they all walked the fifteen miles from Athens to Eleusis, we rode in a carriage, the emperor and I. He sat in quiet contemplation beside me until at last, his whisper cut through the silence. "This is a new beginning for me. I shall be a different kind of ruler, Selene. A different sort of man."

"May the goddess will it," I said, closing my eyes. It was all a dream, yet I wasn't asleep. I floated somehow apart, observing on high, the performance of myself.

The next morning, we were awakened by a call to the sea. I left Isidora with Tala, and then with the rest of the initiates, the emperor and I dressed in plain garments. A rough-hewn tunic for him, no doubt woven by Livia. For me, a simple white *chiton* that fell to my ankles and fastened at my waist with a thin leather cord. We both carried piglets in our arms, animals meant for tribute to the temples. As my feet found purchase in the sand and the surf lifted my dress to my knees, I thought that once again I'd come to the goddess to be purified. But even with the emperor's gaze on me, I could never feel the water on my skin and not think of Helios.

I remembered how he first bathed me. The way his palms spanned the expanse of my hips, how his lips tasted like the sea. After, with squealing piglets running at our feet as we dried ourselves in the sun, we made ready to return to Athens. This travel between the two cities was to bring us closer to the travails of Demeter, who had walked the world to find her lost daughter. Closer to Isis, who had searched far and wide for her lost Osiris. That night was a night of fasting, and I curled round the hunger in my belly, embracing the emptiness.

On the fifth day, with saffron ribbons tied at our wrists, we passed over the narrow bridge that would take us back to Eleusis, and jesters hurled insults to amuse the crowd. When it was dark, the women carried candles and danced while I prepared myself for the role of a temple prostitute. You may think I use this phrase with derision or scorn, but all the stories of goddesses were now coming together in mine.

On the sixth day, when the stars came out, I was weak with hunger. Humbled. When I felt the grief of my goddess in my throat, when my own eyes were filled with tears for her, I thought, *Isis must have a throne. I must restore her to Egypt . . .* But somehow, my thoughts were of a *new* temple. A giant Iseum that I wished to build in Mauretania, with pools filled with Nile water and sacred crocodiles. My thoughts weren't of Egypt but Mauretania, and I cursed my guilty heart for it.

Late that night, we were sent scrambling through the dark, torches in hand, jostling against one another. As queen, I'd seldom felt the touch of commoners against me, but now I was carried along with the tumultuous flow of the crowd as the priests brought out the sacred *kykeon*. It was a mysterious mixture of meal and pennyroyal, but when a cup was poured for me I tasted something else that sent my mind swirling into a *heka*-infused abyss. For a moment, I sensed Helios here in the crowd and squinted my eyes for a flash of that golden hair.

The night was alive with shrieks and dancing, of celebration in the forest. Of life and death, and an awareness that there *was* life after death. I had always come to the goddess sober and clear-eyed, but that wasn't the tradition in Athens so I sipped again from my cup. The emperor drank deeply from his, swallowing it all at once, while the others cried out like maenads in a Bacchic frenzy. The light of the torches danced before my eyes, and the trees themselves loomed like the bony hands of Set reaching for me all the way from the desert.

A gong rang in the night and Augustus grabbed my wrists, crying, "Now!"

I shuddered, thinking that he meant to lay me down here on the earth, where the whole world might witness our joining. But as the emperor pulled me to the temple, I was dizzied and dropped my cup, its sacred fluid soaking the ground. "The hierophant invokes the goddess," the emperor said. "Tonight I shall take the place of the hierophant and you shall take the place of the high priestess. We'll join together in the anteroom of the temple for the sacred marriage."

Just then, I saw Caesarion in the crowd and gave a startled cry. I saw Philadelphus. Then my mother. My father too. And poor Antyllus, or was it Iullus? No. *Antyllus*, for here, we'd parted the veil between this life and the next. These were all my beloved dead. Isis was here, her magic was here, and now we could glimpse her as the queen of the underworld.

I confess that I don't recall how we came away from the crowd. I found myself in the stillness of the temple, adorned in flower garlands, my knees upon a glorious bed of silken sheets, piled high with cushions, the scent of frankincense in the air. Above us was the statue of the goddess. Demeter. Kore. Tanit. Isis. All the same. I knew her, and it comforted me, for I'd made love in a temple before.

"I have something for you," Augustus said, laying a wooden chest beside us. Gracing the top of the box was a golden Ptolemy Eagle laid over a silver bolt of lightning. The box itself was studded with carnelian and a broken lock dangled from its fastening. "Open it."

Dizzied by the *kykeon*, it took me several tries to pull the latch and reveal the contents. There, upon a pillow of purple, was my mother's beaded diadem and gem-encrusted scepter glowing with golden magnificence. These were the insignias of her rule; she'd surrendered them to the emperor before she died in the hopes that he would spare her children and her kingdom.

"Queen of Egypt," Augustus said, reverently placing the crown upon my head. It was happening as Philadelphus had foreseen it. No rumbling mountain has ever quaked as I did in that moment. I couldn't speak, overcome by the enormity of it. My mouth went dry and I lost all possession of myself. I couldn't even hold the scepter when he placed it in my trembling hands. It fell to the bed, and when I stooped to retrieve it a keening sound escaped me. My mother's golden scepter . . . I must hold it. I must wrap my fingers where hers had been and never let it go.

"You *are* a goddess," the emperor rasped, stroking my shoulders. "I've come to do you homage. I'm the god come to meet you."

I could think only of the scepter, but when I reached for it he pushed the box from the bed and it landed on the floor with a clatter. *The scepter.* I must have the scepter. Why could I not stop my mind from spinning long enough to find it, to seize it? Forcing my eyes open in the flickering light, I saw scraggly hairs above the line of the emperor's ribs. When had he become undressed? His nakedness moved nothing in me. He didn't look like a god; he looked as he did when he swam in the pools or played ball with the boys in the yard in Rome.

But his eyes weren't his own. Those chilly gray depths were unfocused, his jaw lax. The emperor pulled me down with him. How small and spindly he seemed. When my hands came to rest on his shoulders, I thought I might crush him. He seemed just a man. Just a man who wanted a son. It was that simple, natural human desire that made me reach for the belt of my gown and loosen it. This time, I wouldn't be held down and forced. This time, I'd come to him, like the primordial sky spreads herself over the earth. I didn't recoil as his hands roamed freely over my body. I must have stroked him, for I found him erect in my hand. I had put the whole of myself into my *khaibit* and watched now only from a shadow.

"I'll give you a son," I whispered, inviting the goddess into me, feeling the *heka* swirl warm round my womb. Outside we heard shrieks and howls, the cymbal and drums, and strange noises, unreal. The sounds of the underworld. Like the goddess, I would bring life from death. I was the Resurrection, was I not?

So insensible was Augustus under the influence of the *kykeon* that as I crawled over him he snorted with pleasure as if he thought himself already inside me. "Yes, yes. Such exquisite pleasure!" He rubbed against me, an obscene motion, and I felt a spurt of seed. Whether it was the whole of his orgasm or only a prelude, I couldn't tell because the gong outside rang again, then again, only to be followed by a bang. It was an impossibly large crash that even in our various states of undressed ecstasy, we couldn't ignore. Was it a door being slammed open?

A breeze caressed my neck, then all the torches guttered out, plunging us into blackness until everything flared bright again. A figure appeared in the doorway, all aglow in an aura of *heka*.

It was Helios.

AUGUSTUS was helpless, unarmored, unarmed, unclothed, and intoxicated on the sacred *kykeon*. The emperor was seldom unguarded, but we'd come to this chamber alone, for who would dare harm him during the most holy ceremony of the civilized world? Slow to respond to the bronze-clad warrior whose beloved hand drew a sword from its sheath, Augustus rose to a seated position to protect me, as if I were the one in danger. "It's only a vision of the underworld," he said. "You're safe, Selene."

"But you aren't, Octavian," Helios said, fingers gripping the pommel of his sword.

At last, the emperor's face showed some sign of recognition. "It can't be . . ."

Helios squared his shoulders, his voice low, filled with a pious resolution. "I come to avenge Egypt. To avenge my father, my mother, my brothers . . . and most of all, to avenge Selene."

"Don't," I said to Helios, finally finding my voice. "For the love of Isis, don't kill him!"

My twin's glance flickered my way and seeing me undressed seemed only to make his rage burn hotter. His blade glinted in the light, the tendons of his thick forearm twitching. "I'll kill him swiftly, which is more than he deserves."

"No!" I cried, clambering over the emperor's body, shielding him with my own.

Augustus was filled with *kykeon* and hubris. He shoved himself up to his feet, knocking me to the ground. My hands hit the stone floor, the resounding impact rattling my bones. "We're here to be shown the secrets of the afterlife, Selene. The goddess challenges me to grapple with him, like Hector and Achilles!"

The *kykeon* was in me too, and I was disoriented, wondering if I wasn't imagining all of this. But not even in a vision would I allow any man to be slain in a temple. The emperor staggered toward Helios as my twin's muscular arm arced back for the killing blow. The deadly point would strike true, at the vulnerable place between the emperor's ribs where his heart would beat its last. In desperation, I threw out my arm, and the sirocco woke to my call, rushing down my elbow and exploding from my fingertips. It was a wild, uncontrolled blast that caught both men and lifted them from the ground. My wind wrenched the sword from Helios's hand, sent it tumbling end over end into the wall where it shattered like glass.

It wasn't the only thing to break.

As if wings flapped behind me, my winds howled through the room, knocking over sconces and ripping tapestries from the wall. Pomegranates rolled upon the floor beside my mother's scepter. Baskets of grain tipped over, spilling their contents, which then flew up into the air, pelting us. As I struggled to my feet, my mother's sparkling diadem tumbled from my hair, which now whipped wild round my head.

The emperor lay on the bed, eyes closed, unmoving, breathing shallowly.

"I don't need a sword to kill him, Selene," my twin said, rage in his eyes. "No one else in the world may dare, but I *can* kill him with my bare hands."

"I can't let you," I shouted over the howling wind. "I *won't* let you."

"I promised that I'd always defend you, Selene, and it's the only promise I can keep. He violated you once and lived. He won't live to do it a second time." Helios pointed at the bed and I felt the spark of fire even before it left the tip of his finger, the flames blazing. The silk upon which the emperor lay ignited around him. Sweet Isis, Helios was going to burn him alive!

I pushed another funnel of air toward the flames, trying to extinguish Helios's fire. Our magic met in burning bed linens and seeds of grain, force against force, Helios and I drawing *heka* from the temple floor to counter each other. Smoke and flame billowed with ribbons of purple silk, soot rising to stain the cult statue of the goddess. "How can you do this?" I cried. "You defile her temple."

"I'm stopping a defilement," Helios replied. "You should ask yourself how *you* can do this. How you can mate with a monster and give him a son."

"Because I must!" I shouted, sending charred bits of silk into the swirling maelstrom. "Do you think I want this? 'Remember Egypt,' our mother said. I'm walking in her footsteps now."

Helios lifted a second hand, orange and yellow fire billowing from both palms, and I stretched my hands to meet them, wondering how long I could hold him back. Which one of us was stronger? "She would have never done this, Selene. What she did, she did for love. Can you say the same?"

No. I was grateful to Augustus. I'd learned to admire him. I'd even forced myself to share in his triumphs and be glad for them. But I loved only Helios. The antechamber became a furnace, an intolerable forging oven in which my inner resolve was melting away. "Our mother took two Romans for politics too. For Egypt . . . she'd have done anything for Egypt."

"Perhaps," my twin said, his eyes squeezing shut. "It was her kingdom. It isn't ours."

Not ours? My winds faltered and his fire seared my fingertips. What could he mean? Some dark voice inside me knew, and I redou-

bled my efforts, blowing the flames back at him until they shot toward
the ceiling, a pillar of fire between us. "Don't say that to me, Helios.
Not to me. Not after all the blood. After all the struggle. After all the
battles you've fought and the cities that have been destroyed—"

"Do you even remember Alexandria?" Helios asked. "Do you
still count it your home?"

"Yes!" I screamed, angrier than I'd ever been. Angrier still to
know it was a lie. Oh, I remembered Alexandria, and the faith I
had as a child that the lighthouse would guide me home. That
Helios should know my heart and name my guilt made me furious.
Egypt lived in me . . . but I'd taken her elsewhere. I'd taken the
spirit of Alexandria and transplanted her to foreign shores. I'd built
her image in Mauretania, where my palace waited for me by the
sea. *Mauretania*, where my child had been born. Where the people
loved me and where the god of the land had come to me as Osiris
comes to Isis.

"You can't unburn Caesarion," Helios said. "You can't make
our mother and father sit up in their tombs and join the living
again. But if you do this, it may send you to your tomb."

Above the roar, the emperor groaned but didn't open his eyes.
The air whirled dangerously through the heated chamber, the
candle wax melting on the altars and bits of glass and pottery clat-
tering against the walls. And the breath went out of me, my lungs
singed by thoughts I didn't want to acknowledge. I glanced up at
the statue of the goddess, willing her to speak to me. Willing her to
cut into my hands and tell me what she would have of me. But this
was a silent Greek version of my goddess. It was only the words of
Helios that cut me. "You don't have to do this, Selene. You don't
have to be his mistress, his goddess, or the mother of his child."

I'd spent my life scheming, spinning such a web of deceit that
even I no longer knew what I actually felt or only pretended to feel.
I wondered what it would be like to be free of all this. To be myself
and not a new incarnation of my mother. What might it be like to
let it all go . . .

At that moment, Augustus roused himself, his eyes opening, his hands raised against the storm of debris. My brother's determination was renewed at the sight of the emperor's struggle and Helios launched a ball of fire from his hands, sending it spiraling toward the emperor, rolling like one of those pomegranates upon the floor.

I leapt in front of it. It struck me in the shoulder and my gown burst into flame.

"No!" Helios roared, tackling me to smother the fire.

What hair remained on my forearms burned away, and as Helios dragged me to the floor I screamed at the emperor, "Run!"

Naked, Augustus managed to stagger past us, stumbling into the dark corridor beyond while Helios beat the flames from my body. My arm was red in patches where I'd been burned, and I'd skinned my hands in my fall. Helios held them now, staring as my blood pooled up in the wounds. "Forgive me, forgive me, Selene."

"Just go, Helios. Go now, before the emperor summons his guards. There are only precious moments. Or will you spill more blood in a temple?"

"I would have only the blood of Octavian on my hands here, not yours! Never yours!"

There was no time to argue. The room was burning and I imagined that I heard the stomping feet of the emperor's praetorians. I took my twin's soot-covered face in my hands and made him look at me. "Will you go or force me to watch you be cut down?"

"Come with me," Helios said. This room would burn. The world might think I'd burned with it. I could die as Helios had died in Thebes and be free. Free as my father had been when he fell upon his sword. Free as my mother had been when she put her hand in that basket of figs . . .

We both knew it wasn't possible. "I can't leave Isidora."

Helios gulped in smoke. "Then you must get free of him. You must swear to me that you'll get free of Augustus or I'll stand here and meet whatever fate."

"We'll speak of it later. You'll find me again and—"

"Selene, before the goddess, vow that you'll get free of him. Find a way, *any way*, to get free of him!"

I knew that if I didn't swear, my twin would stand here and die like the proud fool he was, so the words fell easily from my lips. "I swear to you by Isis, I will get free of Augustus."

Helios pulled me into a desperate kiss. One that tasted of life and death. I scented the smoke and the grain and the incense. And beyond that, in the revelry outside, the scent of grilling meats and celebration. The scents and sounds that we'd been born to. He kissed me, and kissed me, and our fingers twined together before I felt the tug of *heka* as he drew the remaining flames back inside him. The fire went out. The room went still. We broke apart, one last look into one another's eyes before he turned and fled.

In the scorched but silent chamber, I stood coughing uncontrollably. I fastened my gown, pulling my hair behind my shoulders, trying to think of what lie I'd have to spin to absolve me of guilt when the guards rushed into this sacred room. The silence stretched on until I thought I'd go insane waiting for the inevitable clatter of Roman armor. It never came. Instead, the emperor staggered back in the door, bony fingers clutching at me as if to prove I was real. "The goddess has given me a vision!"

My senses failed me, one at a time. My vision narrowed. My lips numbed. After that, I remember nothing more.

Thirty-eight

✿

NOT knowing where I was, my eyes fluttered open to find the emperor's physician hovering over me. I sprawled upon a well-appointed bed, my arm bandaged where it had been burned. With *heka* sickness ravaging my bones, I also became aware of the burning pain in my arm. Both were agony. *Isidora.* I moaned her name. Given what had happened in the temple, Augustus would be consumed with rage, bent on vengeance. I didn't fear for myself but for my daughter. I should have sent her back to Mauretania. Back to Juba. A certain softness stole over me at the realization that he'd protect her. Whatever troubles had ever been between us, I could trust Juba with my daughter; I despaired of having never appreciated this about him before.

As regret consumed me, the emperor's grim face appeared over my sickbed, his eyes troubled. "She wakes. Kore rises from the underworld yet again."

He would have more questions than I could safely answer. He would know me for the scheming liar I'd always been . . .

"You must've overturned a brazier in the night," Musa said as I groaned in pain again. "The initiates claim there was a storm and fire swirled around the temple, but men see such terrors when they indulge in the *kykeon*. It's a miracle you weren't both burned alive."

"Yes, a miracle," the emperor agreed quietly. "Can you give her something for the pain?"

"No," I whispered, refusing with a shaky hand the concoction that Musa tried to force to my lips. I couldn't afford dull senses now.

"She doesn't want it," the emperor said, pulling a chair close to my bedside. "Leave us."

Once Musa was gone, I thought it strange to see Augustus sitting vigil beside me as I'd once done beside him. "I hadn't believed there was a world beyond this one, Selene. Not when words carved in blood and flesh upon your arms, not even when I first saw you raise your hands and call the winds did I believe . . . but now I've seen the power of your goddess and the terrors of the underworld."

The terrors of the underworld were nothing compared to my fears of what Augustus might do if he thought himself betrayed. But I saw neither rage in his eyes nor wrath in his posture as he sat beside me, his gaze far away and haunted, one hand slowly stroking his chin as if to relearn the contours of his own face. "Do you know what happened upon our return to Athens?"

I didn't remember. I hadn't been conscious. I shook my head.

"Zarmanochegas, the holy man in the Indian delegation, burned himself alive. He was inspired by the flames and the storm. Just as my litter bore you into Athens, this man stood before me and immolated himself."

Augustus was shaken as I hadn't seen him shaken in a very long time. Not since he believed that my mother was still alive. Not since he first saw the messages of Isis on my arms. "It must have been a terrible thing to see a man burn alive."

"No," he said, turning to me with naked zeal in his eyes. "It was a thing of wonder. A sacrifice worthy of *me*, a man to whom goddesses send visions."

He hadn't mentioned Helios, so I nodded, wary as if I faced a cobra, ready to dodge its strike. "What did you see?"

"Did we not journey into the underworld together?"

"Yes, but—I want to know if we were sent the same vision."

He moved from the chair to the bed, not seeming to notice when I hissed in pain, cradling my burned arm against me. "I saw ecstasy, terrors, and salvation. I saw the assassins. Brutus. Cassius too. And the boy. Caesarion. Did you see him?"

"Yes," I admitted, fascinated.

"Then I *became* Caesar," he continued. "I put the crown upon Cleopatra's head. I put the scepter in her hands . . . and she spread her body over me like the stars over the earth. Then it was your body. Warm and real. You and I, joined together at last . . ."

I stole a glance to see if he were taunting me, but he wasn't. He went rigid with desire, and my mouth fell slightly agape. Did he not recall that we'd been interrupted? Or was I the one who misremembered, only wishing under the influence of the *kykeon* that the deed hadn't been done? He'd been drunk on the *kykeon*, whereas I'd had only a few swallows. Perhaps it had been enough to distort my memories too.

"I took you as my bride," the emperor recalled, and for one paralyzing moment I thought he might stroke himself with the hand that drifted between his legs. Then he stilled. "Death came for me as a pillar of fire." I swallowed, remembering the glint of Helios's sword and the flames, trying to find the words that might excuse me of conspiracy. "It was your father's shade. I'd know Antony's hulking shoulders anywhere, though his hair was all yellow flame. It was a warning. A warning of some kind. A warning against touching you, I think."

He looked down at me, fearful. He was very near the precipice of something. I need only push him. *Vow to me that you'll get free of him!* I squeezed my eyes shut against the agonizing pain and my twin's impetuous demand. I'd said only what must be said to make him flee and save his life. Vows could be broken. What was one more deception upon the weight I already carried in my heart? "In my vision, I was your salvation, Caesar."

Now the emperor brightened, hopeful. "Yes. The goddess came to me in your guise and beat death back with the air from her wings and a flood of grain. With *seed*. I always thought that damnable frog amulet at your throat meant that you were a resurrection of your mother. Perhaps you're *my* resurrection. You'll give me a son to live on after me. And when I'm gone, you'll preserve my legacy . . ."

It's what you want to believe, I thought. I had only to reassure him. Stoke the fantasy that he desired, as I'd always done, and he'd remember that he made me Queen of Egypt. He'd remember his promise to marry me and set Livia aside. Nothing I'd ever done would be easier than to reassure him that he'd been cleansed by fire, that the deeds of his past had all been burned away to make way for a new Golden Age. He'd believe me. So why couldn't I do it?

I'd made a vow to my goddess. A vow to Helios. A vow to myself . . .

My mother had chosen one River of Time for her own. Now I must choose another, even as all other possibilities flowed away. My mother's calling was not mine. Isis had called me to something different. To break free of Augustus was to accept that I might never see Egypt again. To accept that when I died, I'd be buried in a tomb built for my twin, on a hill in Mauretania that had blossomed forth with flowers to celebrate the child in my womb.

"What is it, Selene? What did you see?" Augustus asked, leaning forward.

Child of Isis, you are more than flesh. That is what my goddess wished to teach me. What I wished to teach my daughter. I was more than a body to give this man a child. My heart was made to hold so much more than hatred. And I didn't have to destroy this man to triumph over him. Turning away from the emperor, a sound of mingled grief and victory escaped me.

"Tell me, Selene. I command you."

I remembered my twin's fury and confusion as I fought his magic with my own. I'd been stronger. Strong enough to save the emperor's life. Maybe now I could be strong enough to save myself. "I saw the scepter of Egypt fall from my hands," I whispered. "The crown flew from my head, and in my vision, Caesar, I could only protect you from death by giving up what I wanted most."

He reeled back. "What are you saying? You're saying that it *was* a warning?"

One little word that would change my destiny. It came out as a sob. "Yes."

His hands went to his hair, pulling at it by the fistful. "No, but the seed . . ."

"Spilled seed. Cornucopias overflowing. Isn't that one of your symbols? One of your tokens of the Golden Age? It was prophesied upon my birth that I must help bring about a Golden Age, but it won't be mine; it will be *yours*, Caesar. I'll ensure your glory as your obedient daughter and client queen. That's how I can help lift the curse my goddess placed upon you."

He was on his feet in a flash. "You and the games you play! If you think that you'll rule Egypt and deny me a son—"

"I can deny you nothing, but you already have a son. Claim Julia's little boy."

"No," Augustus said, shaking his head, distraught.

"You would've made Julia's child with Marcellus your heir. You need only adopt your grandson by Agrippa. Let Julia's little boy be a Caesar. It's what you always intended. If you search your heart, you know it was always your plan."

"Gaius is Agrippa's son and Agrippa has made himself my enemy!"

"Admiral Agrippa is still your friend. You can reconcile with Agrippa . . ."

Now anger crept into his features. "You're just afraid. We've come so far, you and I. To the edge of greatness. Where is my *Cleopatra*? Who is this timid creature who turns away when offered the world?"

I was Cleopatra's daughter, Isidora's mother, the Queen of Mauretania, beloved of Isis. I was myself. I didn't need to be anyone else. *He* did. "I'm your temptation, Caesar. Your Dido."

At this, the emperor's eyes snapped to mine. *"What?"*

"I've always been your temptation. You must send me away. The gods demand it of you as they demanded it of Aeneas."

At the reminder of his forefather, Augustus blinked several times. He'd said that he wanted to be Caesar and wanted in me his own Cleopatra, but those ambitions weren't lofty enough for him. He wanted to be *Aeneas*, a thing I'd always known, a desire I'd fueled in him from the start. *Aeneas*, the great Trojan hero, forefather of Rome. Aeneas, who was, in Virgil's epic, the stalwart hero who must abandon his African queen to meet his destiny.

"No, it cannot be," he whispered, even as he looked down upon my charred dress, a sure reminder of Dido, who had thrown herself upon a pyre for lost love. "You're mistaken," he said, fury turning his face crimson. "You told me once, words in vivid red blood on your hands, that there would never be an end to it between us and you were right. I'll never let you go."

But it was done. Like a Roman *pilum*, my javelin had arced through the air, struck his shield, and *stuck*. The idea would drag upon him no matter how valiantly he tried to fight it. He would send me away—with protestations and self-pity and tears at ruthless fate—but he would send me away. Perhaps even this very night.

AS my ship slipped from the harbor into the Aegean, the mood of my courtiers was decidedly somber. Lady Lasthenia wouldn't meet my eyes, her disappointment palpable. Lady Hybrida blubbered, waving away anyone who tried to hush her. One could rarely tell what Memnon thought about anything, but his shoulders rounded in defeat beneath his bloodred cloak. Crinagoras couldn't even bring himself to make a self-congratulatory remark. None of them knew that the emperor had placed my mother's diadem on my brow and her scepter in my hands; they believed I'd failed them, yet somehow they sought to reassure me.

"Majesty, he'll send for you again," Crinagoras said. "Augustus has too much of a poet's soul to let it end like this."

Perhaps, I thought. *Perhaps not*. Maybe the Eleusinian Mysteries made an end of it for him. It wouldn't surprise me, for I had, in some sense, made a different man of the emperor. Augustus might go on to his destiny as the father of Rome and never turn back. Or perhaps he would summon me again, the game between us timeless. Eternal.

It was too much to contemplate now. My burned arm throbbed painfully beneath my clothes and I wanted wine and oblivion. During the days, I slept in my berth, lulled by the sound of the oars below as we journeyed back to Africa. At night, I drank to excess and I drank alone. I shunned moonlight and pined for those lost nights with Helios on the beach. I shunned sunlight too, for it reminded me of his hair. I felt as if I'd been roused from a long dream, like *kykeon* had been my whole life and only now was I awakening.

Gulls cried and I heard the little running steps of Isidora and Tala's boy as they chased after one another. Someday, my daughter might hate me for choosing these simpler pleasures for her, but heart, be still, listen to her laugh! I clasped my hands over my mouth, overcome, but did nothing to disguise my tears. I let them roll down my cheeks, wet and salty.

It would all be different now. It must all be different now. Augustus believed that *I* was the wronged party, that he'd abandoned me and left me wounded. Scorned. To assuage his worries that I might throw myself into a pyre for love of him, he'd be generous with me. I would do as I pleased and Augustus would say nothing against it.

I loved coins—for they endured. Men had made coins for me, but now I would mint my own. Coins to honor my mother. Coins of Isis. Coins of a crocodile, free, unfettered, unchained. And I would build an Iseum, a bright and beautiful sanctuary for my goddess in the midst of a hostile Roman world. A place where Memnon and all my faithful could worship, where Euphronius could work his magic, and where I could teach Isidora.

It would be a triumph of its own, twice as worthy as anything else I'd ever done.

WHEN I heard the cry of landfall, I emerged, cramped from the womb of my berth, blinking into the sunlight. My eyes burned as if I saw daylight for the first time. A tower of gleaming white light rose before me, a city behind it, all aglow. My lighthouse was complete. Stone by stone, it stood up from the blue sea to tower over my harbor, a guide to bring me home. At the sight of my purple sails, a trumpeter bellowed my homecoming and shouts of gladness went up in the streets. "The queen!" A bustle of activity beset the shore-line while citizens poured out onto balconies and rooftops to cheer my return. The sight of them made me smile through my tears, but not wishing to be feted like a conqueror I went quickly ashore.

Wooden construction cranes with dangling ropes dotted the landscape, as ubiquitous as palm trees, and I saw that Iol-Caesaria was much changed in the years that I'd been away. It was bigger, grander. Buildings of modern design rose tall and majestic over the new city wall. My palace . . . why it was almost finished now.

I didn't dally. Before the staff could even assemble to welcome me, I passed through the gates and took the stairs two at a time. My shawl came loose in the wind and fluttered behind me, but I didn't stop for it. Inside the receiving hall, servants chased after me and stunned courtiers poured out of every crevasse of the palace. Chryssa and Maysar both helped Euphronius, stooped as he was over his divination staff. *My loved ones,* I thought. How bittersweet to see them again with nothing in my hands, when I could have brought them everything.

"Majesty!" Chryssa shrieked with joy, jostling to be the first to welcome me.

"Oh, beloved queen," Euphronius said. "Come closer so I know my old eyes don't deceive me."

"Is this merely a visit?" Maysar asked with a smirk.

"No," I replied, my eyes clear, my voice unwavering. "I've come home."

The Berber chieftain gave a brilliant smile, then lowered to kiss my hands.

"The king is in his chambers," Chryssa said, her own smile wide and teary. "Surely, someone has informed him . . ."

This upset my balance. I'd expected that Juba would still be in Spain with Agrippa. I thought I'd have more time to prepare. Time to consider what I wanted. On the other hand, maybe what lay between Juba and I had always been too well considered. That he was here now was an omen and an opportunity that might not come again.

I strode purposefully to Juba's rooms. His two guards scattered before me as if I were the sirocco itself. They both spoke at once. "Majesty, the king is dressing," one said. "Majesty, the king is sleeping," said the other. I pressed my hands to the big double doors, letting my weight swing them open. It would seem that both guards had been telling the truth, after a fashion. The King of Mauretania was unshaven, his eyes heavy with sleep as one slave tried to tug his arm into his tunic and another laced up his sandals. Juba looked up at me and blinked slowly, as if he couldn't make his bloodshot eyes obey him. "Selene?" Juba coughed into his hand, then snapped at his slaves. "Go!"

The slaves slipped past me and I eyed the king's pallor warily. "Are you feverish?"

"I'm drunk." Juba pulled at the laces of his sandal, irritated by his inability to tie them. "Or at least I was drunk and now I'm ill. Or perhaps I'm *still* drunk and imagining you. Perhaps Dionysus is inside me."

Making my way to his side, I stooped and put my hand over his. "You're not imagining me. And you aren't Dionysus."

"Nay." He drew his hand from mine and let the offending sandal fall to the floor. "That must be Augustus. If you're the New Isis and Queen of Egypt, your consort must be Osiris, or is it Serapis to the Greeks? Dead gods who rise to be lovers befuddle me."

"I thought you were in Spain. With Agrippa."

"I was," Juba said, leaning back on his pillows and shielding his eyes from the light. "I saw Julia too."

Julia. How I missed her. Seating myself at the edge of Juba's bed, I asked, "How does she fare?"

"Better than her new husband, I think. Now that she has a babe, Agrippa wants her to return to Rome but fears the mischief she'd make without him. As it is, Julia loves traveling with the soldiers, meeting the people in the provinces, and indulging in their scandalous customs."

"She always wanted to see the world," I said, sentimental.

"At this rate, she'll see Agrippa into an early grave," Juba said, one arm slung over his brow. "If it isn't Julia's ambition in life to make Agrippa miserable, it's merely an incidental delight."

I smirked, my heart warming at the realization that Julia always overcame every calamity, her spirit unbreakable. "So she's making the best of it."

"She hoped you'd approve," Juba said, finally lowering his arm so that he could look at me. "She mused that half of everything we all do is calculated to win your approval. She thinks Augustus nearly went to war with Parthia just to impress you. The least I could do is learn to be King of Mauretania."

"That's why you came back from Spain?"

Though his expression was guarded, his answer sounded raw and vulnerable. "You were well named, Selene, after the moon. Though we know you only in darkness, like the tides, we're all swayed by your pull, wanting nothing more than to shine in your mysterious light . . ." He looked away. Embarrassed. "There. I've finally become a poet for you, though not a very good one."

The man I'd married had no parents, no siblings to share his pains, no faith to give him strength. He'd adapted and survived on his own. Even now, stinking of wine, he was still changing. Like green shoots of wheat before it grows tall, he was a man still growing, still filled with promise. "You excel at everything you put your mind to, Juba. Whether it's poetry or kingship, you simply have to decide to be good at it."

He propped himself up on a pillow to stare at me. "Why have *you* come back, Selene?"

Shaking my head, I simply said, "He's let me go."

Juba laughed. A harsh sound. "You're cruel to mock me."

"It's true."

Juba launched up from the bed to stand on slightly wobbly legs. "Don't worry, Selene. Augustus will try to forget you; he'll tell himself he can have his pick of any girl in the empire. But then he'll see an image of your mother or hear a song you played for him on your *kithara* harp, and he'll summon you again. When he's eliminated all rivals, he may even make you Queen of Egypt. You'll have Egypt and you'll rule the man who rules the world. Be patient just a little while longer and you'll have your heart's desire."

"That isn't my heart's desire," I whispered. All my life, I'd woven a web of obsession to ensnare others and found myself caught. I'd been a prisoner since the age of ten; I was more than twenty now. I wanted to be free. I wanted freedom. Freedom from the dead that haunted me and from the heartbreak in my wake. Freedom from the cold winter in the emperor's eyes and freedom to take joy in the world my goddess gifted to me. I knew that there must be compromise for these things. Kore could not return to her mother, to the sunshine, without paying a price. To be free of Augustus, I must reach accord with Juba. I caught his hand to make him turn and look at me.

When he did, he frowned. "You don't expect me to believe that you chose *me*."

At the sound of the ocean breeze sweeping through our courtyard, carrying to me the scent of salt and mint and wine, I said, "I chose Mauretania. And you are Mauretania's king. That's a start."

His fingers closed over mine and he swallowed. "A start . . . where would we go next? We've quarreled our whole marriage. There's nothing I can do to please you. Nothing you want that I can give you."

"You can give me a son," I said, finding the courage to look into his startled amber eyes.

His expression turned hopeful. Mine must have too. Like Kore, I would have my reprieve. Until Augustus dragged me back into the cold winter depths, I would dance in summer fields with my daughter. I would abandon my dead to keep my covenant with the living. And I would gather flowers for my tables, not for tombs.

AUTHOR'S NOTE

CLEOPATRA Selene and Juba II would rule Mauretania for at least another fourteen years, during which Selene issued a series of provocative coins honoring Isis and her mother, and hinting at her status as the Queen of Egypt in exile by showing a crocodile unchained. In spite of these belligerent actions, she seems never to have fallen afoul of Augustus. Her reign with Juba was one of relative peace and prosperity, and though Isis was banned in Rome, adherents of the goddess would find a sanctuary in Mauretania, where Selene and Juba built an Iseum complete with sacred crocodiles.

That Cleopatra's daughter memorialized her dead is evidenced by several relics. First, the coins honoring her mother. Second, a stylized Egyptian statue of Petubastes, a priest of Ptah thought to be Selene's cousin, who died just before the fall of Actium when she was still a little girl. Third, a platter depicting Selene as an African queen with Helios nearby. I pieced together her character from these and other indications that Selene never forgot her past.

As the daughter of two of the world's most notoriously fertile rulers, it's possible that Selene gave birth to many children, but we know only of the survival of a son and a daughter. Though speculation abounds, the evidence for Selene's daughter is an Athenian inscription in which the girl is not named. I chose the name Cleopatra Isidora because of the single most telling historical fact that we know about Selene: She named her son *Ptolemy*. Reaching into *her* heritage rather than that of her husband's bespeaks her extraordinary power as a client queen in the Augustan Age and I wanted to reflect that here.

Selene's husband Juba wasn't just a dabbler in the scholarly arts, but a respected geographer whose works would later be cited by Pliny, Plutarch, and Strabo. Though Berbers can and should take pride in Juba's many accomplishments, if his coins are any indication, he was a thoroughly Romanized king. His wit is documented by way of his centaur jest to an irate woman he'd spattered with mud. He seems also to have been a client king of judicious temperament, making him somewhat of an anomaly in an era of bloody tyrants like King Herod.

Juba and Selene are believed to have been buried in the Royal Mausoleum of Mauretania, located in modern-day Algeria. It bears a striking resemblance to the tomb that Augustus built for himself in Rome. It may have been adorned with an *ankh*, a symbol later adopted by Coptic Christians, which could account, in part, for the fact that the tomb was known for many years as the Tomb of the Christian Woman.

These are the things we know about Selene and her husband. Now the time comes to confess my sins.

Selene and Helios were first introduced in *Lily of the Nile* at the age of ten when they would have actually been nine years old. I did this because I wanted older, more relatable, protagonists. In *this* novel, the children of Cleopatra are all aged accurately. However, because of my earlier choice, observant readers may have noticed a small narrowing in the age difference between Selene and Philadelphus.

A rebellion *did* result in the razing of Thebes, a revolt in Alexandria, and the subsequent recall of the Roman Prefect of Egypt, Cornelius Gallus, who was forced to commit suicide under mysterious circumstances. However, the entire chain of events occurred earlier than I have posited and any involvement of Alexander Helios in this rebellion is exceedingly unlikely. For all intents and purposes, after Octavian's triumph, the two sons of Cleopatra and Antony simply disappear from history.

Every novelist to tackle the life of Cleopatra Selene has dealt with the matter of the boys in a different fashion. Some historians have posited that Alexander Helios and Ptolemy Philadelphus went to Mauretania to live unremarkable lives. Modern scholarship disputes this idea, interpreting the silence of ancient sources as evidence that the boys both died young. Ultimately, I took my own approach, and embraced the sense of mystery that surrounds their fate.

As for Selene's half siblings, more is known. Selene's half brother, Iullus Antonius, appears to have held a number of elective offices, so I filled in the blanks, ensuring that he received the military training that would have qualified him for higher office. His relationship with Julia is borne out by the historical record. Both of Selene's half sisters, Antonia Major and Antonia Minor, would go on to play prominent roles in the Julio-Claudian dynasty. Their descendants would eventually restore Isis to great prominence in Rome and Selene's influence is as likely an explanation for that as any.

The favoritism shown to Cleopatra Selene by the imperial family, as well as the remarkable latitude she was allowed as queen, tells us that her relationship with Augustus was extraordinary. There is no evidence, however, that this extraordinary relationship was *amorous*. That Augustus was an adulterer is attested to by several sources, but my portrayal of him as a despoiler of virgins comes from Suetonius, who also mentions Livia as a possible partner in her husband's proclivities. With this in mind, I invented the emperor's obsession with Selene as a consistent rationale for the unexplained turns in her life, and imagined that it stemmed from Augustus's preoccupation with Cleopatra VII as explored by Diana E. E. Kleiner in *Cleopatra and Rome*. Once I took this theory to its natural conclusion, it helped to explain several mysteries in the life of Augustus as well—including Marcus Vipsanius Agrippa's brief self-imposed exile and apparent estrangement. (Although Augustus's illness and the episode with his signet ring has a factual basis, I chose not to explore the Murena Conspiracy except by alluding to the unrest in Rome.)

Though we know that Mauretania was one of the few parts of

his empire in which Augustus never set foot, Rome wasn't a far journey from Iol-Caesaria, and Selene would have almost assuredly visited the capital. There are several indications that she and Juba owned a house in Rome as at least one of Juba's retainers—a mime named Ecloga—is thought to have died there. Precedence for political visits by sitting monarchs can be found in the doings of King Herod, but Selene had more than political reasons to return to Rome; she had family there.

By contrast, there is no evidence that Selene visited Augustus during his sojourn on the Isle of Samos or that she was present for the negotiations with the Kandake of Meroë. If she *was* there, however, she would have almost certainly missed seeing Agrippa, who left the East in 22 B.C. to suppress Isis worshippers.

If Augustus ever gave serious consideration to restoring the Ptolemies in Egypt, the only evidence of it is on Selene's coins, which display her clear intent to restore her dynasty. In any case, it must be remembered that Augustus's residence on the Isle of Samos was actually a succession of visits that took place over the course of three years, during which he settled matters in the Eastern kingdoms, entertained an embassy from India, forged a peace treaty with Meroë, replaced Artaxias in Armenia, and made a show of force on the Parthian border that successfully led to the return of Roman battle standards. The invasion of Egypt by the Kandake of Meroë and her subsequent peace treaty with Augustus were more complex than presented here and the negotiations with Phraates of Parthia, including the return of his hostage son, took place over the course of several years. However, in the interest of brevity, I compressed these events in favor of the fascinating trip to Athens during which Augustus was initiated into the mysteries and witnessed the self-immolation of an Indian ambassador. While the exact ingredients of *kykeon* are unknown, it has been described as a simple mixture of barley water and pennyroyal, but the wide variety of magical revelations described by initiates has led scientists and scholars, including Robert Graves, to posit that the drink was laced with hallucinogens.

Augustus's personal interest in religion at this juncture might strike some as unusual, but it was part of a larger campaign to reshape his image and purge the Roman world of beliefs that ran counter to his propaganda. (Much more unusual is the coin issued by King Herod honoring Kore. Keen not to anger his Jewish subjects, Herod avoided depicting deities or human likenesses on his coins. That Herod made an exception for Kore, quite possibly on the eve of Augustus being initiated into the cult, struck me as significant.) Long after Alexander Helios disappears from the historical record, Augustus continued his posthumous argument with Cleopatra about the true bringer of a Golden Age. Virgil's *Aeneid* was intended to promote Augustus's image as a savior. Any contrary imagery or ideas had to be burned from memory. Indeed, Augustus would eventually seize the Syballine Books and destroy the parts he deemed fraudulent or, one presumes, inexpedient.

The *Aeneid* does mention Marcellus, and that mention did make Octavia swoon, but Virgil's affair with Marcellus is my own invention based on the former's suspected sexual proclivities.

The traditional notion that Juba was granted his ancestral lands, and that he and Selene started their rule in Numidia, has been disputed by Dr. Duane Roller in his book *The World of Juba II and Kleopatra Selene*. Consequently, I decided to short-circuit what would have been an interesting journey through Carthage and Africa Nova, in favor of a direct route to Iol, in Mauretania.

Due to thousands of years of deforestation and depletion of natural resources, today's growing seasons in the region may be slightly different from those enjoyed in the land Juba and Selene settled, but I adopted relatively modern climate patterns. Juba's subsequent explorations of his new kingdom posed the basis for one of his many geographic works, entitled *Libya*. It was in this seminal work that Juba claimed to have discovered the source of the Nile in Mauretania. As a matter of geography, he was wrong, but his theory about the Nile wasn't definitively disproved for almost another two thousand years! If, however, Juba's claim about the Nile was a bit of political poetry to woo Cleopatra Selene by tying her new kingdom to Egypt, it must have been very well received.

As for Selene and Juba's court, I mixed known historical figures with those of my own creation. Leonteus of Argos and Gnaios the gem cutter are known courtiers and funeral inscriptions of those descended from Selene's intimates give us names like Cleopatra Antonianus. (Ecloga is thought to have died circa 30 B.C. but as she's used as evidence by scholars of Selene and Juba's connection to Rome, I had her survive into their reign, which is not out of range of that approximate date.) The fragmentary literary evidence for Selene's life comes down to us from Crinagoras of Mytilene— both her wedding poem as well as one written at her death, so I adopted the theory that he was a member of her court at some time. That he seems to have maintained ties to Antonia Minor doesn't argue against this possibility, as Selene and her half sister may have been in frequent contact. Crinagoras was also an ambassador who wrote on political themes. He dedicated poetry to Tiberius during the latter's excursion into Armenia, lending support to my notion that Selene visited the court of Augustus on the Isle of Samos or, at the very least, was acutely aware of what was happening during this crucial political transition.

Lucius Cornelius Balbus the Younger owned many plantations in Spain and North Africa and seems to have had intimate dealings with the Mauretanian King Bogud, an ally of Antony. Yet, after Augustus came to power, Balbus was eventually made a proconsul in Africa. As such, he'd have been quite invested in the progress of the Mauretanian client kingdom before his eventual role in the war against the Garamantes, so when searching for a representative of the type of settler that Selene would have had to deal with in the early years of her reign, I could think of no better example.

While Lasthenia and Circe are both invented characters, they are archetypes of women who did exist at the time. Several female Pythagorean scholars took the name Lasthenia, and Mauretania would later be noted for the elevated status of women that has been credited to Selene and the relatively egalitarian influence of the Alexandrian culture she imported.

Euphronius (or Euphronios) is an actual historical figure, refer-

enced in ancient sources as a tutor to Cleopatra's children. Euphorbus
Musa was also a historical figure. He was brother to the more famous
Antonius Musa and Juba's court physician, after whom the plant family Euphorbia is named. With some regret and great trepidation, I
combined the two men because of the similarities of their names and
because they would serve essentially the same function in the novel.

Yet, it was the made-up characters of Maysar and Tala who
posed the greatest difficulty for me as an author. The Roman-era
culture of the Berbers in general and the Mauri and Gaetulians
specifically are largely lost to us. Strabo, Herodotus, and other
ancient geographers give us little to differentiate the tribes of
Mauretania from those in Numidia and elsewhere, but what information they give, I have incorporated. Slavery seems to have fallen
off sharply in Mauretania after the initial influx from Rome when
Selene and Juba arrived. Whether or not this was because of a personal abhorrence to the practice on the part of the rulers or their
Berber subjects is unclear. We know that Garamantes were slave
traders, but the Berbers in general declared themselves free
people, so it seemed reasonable to ascribe to them a distaste for
slavery. Unfortunately, modern-day examples of Berber culture are
of limited utility. For example, ancient proto-Berber men are often
depicted in art as wearing a great deal of jewelry but modern Berber men largely eschew it. Moreover, because the indigenous Berber culture in modern Algeria has been suppressed, it's difficult to
reconstruct what these North African people must have been like
before the spread of Islam. Indeed, it's always dangerous to assume
that the cultural anthropology of tribes as we observe them now
has anything to do with their identity in ancient times. Even so, I
decided to risk extrapolating known Berber customs of the Tuaregs,
including their jewelry and indigo dye, back through time. Certainly, Berber culture outside urban settings such as Iol-Caesaria
deserves a more in-depth look than the one presented here, and it's
something I hope to tackle in the next book of this series.

For a more thorough discussion of the history surrounding the
life of Cleopatra Selene, please visit stephaniedray.com.

SONG OF THE NILE

On the Story

1. Is Helios alive, or is he a manifestation of the part of Selene's soul that helps her survive the worst moments of her life?

2. After Selene was raped, Livia offered her a cup of poison to wash away the dishonor. Did Selene have anything to be ashamed of?

3. Selene's mother chose death over dishonor, but Selene chose not to drink the poison. What does that say about her?

4. What does Isis mean when she tells Selene, *Child of Isis, you are more than flesh*?

5. Why does Livia do the wicked things she does? Is she motivated by fear, ambition, or something else?

6. Selene holds grudges and can be vengeful. Do you think she was wrong to instigate the death of Cornelius Gallus, Prefect of Egypt? Should she have forgiven Euphronius sooner? Should she forgive Juba at all?

7. Were Marcellus and Philadelphus poisoned? If so, by whom and for what reason?

8. What does it say about Selene's character that she kept the tattered, bloodstained dress that she wore as a child in the emperor's Triumph? Why did she give it back to the King of Emesa?

9. Is Maysar right when he says Selene punishes herself for being alive when all her family is dead? How does Selene's survivor's guilt influence her choices in the novel?

10. What are Selene's strengths and weaknesses? How is she like Augustus and how does she differ from him?

11. What lessons did Selene learn from her mother and father?

12. What did Selene learn from Circe and Livia? What did she learn from the emperor? Can we all learn things from our enemies?

13. Is Augustus truly Selene's enemy? She says that she hates him, but her feelings toward him are always evolving. Why do you think her feelings toward the emperor are so complicated?

14. How does Juba change over the course of the novel? What about Octavia? Helios? Chryssa?

15. What is behind the emperor's obsession with Selene and why does Augustus allow her so much power and influence over him?

16. How is the myth of Persephone and Hades reflected in Selene's life?

17. Should Selene have sacrificed her happiness in Mauretania in order to regain her mother's throne? Did she owe it to her dead family to dedicate her life to Egypt? What about her Alexandrian courtiers and all the other people who want her to become the Queen of Egypt?

18. What would Selene's mother, Cleopatra the Great, have to say about her daughter's choice to return to Mauretania?

19. Why does Augustus eventually send Selene away?

20. If Selene has Juba's son, how will it affect her relationship with Augustus? Do you think he'll ever summon Selene again?

On the History, Culture, and Religion

21. Historically speaking, Philadelphus and Helios disappear from the record. Some historians have theorized that the two boys went to Mauretania to live in obscurity with Selene. Others believe they died or that Augustus had them killed. *Song of the Nile* embraces the ambiguity about their fates, but what do you think happened to the boys?

22. One of the few things we know about the historical King Juba is that he rode past a woman at the side of the road, who berated him for having

spattered her with mud with his hooves. He replied, "Madam, do you take me for a *centaur*?" What does this tell us about the character of Juba?

23. Instead of invading Parthia, Augustus settled upon a negotiation for the lost battle standards of Rome. Why did he make peace with them instead of fighting for treasure and conquest?

24. Augustus took a serious interest in the prophecies of the Sibyl, going so far as to hunt down "unauthorized" prophecies and burning them. He eventually stored his own "official" version of the Sibylline Books in the Temple of Apollo. Why did he do this?

25. In the ancient world, to be initiated into the Eleusinian Mysteries was a hallmark of a civilized person. The faithful claimed to have seen visions of the dead and terrors of the night. A modern theory is that the sacred *kykeon* brew contained hallucinogenics. Do you think these visions were true spiritual ones or drug-induced illusions or both?

26. While Rome was generally tolerant toward other religions and Isis would go on to dominate the ancient world until the rise of Christianity, Isis worship was out of favor during Selene's lifetime. What does it say about Cleopatra Selene that she never renounced Isis as her patron deity and continued to be a proponent of her faith in spite of the emperor's enmity for the cult?

27. After Cleopatra's death, her daughter Selene was the most prominent client queen in the Roman Empire. Selene had the power to mint her own coins, and her children were named after *her* side of the family. Do you think this is because of her prestige as a Ptolemaic queen, the fact that she had an extraordinary relationship with Augustus, or that Juba couldn't control her?

28. Though Selene and Juba are thought to have been married in 25 B.C., she would not appear on the coinage of the realm as a coruler of Mauretania until 20 B.C. Juba's coins are in Latin and deferential to Rome. Selene's coins are always in Greek, often flouting the emperor's official narrative by celebrating her dead mother—an enemy of Rome—elevating the goddess Isis, and hinting that either Egypt would soon break free of its bonds or that she represented the throne

of Egypt in exile. Does this represent a political split between the two monarchs, or could it have been a calculated strategy between Selene and Juba to appeal to different political elements in their kingdom?

29. Juba claimed to have discovered the source of the Nile in Maureta-nia. It would take hundreds of years before he was proved wrong. Do you think Juba stretched the truth for political reasons—perhaps to flatter Cleopatra Selene and make her feel more at home? Or do you believe that he simply made a mistake?

30. The end of the Republic and the founding of the Julio-Claudian dynasty looks inevitable in retrospect, but what stumbling blocks and dangers did Augustus face on his path to absolute power?